Sarah Morgan [...] bestselling auth [...] women's fiction. [...] million copies of [...] and warmth hav [...] Sarah lives with her family near London, England, where the rain frequently keeps her trapped in her office. Visit her at www.sarahmorgan.com

Award-winning author **Jennifer Hayward** emerged on the publishing scene as the winner of Mills & Boon's So You Think You Can Write global writing contest. The recipient of *Romantic Times Magazine*'s Reviewer's Choice Award for Best Mills & Boon Modern of 2014, Jennifer's careers in journalism and PR, including years of working alongside powerful, charismatic CEOs and travelling the world, have provided perfect fodder for the fast-paced, sexy stories she likes to write.

Anne Fraser always loved reading and never imagined that one day she would be writing for a living. She started life as a nurse and helpfully, for a writer of medical romances, is married to a hospital doctor! Anne and husband have lived and worked all over the world, including South Africa, Canada and Australia and many of their experiences as well as the settings find their way into her books. Anne lives in Glasgow with her husband and two children.

The Gorgeous Greeks

COLLECTION

Playing
Her Games

SARAH MORGAN

JENNIFER HAYWARD

ANNE FRASER

MILLS & BOON

First Published in Great Britain 2020
By Mills & Boon, an imprint of HarperCollins*Publishers*
1 London Bridge Street, London, SE1 9GF

GORGEOUS GREEKS: PLAYING HER GAMES © 2020
Harlequin Books S.A.

Playing by the Greek's Rules © 2015 Sarah Morgan
Changing Constantinou's Game © 2014 Jennifer Drogell
Falling For Dr Dimitriou © 2014 Anne Fraser

ISBN: 978-0-263-28158-3

MIX
Paper from responsible sources
FSC
www.fsc.org
FSC™ C007454

This book is produced from independently certified FSC™ paper to ensure responsible forest management.

For more information visit: www.harpercollins.co.uk/green

Printed and bound in Spain
by CPI, Barcelona

PLAYING BY THE GREEK'S RULES

SARAH MORGAN

To the wonderful Joanne Grant, for her enthusiasm, encouragement and for always keeping the door open.

CHAPTER ONE

LILY PULLED HER hat down to shade her eyes from the burn of the hot Greek sun and took a large gulp from her water bottle. 'Never again.' She sat down on the parched, sunbaked earth and watched as her friend carefully brushed away dirt and soil from a small, carefully marked section of the trench. 'If I ever, *ever* mention the word "love" to you, I want you to bury me somewhere in this archaeological site and never dig me up again.'

'There is an underground burial chamber. I could dump you in there if you like.'

'Great idea. Stick a sign in the ground. *"Here lies Lily, who wasted years of her life studying the origin, evolution and behaviour of humans and still couldn't understand men".*' She gazed across the ruins of the ancient city of Aptera to the sea beyond. They were high on a plateau. Behind them, the jagged beauty of the White Mountains shimmered in the heat and in front lay the sparkling blue of the Sea of Crete. The beauty of it usually lifted her mood, but not today.

Brittany sat up and wiped her brow with her forearm. 'Stop beating yourself up. The guy is a lying, cheating rat bastard.' Reaching for her backpack, she glanced across the site to the group of men who were deep in conversation. 'Fortunately for all of us he's flying back to London tomorrow to his wife. And all I can say to that is, God help the woman.'

Lily covered her face with her hands. 'Don't say the word "wife". I am a terrible person.'

'Hey!' Brittany's voice was sharp. 'He told you he was single. He *lied*. The responsibility is all his. After tomorrow you won't have to see him again and I won't have to struggle not to kill him.'

'What if she finds out and ends their marriage?'

'Then she might have the chance of a decent life with someone who respects her. Forget him, Lily.'

How could she forget when she couldn't stop going over and over it in her head?

Had there been signs she'd missed?

Had she asked the wrong questions?

Was she so desperate to find someone special that she'd ignored obvious signs?

'I was planning our future. We were going to spend August touring the Greek Islands. That was before he pulled out a family photo from his wallet instead of his credit card. Three little kids wrapped around their dad like bindweed. He should have been taking them on holiday, not me! I can't bear it. How could I have made such an appalling error of judgement? That is a line I *never* cross. Family is sacrosanct to me. If you asked me to pick between family and money, I'd pick family every time.' It crossed her mind that right now she had neither. No money. No family. 'I don't know which is worse—the fact that he clearly didn't know me *at all*, or the fact that when I checked him against my list he was perfect.'

'You have a list?'

Lily felt herself grow pink. 'It's my attempt to be objective. I have a really strong desire for permanent roots. Family.' She thought about the emotional wasteland of her past and felt a sense of failure. Was the future going to look the same way? 'When you want something badly it can distort your decision-making process, so I've put in some layers of protection for myself. I know the basic qualities I need in a man to be happy. I never date anyone who doesn't score highly on my three points.'

Brittany looked intrigued. 'Big wallet, big shoulders and big—'

'No! And you are appalling.' Despite her misery, Lily laughed. 'First, he has to be affectionate. I'm not interested in a man who can't show his feelings. Second, he has to be honest, but short of getting him to take a lie detector test I don't know how to check that one. I thought Professor Ashurst was honest. I'm never calling him David again, by the way.' She allowed herself one glance at the visiting archaeologist who had dazzled her during their short, ill-fated relationship. 'You're right. He's a rat pig.'

'I didn't call him a rat pig. I called him a rat b—'

'I know what you called him. I never use that word.'

'You should. It's surprisingly therapeutic. But we shouldn't be wasting this much time talking about him. Professor Asshat is history, like this stuff we're digging up.'

'I can't believe you called him that.'

'You should be calling him far worse. What's the third thing on your list?'

'I want a man with strong family values. He has to want a family. But not several different families at the same time. Now I know why he gave off all those signals about being a family man. Because he already *was* a family man.' Lily descended into gloom. 'My checklist is seriously flawed.'

'Not necessarily. You need a more reliable test for honesty and you should maybe add "single" to your list, that's all. You need to chill. Stop looking for a relationship and have some fun. Keep it casual.'

'You're talking about sex? That doesn't work for me.' Lily took another sip of water. 'I have to be in love with a guy to sleep with him. The two are welded together for me. How about you?'

'No. Sex is sex. Love is love. One is fun and the other is to be avoided at all costs.'

'I don't think like that. There is something wrong with me.'

'There's nothing wrong with you. It's not a crime to want a relationship. It just means you get your heart broken more than the average person.' Brittany pushed her hat back from her face. 'I can't believe how hot it is. It's not even ten o'clock and already I'm boiling like a lobster.'

'And you know all about lobsters, coming from Maine. It's summer and this is Crete. What did you expect?'

'Right now I'd give anything for a few hours back home. I'm not used to summers that fry your skin from your body. I keep wanting to remove another layer of clothing.'

'You've spent summers at digs all over the Mediterranean.'

'And I moaned at each and every one.' Brittany stretched out her legs and Lily felt a flash of envy.

'You look like Lara Croft in those shorts. You have amazing legs.'

'Too much time hiking in inhospitable lands searching for ancient relics. I want your gorgeous blonde hair.' Brittany's hair, the colour of polished oak, was gathered up from her neck in a ponytail. Despite the hat, her neck was already showing signs of the sun. 'Listen, don't waste another thought or tear on that man. Come out with us tonight. We're going to the official opening of the new wing at the archaeological museum and afterwards we're going to try out that new bar on the waterfront. My spies tell me that Professor Asshat won't be there, so it's going to be a great evening.'

'I can't. The agency rang this morning and offered me an emergency cleaning job.'

'Lily, you have a masters in archaeology. You shouldn't be taking these random jobs.'

'My research grant doesn't pay off my college loans and

I want to be debt free. And anyway, I love cleaning. It relaxes me.'

'You love cleaning? You're like a creature from another planet.'

'There's nothing more rewarding than turning someone's messy house into a shiny home, but I do wish the job wasn't tonight. The opening would have been fun. A great excuse to wash the mud off my knees and dress up, not to mention seeing all those artefacts in one place. Never mind. I'll focus on the money. They're paying me an emergency rate for tonight.'

'Cleaning is an emergency?'

Lily thought about the state of some of the houses she cleaned. 'Sometimes, but in this case it's more that the owner decided to arrive without notice. He spends most of his time in the US.' She dug in her bag for more sunscreen. 'Can you imagine being so rich you can't quite decide which of your many properties you are going to sleep in?'

'What's his name?'

'No idea. The company is very secretive. We have to arrive at a certain time and then his security team will let us in. Four hours later I add a gratifyingly large sum of money to my bank account and that's the end of it.'

'Four hours? It's going to take five of you four hours to clean one house?' Brittany paused with the water halfway to her mouth. 'What is this place? A Minoan palace?'

'A villa. It's big. She said I'd be given a floor plan when I arrive, which I have to return when I leave and I'm not allowed to make copies.'

'A *floor plan*?' Brittany choked on her water. 'Now I'm intrigued. Can I come with you?'

'Sure—' Lily threw her a look '—because scrubbing out someone's shower is so much more exciting than having cocktails on the terrace of the archaeological museum while the sun sets over the Aegean.'

'It's the Sea of Crete.'

'Technically it's still the Aegean, and either way I'm missing a great party to scrub a floor. I feel like Cinderella. So what about you? Are you going to meet someone tonight and do something about your dormant love life?'

'I don't have a love life, I have a sex life, which is not at all dormant fortunately.'

Lily felt a twinge of envy. 'Maybe you're right. I need to lighten up and use men for sex instead of treating every relationship as if it's going to end in confetti. You were an only child, weren't you? Did you ever wish you had brothers or sisters?'

'No, but I grew up on a small island. The whole place felt like a massive extended family. Everyone knew everything, from the age you first walked, to whether you had all A's on your report card.'

'Sounds blissful.' Lily heard the wistful note in her own voice. 'Because I was such a sickly kid and hard work to look after, no one took me for long. My eczema was terrible when I was little and I was always covered in creams and bandages and other yucky stuff. I wasn't exactly your poster baby. No one wanted a kid who got sick. I was about as welcome as a stray puppy with fleas.'

'Crap, Lily, you're making me tear up and I'm not even a sentimental person.'

'Forget it. Tell me about your family instead.' She loved hearing about other people's families, about the complications, the love, the experiences woven into a shared history. To her, family seemed like a multicoloured sweater, with all the different coloured strands of wool knitted into something whole and wonderful that gave warmth and protection from the cold winds of life.

She picked absently at a thread hanging from the hem of her shorts. It felt symbolic of her life. She was a single fibre, loose, bound to nothing.

Brittany took another mouthful of water and adjusted the angle of her hat. 'We're a normal American family, I guess. Whatever that is. My parents were divorced when I was ten.

My mom hated living on an island. Eventually she remarried and moved to Florida. My dad was an engineer and he spent all his time working on oil rigs around the world. I lived with my grandmother on Puffin Island.'

'Even the name is adorable.' Lily tried to imagine growing up on a place called Puffin Island. 'Were you close to your grandmother?'

'Very. She died a few years ago, but she left me her cottage on the beach so I'd always have a home. I take several calls a week from people wanting to buy the place but I'm never going to sell.' Brittany poked her trowel into the ground. 'My grandmother called it Castaway Cottage. When I was little I asked her if a castaway ever lived there and she said it was for people lost in life, not at sea. She believed it had healing properties.'

Lily didn't laugh. 'I might need to spend a month there. I need to heal.'

'You'd be welcome. A friend of mine is staying at the moment. We use it as a refuge. It's the best place on earth and I always feel close to my grandmother when I'm there. You can use it any time, Lil.'

'Maybe I will. I still need to decide what I'm going to do in August.'

'You know what you need? Rebound sex. Sex for the fun of it, without all the emotional crap that goes with relationships.'

'I've never had rebound sex. I'd fall in love.'

'So pick someone you couldn't possibly fall in love with in a million years. Someone with exceptional bedroom skills, but nothing else to commend him. Then you can't possibly be at risk.' She broke off as Spyros, one of the Greek archaeologists from the local university, strolled across to them. 'Go away, Spy, this is girl talk.'

'Why do you think I'm joining you? It's got to be more interesting than the conversation I just left.' He handed Lily a can of chilled Diet Coke. 'He's a waste of space, *theé mou.*' His voice was gentle and she coloured, touched by his kindness.

'I know, I know.' She lifted the weight of her hair from her neck, wishing she'd worn it up. 'I'll get over it.'

Spy dropped to his haunches next to her. 'Want me to help you get over him? I heard something about rebound sex. I'm here for you.'

'No thanks. You're a terrible flirt. I don't trust you.'

'Hey, this is about sex. You don't need to trust me.' He winked at her. 'What you need is a real man. A Greek man who knows how to make you feel like a woman.'

'Yeah, yeah, I know the joke. You're going to hand me your laundry and tell me to wash it. This is why you're not going to be my rebound guy. I am not washing your socks.' But Lily was laughing as she snapped the top of the can. Maybe she didn't have a family, but she had good friends. 'You're forgetting that when I'm not cleaning the villas of the rich or hanging out here contributing nothing to my college fund, I work for the ultimate in Greek manhood.'

'Ah yes.' Spyros smiled. 'Nik Zervakis. Head of the mighty ZervaCo. Man of men. Every woman's fantasy.'

'Not mine. He doesn't tick a single box on my list.'

Spy raised his eyebrows and Brittany shook her head. 'You don't want to know. Go on, Lily, dish the dirt on Zervakis. I want to know everything from his bank balance to how he got that incredible six pack I saw in those sneaky photos of him taken in that actress's swimming pool.'

'I don't know much about him, except that he's super brilliant and expects everyone around him to be super brilliant, too, which makes him pretty intimidating. Fortunately he spends most of his time in San Francisco or New York so he isn't around much. I've been doing this internship for two months and in that time two personal assistants have left. It's a good job he has a big human resources department because I can tell you he gets through *a lot* of human resources in the average working week. And don't even start me on the girl-friends. I need a spreadsheet to keep it straight in my head.'

'What happened to the personal assistants?'

'Both of them resigned because of the pressure. The work-load is inhuman and he isn't easy to work for. He has this way of looking at you that makes you wish you could teleport. But he *is* very attractive. He isn't my type so I didn't pay much attention, but the women talk about him all the time.'

'I still don't understand why you're working there.'

'I'm trying different things. My research grant ends this month and I don't know if I want to carry on doing this. I'm exploring other options. Museum work doesn't pay much and anyway, I don't want to live in a big city. I could never teach—' She shrugged, depressed by the options. 'I don't know what to do.'

'You're an expert in ceramics and you've made some beautiful pots.'

'That's a hobby.'

'You're creative and artistic. You should do something with that.'

'It isn't practical to think I can make a living that way and dreaming doesn't pay the bills.' She finished her drink. 'Sometimes I wish I'd read law, not archaeology, except that I don't think I'm cut out for office work. I'm not good with technology. I broke the photocopier last week and the cof-fee machine hates me, but apparently having ZervaCo on your résumé makes prospective employers sit up. It shows you have staying power. If you can work there and not be intimidated, you're obviously robust. And before you tell me that an educated woman shouldn't allow herself to be intimidated by a guy, try meeting him.'

Spyros rose to his feet. 'Plenty of people would be intimi-dated by Nik Zervakis. There are some who say his name along with the gods.'

Brittany pushed her water bottle back into her backpack.

'Those would be the people whose salary he pays, or the women he sleeps with.'

Lily took off her hat and fanned herself. 'His security team is briefed to keep them away from him. We are not allowed to put any calls through to him unless the name is on an approved list and that list changes pretty much every week. I have terrible trouble keeping up.'

'So his protection squad is there to protect him from women?' Brittany looked fascinated. 'Unreal.'

'I admire him. They say his emotions have never played a part in anything he does, business or pleasure. He is the opposite of everything I am. No one has ever dumped him or made him feel less of a person and he always knows what to say in any situation.' She glanced once across the heat-baked ruins of the archaeological site towards the man who had lied so glibly. Thinking of all the things she could have said and hadn't plunged her into another fit of gloom. 'I'm going to try and be more like Nik Zervakis.'

Brittany laughed. 'You're kidding, right?'

'No, I'm not kidding. He is like an ice machine. I want to be like that. How about you? Have either of you ever been in love?'

'No!' Spy looked alarmed, but Brittany didn't answer. Instead she stared sightlessly across the plateau to the ocean.

'Brittany?' Lily prompted her. 'Have you been in love?'

'Not sure.' Her friend's voice was husky. 'Maybe.'

'Wow. Ball-breaking Brittany, in love?' Spy raised his eyebrows. 'Did you literally fire an arrow through his heart?' He spread his hands as Lily glared at him. 'What? She's a Bronze Age weapons expert and a terrifyingly good archer. It's a logical suggestion.'

Lily ignored him. 'What makes you think you might have been in love? What were the clues?'

'I married him.'

Spyros doubled up with soundless laughter and Lily stared. 'You—? Okay. Well that's a fairly big clue right there.'

'It was a mistake.' Brittany tugged the trowel out of the ground. 'When I make mistakes I make sure they're *big*. I guess you could call it a whirlwind romance.'

'That sounds more like a hurricane than a whirlwind. How long did it last?'

Brittany stood up and brushed dust off her legs. 'Ten days. Spy, if you don't wipe that smile off your face I'm going to kick you into this trench and cover your corpse with a thick layer of dirt and shards of pottery.'

'You mean ten *years*,' Lily said and Brittany shook her head.

'No. I mean days. We made it through the honeymoon without killing each other.'

Lily felt her mouth drop open and closed it again quickly. 'What happened?'

'I let my emotions get in the way of making sane decisions.' Brittany gave a faint smile. 'I haven't fallen in love since.'

'Because you learned how not to do it. You didn't go and make the same mistake again and again. Give me some tips.'

'I can't. Avoiding emotional entanglement came naturally after I met Zach.'

'Sexy name.'

'Sexy guy.' She shaded her eyes from the sun. 'Sexy rat bastard guy.'

'Another one,' Lily said gloomily. 'But you were young and everyone is allowed to make mistakes when they're young. Not only do I not have that excuse, but I'm a habitual offender. I should be locked up until I'm safe to be rehabilitated. I need to be taken back to the store and reprogrammed.'

'You do not need to be reprogrammed.' Brittany stuffed her trowel into the front of her backpack. 'You're warm, friendly and lovable. That's what guys like about you.'

'That and the fact it takes one glance to know you'd look great naked,' Spy said affably.

Lily turned her back on him. 'Warm, friendly and lovable are great qualities for a puppy, but not so great for a woman. They say a person can change, don't they? Well, I'm going to change.' She scrambled to her feet. 'I am not falling in love again. I'm going to take your advice and have rebound sex.'

'Good plan.' Spy glanced at his watch. 'You get your clothes off, I'll get us a room.'

'Not funny.' Lily glared at him. 'I am going to pick someone I don't know, don't feel anything for and couldn't fall in love with in a million years.'

Brittany looked doubtful. 'Now I'm second-guessing myself. Coming from you it sounds like a recipe for disaster.'

'It's going to be perfect. All I have to do is find a man who doesn't tick a single box on my list and have sex with him. It can't possibly go wrong. I'm going to call it Operation Ice Maiden.'

Nik Zervakis stood with his back to the office, staring at the glittering blue of the sea while his assistant updated him. 'Did he call?'

'Yes, exactly as you predicted. How do you always know these things? I would have lost my nerve days ago with those sums of money involved. You don't even break out in a sweat.'

Nik could have told him the deal wasn't about money, it was about power. 'Did you call the lawyers?'

'They're meeting with the team from Lexos first thing tomorrow. So it's done. Congratulations, boss. The US media have turned the phones red-hot asking for interviews.'

'It's not over until the deal is signed. When that happens I'll put out a statement, but no interviews.' Nik felt some of the tension leave his shoulders. 'Did you make a reservation at The Athena?'

'Yes, but you have the official opening of the new museum wing first.'

Nik swore softly and swung round. 'I'd forgotten. Do you have a briefing document on that?'

His PA paled. 'No, boss. All I know is that the wing has been specially designed to display Minoan antiquities in one place. You were invited to the final meeting of the project team but you were in San Francisco.'

'Am I supposed to give a speech?'

'They're hoping you will agree to say a few words.'

'I can manage a few words, but they'll be unrelated to Minoan antiquities.' Nik loosened his tie. 'Run me through the schedule.'

'Vassilis will have the car here at six-fifteen, which should allow you time to go back to the villa and change. You're picking up Christina on the way and your table is booked for nine p.m.'

'Why not pick her up after I've changed?'

'That would have taken time you don't have.'

Nik couldn't argue with that. The demands of his schedule had seen off three assistants in the last six months. 'There was something else?'

The man shifted uncomfortably. 'Your father called. Several times. He said you weren't picking up your phone and asked me to relay a message.'

Nik flicked open the button at the neck of his shirt. 'Which was?'

'He wants to remind you that his wedding is next weekend. He thinks you've forgotten.'

Nik stilled. *He hadn't forgotten.* 'Anything else?'

'He is looking forward to having you at the celebrations. He wanted me to remind you that of all the riches in this world, family is the most valuable.'

Nik, whose sentiments on that topic were a matter of public record, made no comment.

He wondered why anyone would see a fourth wedding as a cause for celebration. To him, it shrieked of someone who hadn't learned his lesson the first three times. 'I will call him from the car.'

'There was one more thing—' The man backed towards the door like someone who knew he was going to need to make a rapid exit. 'He said to make sure you knew that if you don't come, you'll break his heart.'

It was a statement typical of his father. Emotional. Unguarded.

Reflecting that it was that very degree of sentimentality that had made his father the victim of three costly divorces, Niklaus strolled to his desk. 'Consider the message delivered.'

As the door closed he turned back to the window, staring over the midday sparkle of the sea.

Exasperation mingled with frustration and beneath that surface response lay darker, murkier emotions he had no wish to examine. He wasn't given to introspection and he believed that the past was only useful when it informed the future, so finding himself staring down into a swirling mass of long-ignored memories was an unwelcome experience.

Despite the air conditioning, sweat beaded on his forehead and he strode across his office and pulled a bottle of iced water from the fridge.

Why should it bother him that his father was marrying again?

He was no longer an idealistic nine-year-old, shattered by a mother's betrayal and driven by a deep longing for order and security.

He'd learned to make his own security. Emotionally he was an impenetrable fortress. He would never allow a relationship to explode the world from under his feet. He didn't believe in love and he saw marriage as expensive and pointless.

Unfortunately his father, an otherwise intelligent man, didn't share his views. He'd managed to build a successful business from nothing but the fruits of the land around him, but for some reason he had failed to apply that same intellect to his love life.

Nik reflected that if he approached business the way his father approached relationships, he would be broke.

As far as he could see his father performed no risk analysis, gave no consideration to the financial implications of each of his romantic whims and approached each relationship with the romantic optimism entirely inappropriate for a man on his fourth marriage.

Nik's attempts to encourage at least some degree of circumspection had been dismissed as cynical.

To make the situation all the more galling, the last time they'd met for dinner his father had actually lectured him on his lifestyle as if Nik's lack of divorces suggested a deep character flaw.

Nik closed his eyes briefly and wondered how everything in his business life could run so smoothly while his family was as messy as a dropped pan of spaghetti. The truth was he'd rather endure the twelve labours of Hercules than attend another of his father's weddings.

This time he hadn't met his father's intended bride and he didn't want to. He failed to see what he would bring to the proceedings other than grim disapproval and he didn't want to spoil the day.

Weddings depressed him. All the champagne bubbles in the world couldn't conceal the fact that two people were paying a fortune for the privilege of making a very public mistake.

Lily dumped her bag in the marble hallway and tried to stop her jaw from dropping.

Palatial didn't begin to describe it. Situated on the headland overlooking the sparkling blue of the sea, Villa Harmonia epitomised calm, high-end luxury.

Wondering where the rest of the team were, she wandered out onto the terrace.

Tiny paths wound down through the tumbling gardens to a private cove with a jetty where a platform gave direct swimming access to the sea.

'I've died and gone to heaven.' Disturbed from her trance by the insistent buzz of her phone, she dug it out of her pocket. Her simple uniform was uncomfortably tight, courtesy of all the delicious thyme honey and Greek yoghurt she'd consumed since arriving in Crete. Her phone call turned out to be the owner of the cleaning company, who told her that the rest of the team had been involved in an accident and wouldn't make it.

'Oh no, are they hurt?' On hearing that no one was in hospital but that the car was totalled, Lily realised she was going to be on her own with this job. 'So if it normally takes four of us four hours, how is one person going to manage?'

'Concentrate on the living areas and the master suite. Pay particular attention to the bathroom.'

Resigned to doing the best she could by herself, Lily set to work. Choosing Mozart from her soundtrack, she pushed in her earbuds and sang her way through *The Magic Flute* while she brushed and mopped the spacious living area.

Whoever lived here clearly didn't have children, she thought as she plumped cushions on deep white sofas and polished glass tables. Everything was sophisticated and understated.

Realising that dreaming would get her fired, Lily hummed her way up the curving staircase to the master bedroom and stopped dead.

The tiny, airless apartment she shared with Brittany had a single bed so narrow she'd twice fallen out of it in her sleep. *This* bed, by contrast, was large enough to sleep a family of six comfortably. It was positioned to take advantage of the incredible view across the bay and Lily stood, drooling with envy, imagining how it must feel to sleep in a bed this size. How many times could you roll over before finding yourself on the floor? If it were hers, she'd spread out like a starfish.

Glancing quickly over her shoulder to check there was no sign of the security team, she unclipped her phone from her pocket and took a photo of the bed and the view.

One day, she texted Brittany, I'm going to have sex in a bed like this.

Brittany texted back, I don't care about the bed, just give me the man who owns it.

With a last wistful look at the room, Lily tucked her phone carefully into her bag and strolled into the bathroom. A large tub was positioned next to a wall of glass, offering the owner an uninterrupted view of the ocean. The only way to clean something so large was to climb inside it, so she did that, extra careful not to slip.

When it was gleaming, she turned her attention to the large walk-in shower. There was a sophisticated control panel on the wall and she looked at it doubtfully. Remembering her disastrous experience with the photocopier and the coffee machine, she was reluctant to touch anything, but what choice was there?

Lifting her hand, she pressed a button cautiously and gasped as a powerful jet of freezing water hit her from the opposite wall.

Breathless, she slammed her hand on another button to try and stop the flow but that turned on a different jet and she was blasted with water until her hair and clothes were plastered to her body and she couldn't see. She thumped the wall blindly and was alternately scalded and frozen until finally she managed to turn off the jets. Panting, her hair and clothes plastered to her body, she sank to the floor while she tried to get her breath back, shivering and dripping like a puppy caught in the rain.

'I hate, hate, *hate* technology.' She pushed her hair back from her face, took it in her hands and twisted it into a rope, squeezing to remove as much of the water as she could. Then she stood up, but her uniform was dripping and stuck to her skin. If she walked back through the villa like this, she'd drip water everywhere and she didn't have time to clean the place again.

Peeling off her uniform, she was standing in her underwear wringing out the water when she heard a sound from the bedroom.

Assuming it must be one of the security team, she gave a whimper of horror. 'Hello? If there's anyone out there, don't come in for a moment because I'm just—' She stilled as a woman appeared in the doorway.

She was perfectly groomed, her slender body sheathed in a silk dress the colour of coral, her mouth a sheen of blended lipstick and lip-gloss.

Lily had never felt more outclassed in her life.

'Nik?' The woman spoke over her shoulder, her tone icy. 'Your sex drive is, of course, a thing of legend but for the record it's always a good idea to remove the last girlfriend before installing a new one.'

'What are you talking about?' The male voice came from the bedroom, deep, bored and instantly recognisable.

Still shivering from the impact of the cold water, Lily closed her eyes and wondered if any of the buttons on the control panel operated an ejector seat.

Now she knew who owned the villa.

Moments later he appeared in the doorway and Lily peered through soaked lashes and had her second ever look at Nik Zervakis. Confronted by more good looks and sex appeal than she'd ever seen concentrated in one man before, her tummy tumbled and she felt as if she were plunging downhill on a roller coaster.

He stood, legs braced apart, his handsome face blank of expression as if finding a semi-naked woman in his shower wasn't an event worthy of an emotional response. 'Well?'

That was all he was going to say?

Braced for an explosion of volcanic proportions, Lily gulped. 'I can explain—'

'I wish you would.' The woman's voice turned from ice

to acid and her expensively shod foot tapped rhythmically on the floor. 'This should be worth hearing.'

'I'm the cleaner—'

'Of course you are. Because "cleaners" always end up naked in the client's shower.' Vibrating with anger, she turned the beam of her angry glare onto the man next to her. 'Nik?'

'Yes?'

Her mouth tightened into a thin, dangerous line. 'Who is she?'

'You heard her. She's the cleaner.'

'*Obviously* she's lying.' The woman bristled. 'No doubt she's been here all day, sleeping off the night before.'

His only response to that was a faint narrowing of those spectacular dark eyes.

Recalling someone warning her on her first day with his company that Nik Zervakis was at his most dangerous when he was quiet, Lily felt her anxiety levels rocket but apparently her concerns weren't shared by his date for the evening, who continued to berate him.

'Do you know the worst thing about this? Not that you have a wandering eye, but that your eye wanders to someone as fat as her.'

'*Excuse* me? I'm not fat.' Lily tried vainly to cover herself with the soaking uniform. 'I'll have you know that my BMI is within normal range.'

But the woman wasn't listening. 'Was she the reason you were late picking me up? I *warned* you, Nik, no games, and yet you do this to me. Well, you gambled and you lost because I don't do second chances, especially this early in a relationship and if you can't be bothered to give an explanation then I can't be bothered to ask for one.' Without giving him the chance to respond, his date stalked out of the room and Lily flinched in time with each furious tap of those skyscraper heels.

She stood in awkward silence, her feelings bruised and her spirits drenched in cold water and guilt. 'She's very upset.'

'Yes.'

'Er—is she coming back?'

'I sincerely hope not.'

Lily wanted to say that he was well rid of her, but decided that protecting her job was more important than honesty. 'I'm *really* sorry—'

'Don't be. It wasn't your fault.'

Knowing that wasn't quite true, she squirmed. 'If I hadn't had an accident, I would have had my clothes on when she walked into the room.'

'An accident? I've never considered my shower to be a place of danger but apparently I was wrong about that.' He eyed the volume of water on the floor and her drenched clothing. 'What happened?'

'Your shower is like the flight deck of a jumbo jet, that's what happened!' Freezing and soaked, Lily couldn't stop her teeth chattering. 'There are no instructions.'

'I don't need instructions.' His gaze slid over her with slow, disturbing thoroughness. 'I'm familiar with the workings of my own shower.'

'Well I'm not! I had no idea which buttons to press.'

'So you thought you'd press all of them? If you ever find yourself on the flight deck of a Boeing 747 I suggest you sit on your hands.'

'It's not f-f-funny. I'm soaking wet and I didn't know you were going to come home early.'

'I apologise.' Irony gleamed in those dark eyes. 'I'm not in the habit of notifying people of my movements in advance. Have you finished cleaning or do you want me to show you which buttons to press?'

Lily summoned as much dignity as she could in the circumstances. 'Your shower is clean. Extra clean, because I wiped myself around it personally.' Anxious to make her exit as fast as possible, she kept her eyes fixed on the door and away from that tall, powerful frame. 'Are you sure she isn't coming back?'

'No.'

Lily paused, torn between relief and guilt. 'I've ruined another relationship.'

'Another?' Dark eyebrows lifted. 'It's a common occurrence?'

'You have no idea. Look—if it would help I could call my employer and ask her to vouch for me.' Her voice tailed off as she realised that would mean confessing she'd been caught half naked in the shower.

He gave a faint smile. 'Unless you have a very liberal-minded employer, you might want to rethink that idea.'

'There must be some way I can fix this. I've ruined your date, although for the record I don't think she's a very kind person so she might not be good for you in the long term and with a body that bony she won't be very cuddly for your children.' She caught his eye. 'Are you laughing at me?'

'No, but the ability to cuddle children isn't high on my list of necessary female attributes.' He flung his jacket carelessly over the back of a sofa that was bigger than her bed at home.

She stared in fascination, wondering if he cared at all that his date had walked out. 'As a matter of interest, why didn't you defend yourself?'

'Why would I defend myself?'

'You could have explained yourself and then she would have forgiven you.'

'I never explain myself. And anyway—' he shrugged '—you had already given her an explanation.'

'I don't think she saw me as a credible witness. It might have sounded better coming from you.'

He stood, legs spread, his powerful shoulders blocking the doorway. 'I assume you told her the truth? You're the cleaner?'

'Of course I told her the truth.'

'Then there was nothing I could have added to your story.'

In his position she would have died of humiliation, but he seemed supremely indifferent to the fact he'd been publicly dumped. 'You don't seem upset.'

'Why would I be upset?'

'Because most people are upset when a relationships ends.'

He smiled. 'I'm not one of those.'

Lily felt a flash of envy. 'You're not even a teeny tiny bit sad?'

'I'm not familiar with that unit of measurement but no, I'm not even a "teeny tiny" bit sad. To be sad I'd have to care and I don't care.'

To be sad I'd have to care and I don't care.

Brilliant, Lily thought. *Why* couldn't she have said that to Professor Ashurst when he'd given her that fake sympathy about having hurt her? She needed to memorise it for next time. 'Excuse me a moment.' Leaving a dripping trail behind her, she shot past him, scrabbled in her bag and pulled out a notebook.

'What are you doing?'

'I'm writing down what you said. Whenever I'm dumped I never know the right thing to say, but next time it happens I'm going to say *exactly* those words in exactly that tone instead of producing enough tears to power a water feature at Versailles.' She scribbled, dripping water onto her notebook and smearing the ink.

'Being "dumped" is something that happens to you often?'

'Often enough. I fall in love, I get my heart broken, it's a cycle I'm working on breaking.' She wished she hadn't said anything. Although she was fairly open with people, she drew the line at making public announcements about not being easy to love.

That was her secret.

'How many times have you fallen in love?'

'So far?' She shook the pen with frustration as the ink stalled on the damp page, 'Three times.'

'*Cristo*, that's unbelievable.'

'Thanks for not making me feel better. I bet you've never been unlucky in love, have you?'

'I've never been in love at all.'

Lily digested that. 'You've never met the right person.'

'I don't believe in love.'

'You—' She rocked back on her heels, her attention caught. 'So what do you believe in?'

'Money, influence and power.' He shrugged. 'Tangible, measurable goals.'

'You can measure power and influence? Don't tell me— you stamp your foot and it registers on the Richter scale.'

He loosened his tie. 'You'd be surprised.'

'I'm already surprised. Gosh, you are *so* cool. You are my new role model.' Finally she managed to coax ink from the pen. 'It is never too late to change. From now on I'm all about tangible, measurable goals, too. As a matter of interest, what is your goal in relationships?'

'Orgasm.' He gave a slow smile and she felt herself turn scarlet.

'Right. Well, that serves me right for asking a stupid question. That's definitely a measurable goal. You're obviously able to be cold and ruthlessly detached when it comes to relationships. I'm aiming for that. I've dripped all over your floor. Be careful not to slip.'

He was leaning against the wall, watching her with amusement. 'This is what you look like when you're being cold and ruthlessly detached?'

'I haven't actually started yet, but the moment my radar warns me I might be in danger of falling for the wrong type, *bam*—' she punched the air with her fist '—I'm going to turn on my freezing side. From now on I have armour around my heart. Kevlar.' She gave him a friendly smile. 'You think I'm crazy, right? All this is natural to you. But it isn't to me. This is the first stage of my personality transplant. I'd love to do the whole thing under anaesthetic and wake up all new and perfect, but that isn't possible so I'm trying to embrace the process.'

A vibrating noise caught her attention and she glanced across the room towards his jacket. When he didn't move, she looked at him expectantly. 'That's your phone.'

He was still watching her, his gaze disturbingly intent. 'Yes.'

'You're not going to answer it?' She scrambled to her feet, still clutching the towel. 'It might be her, asking for your forgiveness.'

'I'm sure it is, which is why I don't intend to answer it.'

Lily absorbed that with admiration. 'This is a perfect example of why I need to be like you and not like me. If that had been my phone, I would have answered it and when whoever was on the end apologised for treating me badly, I would have told him it was fine. I would have forgiven them.'

'You're right,' he said. 'You do need help. What's your name?'

She shifted, her wet feet sticking to the floor. 'Lily. Like the flower.'

'You look familiar. Have we met before?'

Lily felt the colour pour into her cheeks. 'I've been working as an intern at your company two days a week for the past couple of months. I'm second assistant to your personal assistant.' *I'm the one who broke the photocopier and the coffee machine.*

Dark eyebrows rose. 'We've met?'

'No. I've only seen you once in person. I don't count the time I was hiding in the bathroom.'

'You hid in the bathroom?'

'You were on a firing spree. I didn't want to be noticed.'

'So you work for me two days a week, and on the other three days you're working as a cleaner?'

'No, I only do that job in the evenings. The other three days I'm doing fieldwork up at Aptera for the summer. But that's almost finished. I've reached a crossroads in my life and I've no idea which direction to take.'

'Fieldwork?' That sparked his interest. 'You're an archae-ologist?'

'Yes, I'm part of a project funded by the university but that part doesn't pay off my massive college loans so I have other jobs.'

'How much do you know about Minoan antiquities?'

Lily blinked. 'Probably more than is healthy for a woman of twenty-four.'

'Good. Get back into the bathroom and dry yourself off while I find you a dress. Tonight I have to open the new wing of the museum. You're coming with me.'

'Me? Don't you have a date?'

'I had a date,' he said smoothly. 'As you're partially re-sponsible for the fact she's no longer here, you're coming in her place.'

'But—' She licked her lips. 'I'm supposed to be clean-ing your villa.'

His gaze slid from her face to the wash of water covering the bathroom floor. 'I'd say you've done a pretty thorough job. By the time we get home, the flood will have spread down the stairs and across the living areas, so it will clean itself.'

Lily gave a gurgle of laughter. She wondered if any of his employees realised he had a sense of humour. 'You're not going to fire me?'

'You should have more confidence in yourself. If you have knowledge of Minoan artefacts then I still have a use for you and I never fire people who are useful.' He reached for the towel and tugged it off, leaving her clad only in her soaking wet underwear.

'What are you doing?' She gave a squeak of embarrass-ment and snatched at the towel but he held it out of reach.

'Stop wriggling. I can't be the first man to see you half naked.'

'Usually I'm in a relationship when a man sees me naked.

And being stared at is very unnerving, especially when you've been called fat by someone who looks like a toast rack—' Lily broke off as he turned and strolled away from her. She didn't know whether to be relieved or affronted. 'If you want to know my size you could ask me!'

He reached for his phone and dialled. While he waited for the person on the other end to answer, he scanned her body and gave her a slow, knowing smile. 'I don't need to ask, *theé mou*,' he said softly. 'I already know your size.'

CHAPTER TWO

NIK LOUNGED IN his seat while the car negotiated heavy evening traffic. Beside him Lily was wriggling like a fish dropped onto the deck of a boat.

'Mr Zervakis? This dress is far more revealing than anything I would normally wear. And I've had a horrible thought.' Her voice was breathy and distracting and Nik turned his head to look at her, trying to remind himself that girls with sweet smiles who were self-confessed members of Loveaholics Anonymous were definitely off his list.

'Call me Nik.'

'I can't call you Nik. It would feel wrong while I'm working in your company. You pay my salary.'

'I pay you? I thought you said you were an intern.'

'I am. You pay your interns far more than most companies, but that's a different conversation. I'm still having that horrible thought by the way.'

Nik dragged his eyes from her mouth and tried to wipe his brain of X-rated thoughts. 'What horrible thought is that?'

'The one where your girlfriend finds out you took me as your date tonight.'

'She will find out.'

'And that doesn't bother you?'

'Why would it?'

'Isn't it obvious? Because she didn't believe I was the cleaner. She thought you and I—well...' she turned scarlet

'…if she finds out we were together tonight then it will look as if she was right and we were lying, even though if people used their brains they could work out that if she's your type then I couldn't possibly be.'

Nik tried to decipher that tumbled speech. 'You're concerned she will think we're having sex? Why is that a horrible thought? You find me unattractive?'

'That's a ridiculous question.' Lily's eyes flew to his and then away again. 'Sorry, but that's like asking a woman if she likes chocolate.'

'There are women who don't like chocolate.'

'They're lying. They might not eat it, but that doesn't mean they don't like it.'

'So I'm chocolate?' Nik tried to remember the last time he'd been this entertained by anyone.

'If you're asking if I think you're very tempting and definitely bad for me, the answer is yes. But apart from the fact we're totally unsuited, I wouldn't be able to relax enough to have sex with you.'

Nik, who had never had trouble helping a woman relax, rose to the challenge. 'I'm happy to—'

'No.' She gave him a stern look. 'I know you're competitive, but forget it. I saw that photo of you in the swimming pool. No way could I ever be naked in front of a man with a body like yours. I'd have to suck everything in and make sure you only saw my good side. The stress would kill any passion.'

'I've already seen you in your underwear.'

'Don't remind me.'

Nik caught his driver's amused gaze in the mirror and gave him a steady stare. Vassilis had been with him for over a decade and had a tendency to voice his opinions on Nik's love life. It was obvious he thoroughly approved of Lily.

'It's true that if you turn up as my guest tonight there will be people who assume we are having sex.' Nik returned his attention to the conversation. 'I can't claim to be intimately acquainted with the guest list, but I'm assuming a few of the people there will be your colleagues. Does that bother you?'

'No. It will send a message that I'm not broken-hearted, which is good for my pride. In fact the timing is perfect. Just this morning I embarked on a new project. Operation Ice Maiden. You're probably wondering what that is.'

Nik opened his mouth to comment but she carried on without pausing.

'I am going to have sex with no emotion. That's right.' She nodded at him. 'You heard me correctly. Rebound sex. I am going to climb into bed with some guy and I'm not going to feel a thing.'

Hearing a sound from the front of the car, Nik pressed a button and closed the screen between him and Vassilis, giving them privacy.

'Do you have anyone in mind for—er—Operation Ice Maiden?'

'Not yet, but if they happen to think it's you that's fine. You'd look good on my romantic résumé.'

Nik leaned his head back against the seat and started to laugh. 'You, Lily, are priceless.'

'That doesn't sound like a compliment.' She adjusted the neckline of her dress and her breasts almost escaped in the process. 'You're basically saying I'm not worth anything.'

Dragging his gaze from her body, Nik decided this was the most entertaining evening he'd had in a long time.

'There are photographers.' As they pulled up outside the museum Lily slunk lower in her seat and Nik closed his hand around her wrist and hauled her upright again.

'You look stunning. If you don't want them all surmising that we climbed out of bed to come here then you need to stop looking guilty.'

'I saw several TV cameras.'

'The opening of a new wing of the museum is news.'

'The neckline of this dress might also be news.' She

tugged at it. 'My breasts are too big for this plunging style. Can I borrow your jacket?'

'Your breasts deserve a dress like that and no, you may not borrow my jacket.' His voice was a deep, masculine purr and she felt the sizzle of sexual attraction right through her body.

'Are you flirting with me?' He was completely different from the safe, friendly men who formed part of her social circle. There was a brutal strength to him, a confidence and assurance that suggested he'd never met a man he hadn't been able to beat in a fight, whether in the bar or the boardroom.

Her question appeared to amuse him. 'You're my date. Flirting is mandatory.'

'It unsettles me and I'm already unsettled at the thought of tonight.'

'Because you're with me?'

No way was she confessing how being with him really made her feel. 'No, because the opening of this new museum wing is a really momentous occasion.'

'You and I have a very different idea of what constitutes a momentous occasion, Lily.' There was laughter in his eyes. 'Never before has my ego been so effectively crushed.'

'Your ego is armour plated, like your feelings.'

'It's true that my feelings of self-worth are not dependent on the opinion of others.'

'Because you think you're right and everyone else is wrong. I wish I were more like you. What if the reporters ask who I am? What do I say? I'm a fake.'

'You're the archaeologist. I'm the fake. And you say whatever you want to say. Or say nothing. Your decision. You're the one in charge of your mouth.'

'You have no idea how much I wish that was true.'

'Tell me why you're excited about tonight.'

'You mean apart from the fact I get to dress up? The new wing houses the biggest collection of Minoan antiquities anywhere in Greece. It has a high percentage of provenanced material, which means archaeologists will be able to restudy material from old excavations. It's exciting. And I love the dress by the way, even though I'll never have any reason to wear it again.'

'Chipped pots excite you?'

She winced. 'Don't say that on camera. The collection will play an active role in research and in university teaching as well as offering a unique insight for the general public.'

As the car pulled up outside the museum one of Nik's security team opened the door and Lily emerged to what felt like a million camera flashes.

'Unreal,' she muttered. 'Now I know why celebrities wear sunglasses.'

'Mr Zervakis—' Photographers and reporters gathered as close as they could. 'Do you have a statement about the new wing?'

Nik paused and spoke directly to the camera, relaxed and at ease as he repeated Lily's words without a single error.

She stared at him. 'You must have an incredible short-term memory.'

A reporter stepped forward. 'Who's your guest tonight, Nik?'

Nik turned towards her and she realised he was leaving it up to her to decide whether to give them a name or not.

'I'm a friend,' she muttered and Nik smiled, took her hand and led her up the steps to the welcome committee at the top.

The first person she spotted was David Ashurst and she stopped in dismay. In answer to Nik's questioning look, she shook her head quickly, misery and panic creating a sick cocktail inside her. 'I'm fine. I saw someone I didn't expect to see, that's all. I didn't think he'd have the nerve to show up.'

'That's him?' His gaze travelled from her face to the man looking awkward at the top of the steps. 'He is the reason you're hoping for a personality transplant?'

'His name is Professor Ashurst. He has a *wife*,' she muttered in an undertone. 'Can you believe that? I actually cried over that loser. Do I have time to get my notebook out of my bag? I can't remember what I wrote down.'

'I'll tell you what to say.' He leaned closer and whispered something in her ear that made her gasp.

'I can't say that.'

'No? Then how's this for an alternative?' Sliding his arm round her waist, he pressed his hand to the base of her spine and flattened her against him. She looked up at him, hypnotised by those spectacular dark eyes and the raw sexuality in his gaze. Before she could ask what he was doing he lowered his head and kissed her.

Pleasure screamed through her, sensation scorching her skin and stoking a pool of heat low in her belly. She'd been kissed before, but never like this. Nik used his mouth with slow, sensual expertise and she felt a rush of exquisite excitement burn through her body. Her nerve endings tingled, her tummy flipped like a gymnast in a competition, and Lily was possessed by a deep, dark craving that was entirely new to her. Oblivious to their audience, she pushed against his hard, powerful frame and felt his arms tighten around her in a gesture that was unmistakably possessive. It was a taste rather than a feast, but it left her starving for more so that when he slowly lifted his head she swayed towards him dizzily, trying to balance herself.

'Wh-why did you do that?'

He dragged his thumb slowly across her lower lip and released her. 'Because you didn't know what to say and sometimes actions speak louder than words.'

'You're an amazing kisser.' Lily blinked as a flashbulb went off in her face. 'Now there's *no* chance your girlfriend will believe I'm the cleaner.'

'No chance.' His gaze lingered on her mouth. 'And she isn't my girlfriend.'

Her head spun and her legs felt shaky. She was aware of the women staring at her enviously and David gaping at her, shell-shocked.

As she floated up the last few steps to the top she smiled at him, feeling strong for the first time in days. 'Hi, Professor Ass—Ashurst.' She told herself it was the heat that was making her dizzy and disorientated, not the kiss. 'Have a safe flight home tomorrow. I'm sure your family has missed you.'

There was no opportunity for him to respond because the curator of the museum stepped forward to welcome them, shaking Nik's hand and virtually prostrating himself in gratitude.

'Mr Zervakis—your generosity—this wing is the most exciting moment of my career—' the normally articulate man was stammering. 'I know your schedule is demanding but we'd be honoured if you'd meet the team and then take a quick tour.'

Lily kept a discreet distance but Nik took her hand and clamped her next to his side, a gesture that earned her a quizzical look from Brittany, who was looking sleek and pretty in a short blue dress that showed off her long legs. She was standing next to Spy, whose eyes were glued to Lily's cleavage, confirming all her worst fears about the suitability of the dress.

The whole situation felt surreal.

One moment she'd been half naked and shivering on the bathroom floor, the next she'd been whisked into an elegant bedroom by a team of four people who had proceeded to style her hair, do her make-up and generally make her fit to be seen on the arm of Nik Zervakis.

Three dresses had magically appeared and Nik had strolled into the room in mid phone call, gestured to one of them and then left without even pausing in his conversation.

It had been on the tip of Lily's tongue to select a different dress on principle. Then she'd reasoned that not only had he provided the dress, thus allowing her to turn up at the museum opening in the first place, but that he'd picked the dress she would have chosen herself.

All the same, she felt self-conscious as her friends and

colleagues working on the project at Aptera stood together while she was treated like a VIP.

As the curator led them towards the first display Lily forgot to be self-conscious and examined the pot.

'This is early Minoan.'

Nik stared at it with a neutral expression. 'You know that because it's more cracked than the others?'

'No. Because their ceramics were characterised by linear patterns. Look—' She took his arm and drew him closer to the glass. 'Spirals, crosses, triangles, curved lines—' She talked to him about each one and he listened carefully before strolling further along the glass display cabinet.

'This one has a bird.'

'Naturalistic designs were characteristic of the Middle Minoan period. The sequencing of ceramic styles has helped archaeologists define the three phases of Minoan culture.'

He stared down in her eyes. 'Fascinating.'

Her heart bumped hard against her chest and as the curator moved away to answer questions from the press she stepped closer to him. 'You're not really fascinated, are you?'

'I am.' His eyes dropped to her mouth with blatant interest. 'But I think it might be because you're the one saying it. I love the way you get excited about things that put other people to sleep, and your mouth looks cute when you say "Minoan". It makes you pout.'

She tried not to laugh. 'You're impossible. To you it's an old pot, but it can have tremendous significance. Ceramics help archaeologists establish settlement and trading patterns. We can reconstruct human activity based on the distribution of pottery. It gives us an idea of population size and social complexity. Why are you donating so much money to the museum if it isn't an interest of yours?'

'Because I'm interested in preserving Greek culture. I donate the money. It's up to them to decide how to use it. I don't micromanage and gifts don't come with strings.'

'Why didn't you insist that it was called "The Zervakis

Wing" or something? Most benefactors want their name in the title.'

'It's about preserving history, not about advertising my name.' His eyes gleamed. 'And ZervaCo is a modern, forward-thinking company at the cutting edge of technology development. I don't want the name associated with a museum.'

'You're joking.'

'Yes, I'm joking.' His smile faded as Spy and Brittany joined them.

'They're good friends of mine,' Lily said quickly, 'so you can switch off the full-wattage intimidation.'

'If you're sure.' He introduced himself to both of them and chatted easily with Spy while Brittany pulled Lily to one side.

'I don't even know where to start with my questions.'

'Probably just as well because I wouldn't know where to start with my answers.'

'I'm guessing he's the owner of Villa You-Have-to-be-Kidding-Me.'

'He is.'

'I'm not going to ask,' Brittany muttered and then grinned. 'Oh hell, yes I am. I'm asking. What happened? He found you in the cellar fighting off the ugly sisters and decided to bring you to the ball?'

'Close. He found me on the floor of his bathroom where I'd been attacked and left for dead by his power shower. After I broke up his relationship, he needed a replacement and I was the only person around.'

Brittany started to laugh. 'You were left for dead by his power shower?'

'You said you wouldn't ask.'

'These things only ever happen to you, Lily.'

'I am aware of that. I am really not good with technology.'

'Maybe not, but you know how to pick your rebound guy. He is spectacular. And you look stunning.' Brittany's curious gaze slid over her from head to foot. 'It's a step up from dusty shorts and hiking boots.'

Lily frowned. 'He isn't my rebound guy.'

'Why not? He is smoking hot. And there's something about him.' Her friend narrowed her eyes as she scanned Nik's broad shoulders and powerful frame. 'A suggestion of the uncivilised under the civilised, if you know what I mean.' Brittany put her hand on her arm and her voice was suddenly serious. 'Be careful.'

'Why would I need to be careful? I'm never setting foot in his shower again, if that's what you mean.'

'It isn't what I mean. That man is not tame.'

'He's surprisingly amusing company.'

'That makes him even more dangerous. He's a tiger, not a pussycat and he hasn't taken his eyes off you for five seconds. I don't want to see you hurt again.'

'I have never been in less danger of being hurt. He isn't my type.'

Brittany looked at her. 'Nik Zervakis is the man equivalent of Blood Type O. He is everyone's type.'

'Not mine.'

'He kissed you,' Brittany said dryly, 'so I'm guessing he might have a different opinion on that.'

'He kissed me because I didn't know what to say to David. I was in an awkward position and he helped me out. He did that for me.'

'Lily, a guy like him does things for himself. Don't make a mistake about that. He does what he wants, with whoever he wants to do it, at a time that suits him.'

'I know. Don't worry about me.' Smiling at Brittany, she moved back to Nik. 'Looks like the party is breaking up. Thanks for a fun evening. I'll post you the dress back and any time you need your shower cleaned let me know. I owe you.'

He stared down at her for a long moment, ignoring everyone around them. 'Have dinner with me. I have a reservation at The Athena at nine.'

She'd heard of The Athena. Who hadn't? It was one of the most celebrated restaurants in the whole of Greece. Eating there was a once-in-a-lifetime experience for most people and a never-in-this-lifetime experience for her.

Those incredible dark eyes held hers and Brittany's voice flitted into her head.

He's a tiger, not a pussycat.

From the way he was looking at her mouth, she wondered if he intended her to be the guest or the meal.

'That's a joke, right?' She gave a half-smile and looked away briefly, awkward, out of her depth. When she looked back at him she was still the only one smiling.

'I never joke about food.'

Something curled low in her stomach. 'Nik…' she spoke softly '…this has been amazing. Really out of this world and something to tell my kids one day, but you're a gazillionaire and I'm a—a—'

'Sexy woman who looks great in that dress.'

There was something about him that made her feel as if she were floating two feet above the ground.

'I was going to say I'm a dusty archaeologist who can't even figure out how to use your power shower.'

'I'll teach you. Have dinner with me, Lily.' His soft command made her wonder if anyone had ever said no to him.

Thrown by the look in his eyes and the almost unbearable sexual tension, she was tempted. Then she remembered her rule about never dating anyone who didn't fit her basic criteria. 'I can't. But I'll never forget this evening. Thank you.' Because she was afraid she'd change her mind, she turned and walked quickly towards the exit.

What a crazy day it had been.

Part of her was longing to look back, to see if he was watching her.

Of course he wouldn't be watching her. Look at how quickly he'd replaced Christina. Within two minutes of her refusal, Nik Zervakis would be inviting someone else to dinner.

David stood in the doorway, blocking her exit. 'What are you doing with him?'

'None of your business.'

His jaw tightened. 'Did you kiss him to make me jealous or to help you get over me?'

'I kissed him because he's a hot guy, and I was over you the moment I found out you were married.' Realising it was true, Lily felt a rush of relief but that relief was tempered by the knowledge that her system for evaluating prospective life partners was seriously flawed.

'I know you love me.'

'You're wrong. And if you really knew me, you'd know I'm incapable of loving a man who is married to another woman.' Her voice and hands were shaking. 'You have a wife. A family.'

'I'll work something out.'

'Did you really just say that to me?' Lily stared at him, appalled. 'A family is *not* disposable. You don't come and go as it suits you, nor do you "work something out". You stick by them through thick and thin.' Disgusted and disillusioned, she tried to step past him but he caught her arm.

'You don't understand. Things are tough right now.'

'I don't care.' She dug her fingers into clammy palms. Knowing that her response was deeply personal, she looked away. 'A real man doesn't walk away when things get tough.'

'You're forgetting how good it was between us.'

'And you're forgetting the promises you made.' She dragged her arm out of his grip. 'Go back to your wife.'

He glanced over her shoulder towards Nik. 'I never thought you were the sort to be turned on by money, but obviously I was wrong. I hope you know what you're doing because all that man will ever give you is one night. A man like him is only interested in sex.'

'What did you say?' Lily stared at him and then turned her

head to look at Nik. The sick feeling in her stomach eased and her spirits lifted. 'You're right. Thank you so much.'

'For making you realise he's wrong for you?'

'For making me realise he's perfect. Now stop looking down the front of my dress and go home to your wife and kids.' With that, she stalked past him and spotted the reporter who had asked her identity on the way in. 'Lily,' she said clearly. 'Lily Rose. That's my name. And yes, Rose is my second name.'

Then she turned and stalked back into the museum, straight up to Nik, who was deep in conversation with two important-looking men in suits.

All talk ceased as Lily walked up to him, her heels making the same rhythmic tapping sound that Christina's had earlier in the evening. She decided heels were her new favourite thing for illustrating mood. 'What time is that restaurant reservation?'

He didn't miss a beat. 'Nine o'clock.'

'Then we should leave, because we don't want to be late.' She stood on tiptoe and planted a kiss firmly on his mouth. 'And just so that you know, whatever you're planning on doing with the dress, I'm keeping the shoes.'

CHAPTER THREE

THE ATHENA WAS situated on the edge of town, on a hill overlooking Souda Bay with the White Mountains dominating the horizon behind them.

Still on a high after her confrontation with David, Lily sailed into the restaurant feeling like royalty. 'You have no idea how good it felt to tell David to go home to his wife. I felt like punching the air. You see what a few hours in your company has done for me? I'm already transformed. Your icy control and lack of emotional engagement is contagious.'

Nik guided her to his favourite table, tucked away behind a discreet screen of vines. 'You certainly showed the guy what he was missing.'

Lily frowned. 'I didn't want to show him what he was missing. I wanted him to learn a lesson and never lie or cheat again. I wanted him to think of his poor wife. Marriage should be for ever. No cheating. Mess around as much as you like before if that's what you want, but once you've made that commitment, that's it. Don't you agree?'

'Definitely. Which is why I've never made that commitment,' he said dryly. 'I'm still at the "messing around" stage and I expect to stay firmly trapped in that stage for the rest of my life.'

'You don't want a family? We're very different. It's brilliant.' She smiled at him and his eyes narrowed.

'Why is that brilliant?'

'Because you're completely and utterly wrong for me. We don't want the same things.'

'I'm relieved to hear it.' He leaned back in his chair. 'I hardly dare ask what you want.'

She hesitated. 'Someone like you will think I'm a ridiculous romantic.'

'Tell me.'

She dragged her gaze from his and looked over the tumbling bougainvillea to the sea beyond. *Was she a ridiculous romantic?*

Was she setting herself unachievable goals?

Seduced by the warmth of his gaze and the beauty of the spectacular sunset, she told the truth. 'I want the whole fairy tale.'

'Which fairy tale? The one where the stepmother poisons the apple or the one where the prince has to deal with a heroine with narcolepsy?'

She laughed. 'The happy-ending part. I want to fall in love, settle down and have lots of babies.' Enjoying herself, she looked him in the eye. 'Am I freaking you out yet?'

'That depends. Are you expecting to do any of that with me?'

'No! Of course not.'

'Then you're not freaking me out.'

'I start every relationship in the genuine belief it might go somewhere.'

'I presume you mean somewhere other than bed?'

'I do. I have never been interested in sex for the sake of sex.'

Nik looked amused. 'That's the only sort of sex I'm interested in.'

She sat back in her chair and looked at him. 'I've never had sex with a man I wasn't in love with. I fall in love, then I have sex. I think sex cements my emotional connection to someone.' She sneaked another look at him. 'You don't have that problem, do you?'

'I'm not looking for an emotional connection, if that's what you're asking.'

'I want to be more like you. I decided this morning I'm going to have cold, emotionless rebound sex. I'm switching everything off. It's going to be wham, bam, thank you, man.'

The corners of his mouth flickered. 'Do you have anyone in mind for this project?'

She sensed this wasn't the moment to confess he was right at the top of her list. 'I'm going to pick a guy I couldn't possibly fall in love with. Then I'll be safe. It will be like—' she struggled to find the right description '—emotional contraception. I'll be taking precautions. Wearing a giant condom over my feelings. Protecting myself. I bet you do that all the time.'

'If you're asking if I've ever pulled a giant condom over my feelings, the answer is no.'

'You're laughing at me, but if you'd been hurt as many times as I have you wouldn't be laughing. So if emotions don't play a part in your relationships, what exactly is sex to you?'

'Recreation.' He took a menu from the waiter and she felt a rush of mortification. As soon as he walked away, she gave a groan.

'How long had he been standing there?'

'Long enough to know you're planning on having cold, unemotional rebound sex and that you're thinking of wearing a giant condom over your feelings. I think that was the point he decided it was time to take our order.'

She covered her face with her hands. 'We need to leave. I'm sure the food here is delicious, but we need to eat somewhere different or I need to take my plate under the table.'

'You're doing it again. Letting emotions govern your actions.'

'But he *heard* me. Aren't you embarrassed?'

'Why would I be embarrassed?'

'Aren't you worried about what he might think of you?'

'Why would I care what he thinks? I don't know him. His role is to serve our food and make sure we enjoy ourselves sufficiently to want to come back. His opinion on anything else is irrelevant. Carry on with what you were saying. It was fascinating. Dining with you is like learning about an alien species. You were telling me you're going to pick a guy you can't fall in love with and use him for sex.'

'And you were telling me sex is recreation—like football?'

'No, because football is a group activity. I'm possessive, so for me it's strictly one on one.'

Her heart gave a little flip. 'That sounds like a type of commitment.'

'I'm one hundred per cent committed for the time a woman is in my bed. She is the sole focus of my attention.'

Her stomach uncurled with a slow, dangerous heat. 'But that might only be for a night?'

He simply smiled and she leaned back with a shocked laugh.

'You are so *bad*. And honest. I love that.'

'As long as you don't love *me*, we don't have a problem.'

'I could never love you. You are so wrong for me.'

'I think we should drink to that.' He raised a hand and moments later champagne appeared on the table.

'I can't believe you live like this. A driver, bottles of champagne—' She lifted the glass, watching the bubbles. 'Your villa is bigger than quite a few Greek islands and there is only one of you.'

'I like space and light and property is always a good investment.' He handed the menu back to the waiter. 'Is there any food you don't eat?'

'I eat everything.' She paused while he spoke to the waiter in Greek. 'Are you seriously ordering for me?'

'The menu is in Greek and you were talking about sex so I was aiming to keep the interaction as brief as possible in order to prevent you from feeling the need to dine under the table.'

'In that case I'll forgive you.' She waited until the waiter had walked away with their order. 'So if property is an investment that means you'd *sell* your home?'

'I have four homes.'

Her jaw dropped. 'Four? Why does one person need four homes? One for every season or something?'

'I have offices in New York, San Francisco and London and I don't like staying in hotels.'

'So you buy a house. That is the rich man's way of solving a problem. Which one do you think of as home?' Seeing the puzzled look on his face, she elaborated. 'Where do your family live? Do you have family? Are your parents alive?'

'They are.'

'Happily married?'

'Miserably divorced. In my father's case three times so far, but he's always in competition with himself so I'm expecting a fourth as soon as the wedding is out of the way.'

'And your mother?' She saw a faint shift in his expression.

'My mother is American. She lives in Boston with her third husband who is a divorce lawyer.'

'So do you think of yourself as Greek American or American Greek?'

He gave a careless lift of his broad shoulders. 'Whichever serves my purpose at the time.'

'Wow. So you have this big, crazy family.' Lily felt a flash of envy. 'That must be wonderful.'

'Why?'

'You don't think it's wonderful? I guess we never appreciate something when we have it.' She said it lightly but felt his dark gaze fix on her across the table.

'Are you going to cry?'

'No, of course not.'

'Good. Because tears are the one form of emotional expression I don't tolerate.'

She stole an olive from the bowl on the table. 'What if someone is upset?'

'Then they need to walk away from me until they've sorted themselves out, or be prepared for me to walk away. I never allow myself to be manipulated and ninety-nine per cent of tears are manipulation.'

'What about the one per cent which are an expression of genuine emotion?'

'I've never encountered that rare beast, so I'm willing to play the odds.'

'If that's your experience, you must have met some awful women in your time. I don't believe you'd be that unsympathetic.'

'Believe it.' He leaned back as the waiter delivered a selection of dishes. 'These are Cretan specialities. Try them.' He spooned beans in a rich tomato sauce onto her plate and added local goat's cheese.

She nibbled the beans and moaned with pleasure. 'These are delicious. I still can't believe you ordered for me. Do you want to feed me, too? Because I could lie back and let you drop grapes into my mouth if that would be fun. Or you could cover my naked body with whipped cream. Is that the sort of stuff you do in bed?'

There was a dangerous glitter in his eyes. 'You don't want to know the sort of "stuff" I do in bed, Lily. You're far too innocent.'

She remembered what Brittany had said about him not being tame. 'I'm not innocent. I have big eyes and that gives people a false impression of me.'

'You remind me of a kitten that's been abandoned by the side of the road.'

'You've got me totally wrong. I'd say I'm more of a panther.' She clawed the air and growled. 'A little bit predatory. A little bit dangerous.'

He gave her a long steady look and she blushed and lowered her hand.

'All right, maybe not a *panther* exactly but not a kitten either.' She thought about what lay in her past. 'I'll have you know I'm pretty tough. Tell me more about your family. So you have a father and a few stepmothers. How about siblings?'

'I have one half-sister who is two.'

Lily softened. 'I love that age. They're so busy and into everything. Is she adorable?'

'I've no idea. I've never met her.'

'You've—' She stared at him, shocked. 'You mean it's been a while since you've seen her.'

'No. I mean I've never seen her.' He lifted his champagne. 'Her mother extracted all the money she could from my father and then left. She lives in Athens and visits when she wants something.'

'Oh, my God, that's *terrible.*' Lily's eyes filled. 'Your poor, poor father.'

He put his glass down slowly. 'Are you crying for my father?'

'No.' Her throat was thickened. 'Maybe. Yes, a little bit.'

'A man you've never met and know nothing about.'

'Maybe I'm the one per cent who cares.' She sniffed and he shook his head in exasperation.

'This is your tough, ruthless streak? How can you be sad for someone you don't know?'

'Because I sympathise with his situation. He doesn't see his little girl and that must be so hard. Family is the most important thing in the world and it is often the least appreciated thing.'

'If you let a single tear fall onto your cheek,' he said softly, 'I'm walking out of here.'

'I don't believe you. You wouldn't be that heartless. I think it's all a big act you put on to stop women slobbering all over you.'

'Do you want to test it?' His tone was cool. 'Because I suggest you wait until the end of the meal. The lamb *kleftiko* is the best anywhere in Greece and they make a house special with honey and pistachio nuts that you wouldn't want to miss.'

'But if you're the one walking out, then I can stay here and eat your portion.' She helped herself to another spoonful of food from the dish closest to her. 'I don't know why you're so freaked out by tears. It's not as if I was expecting you to hug me. I've taught myself to self-soothe.'

'Self-soothe?' Some of the tension left him. 'You hug yourself?'

'It's important to be independent.' She'd been self-sufficient from an early age, but the ability to do everything for herself hadn't removed the deep longing to share her life with someone. 'Why did your dad and his last wife divorce?'

'Because they married,' he said smoothly, 'and divorce is an inevitable consequence of marriage.'

She wondered why he had such a grim view of marriage. 'Not all marriages.'

'All but those infected with extreme inertia.'

'So you're saying that even people who stay married would divorce if they could be bothered to make the effort.'

'I think there are any number of reasons for a couple to stay together, but love isn't one of them. In my father's case, wife number three married him for his money and the novelty wore off.'

'Does "wife number three" have a name?'

'Callie.' His hard tone told her everything she needed to know about his relationship with his last stepmother.

'You don't like her?'

'Are you enjoying your meal?'

She blinked, thrown by the change of subject. 'It's delicious, but—'

'Good. If you're hoping to sample dessert, you need to talk about something other than my family.'

'You control everything, even the conversation.' She wondered why he didn't want to talk about his family. 'Is this where you bring all the women you date?'

'It depends on the woman.'

'How about that woman you were with earlier—Christina? She definitely wouldn't have eaten any of this. She had carb-phobia written all over her.'

Those powerful shoulders relaxed slightly. 'She would have ordered green salad, grilled fish and eaten half of it.'

'So why didn't you order green salad and grilled fish for me?'

'Because you look like someone who enjoys food.'

Lily gave him a look. 'I'm starting to understand why women cry around you. You basically called me fat. For your information, most women would storm out if you said that to them.'

'So why didn't you storm out?'

'Because eating here is a once-in-a-lifetime experience and I don't want to miss it. And I don't think you meant it that way and I like to give people the benefit of the doubt. Tell me what happens next on a date. You bring a woman to a place like this and then you take her back to your villa for sex in that massive bed?'

'I never talk about my relationships.'

'You don't talk about your family and you don't talk about your relationships.' Lily helped herself to rich, plump slices of tomato salad. 'What do you want to talk about?'

'You. Tell me about your work.'

'I work in your company. You know more about what goes on than I do, but one thing I will say is that with all these technology skills at your disposal you need to invent an app that syncs all the details of the women who call you. You have a busy sex life and it's easy to get it mixed up, especially as they're all pretty much the same type.' She put her fork down. 'Is that the secret to staying emotionally detached? You date women who are clones, no individual characteristics to tell them apart.'

'I do not date clones, and I don't want to talk about my work, I want to talk about your work. Your archaeological work.' His eyes gleamed. 'And try to include the word "Minoan" at least eight times in each sentence.'

She ignored that. 'I'm a ceramics expert. I did a masters in archaeology and since then I've been working on an internationally funded project replicating Minoan cooking fabrics. Among other things we've been looking at the technological shift Minoan potters made when they replaced hand-building methods with the wheel. We can trace patterns of production, but also the context of ceramic consumption. The word ceramic comes from the Greek, *keramikos,* but you probably already know that.'

He reached for his wine glass. 'I can't believe you were cleaning my shower.'

'Cleaning your shower pays well and I have college debts.'

'If you didn't have college debts, what would you be doing?'

She hesitated, unwilling to share her dream with a stranger, especially one who couldn't possibly understand having to make choices driven by debt. 'I have no idea. I can't afford to think like that. I have to be practical.'

'Why Crete?'

'Crete had all the resources necessary to produce pottery. Clay, temper, water and fuel. Microscopic ceramic fabric analysis indicate those resources have been used for at least eight thousand years. The most practical way of understanding ancient technology is to replicate it and use it and that's what we've been doing.'

'So you've been trying to cook like a Minoan?'

'Yes. We're using tools and materials that would have been available during the Cretan Bronze Age.'

'That's what you're digging for?'

'Brittany and the team have different objectives, but while they're digging I'm able to access clay. I spend some of my time on site and some of my time at the museum with a small team, but that's all coming to an end now. Tell me what you do.'

'You work in my company. You should know what I do.'

'I don't know *specifically* what you do. I know you're a technology wizard. I guess that's why you have a shower that looks like something from NASA. I bet you're good with computers. Technology isn't really my thing, but you probably already know that.'

'If technology isn't your thing, why are you working in my company?'

'I'm not dealing with the technology side. I'm dealing with people. I did a short spell in Human Resources—you keep them busy by the way—and now I'm working with your personal assistants. I still haven't decided what I want to do with my life so I'm trying different things. It's only two days a week and I wanted to see how I enjoyed corporate life.'

'And how are you enjoying "corporate life"?'

'It's different.' She dodged the question and he gave her a long, speculative look.

'Tell me why you became involved with that guy who looked old enough to be your father.'

Her stomach lurched. *Because she was an idiot.* 'I never talk about my relationships.'

'On short acquaintance I'd say the problem is stopping you talking, not getting you talking. Tell me.' Something about that compelling dark gaze made it impossible not to confide.

'I think I was attracted to his status and gravitas. I was flattered when he paid me attention. A psychologist would probably say it has something to do with not having a father around when I was growing up. Anyway, he pursued me pretty heavily and it got serious fast. And then I found out he was married.' She lowered her voice and pulled a face. 'I hate myself for that, but most of all I hate him for lying to me.' Knowing his views on marriage, she wondered if he'd think she was ridiculously principled but his eyes were hard.

'You cried over this guy?'

'I think perhaps I was crying because history repeated

itself. My relationships always follow the same pattern. I meet someone I'm attracted to, he's caring, attentive and a really good listener—I fall in love, have sex with him, start planning a future and then suddenly that's it. We break up.'

'And this experience hasn't put you off love?'

Perhaps it should have done.

No one had ever stayed in her life.

From an early age she'd wondered what it was about her that made it so easy for people to walk away.

The dishes were cleared away and a sticky, indulgent dessert placed in the centre of the table.

She tried to pull herself together. 'If you have one bad meal you don't stop eating, do you? And by the way this is the best meal I've ever had in my whole life.' She stuck her spoon in the pastry and honey oozed over the plate. She decided this was the perfect time to check a few facts before finally committing herself. 'Tell me what happens in your relationships. We'll talk hypothetically as you don't like revealing specifics. Let's say you meet a woman and you find her attractive. What happens next?'

'I take her on a date.'

'What sort of date?' Lily licked the spoon. 'Dinner? Theatre? Movie? Walk on the beach?'

'Any of those.'

'Let's say it's dinner. What would you talk about?'

'Anything.'

'Anything as long as it isn't to do with your family or relationships.'

He smiled. 'Exactly.'

'So you talk, you drink expensive wine, you admire the romantic view—then what? You take her home or you take her to bed?'

'Yes.' He paused as their waiter delivered a bottle of clear liquid and two glasses and Lily shook her head.

'Is that raki? Brittany loves it, but it gives me a headache.'

'We call it *tsikoudia.* It is a grape liqueur—an important part of Cretan hospitality.'

'I know. It's been around since Minoan times. Archaeologists have found the petrified remains of grapes and grape pips inside *pithoi,* the old clay storage jars, so it's assumed they knew plenty about distillation. Doesn't change the fact it gives me a headache.'

'Then you didn't drink it with enough water.' He handed her a small glass. 'The locals think it promotes a long and healthy life.'

Lily took a sip and felt her throat catch fire as she swallowed. 'So now finish telling me about your typical date. You don't fall in love, because you don't believe in love. So when you take a woman to bed, there are no feelings involved at all?'

'There are plenty of feelings involved.' The look he gave her made her heart pump faster.

'I mean emotions. You have emotionless sex. You don't say *I love you.* You don't feel anything here—' Lily put her hand on her heart. 'No feelings. So it's all about physical satisfaction. This is basically a naked workout, yes? It's like a bench press for two.'

'Sex may not be emotional, but it's intimate,' he said softly. 'It requires the ultimate degree of trust.'

'You can do that and still not be emotionally involved?'

'When I'm with a woman I care about her enjoyment, her pleasure, her happiness and her comfort. I don't love her.'

'You don't love women?'

'I do love women.' The corners of his mouth flickered. 'I just don't want to love one specific woman.'

Lily stared at him in fascination.

There was no way, *no way,* she would ever fall in love with a man like Nik. She didn't even need to check her list to know he didn't tick a single one of the boxes.

He was perfect.

'There's something I want to say to you and I hope you're

not going to be shocked.' She put her glass down and took a deep breath. 'I want to have rebound sex. No emotions involved. Sex without falling in love. Not something I've ever done before, so this is all new to me.'

He watched her from under lowered lids, his expression unreadable. There was a dangerous stillness about him. 'And you're telling me this because—?'

'Because you seem to be the expert.' Her heart started to pound. 'I want you to take me to bed.'

CHAPTER FOUR

Nik scanned her in silence. The irony was that his original plan had been to do exactly that. Take her to bed. She was fun, sexy and original but the longer he spent in her company the more he realised how different her life goals were from his own. By her own admittance, Lily wasn't the sort to emotionally disengage in a relationship. In the interests of self-protection, logic took precedence over his libido.

'It's time I took you home.'

Far from squashing her, the news appeared to cheer her. 'That's what I was hoping you'd say. I promise you won't regret it. What I lack in experience I make up for in enthusiasm.'

She was as bright as she was pretty and he knew her 'misunderstanding' was deliberate.

'*Theé mou*, you should *not* be saying things like that to a man. It could be taken the wrong way.'

She sliced into a tomato. 'You're taking it the way I intended you to take it.'

Nik glanced at the bottle of champagne and tried to work out how much she'd had. 'I'm not taking you to my home, I'm taking you to *your* home.'

'You don't want to do that. My bed is smaller than a cat basket and you're big. I have a feeling we're going to get very hot and sweaty, and I don't have air conditioning.'

Nik's libido was fighting against the restraining bonds of logic. 'I will give you a lift home and then I'm leaving.'

'Leaving?' Disappointment mingled with uncertainty. 'You don't find me attractive?'

'You're sexy as hell,' he drawled, 'but you're not my type.'

'That doesn't make any sense. You don't like sexy?'

'I like sexy. I don't like women who want to fall in love, settle down and have lots of babies.'

'I thought we'd already established I didn't want to do any of that with you. You don't score a single point on my checklist, which is *exactly* why I want to do this. I know I'd be safe. And so would you!'

He decided he didn't even want to know about her checklist. 'How much champagne have you had?'

'I'm not drunk, if that's what you're suggesting. Ask me anything. Make me walk in a straight line. I'll touch my nose with my eyes closed, or I'll touch *your* nose with my eyes closed if you prefer. Or other parts of you—' She gave a wicked grin and leaned forward. 'One night. That's all it would be. You will not regret it.'

Nik deployed the full force of his will power and kept his eyes away from the softness of her breasts. 'You're right. I won't, because it's not going to happen.'

'I do yoga. I'm very bendy.'

Nik gave a soft curse. 'Stop talking.'

'I can put my legs behind my head.'

'*Cristo*, you should *definitely* stop talking.' His libido was urging logic to surrender.

'What's the problem? One night of fun. Tomorrow we both go our own ways and if I see you in the office I'll pretend I don't know you. Call your lawyer. I'll sign a contract promising not to fall in love with you. A pre-non-nuptial agreement. All I want is for you to take me home, strip me naked, throw me onto that enormous bed of yours and have sex with me in every conceivable position. After that I will walk out of your door and you'll never see me again. Deal?'

He tried to respond but it seemed her confusing mix of innocence and sexuality had short-circuited his brain. 'Lily—' he spoke through his teeth '—trust me, you do *not* want me to take you home, strip you naked and throw you onto my bed.'

'Why not? It's just sex.'

'You've spent several hours telling me you don't do "just sex".'

'But I'm going to this time. I want to be able to separate sex from love. The next time a man comes my way who might be the one, I won't let sex confuse things. I'll be like Kevlar. Nothing is getting through me. Nothing.'

'You are marshmallow, not Kevlar.'

'That was the old me. The new me is Kevlar. I don't understand why you won't do this, unless—' She studied him for a long moment and then leaned forward, a curious look in her eyes. 'Are you *scared*?'

'I'm sober,' he said softly, 'and when I play, I like it to be with an opponent who is similarly matched.'

'I'm tougher than I look.' A dimple appeared in the corner of her mouth. 'Drink another glass of champagne and then call Vassilis.'

'How do you know my driver's name?'

'I listen. And he has a kind face. There really is no need to be nervous. If rumour is correct, you're a cold, emotionless vacuum and that means you're in no danger from someone like little me.'

He had a feeling 'little me' was the most dangerous thing he'd encountered in a long while. 'If I'm a "cold, emotionless vacuum", why would you want to climb into my bed?'

'Because you are *insanely* sexy and all the things that make you so wrong for me would make you perfect for rebound sex.'

He looked into those blue eyes and tried to ignore the surge of sexual hunger that had gripped him from the moment he'd laid eyes on that pale silky hair tumbling damp round her gleaming wet body.

Never before had doing the right thing felt so wrong.

Nik cursed under his breath and rose to his feet. 'We're leaving.'

'Good decision.' She slid her hand into his, rose on tiptoe and whispered in his ear. 'I'll be gentle with you.'

With her wide smile and laughing eyes, it was like being on a date with a beam of sunshine. He felt heat spread through his body, his arousal so brutal he was tempted to haul her behind the nearest lockable door, rip off that dress and acquaint himself with every part of her luscious, naked body.

Vassilis was waiting outside with the car and Nik bundled her inside and sat as far from her as possible.

All his life, he'd avoided women like her. Women who believed in romance and 'the one'. For him, the myth of love had been smashed in childhood along with Santa and the Tooth Fairy. He had no use for it in his life.

'Where do you live?' He growled the words but she simply smiled.

'You don't need to know, because we're going back to your place. Your bed is almost big enough to be seen from outer space.'

Nik ran his hand over his jaw. 'Lily—'

Her phone signalled a text and she dug around in her bag. 'I need to answer this. It will be Brittany, checking I'm all right. She and Spy are probably worried because they saw me go off with you.'

'Maybe you should pay attention to your friends.'

'Hold that thought—'

Having rebound sex. She mouthed the words as she typed. Speak to you tomorrow.

Nik was tempted to seize the phone and text her friends to come and pick her up. 'Brittany was the girl in the blue dress?'

'She's the female version of you, but without the money.

She doesn't engage emotionally. I found out today that she was married for ten days when she was eighteen. Can you believe that? Ten days. I don't know the details, but apparently it cured her of ever wanting a repeat performance.' She pressed send and slid the phone back into her bag. 'I grew up in foster homes so I don't have any family. I think that's probably why my friends are so important to me. I never really had a sense of belonging anywhere. That's a very lonely feeling as a child.'

He felt something stir inside him, as if she'd poked a stick into a muddy, stagnant pool that had lain dormant and undiscovered for decades. Deeply uncomfortable, he shifted in his seat. 'Why are you telling me this?'

'I thought as we're going to have sex, you might want to know something about me.'

'I don't.'

'That's not very polite.'

'I'm not striving for "polite". This is who I am. It's not too late for my driver to drop you home. Give him the address.'

She leaned forward and pressed the button so that the screen closed between him and the driver. 'Sorry, Vassilis, but I don't want to corrupt you.' She slid across the seat, closed her eyes and lifted her face to his. 'Kiss me. Whatever it is you do, do it now.'

Nik had always considered himself to be a disciplined man but he was rapidly rethinking that assessment. With her, there was no discipline. He looked down at those long, thick eyelashes and the pink curve of her mouth and tried to remember when he'd last been tempted to have sex in the back of his car.

'No.' He managed to inject the word with forceful conviction but instead of retreating, she advanced.

'In that case I'll kiss you. I don't mind taking the initiative.' Her slim fingers slid to the inside of his thigh. He was so aroused he couldn't even remember why he was fighting this, and instead of pushing her away he gripped her hand hard and turned his head towards her.

His gaze swept her flushed cheeks and the lush curve of her mouth. With a rough curse he lowered his head, driving her lips apart with his tongue and taking that mouth in a kiss that was as rough as it was sexually explicit. His intention was to scare her off, so there was no holding back, no diluting of his passion. He kissed her hard, expecting to feel her pull back but instead she pressed closer. She tasted of sugar and sweet temptation, her mouth soft and eager against his as she all but wriggled onto his lap.

The heavy weight of her breasts brushed against his arm and he gave a groan and slid his hand into her hair, anchoring her head for the hard demands of his kiss. She licked into his mouth, snuggling closer like a kitten, those full soft curves pressing against him. It was a kiss without boundaries, an explosion of raw desire that built until the rear of the car shimmered with stifling heat and sexual awareness.

He slid his hand under her dress, over the smooth skin of her thigh to the soft shadows between her legs. It was her thickened moan of pleasure that woke him up.

Cristo, they were in the car, in moving traffic.

Releasing her as if she were a hot coal, he pushed her away. 'I thought you were supposed to be smart.'

Her breathing was shallow and rapid. 'I'm very, very smart. And you're an amazing kisser. Are you as good at everything else?'

His pulse was throbbing and he was so painfully aroused he didn't dare move. 'If you really want to come home with me then you're not as smart as you look.'

'What makes you think that?'

'Because a woman like you should steer clear of men like me. I don't have a love life, I have a sex life. I'll use you. If you're in my bed it will be all about pleasure and nothing else. I don't care about your feelings. I'm not kind. I'm not gentle. I need you to know that.'

There was a long, loaded silence and then her gaze slid to his mouth. 'Okay, I get it. No fluffy kittens in this relationship. Message received and understood. Can this car go any faster because I don't think I've ever been this turned on in my life before.'

She wasn't the only one. His self-control was stretched to breaking point. Why was he fighting it? She was an adult. She wasn't drunk and she knew what she was doing. Logic didn't just surrender to libido, it was obliterated. All the same, something made him open one more exit door. 'Be very sure, Lily.'

'I'm sure. I've never been so sure of anything in my life. Unless you want to be arrested for performing an indecent act in a public place you'd better tell Vassilis to break a few speed limits.'

Lily walked into the villa she'd cleaned earlier, feeling ridiculously nervous. In the romantic setting of the restaurant this had seemed like a good idea. Now she wasn't quite so sure. 'So why did you hire a contract cleaning company?'

'I didn't.' He threw his jacket over the back of a chair with careless disregard for its future appearance. 'I have staff who look after this place. Presumably they arranged it. I didn't give them much notice of my return. I don't care how they do their job as long as it gets done.'

She paced across the living room and stared across the floodlit shimmer of the infinity pool. 'It's pretty at night.' It was romantic, but she knew this had nothing to do with romance. Her other relationships had been with men she knew and cared about. This scenario was new to her. 'Do you have something to drink?'

'You're thirsty?'

Nervous. 'A little.'

He gave her a long look, strolled out of the room and returned moments later carrying a glass of water.

'I want you sober,' he said softly. 'In fact I insist on it.'

Realising they were actually going to do this, she suddenly found she was shaking so much the water sloshed out of the glass and onto the floor. 'Oops. I'm messing up the floor I cleaned earlier.'

He was standing close to her and her gaze drifted to the bronzed skin at the base of his throat and the blue-shadowed jaw. Everything about him was unapologetically masculine. He wasn't just dangerously attractive, he was lethal and suddenly she wondered what on earth she was doing. Maybe she should have taken up Spy's offer of rebound sex, except that Spy didn't induce one tenth of this crazy response in her. A thrilling sense of anticipation mingled with wicked excitement and she knew she'd regret it for ever if she walked away. She knew she took relationships too seriously. If she was going to try a different approach then there was surely no better man to do it with than Nik.

'Scared?' His voice was deep, dark velvet and she gave a smile.

'A little. But only because I don't normally do this and you're not my usual type. It's like passing your driving test and then getting behind the wheel of a Ferrari. I'm worried I'll crash you into a lamppost.' She put the glass down carefully on the glass table and ran her damp hands over her thighs. 'Okay, let's do this. Ignore the fact I'm shaking, go right ahead and do your bad, bad thing, whatever that is.'

He said nothing. Just looked at her, that dark gaze uncomfortably penetrating.

She waited, heart pounding, virtually squirming on the spot. 'I'm not good with delayed gratification. I'm more of an instant person. I like to—'

'Hush.' Finally he spoke and then he reached out and drew her against him, the look in his eyes driving words and thoughts from her head. She felt the warmth of his hand against the base of her spine, the slow, sensitive stroke of his fingers low on her back and then he lifted his hands and cupped her face, forcing her to look at him. 'Lily Rose—'

She swallowed. 'Nik—'

'Don't be nervous.' He murmured the words against her lips. 'There's no reason to be nervous.'

'I'm not nervous,' she lied. 'But I'm not really sure what happens next.'

'I'll decide what happens next.'

Her heart bumped uncomfortably against her ribs. 'So—what do you want me to do?'

His mouth hovered close to hers and his fingers grazed her jaw. 'I want you to stop talking.'

'I'm going to stop talking right now this second.' Her stomach felt as if a thousand butterflies were trying to escape. She hadn't expected him to be so gentle, but those exploring fingers were slow, almost languorous as they stroked her face and slid over her neck and into her hair.

She stood, disorientated by intoxicating pleasure as he trailed his mouth along her jaw, tormenting her with dark, dangerous kisses. Heat uncurled low in her pelvis and spread through her body, sapping the strength from her knees, and she slid her hands over those sleek, powerful shoulders, feeling the hard swell of muscle beneath her palms. His mouth moved lower and she tilted her head back as he kissed her neck and then the base of her throat. She felt the slow slide of his tongue against supersensitive skin, the warmth of his breath and then his hand slid back into her hair and he brought his mouth back to hers. He kissed her with an erotic expertise that made her head spin and her legs grow heavy. With each slow stroke of his tongue, he sent her senses spinning out of control. It was like being drugged. She tried to find her balance, her centre, but just when she felt close to grasping a few threads of control, he used his mouth to drive every coherent thought from her head. Shaky, she lifted her hand to his face, felt the roughness of his jaw against her palm and the lean, spare perfection of his bone structure.

She slid her fingers into his hair and felt his hand slide down her spine and draw her firmly against him.

She felt him, brutally hard through the silky fabric of her dress, and she gave a moan, low in her throat as he trapped her there with the strength of his arms, the power in those muscles reminding her that this wasn't a safe flirtation, or a game.

His kisses grew rougher, more intimate, more demanding and she tugged at his shirt, her fingers swift and sure on the buttons, her movements more frantic with each bit of male muscle she exposed.

His chest was powerful, his abs lean and hard and she felt a moment of breathless unease because she'd never had sex with a man built like him.

He was self-assured and experienced and as she pushed the shirt from his shoulders she tried to take a step backwards.

'I'd like to keep my clothes on, if that's all right with you.'

'It's not all right.' But there was a smile in his voice as he slid his hand from her hips to her waist, pulling her back against him. His fingers brushed against the underside of her breast and she moaned.

'You look as if you spend every spare second of your life working out.'

'I don't.'

'You get this way through lots of athletic sex?'

His mouth hovered close to hers. 'You promised to stop talking.'

'That was before I saw you half naked. I'm intimidated. That photo didn't lie. Now I know what you look like under your clothes I think I might be having body-image problems.'

He smiled, and she felt his hands at the back of her dress and the slow slither of silk as her dress slid to the floor.

Standing in front of him in nothing but her underwear and high heels, she felt ridiculously exposed. It didn't matter that he'd already seen her that way. This was different.

He eased back from her, his eyes slumberous and dangerously dark. 'Let's go upstairs.'

Her knees were shaking so much she wasn't sure she could walk but the next moment he scooped her into his arms and she gave a gasp of shock and dug her hands in his shoulder.

'Don't you dare drop me. I bruise easily.' She had a close-up view of his face and stared hungrily at the hard masculine lines, the blue-black shadow of his jaw and the slim, sensual line of his mouth. 'If I'd known you were planning on carrying me I would have said no to dessert.'

'Dessert was the best part.' They reached the top of the stairs and he carried her into his bedroom and lowered her to the floor next to the bed.

She didn't see him move, and yet a light came on next to the bed sending a soft beam over the silk covers. Glancing around her, Lily realised that if she lay on that bed her body would be illuminated by the wash of light.

'Can we switch the lights off?'

His eyes hooded, he lowered his hands to his belt. 'No.' As he removed the last of his clothes she let her eyes skid downwards and felt heat pour into her cheeks.

It was only a brief glance, but it was enough to imprint the image of his body in her brain.

'Do you model underwear in your spare time? Because seriously—' Her cheeks flooded with colour. 'Okay so I think this whole thing would be easier in the dark—then I won't be so intimidated by your supersonic abs.'

'Hush.' He smoothed her hair back from her face. 'Do you trust me?' His voice was rough and she felt a flutter of nerves low in her belly.

'I—yes. I think so. Why? Am I being stupid?'

'No. Close your eyes.'

She hesitated and then closed them. She heard the sound of a drawer opening and then felt something soft and silky being tied round her eyes.

'What are you doing?' She lifted her hand but he closed

his fingers round her wrist and drew her hands back to her sides.

'Relax.' His voice was a soft purr. 'I'm taking away one of your senses. The one that's making you nervous. There's no need to panic. You still have four remaining. I want you to use those.'

'I can't see.'

'Exactly. You wanted to do this in the dark. Now you're in the dark.'

'I meant that you should put the lights out! It was so you couldn't see me, not so that I couldn't see you.'

'Shh.' His lips nibbled at hers, his tongue stroking over her mouth in a slow, sensual seduction.

She was quivering, her senses straining with delicious anticipation as she tried to work out where he was and where he'd touch her next.

She felt his lips on her shoulder and felt his fingers slide the thin straps of her bra over her arms. Wetness pooled between her thighs and she pressed them together, so aroused she could hardly breathe.

He took his time, explored her neck, her shoulder, the underside of her breast until she wasn't sure her legs would hold her and he must have known that because he tipped her back onto the bed, supporting her as she lost her balance.

She could see nothing through the silk mask but she felt the weight of him on top of her, the roughness of his thigh against hers and the slide of silk against her heated flesh as he stripped her naked.

She was quivering, her senses sharpened by her lack of vision. She felt the warmth of his mouth close over the tip of her breast, the skilled flick of his tongue sending arrows of pleasure shooting through her over-sensitised body.

She gave a moan and clutched at his shoulders. 'Do we need a safe word or something?' She felt him pause.

'Why would you need a safe word?'

'I thought—'

'I'm not going to do anything that makes you uncomfortable.'

'What do I say if I want you to stop?'

His mouth brushed lightly across her jaw. 'You say "stop".'

'That's it?'

'That's it.' There was a smile in his voice. 'If I do one single thing that makes you uncomfortable, tell me.'

'Is embarrassed the same as uncomfortable?'

He gave a soft laugh and she felt the stroke of his palm on her thigh and then he parted her legs and his mouth drifted from her belly to her inner thigh.

He paused, his breath warm against that secret place. 'Relax, *erota mou*.'

She lifted her hands to remove the blindfold but he caught her wrists in one hand and held them pinned, while he used the other to part her and expose her secrets.

Unbearably aroused, melting with a confusing mix of desire and mortification, she tried to close her legs but he licked at her intimately, opening her with his tongue, exploring her vulnerable flesh with erotic skill and purpose until all she wanted was for him to finish what he'd started.

'Nik—' She writhed, sobbed, struggled against him and he released her hands and anchored her hips, holding her trapped as he explored her with his tongue.

She'd forgotten all about removing the blindfold.

The only thing in her head was easing the maddening ache that was fast becoming unbearable.

She dug her fingers in the sheets, moaning as he slid his fingers deep inside her, manipulating her body and her senses until she tipped into excitement overload. She felt herself start to throb round those seeking fingers, but instead of giving her what she wanted he gently withdrew his hand and eased away from her.

'Please! Oh, please—' she sobbed in protest, wondering what he was doing.

Was he leaving her?

Was he stopping?

With a whimper of protest, she writhed and reached for him and then she heard a faint sound and understood the reason for the brief interlude.

Condom, she thought, and then the ability to think coherently vanished because he covered her with the hard heat of his body. She felt the blunt thrust of his erection at her moist entrance and tensed in anticipation, but instead of entering her he cupped her face in his hand and gently slid off the blindfold.

'Look at me.' His soft command penetrated her brain and she opened her eyes and stared at him dizzily just as he slid his hand under her bottom and entered her in a series of slow, deliciously skilful thrusts. He was incredibly gentle, taking his time, murmuring soft words in Greek and then English as he moved deep into the heart of her. Then he paused, kissed her mouth gently, holding her gaze with his.

'Are you all right? Do you want to use the safe word?' His voice was gently teasing but the glitter in his eyes and the tension in his jaw told her he was nowhere near as relaxed as he pretended to be.

In the grip of such intolerable excitement she was incapable of responding, Lily simply shook her head and then moaned as he withdrew slightly and surged into her again, every movement of his body escalating the wickedly agonising pleasure.

She slid her hands over the silken width of his shoulders, down his back, her fingers clamping over the thrusting power of his body as he rocked against her. His hand was splayed on her bottom, his gaze locked on hers as he drove into her with ruthlessly controlled strength and a raw, primitive rhythm. She wrapped her legs around him as he brought pleasure raining down on both of them. She cried out his name and he took her mouth, kissing her deeply, intimately, as the first ripple of orgasm took hold of her body. They didn't stop kissing, mouths locked, eyes locked as her body contracted around his and dragged him over the edge of control. She'd never experienced anything like it, the whole experience a shattering revelation about her capacity for sensuality.

It was several minutes before she was capable of speaking and longer than that before she could persuade her body to move.

As she tried to roll away from him, his arms locked around her. 'Where do you think you're going?'

'I'm sticking to the rules. I thought this was a one-night thing.'

'It is.' He hauled her back against him. 'And the night isn't over yet.'

CHAPTER FIVE

NIK SPENT TEN minutes under a cold shower, trying to wake himself up after a night that had consisted of the worst sleep of his life and the best sex. He couldn't remember the last time he hadn't wanted to leave the bed in the morning.

A ton of work waited for him in the office, but for the first time ever he was contemplating working from home so that he could spend a few more hours with Lily. After her initial shyness she'd proved to be adventurous and insatiable, qualities that had kept both of them awake until the rising sun had sent the first flickers of light across the darkened bedroom.

Eventually she'd fallen into an exhausted sleep, her body tangled around his as dawn had bathed the bedroom in a golden glow.

It had proved impossible to extract himself without waking her so Nik, whose least favourite bedroom activity was hugging, had remained there, his senses bathed in the soft floral scent of her skin and hair, trapped by those long limbs wrapped trustingly around him.

And he had no one to blame but himself.

She'd offered to leave and he'd stopped her.

He frowned, surprised by his own actions. He had no need for displays of affection or any of the other meaningless rituals that seemed to inhabit other people's relationships. To him, sex was a physical need, no different from hunger and thirst. Once satisfied he moved on. He had no desire for anything deeper. He didn't believe anything deeper existed.

When he was younger, women had tried to persuade him differently. There had been a substantial number who had believed they had what it took to penetrate whatever steely coating made his heart so inaccessible. When they'd had no more success than their predecessors they'd withdrawn, bruised and broken, but not before they'd delivered their own personal diagnosis on his sorry condition.

He'd heard it all. That he didn't have a heart, that he was selfish, single minded, driven, too focused on his work. He accepted those accusations without argument, but knew that none explained his perpetually single status. Quite simply, he didn't believe in love. He'd learned at an early age that love could be withdrawn as easily as it was given, that promises could be made and broken in the same breath, that a wedding ring was no more than a piece of jewellery, and wedding vows no more binding than one plant twisted loosely around another.

He had no need for the friendship and affection that punctuated other people's lives.

He'd taught himself to live without it, so to find himself wrapped in the tight embrace of a woman who smiled even when she was asleep was as alien to him as it was unsettling.

For a while, he'd slept, too, and then woken to find her locked against him. Telling himself that she was the one holding him and not the other way round, he'd managed to extract himself without waking her and escaped to the bathroom where he contemplated his options.

He needed to find a tactful way of ejecting her.

He showered, shaved and returned to the bedroom. Expecting to find her still asleep, he was thrown to find her dressed. She'd stolen one of his white shirts and it fell to mid-thigh, the sleeves flapping over her small hands as she talked on the phone.

'Of course he'll be there.' Her voice was as soothing as

warm honey. 'I'm sure it's a simple misunderstanding…well, no I agree with you, but he's very busy…'

She lay on her stomach on the bed, her hair hanging in a blonde curtain over one shoulder, the sheets tangled around her bare thighs.

Nik took one look at her and decided that there was no reason to rush her out of the villa.

They'd have breakfast on the terrace. Maybe enjoy a swim.

Then he'd find a position they hadn't yet tried before sending her home in his car.

Absorbed in her conversation, she hadn't noticed him and he strolled round in front of her and slowly released the towel from his waist.

He saw her eyes go wide. Then she gave him a smile that hovered somewhere between cheeky and innocent and he found himself resenting the person on the end of the phone who was taking up so much of her time.

He dressed, aware that she was watching him the whole time, her conversation reduced to soothing, sympathetic noises.

It was the sort of exchange he'd never had in his life. The sort that involved listening while someone poured out their woes. When Nik had a problem he solved it or accepted it and moved on. He'd never understood the female urge to dissect and confide.

'I know,' she murmured. 'There's nothing more upsetting than a rift in the family, but you need to talk. Clear the air. Be open about your feelings.'

She was so warm and sympathetic it was obvious to Nik that the conversation was going to be a long one. Someone had rung in the belief that talking to Lily would make them feel better and he couldn't see a way that this exchange would ever end as she poured a verbal Band-Aid over whatever wound she was being asked to heal. Who would want to hang up when they were getting the phone equivalent of a massive hug?

Outraged on her behalf, Nik sliced his finger across his throat to indicate that she should cut the connection.

When she didn't, he was contemplating snatching the phone and telling whoever it was to get a grip, sort out their own problems and stop encroaching on Lily's good nature when she gestured to the phone with her free hand.

'It's for you,' she mouthed. 'Your father.'

His *father*?

The person she'd been soothing and placating for the past twenty minutes was his *father*?

Nik froze. Only now did he notice that the phone in her hand was his. 'You answered my phone?'

'I wouldn't have done normally, but I saw it was your dad and I knew you'd want to talk to him. I didn't want you to miss his call because you were in the shower.' Clearly believing she'd done him an enormous favour, she wished his father a cheery, caring goodbye and held out the phone to him. The front of his shirt gapped, revealing those tempting dips and curves he'd explored in minute detail the night before. The scrape of his jaw had left faint red marks over her creamy skin and the fact that he instantly wanted to drop the phone in the nearest body of water and take her straight back to bed simply added to his irritation.

'That's my shirt.'

'You have so many, I didn't think you'd miss one.'

Reflecting on the fact she was as chirpy in the morning as she was the rest of the day, Nik dragged his gaze from her smiling mouth, took the phone from her and switched to Greek. 'You didn't need to call again. I got your last four messages.'

'Then why didn't you call me back?'

'I've been busy.'

'Too busy to talk to your own father? I have rung you every day this week, Niklaus. Every single day.'

Aware that Lily was listening Nik paced to the window, turned his back on her and stared out over the sea. 'Is the wedding still on?'

'Of course it is on! Why wouldn't it be? I love Diandra and she loves me. You would love her, too, if you took the time to meet her and what better time than the day in which we exchange our vows?' There was a silence. 'Nik, come home. It has been too long.'

Nik knew exactly how long it had been to the day.

'I've been busy.'

'Too busy to visit your own family? This is the place of your birth and you never come home. You have a villa here that you converted and you don't even visit. I know you didn't like Callie and it's true that for a long time I was very angry with you for not making more of an effort when she showed you so much love, but that is behind us now.'

Reflecting on exactly what form that 'love' had taken, Nik tightened his hand on the phone and wondered if he'd been wrong not to tell his father the unpalatable truth about his third wife. He'd made the decision that since she'd ended the relationship anyway there was nothing to be gained from revealing the truth, but now he found himself in the rare position of questioning his own judgement.

'Will Callie be at the wedding?'

'No.' His father was quiet. 'I wanted her to bring little Chloe, but she hasn't responded to my calls. I don't mind admitting it's a very upsetting situation all round for everyone.'

Not everyone, Nik thought. He was sure Callie wasn't remotely upset. Why would she be? She'd extracted enough money from his father to ensure she could live comfortably without ever lifting a finger again. 'You would really want her at your wedding?'

'Callie, no. But Chloe? Yes, of course. If I had my way she would be living here with me. I still haven't given up hope that might happen one day. Chloe is my child, Nik. My daughter. I want her to grow up knowing her father. I don't want her thinking I abandoned her or chose not to have her in my life.'

Nik kept his eyes forward and the past firmly suppressed. 'These things happen. They're part of life and relationships.'

His father sighed. 'I'm sorry you believe that. Family is the most important thing in the world. I want that for you.'

'I set my own life goals, and that isn't on the list,' Nik drawled softly. Contemplating the complexity of human relationships, he was doubly glad he'd successfully avoided them himself. Like every other area of his life, he had his feelings firmly under control. 'Would Diandra really want Chloe to be living with you?'

'Of course! She'd be delighted. She wants it as much as I do. And she'd really like to meet you, too. She's keen for us to be a proper family.'

A proper family.

A long-buried memory emerged from deep inside his brain, squeezing itself through the many layers of self-protection he'd used to suppress it.

It had been so long the images were no longer clear, a fact for which he was grimly grateful. Even now, several decades later, he could still remember how it had felt to have those images replaying in his head night after night.

A man, a woman and a young boy, living an idyllic existence under blue skies and the dazzle of the sun. Growing up, he'd learned a thousand lessons about living. How to cook with leaves from the vine, how to distil the grape skins and seeds to form the potent *tsikoudia* they drank with friends. He'd lived his cocooned existence until one day his world had crumbled and he'd learned the most important lesson of all.

That a family was the least stable structure invented by man.

It could be destroyed in a moment.

'Come home, Niklaus,' his father said quietly. 'It has been too long. I want us to put the past behind us. Callie is no longer here.'

Nik didn't tell him that the reason he avoided the island had nothing to do with Callie.

Whenever he returned there it stirred up the same memory of his mother leaving in the middle of the night while he watched in confusion from the elegant curve of the stairs.

Where are you going, Mama? Are you taking us with you? Can we come, too?

'Niklaus?' His father was still talking. 'Will you come?'

Nik dragged his hand over the back of his neck. 'Yes, if that's what you want.'

'How can you doubt it?' There was joy in his father's voice. 'The wedding is Tuesday but many of our friends are arriving at the weekend so that we can celebrate in style. Come on Saturday then you can join in the pre-wedding celebrations.'

'Saturday?' His father expected him to stay for four days? 'I'll have to see if I can clear my diary.'

'Of course you can. What's the point of being in charge of the company if you can't decide your own schedule? Now tell me about Lily. I like her very much. How long have the two of you been together?'

Ten memorable hours. 'How do you know her name?'

'We've been talking, Niklaus! Which is more than you and I ever do. She sounds nice. Why don't you bring her to the wedding?'

'We don't have that sort of relationship.' He felt a flicker of irritation. Was that why she'd spent so much time on the phone talking to his father? Had she decided that sympathy might earn her an invite to the biggest wedding of the year in Greece?

Exchanging a final few words with his father, he hung up. 'Don't ever,' he said with silky emphasis as he turned to face her, 'answer my phone again.' But he was talking to an empty room because Lily was nowhere to be seen.

Taken aback, Nik glanced towards the bathroom and then noticed the note scrawled on a piece of paper by his pillow.

Thanks for the best rebound sex ever. Lily.

The best rebound sex?

She'd left?

Nik picked up the note and scrunched it in his palm. He'd been so absorbed in the conversation with his father he hadn't heard her leaving.

The dress from the night before lay neatly folded on the chair but there was no sign of the shoes or his shirt. He had no need to formulate a plan to eject her from his life because she'd removed herself.

She'd gone.

And she hadn't even bothered saying goodbye.

'No need to ask if you had a good night, it's written all over your face.' Brittany slid her feet into her hiking boots and reached for her bag. 'Nice shirt. Is that silk?' She reached out and touched the fabric and gave a murmur of appreciation. 'The man has style, I'll give him that.'

'Thanks for your text. It was sweet of you to check on me. How was your evening?'

'Nowhere near as exciting as yours apparently. While you were playing Cinderella in the wolf's lair, I was cataloguing pottery shards and bone fragments. My life is so exciting I can hardly bear it.'

'You love it. And I think you're mixing your fairy tales.' Aware that her hair was a wild mass of curls after the relentless exploration of Nik's hands, Lily scooped it into a ponytail. She told herself that eventually she'd stop thinking about him. 'Did you find anything else after I left yesterday?'

'Fragments of plaster, conical cups—' Brittany frowned. 'We found a bronze leg that probably belongs to that figurine that was discovered last week. Are you listening to me?'

Lily was deep in an action replay of the moment Nik had removed the mask from her eyes. 'That's exciting! I'm going to join you later.'

'We're removing part of the stone mound and exploring the North Eastern wall.' Brittany eyed her. 'You might want to rethink white silk. So am I going to hear the details?'

'About what?'

'Oh, please—'

'It was fun. All right, incredible.' Lily felt her cheeks burn and Brittany gave a faint smile.

'That good? Now I'm jealous. I haven't had incredible sex since—well, let's just say it's been a while. So are you seeing him again?'

'Of course not. The definition of rebound sex is that it's just one night. No commitment.' She parroted the rules and tried not to wish it could have lasted a little more than one night. The truth was even in that one night Nik had made her feel special. 'Do we have food in our fridge? I'm starving.'

'He helped you expend all those calories and then didn't feed you before you left? That's not very gentlemanly.'

'He didn't see me leave. He had to take a call.' And judging from the reluctance he'd shown when she'd handed him the phone, if it had been left to him he wouldn't have answered it.

Why not?

Why wouldn't a man want to talk to his father?

It had been immediately obvious that whatever issues Nik might have in expressing his emotions openly weren't shared by his father, who had been almost embarrassingly eager to share his pain.

She'd squirmed with discomfort as Kostas Zervakis had told her how long it was since his son had come home. Even on such a short acquaintance she knew that family was one of the subjects Nik didn't touch. She'd felt awkward listening, as if she were eavesdropping on a private conversation, but at the same time his father had seemed so upset she hadn't had the heart to cut him off.

The conversation had left her feeling ever so slightly sick, an emotion she knew was ridiculous given that she hadn't ever met Kostas and barely knew his son. Why should it bother her that there were clearly problems in their relationship?

Her natural instinct had been to intervene but she'd recognised instantly the danger in that. Nik wasn't a man who appreciated the interference of others in anything, least of all his personal life.

The black look he'd given her had been as much responsible for her rapid exit as her own lack of familiarity with the morning-after etiquette following rebound sex.

She'd taken advantage of his temporary absorption in the phone call to make a hasty escape, but not before she'd heard enough to make her wish for a happy ending. Whatever damage lay in their past, she wanted them to fix their problems.

She always wanted people to fix their problems.

Lily blinked rapidly, realising that Brittany was talking. 'Sorry?'

'So he doesn't know you left?'

'He knows by now.'

'He won't be pleased that you didn't say goodbye.'

'He'll be delighted. He doesn't want emotional engagement. No awkward conversations. He will be relieved to be spared a potentially awkward conversation. We move in different circles so I probably won't ever see him again.' And that shouldn't bother her, should it? Although a one-night stand was new to her, she was the expert at transitory relationships. Her entire life had been a series of transitory relationships. No one had ever stuck in her life. She felt like an abandoned railway station where trains passed through but never stopped.

Brittany glanced out of the window at the street below and raised her eyebrows. 'I think you're going to see him again a whole lot sooner than you think.'

'What makes you say that?'

'Because he's just pulled up outside our apartment.'

Lily's heart felt as if it were trying to escape from her chest. 'Are you sure?'

'Well there's a Ferrari parked outside that costs more than I'm going to earn in a lifetime, so, unless there is someone else living in this building that has attracted his attention, he clearly has things he wants to say to you.'

'Oh *no*.' Lily shrank against the door of the bedroom. 'Can you see his face? Does he look angry?'

'What reason would he have to be angry?' Brittany glanced out of the window again and then back at Lily. 'Is this about the shirt? He can afford to lose one shirt, surely?'

'I don't think he's here because of the shirt,' Lily said weakly. 'I think he's here because of something I did this morning. I'm going to hide on the balcony and you're going to tell him you haven't seen me.'

Brittany looked at her curiously. 'What did you do?'

Lily flinched as she heard a loud hammering on the door. 'Remember—you haven't seen me.' She fled into the bedroom they shared and closed the door.

What was he doing here?

She'd seen the flash of anger in his eyes when he'd realised it was *his* phone she'd answered, but surely he wouldn't care enough to follow her home?

She heard his voice in the doorway and heard Brittany say, 'Sure, come right on in, Nik—is it all right if I call you Nik?—she's in the bedroom, hiding.' The door opened a moment later and Brittany stood there, arms folded, her eyes alive with laughter.

Lily impaled her with a look of helpless fury. 'You're a traitor.'

'I'm a friend and I am doing you a favour,' Brittany murmured. 'The man is seriously *hot*.' Having delivered that assessment, she stepped to one side with a bright smile. 'Go ahead. The space is a little tight, but I guess you folks don't mind that.'

'No! Brittany, don't—er—hi...' Lily gave a weak smile

as Nik strolled into the room. His powerful frame virtually filled the cramped space and she wished she'd picked a different room as a refuge. Being in a bedroom reminded her too much of the night before. 'If you're mad about the shirt, then give me two minutes to change. I shouldn't have taken it, but I didn't want to do the walk of shame through the middle of Chania wearing an evening dress that doesn't belong to me.'

'I don't care about the shirt.' His hair was glossy dark, his eyes dark in a face so handsome it would have made a Greek god weep with envy. 'Do you seriously think I'm here because of the shirt?'

'No. I assume you're mad because I answered your phone, but I saw that it was your father and thought you wouldn't want to miss his call. If I had a dad I'd be ringing him every day.'

His face revealed not a flicker of emotion. 'We don't have that sort of relationship.'

'Well I know that *now,* but I didn't know when I answered the phone and once he started talking he was so upset I didn't want to hang up. He needed to talk to someone and I was in the right place at the right time.'

'You think so?' His voice was silky soft. 'Because I would have said you were in the wrong place at the wrong time.'

'Depends how you look at it. Did you manage to clear the air?' She risked a glance at the hard lines of his face and winced. 'I'm guessing the answer to that is no. If I made it worse by handing you the phone, I'm sorry.'

He raised an eyebrow. 'Are you?'

She opened her mouth and closed it again. 'No, not really. Family is the most important thing in the world. I don't understand how anyone could not want to try and heal a rift. But I could see you were very angry that I'd answered the call and of course your relationship with your father is none of my business.' But she wanted to make it her business so badly she virtually had to sit on her hands to stop herself from interfering.

'For someone who realises it's none of her business, you seem to be showing an extraordinary depth of interest.'

'I feel strongly about protecting the family unit. It's my hot button.'

His searing glance reminded her he was intimately familiar with all her hot buttons. 'Why did you walk out this morning?'

The blatant reminder of the night before brought the colour rushing to her cheeks.

'I thought the first rule of rebound sex was that you rebound right out of the door the next morning. I have no experience of morning-after conversation and frankly the thought of facing you over breakfast after all the things we did last night didn't totally thrill me. And can you honestly tell me you weren't standing in that shower working out how you were going to eject me?' The expression on his face told her she was right and she nodded. 'Exactly. I thought I'd spare us both a major awkward moment and leave. I grabbed a shirt and was halfway out of the door when your father rang.'

'It didn't occur to you to ignore the phone?'

'I thought it might be important. And it was! He was *so* upset. He told me he'd already left a ton of messages.' Concern overwhelmed her efforts not to become involved. 'Why haven't you been home for the past few years?'

'A night in my bed doesn't qualify you to ask those questions.' The look in his eyes made her confidence falter.

'I get the message. Nothing personal. Now back off. Last night you were charming and fun and flirty. This morning you're scary and intimidating.'

He inhaled deeply. 'I apologise,' he breathed. 'It was not my intention to come across as scary or intimidating, but you should *not* have answered the phone.'

'What's done is done. And I was glad to be a listening ear for someone in pain.'

'My father is not in pain.'

'Yes, he is. He misses you. This rift between you is caus-ing him agony. He wants you to go to his wedding. It's break-ing his heart that you won't go.'

'Lily—'

'You're going to tell me it's none of my business and you're right, it isn't, but I don't have a family at all. I don't even have the broken pieces of a family, and you have no idea how much I wish I did. So you'll have to forgive me if I have a tendency to try and glue back together everyone else's chipped fragments. It's the archaeologist in me.'

'Lily—'

'Just because you don't believe in love, doesn't mean you have to inflict that view on others and judge them for their decisions. Your father is happy and you're spoiling it. He loves you and he wants you there. Whatever you are feeling, you should bury it and go and celebrate. You should raise a glass and dance at his wedding. You should show him you love him no matter what, and if this marriage goes wrong then you'll be there to support him.' She stopped, breathless, and waited to be frozen by the icy wind of his disapproval but he surprised her yet again by nodding.

'I agree.'

'You do?'

'Yes. I've been trying to tell you that but you wouldn't stop talking.' He spoke through clenched teeth. 'I am con-vinced that I should go to the wedding, which is why I'm here.'

'What does the wedding have to do with me?'

'I want you to come with me.'

Lily gaped at him. 'Me? Why?'

He ran his hand over the back of his neck. 'I am willing to be present if that is truly what my father wants, but I don't have enough faith in my acting skills to believe I will be able to convince anyone that I'm pleased to be there. No matter how much he tells me Diandra is "the one", I cannot see how this match will have a happy ending. You, however, seem to see happy endings where none exist. I'm hoping that by taking you, people will be blinded in the dazzling beam of your sunny optimism and won't notice the dark thundercloud hovering close by threatening to rain on the proceedings.'

The analogy made her smile. 'You're the dark thundercloud in that scenario?'

His eyes gleamed. 'You need to ask?'

'You really believe this marriage is doomed? How can you say that when you haven't even met Diandra?'

'When it comes to women, my father has poor judgement. He follows his heart and his heart has no sense of direction. Frankly I can't believe he has chosen to get married again after three failed attempts. I think it's insane.'

'I think it's lovely.'

'Which is why you're coming as my guest.' He reached out and lifted a small blue plate from her shelf, tipping off the earrings that were stored there. 'This is stylish. Where did you buy it?'

'I didn't buy it, I made it. And I haven't agreed to come with you yet.'

'You *made* this?'

'It's a hobby of mine. There is a kiln at work and sometimes I use it. The father of one of the curators at the museum is a potter and he's helped me. It's interesting comparing old and new techniques.'

He turned it in his hands, examining it closely. 'You could sell this.'

'I don't want to sell it. I use it to store my earrings.'

'Have you ever considered having an exhibition?'

'Er—no.' She gave an astonished laugh. 'I've made about eight pieces I didn't throw away. They're all exhibited around the apartment. We use one as a soap dish.'

'You've never wanted to do this for a living?'

'What I want to do and what I can afford to do aren't the same thing. It isn't financially viable.' She didn't even allow her mind to go there. 'And where would our soap live? Let's talk about the wedding. A wedding is a big deal. It's intimate and special, an occasion to be shared with friends and loved ones. You don't even know me.' The moment the words left her mouth she realised how ridiculous that statement was given the night they'd spent. 'I mean obviously there are *some* things about me you know very well, but other things like my favourite flower and my favourite colour, you don't know.'

Still holding her plate, he studied her with an unsettling intensity. 'I know all I need to know, which is that you like weddings almost as much as I hate them. Did you study art?'

'Minoan art. This is a sideline. And if I go with you, people will speculate. How would you explain our relationship to your father? Would you want us to pretend to be in a relationship? Are we supposed to have known one another for ages or something?'

'No.' His frown suggested that option hadn't occurred to him. 'There is no need to tell anything other than the truth, which is that I'm inviting you to the wedding as a friend.'

'Friend with benefits?'

He put the plate back down on the shelf and replaced the earrings carefully. 'That part is strictly between us.'

'And if your father asks how we met?'

'Tell him the truth. He'd be amused, I assure you.'

'So you don't want to pretend we're madly in love or anything? I don't have to pose as your girlfriend?'

'No. You'd be going as yourself, Lily.' A muscle flickered in his lean jaw. 'God knows, the wedding will be stressful enough without us playing roles that feel unnatural.'

It was his obvious distaste for lies and games that made up her mind. After David, a man whose instinct was to tell the truth was appealing. 'When would we leave?'

'Next Saturday. The wedding is on Tuesday but there will be four days of celebrations.' It was obvious from his expression he'd rather be dragged naked through an active volcano than join in those celebrations and a horrible thought crept into her mind.

'You're not going because you're planning to break off the wedding, are you?'

'No.' His gaze didn't shift from hers. 'But I won't tell you it didn't cross my mind.'

'I'm glad you rose above your natural impulse to wreck someone else's happiness. And if you really think it would help to have me there, then I'll come, if only to make sure you don't have second thoughts and decide to sabotage your father's big day.' Lily sank down onto the edge of her bed, thinking. 'I'll need to ask for time off.'

'Is that a problem? I could make a few calls.'

'No way!' Imagining how the curator at the museum would respond to personal intervention from Nik Zervakis, Lily recoiled in alarm. 'I'm quite capable of handling it myself. I don't need to bring in the heavy artillery, I'll simply ask the question. I'm owed holiday and my post ends in a couple of weeks anyway. Where exactly are we going? Where is "home" for you?'

'My father owns an island off the north coast of Crete. You will like it. The western part of the island has Minoan remains and there is a Venetian castle on one of the hilltops. It is separated from Crete by a lagoon and the beaches are some of the best anywhere in Greece. When you're not reminding me to smile, I'm sure you'll enjoy exploring.'

'And he *owns* this island? So tourists can't visit.'

'That's right. It belongs to my family.'

Lily looked at him doubtfully. 'How many guests will there be?'

'Does it matter?'

'I wondered, that's all.' She wanted to ask where they'd be sleeping but decided that if his father could afford a private island then presumably there wasn't a shortage of beds. 'I need to go shopping.'

'Given that you are doing me a favour, I insist you allow me to take care of that side of things.'

'No. Apart from last night, which wasn't real, I buy my own clothes. But thanks.'

'Last night didn't feel real?' He gave her a long, penetrating look and she felt heat rush into her cheeks as she remembered all the very real things he'd done to her and she'd done to him.

'I mean it wasn't really my life. More like a dreamy moment you know is never going to happen again.' Realising it was long past time she kept her mouth shut, she gave a weak smile. 'I'll buy or borrow clothes, don't worry. I'm good at putting together a wardrobe. Colours are my thing. The secret is to accessorise. I won't embarrass you even if we're surrounded by people dressed head to toe in Prada.'

'That possibility didn't enter my head. My concern was purely about the pressure on your budget.'

'I'm creative. It's not a problem.' She remembered she was wearing his shirt. 'I'll return this, obviously.'

A smile flickered at the corners of his mouth. 'It looks better on you than it does on me. Keep it.'

His gaze collided with hers and suddenly it was hard to breathe. Sexual tension simmered in the air and she was acutely aware of the oppressive heat in the small room that had no air conditioning. Blistering, blinding awareness clouded her vision until the only thing in her world was him. She wanted so badly to touch him. She wanted to lean into that muscled power, rip off those clothes and beg him to do all the things he'd done to her the night before. Shaken, she assumed she was alone in feeling that way and then saw something flare in his eyes and knew she wasn't. He was sexually aroused and thinking all the things she was thinking.

'Nik—'

'Saturday.' His tone was thickened, his eyes a dark, dangerous black. 'I will pick you up at eight a.m.'

She watched him leave, wondering what the rules of engagement were when one night wasn't enough.

CHAPTER SIX

NIK PUT HIS foot down and pushed the Ferrari to its limits on the empty road that led to the north-western tip of Crete.

He spent the majority of his time at the ZervaCo offices in San Francisco. When he returned to Crete it was to his villa on the beach near Chania, not to the island that had been his home growing up.

For reasons he tried not to think about, he'd avoided the place for the past few years and the closer he got to their destination, the blacker his mood.

Lily, by contrast, was visibly excited. She'd been waiting on the street when he'd arrived, her bag by her feet and she'd proceeded to question him non-stop. 'So will this be like *My Big Fat Greek Wedding*? I loved that movie. Will there be dancing? Brittany and I have been learning the *kalamatianós* at the *taverna* near our apartment so I should be able to join in as long as no one minds losing their toes.' She hummed a Greek tune to herself and he sent her an exasperated look.

'Are you ever *not* cheerful?'

The humming stopped and she glanced at him. 'You want me to be miserable? Did I misunderstand the brief, because I thought I was supposed to be the sunshine to your thundercloud. I didn't realise I had to be a thundercloud, too.'

Despite his mood, he found himself smiling. 'Are you capable of being a thundercloud?'

'I'm human. I have my low moments, same as anyone.'

'Tell me your last low moment.'

'No, because then I might cry and you'd dump me by the side of the road and leave me to be pecked to death by buzzards.' She gave him a cheery smile. 'This is the point where you reassure me that you wouldn't leave me by the side of the road, and that there are no buzzards in Crete.'

'There are buzzards. Crete has a varied habitat. We have vultures, Golden Eagle, kestrel—' he slowed down as he approached a narrow section of the road '—but I have no intention of leaving you by the side of the road.'

'I'd like to think that decision is driven by your inherent good nature and kindness towards your fellow man, but I'm pretty sure it's because you don't want to have to go to this wedding alone.'

'You're right. My actions are almost always driven by self-interest.'

'I don't understand you at all. I love weddings.'

'Even when you don't know the people involved?'

'I support the principle. I think it's lovely that your father is getting married again.'

Nik struggled to subdue a rush of emotion. 'It is not lovely that he is getting married again. It's ill advised.'

'That's your opinion. But it isn't what *you* think that matters, is it? It's what *he* thinks.' She spoke with gentle emphasis. 'And he thinks it's a good idea. For the record, I think it says a lot about a person that he is prepared to get married again.'

'It does.' As they hit a straight section of road, he pushed the car to its limits and the engine gave a throaty roar. 'It says he's a man with an inability to learn from his mistakes.'

'I don't see it that way.' Her hair whipped around her face and she anchored it with her hand and lifted her face to the sun. 'I think it shows optimism and I love that.'

Hearing the breathy, happy note in her voice he shook his head. 'Lily, how have you survived in this world without being eaten alive by unscrupulous people determined to take advantage of you?'

'I've been hurt on many occasions.'

'That doesn't surprise me.'

'It's part of life. I'm not going to let it shatter my belief in human nature. I'm an optimist. And what would it mean to give up? That would be like saying that love isn't out there, that it doesn't exist, and how depressing would *that* be?'

Nik, who lived his life firmly of the conviction that love didn't exist, didn't find it remotely depressing. To him, it was simply fact. 'Clearly you are the perfect wedding guest. You could set up a business, weddingguests.com. Optimists-R-us. You could be the guaranteed smile at every wedding.'

'Your cynicism is deeply depressing.'

'Your optimism is deeply concerning.'

'I prefer to think of it as inspiring. I don't want to be one of those people who think that a challenging past has to mean a challenging future.'

'You had a challenging past?' He remembered that she'd mentioned being brought up in foster care and hoped she wasn't about to give him the whole story.

She didn't. Instead she shrugged and kept her eyes straight ahead. 'It was a bit like a bad version of *Goldilocks and the Three Bears.* I was never "just right" for anyone, but that was my bad luck. I didn't meet the right family. Doesn't mean I don't believe there are loads of great families out there.'

'Doesn't what happened to you cause you to question the validity of any of these emotions you feel? The fact that the last guy lied to you *and* his wife doesn't put you off relationships?'

'It was one guy. I know enough about statistics to know you can't draw a reliable conclusion from a sample of one.' She frowned. 'If I'm honest, I'm working from a bigger sample than that because he's the third relationship I've had, but I still don't think you can make a judgement on the opposite sex based on the behaviour of a few.'

Nik, who had done exactly that, stayed silent and of course she noticed because she was nothing if not observant.

'Put it this way—if I'm bitten by a shark am I going to avoid swimming in the sea? I could, but then I'd be depriving myself of one of my favourite activities so instead I choose to carry on swimming and be a little more alert. Life isn't always about taking the safe option. Risk has to be balanced against the joy of living. I call it being receptive.'

'I call it being ridiculously naïve.'

She looked affronted. 'You're cross and irritable because you're not looking forward to this, but there is no reason to take it out on me. I'm here as a volunteer, remember?'

'You're right. I apologise.'

'Accepted. But for your father's sake you need to work on your body language. If you think you're a thundercloud you're deluding yourself because right now you're more of a tropical cyclone. You have to stop being judgemental and embrace what's happening.'

Nik took the sharp right-hand turn that led down to the beach and the private ferry. 'I am finding it hard to embrace something I know to be a mistake. It's like watching someone driving their car full speed towards a brick wall and not trying to do something to stop it.'

'You don't know it's a mistake,' she said calmly. 'And even if it is, he's an adult and should be allowed to make his own decisions. Now smile.'

He pulled in, killed the engine and turned to look at her.

Those unusual violet eyes reminded him of the spring flowers that grew high in the mountains. 'I will not be so hypocritical as to pretend I am pleased, but I promise not to spoil the moment.'

'If you don't smile then you *will* spoil the moment! Poor Diandra might take one look at your face and decide she doesn't want to marry into your family and then your father would be heartbroken. I can't believe I'm saying this, but be hypocritical if that's what it takes to make you smile.'

'Poor Diandra will not be poor for long so I think it unlikely she'll let anything stand in the way of her wedding, even my intimidating presence.'

Her eyes widened. 'Is that what this is about? You think she's after his money?'

'I have no idea but I'd be a fool not to consider it.' Nik saw no reason to be anything but honest. 'He is mega wealthy. She was his cook.'

'What does her occupation have to do with it? Love is about people, not professions. And I find it very offensive that you'd even think that. You can't judge a person based on their income. I know plenty of wealthy people who are slimeballs. In fact if we're going with stereotypes here, I'd say that generally speaking in order to amass great wealth you have to be prepared to be pretty ruthless. There are plenty of wealthy people who aren't that nice.'

Nik, who had never aspired to be 'nice', was careful not to let his expression change. 'Are you calling me a slimeball?'

'I'm simply pointing out that income isn't an indicator of a person's worth.'

'You mean because you don't know the level of expenditure?'

'No! Why is everything about money with you? I'm talking about *emotional* worth. Your father told me about Diandra. He was ill with flu last winter after Callie left. He was so ill at one point he couldn't drag himself from the bed. I sympathised because it happened to me once and I hope I never get flu again. Anyway, Diandra cared for him the whole time. She was the one who called the doctor. She made all his meals. That was kind, don't you think?'

'Or opportunistic.'

'If you carry on thinking like that you are going to die lonely. He met her when she cooked him her special moussaka to try and tempt him to eat. I *love* that he doesn't care what she does.'

'He should care. She stands to gain an enormous amount financially from this wedding.'

'That's horrible.'

'It is truly horrible. Finally we find something we agree on.'

'I wasn't agreeing with you! It's your attitude that's horrible, not this wedding. You're not only a judgemental cynic, you're also a raging snob.'

Nik breathed deeply. 'I am not a raging snob, but I am realistic.'

'No, what you are is damaged. Not everything has a price, Nik, and there are things in life that are far more important than money. Your father is trying to make a family and I think that's admirable.' She fumbled with the seat belt. 'Get me out of this car before I'm contaminated by you. Your thundercloud is about to rain all over my sunny patch of life.'

Your father is trying to make a family.

Nik thought about everything that had gone before.

He'd buried the pain and hurt deep and it was something he had never talked about with anyone, especially not his father, who had his own pain to deal with. What would happen when this relationship collapsed?

'If my father entered relationships with some degree of caution and objective contemplation then I would be less concerned, but he makes the same mistake you make. He confuses physical intimacy with love.' He saw the colour streak across her cheeks.

'I'm not confused. Have I spun fairy tales about the night we spent together? Have I fallen in love with you? No. I know exactly what it was and what we did. You're in a little compartment in my brain labelled "Once in a Lifetime Experiences" along with skydiving and a helicopter flight over the New York skyline. It was amazing by the way.'

'The helicopter flight was amazing?'

'No, I haven't done that yet. I was talking about the night with you, although there were moments that felt as nerve-racking as skydiving.' Her mouth tilted into a self-conscious smile. 'Of course it's also a little embarrassing looking at you in daylight after all those things we did in the dark, but I'm trying not to think about it. Now stop being annoying. In fact, stop talking for a while. That way I'm less likely to kill you before we arrive.'

Nik refrained from pointing out she'd been the only one in the dark. He'd had perfect vision and he'd used it to his own shameless advantage. There wasn't a single corner of her body he hadn't explored and the memory of every delicious curve was welded in his brain.

He tried to work out what it was about her that was so appealing. Innocence wasn't a quality he generally admired in a person so he had to assume the power of the attraction stemmed from the sheer novelty of being with someone who had managed to retain such an untarnished view of the world.

'Are you embarrassed about the night we spent together?'

'I would be if I thought about it, so I'm not thinking about it. I'm living in the moment.' Having offered that simple solution to the problem, she reached into the back of the car for her hat. 'You could take the same approach to the wedding. You're not here to fix it or protect anyone. You're here as a guest and your only responsibility is to smile and look happy. Is this it? Are we here? Because I don't see an island. Maybe your father might have changed the venue when he saw the black cloud of your presence approaching over the horizon.'

Nik dragged his gaze from her mouth to the jetty. 'This is it. From here, we go by boat.'

Lily stood in the prow of the boat feeling the cool brush of the wind on her face and tasting the salty air. The boat skimmed and bounced over the sparkling ocean towards the large island in the distance, sending a light spray over her face and tangling her hair.

Nik stood behind the wheel, legs braced, eyes hidden behind a pair of dark glasses. Despite the unsmiling set of his mouth, he looked more approachable and less the hard-headed businessman.

'This is so much fun. I think I might love it more than your Ferrari.'

He gave a smile that turned him from insanely good-looking to devastating, and she felt the intensity of the attraction like a physical punch.

It was true he didn't seem to display any of the family values that were so important to her, but that didn't do anything to diminish the sexual attraction.

As far as she could tell, he couldn't be more perfect for a short-term relationship.

For the whole trip in the car she'd been aware of him. As he'd shifted gear his hand had brushed against her bare thigh and she'd discovered that being with him was an exciting, exhilarating experience that was like nothing she'd experienced before.

There had been a brief moment when they'd pulled into the car park that she'd thought he might be about to kiss her. He'd looked at her mouth the way a panther looked at its prey before it devoured it, but just when she'd been about to close her eyes and take a fast ride to bliss, he'd sprung from the car, leaving her to wonder if she'd imagined it.

She'd followed him to the jetty, watching in fascination as the group of people gathered there sprang to attention. If she needed any more evidence of the power he wielded, she had only to observe the way people responded to him. He behaved with an authority that was instinctive, his air of command unmistakable even in this apparently casual setting.

It was a good job he didn't possess any of the qualities she was looking for, she thought, otherwise she'd be in trouble.

Her gaze lingered on his bronzed throat, visible at the open neck of his shirt. He handled the boat with the same confident assurance he displayed in everything and she was sure that no electrical device had ever dared to misbehave under his expert touch.

Trying not to think about just how expert his touch had been, she anchored her hair and shouted above the wind. 'The beaches are beautiful. People aren't allowed to bathe here?'

'You can bathe here. You're my guest.' As they approached the island, he slowed the speed of the boat and skilfully steered against the dock.

Two men instantly jumped forward to help and Nik sprang from the boat and held out his hand to her.

'I need to get my bag.'

'They will bring our luggage up to the villa later.'

'I have a gift for your father and it's only one bag,' she muttered. 'I can carry a single bag.'

'You bought a gift?'

'Of course. It's a wedding. I couldn't come without a small gift.' She stepped out of the bobbing boat and allowed herself to hold his hand for a few seconds longer than was necessary for balance. She felt warmth and strength flow through her fingers and had to battle the temptation to press herself against him. 'So how many bedrooms does your father have? Are you sure there is room for me to stay?'

The question seemed to amuse him. 'There will be room, *theé mou*, don't worry. As well as the main villa, there are several other properties scattered around the island. We will be staying in one of those.'

As they walked up a sandy path she breathed in the wonderful scents of sea juniper and wild thyme. 'One of the things I love most about Crete is the thyme honey. Brittany and I eat it for breakfast.'

'My father keeps bees so he will be very happy to hear you say that.'

The path forked at the top and he turned right and took the path that led down to another beach. There, nestling in the small horseshoe bay of golden sand with the water almost lapping at the whitewashed walls, was a beautiful contemporary villa.

Lily stopped. '*That's* your father's house?' The position

was idyllic, the villa stunning, but it looked more like a honeymoon hideaway than somewhere to accommodate a large number of high-profile international guests.

'No. This is Camomile Villa. The main house is fifteen minutes' walk in the other direction, towards the small Venetian fort. I thought we'd unpack and breathe for an hour or so before we face the guests.'

Witnessing his tension, she felt a rush of compassion. 'Nik—' She put her hand on his cheek and turned his face to hers. 'This is a wedding, not the sacking of Troy. You do not need to find your strength or breathe. Your role is to smile and enjoy yourself.'

His gaze locked on hers and she wished she hadn't touched him. His blue-shadowed jaw was rough beneath her fingers and suddenly she was remembering that night in minute detail.

Seriously unsettled, she started to pull her hand away but he caught her wrist in his fingers and held it there.

'You are a very unusual woman.' His voice was husky and she gave a faint smile, ignoring the wild flutter of nerves low in her stomach.

'I am not even going to ask what you mean by that. I'm simply going to take it as a compliment.'

'Of course you are.' There was a strange gleam in his eyes. 'You see positive in everything, don't you?'

'Not always.' She could have told him that she saw very little positive in being alone in the world, having no family, but given his obvious state of tension she decided to keep that confidence to herself. 'So how do you know we're staying in Camomile Villa? Cute name, by the way. Maybe your father has given it to one of the other guests. Shouldn't you go and check?'

'Camomile belongs to me.'

Lily digested that. 'So actually you own five properties, not four.'

'I don't count this place.'

'Really? Because if I owned this I'd be spending every spare minute here.' She walked up the path, past silvery green olive trees, nets lying on the ground ready for harvesting later in the year. A small lizard lay basking in the hot sun and she smiled as it sensed company and darted for safety into the dry, dusty earth.

The path leading down to the villa cut through a garden of tumbling colour. Bougainvillaea in bright pinks and purples blended and merged against the dazzling white of the walls and the perfect blue of the sky.

Nik opened the door and Lily followed him inside.

White beamed ceilings and natural stone floors gave the interior a cool, uncluttered feel and the elegant white interior was lifted by splashes of Mediterranean blue.

'If you don't want this place, I might live here.' Lily looked at the shaded terrace with its beautiful infinity pool. 'Why does anyone need a pool when the sea is five steps from the front door?'

'Some people don't like swimming in the sea.'

'I'm not one of those people. I adore the sea. Nik, this place is—' she felt a lump in her throat '—it's really special.'

He opened the doors to the terrace and gave her a wary look. 'Are you going to cry?'

'It's perfect.' She blinked. 'And I'm fine. Happy. And excited. I love Crete, but I never get the chance to enjoy it like a tourist. I'm always working.' And never in her life had she experienced this level of luxury.

She and Brittany were always moaning about the mosquitoes and lack of air conditioning in their tiny apartment. At night they slept with the windows open to make the most of the breeze from the sea, but in the summer months it was almost unbearable indoors.

'You are the most unusual woman I've ever met. You enjoy small things.'

'This is not a small thing. And you're the unusual one.' She picked up her bag. 'You take this life for granted.'

'That is not true. I know how fortunate I am.'

'I don't think you do, but I'm going to be pointing it out to you every minute for the next few days so hopefully by the time we leave you will.' She glanced around her and then looked at him expectantly. 'My bedroom?'

For a wild, unnerving moment she hoped he was going to tell her there was just one bedroom, but he gestured to a door that led from the large spacious living area.

'The guest suite is through there. Make yourself comfortable.'

Guest suite.

So he didn't intend them to share a room. For Nik, it really had been one night.

Telling herself it was probably for the best, she followed his directions and walked through an open door into a bright, airy bedroom. The bed was draped in layers of cream and white, deep piles of cushions and pillows inviting the occupant to lounge and relax. The walls were hung with bold, contemporary art, slashes of deep blue on large canvases that added a stylish touch to the room. In one corner stood a tall, elegant vase in graduated blues, the colour shifting under the dazzling sunlight.

Lily recognised it instantly. 'That's one of Skylar's pots.'

He looked at her curiously. 'You know the artist?'

'Skylar Tempest. She and Brittany were roommates at college. They're best friends, as close as sisters. I would know her work anywhere. Her style, her use of colour and composition is unique, but I know that pot specifically because I talked to her about it. Brittany introduced us because Skylar wanted to talk to me about ceramics. She's incorporated a few Minoan designs into some of her work, modernised, of course.' She knelt down and slid her hand over the smooth surface of the glass. 'This is from her *Mediterranean Sky* collection. She had a small exhibition in New York, not only glass and pots but jewellery and a couple of paintings. She's insanely talented.'

'You were at that exhibition?'

'Sadly no. I don't move in those circles. Nor do I pretend to claim any credit for any of her incredible creations, but I did talk to her about shapes and style. Of course the Minoans used terracotta clay. It was Sky's idea to reproduce the shape in glass. Look at this—' She trailed her finger lightly over the surface. 'The Minoans usually decorated their pots with dark on light motifs, often of sea creatures, and she's taken her inspiration from that. It's genius. I can't believe you own it. Where did you find it?'

'I was at the exhibition.'

'In New York? How did you even know about her?'

'I saw her work in a small artisan jewellers in Greenwich Village and I bought one of her necklaces for—' He broke off and Lily looked at him expectantly.

'For? For one of your women? We're not in a relationship, Nik. You don't have to censor your conversation. And even if we were in a relationship you still wouldn't need to censor it.'

'In my experience, most women do not appreciate hearing about their predecessors.'

'Yes, well the more I hear about the women you've known in your life, the more I'm not surprised. Now tell me about how you discovered Skylar.'

'I asked to see more of her work and was told she was having an exhibition. I managed to get myself invited.'

Lily rocked back on her heels. 'She never mentioned that she met you.'

'We never met. I didn't introduce myself. I went on the first night and she was surrounded by well-wishers, so I simply bought a few pieces and left. That was two years ago.'

'So she doesn't know she sold pieces to Nik Zervakis?'

'A member of my team handled the actual transaction.'

Lily scrambled to her feet. 'Because you don't touch real money? She would be so excited if she knew her work was here in your villa. Can I tell her?'

He looked amused. 'If you think it would interest her, then yes.'

'Interest her? Of course it would interest her.' Lily pulled her phone out of her bag and took a photo. 'I must admit that pot looks perfect there. It needs a large room with lots of light. Did you know she has another exhibition coming up?' She slipped her phone back into her bag. 'December in London. An upmarket gallery in Knightsbridge is showing her work. She's really excited. Her new collection is called *Ocean Blue*. It's still sea themed. Brittany showed me some photos.'

'Will you be going?'

'To an exhibition in Knightsbridge? Sure. I thought I'd fly in on my private jet, spend a night in the Royal Suite at The Savoy and then get my driver to take me to the exhibition.' She laughed and then saw something flicker in his eyes. 'Er—that's exactly what you're going to be doing, isn't it?'

'My plans aren't confirmed.'

'But you do have a private jet.'

'ZervaCo owns a Gulfstream and a couple of Lear jets.' He said it as if it was normal and she shook her head, trying not to be intimidated.

For her, wealth was people and family, not money, but still—

'Seriously, Nik. What am I doing here? To you a Gulfstream is a mode of transport, to me it's a warm Atlantic current. I used to own a rusty mountain bike until the wheel fell off. I'm the one who works in a dusty museum, digs in the dirt in the summer and cleans other people's houses to give myself enough money to live. And living doesn't include jetting across Europe to a friend's exhibition. I have no idea where I'll even be in December. I'm job hunting.'

'Wherever you are, I'll fly you there. And for your information, I wouldn't be staying in the Royal Suite.'

'Because you already own an apartment that most royals would kill for.' His lack of response told her she was right and she rolled her eyes. 'Nik, we had an illuminating conversation earlier during which you confessed that you think your new stepmother is only interested in your father's money. Money is obviously a very big deal to you, so I'm hardly likely to take you up on your offer of a ride in your private jet, am I?'

'That is different. I'm grateful that you agreed to come here with me,' he said softly, 'and taking you to Skylar's exhibition would be my way of saying thank you.'

'I don't need a thank you. And to be honest I'm here because of the conversation I had with your father. My decision didn't have anything to do with you. We had one night, that's all. I mean, the sex was great, but I had no trouble walking out of your door that morning. There were no feelings involved.' She shook her head to add emphasis. 'Kevlar, that's me.'

He gave her a long, steady look. 'I have never met anyone who less resembles that substance.'

'Up until a week ago I would have agreed with you, but now I'm a changed person. Seriously, I'm enjoying being with you. You're smoking hot and surprisingly entertaining despite your warped view of relationships, but I am no more in love with you than I am with your supersonic shower. And you don't owe me anything for bringing me here—in fact I owe you.' She glanced across the room to the terrace outside. 'This is the nearest I've come to a vacation in a long time. It's not exactly a hardship being here. I am going to lie in the sun like that lizard out there.'

'You haven't met my family yet.' He paused, his gaze fixed on hers. 'Think about it. If you change your mind about coming to Skylar's London exhibition, let me know. The invitation stands. I won't withdraw it.'

It was a different world.

What would it be like, she wondered, not to have to think about your budget? Not to have to make choices between forfeiting one thing to buy another?

This close she could see the flecks of gold in those dark eyes, the blue-black shadow of his jaw and the almost un-believably perfect lines of his bone structure. If a scale had been invented to measure sex appeal, she was pretty sure he would have shattered it. She couldn't look at his mouth without remembering all the ways he'd used it on her body and remembering made her want it again. She wanted to reach out and slide her fingers into that silky dark hair and press her mouth to his. And this time she wanted to do it without the blindfold.

Aware that her mind was straying into forbidden territory she took a step back, reminding herself that money came a poor second to family and this man seemed to be virtually estranged from his father.

'I won't change my mind.'

Dragging her gaze from his, she dropped her bag on the floor and unzipped it. 'I need to hang up my dresses or they'll be creased. I don't want to make a bad impression.'

'There are staff over in the main villa who will help you unpack. I can call them.'

'Are you kidding?' Amused by yet more evidence of the differences between their respective lifestyles, she pulled out her clothes. 'This will take me five minutes at most. And I'd be embarrassed to ask anyone else to hang up a tee shirt that cost the same amount as a cup of coffee. So what happens next?'

'We are joining my father and Diandra for lunch.'

'Sounds good to me.'

The expression on his face told her he didn't share her sentiments. 'I need to make some calls. Make yourself at home. The fridge is stocked, there are books in the living room. Feel free to use the pool. If there is anything you need, let me know. I'll be using the office on the other side of the living room.'

What else could she possibly need?

Lily glanced round the villa, which was by far the most luxurious and exclusive place she'd ever stayed.

She had a feeling the only thing she was going to need was a reality check.

He hadn't been back here since that summer five years before. It had been an attempt to put the past behind him, but ironically it had succeeded only in making things worse.

The memory of his last visit sat in his head like a muddy stain.

Nik strolled out onto the terrace, hoping the view would relieve his tension, but being here took him right back to his childhood and that was a place he made a point of avoiding.

With a soft curse, he walked back into the room he'd had converted into an office and switched on his laptop.

For the next hour he took an endless stream of calls and then finally, when he couldn't postpone the moment any longer, he took a quick shower and changed for lunch.

Another day, another wedding.

Mouth grim, he pocketed his phone and strolled through the villa to find Lily.

She was sitting in the shade on the terrace, a glass of iced lemonade by her hand and a book in her lap, staring out across the bright turquoise blue of the bay.

She hadn't noticed him and he stood for a moment, watching her. The tension left him to be replaced by tension of a different source. That one night he'd spent with her hadn't been anywhere near long enough.

He wanted to rip off that pretty blue sundress and take her straight back to bed but he knew that, no matter what she said, she wasn't the sort of woman to be able to keep her emotions out of the bedroom so he gave her a cool smile as he strolled onto the terrace.

'Are you ready?'

'Yes.' She slid her feet into a pair of silver ballet flats and put her book on the table. 'Is there anything I should know? Who will be there?'

'My father and Diandra. They wanted this lunch to be family only.'

'In other words your father doesn't want your first meeting for a long while to be in public.' She reached for her glass and finished her drink. 'Don't worry about me while we're here. I'm sure I can find a few friendly faces to talk to while you're mingling.'

He looked down at the curve of her cheeks and the dimple in the corner of her mouth and decided she was the one with the friendly face. If he had to pick a single word to describe her, it would be approachable. She was warm, friendly and he was sure there would be no shortage of guests eager to talk to her. The thought should have reduced his stress because it gave him one less responsibility, but it didn't.

Despite her claims to being made of Kevlar, he wasn't convinced she'd managed to manufacture even a thin layer of protection for herself.

He offered to drive her to avoid the heat but she chose to walk and on the way up to the main house she grilled him about his background. Did his father still work? What exactly was his business? Did he have any other family apart from Nik?

His suspicion that she was more comfortable with this gathering than him was confirmed as soon as he walked onto the terrace.

He saw the table by the pool laid for four and felt Lily sneak her hand into his.

'He wants you to get to know Diandra. He's trying to build bridges,' she said softly, her fingers squeezing his. 'Don't glare.'

Before he could respond, his father walked out onto the terrace.

'Niklaus—' His voice shook and Nik saw the shimmer of tears in his father's eyes.

Lily extracted her hand from his. 'Hug him.' She made it sound simple and Nik wondered whether bringing someone as idealistic as Lily to a reunion as complicated as this one had been entirely sensible, but she and his father obviously thought alike because he walked towards them, arms outstretched.

'It's been too long since you were home. Far too long, but the past is behind us. All is forgiven. I have such news to tell you, Niklaus.'

Forgiven?

His feet nailed to the floor by the past and the weight of the secrets his father didn't know, Nik didn't move and then he felt Lily's small hand in his back pushing, harder this time, and he then stepped forward and was embraced by his father so tightly it knocked the air from his lungs.

He felt a heaviness in his chest that had nothing to do with the intensity of his father's grip. Emotions rushed towards him and he was beginning to wish he'd never agreed to this reunion when Lily stepped forward, breaking the tension of the moment with her warmest, brightest smile and an extended hand that gave his father no choice but to release Nik.

'I'm Lily Rose. We spoke on the phone. You have a very beautiful home, Mr Zervakis. It's kind of you to invite me to share your special day.' Blushing charmingly, she then attempted to speak a few words of Greek, a gesture that both distracted his father and guaranteed a lifetime of devotion.

Nik watched as his dazzled father melted like butter left in the hot sun.

He kissed her hand and switched to heavily accented English. 'You are welcome in my home, Lily. I'm so happy you are able to join us for what is turning out to be the most special week of my life. This is Diandra.'

For the first time Nik noticed the woman hovering in the background.

He'd assumed she was one of his father's staff, but now she stepped forward and quietly introduced herself.

Nik noticed that she didn't quite meet his eye, instead she focused all her attention on Lily as if she were the lifebelt floating on the surface of a deep pool of water.

Diandra clearly had sophisticated radar for detecting sympathy in people, Nik thought, wondering what 'news' his father had for them.

Experience led him to assume it was unlikely to be good.

'I've brought you a small gift. I made it myself.' Lily delved into her bag and handed over a prettily wrapped parcel.

It was a ceramic plate, similar to the one he'd admired in her apartment, decorated with the same pattern of swirling blues and greens.

Nik could see she had real talent and so, apparently, did his father.

'You made this? But this isn't your business?'

'No. I'm an archaeologist. But I did my dissertation on Minoan ceramics so it's an interest of mine.'

'You must tell me all about it. And all about yourself. Lily Rose is a beautiful name.' His father led her towards the table that had been laid next to the pool. Silver gleamed in the sunlight and bowls of olives gleamed glossy dark in beautiful blue bowls. Kostas put Lily's plate in the centre of the table. 'Your mother liked flowers?'

'I don't know. I didn't know my mother.' She shot Nik an apologetic look. 'That's too much information for a first meeting. Let's talk about something else.'

But Kostas Zervakis wasn't so easily deflected. 'You didn't know your mother? She passed away when you were young, *koukla mou*?'

Appalled by that demonstration of insensitivity, Nik shot him an exasperated look and was about to steer the conversation away from such a deeply personal topic when Lily answered.

'I don't know what happened to her. She left me in a basket in Kew Gardens in London when I was a few hours old.'

Whatever he'd expected to hear, it hadn't been that and Nik, who made a point of never asking about a woman's past, found himself wanting to know more. 'A basket?' Her eyes lifted to his and for a moment the presence of other people was forgotten.

'Yes. I was found by one of the staff and taken to hospital. They called me Lily Rose because I was found among the flowers. They never traced my mother. They assumed she was a teenager who panicked.' She spoke in a matter-of-fact tone but Nik knew she wasn't matter-of-fact about the way she felt.

This was why she had shown so much wistful interest in the detail of his family. At the time he hadn't been able to understand why it would make an interesting topic of conversation, but now he understood that, to her, it was not a frustration or a complication. It was an aspiration.

This was why she dreamed of happy endings, both for herself and other people.

He felt something stir inside him, an emotion that was entirely new to him.

He'd believed himself immune to even the most elaborately constructed sob story, but Lily's revelation had somehow managed to slide under those steely layers of protection he'd constructed for himself. For some reason, her simply stated story touched him deeply.

Unsettled, he dragged his eyes from her soft mouth and promised himself that no matter how much he wanted her, he wasn't going to touch her again. It wouldn't be fair, when their expectations of life were so different. He had no concerns about his own ability to keep a relationship superficial. He did, however, have deep concerns about her ability to do the same and he didn't want to hurt her.

His father, predictably, was visibly moved by the revelation about her childhood.

'No family?' His voice was roughened by emotion. 'So who raised you, *koukla mou*?'

'I was brought up in a series of foster homes.' She poked absently at her food. 'And now I think we should talk about something else because this is *definitely* too much detail for a first meeting, especially when we're here to celebrate a wedding.' Superficially she was as cheerful as ever but Nik knew she was upset.

He was about to make another attempt to change the topic when his father reached out and took Lily's hand.

'One day you will have a family of your own. A big family.'

Nik ground his teeth. 'I don't think Lily wants to talk about that right now.'

'I don't mind.' Lily sent him a quick smile and then turned back to his father. 'I hope so. I think family makes you feel anchored and I've never had that.'

'Anchors keep a boat secured in one place,' Nik said softly, 'which can be limiting.'

Her gaze met his and he knew she was deciding if his observation was random or a warning.

He wasn't sure himself. All he knew was that he didn't want her thinking this was anything other then temporary. He could see she'd had a tough life. He didn't want to be the one to shatter that optimism and remove the smile from her face.

His father gave a disapproving frown. 'Ignore him. When it comes to relationships my son behaves like a child in a sweetshop. He gorges his appetites without learning the benefits of selectivity. He enjoys success in everything he touches except, sadly, his private life.'

'I'm very selective.' Nik reached for his wine. 'And given that my private life is exactly the way I want it to be, I consider it an unqualified success.'

He banked down the frustration, wondering how his father, thrice divorced, could consider himself an example to follow.

His father looked at him steadily. 'All the money in the

world will not bring a man the same feeling of contentment as a wife and children, don't you agree, Lily?'

'As someone with massive college loans, I wouldn't dismiss the importance of money,' Lily said honestly, 'but I agree that family is the most important thing.'

Feeling as if he'd woken up on the set of a Hollywood rom-com in which he'd been cast in the role of 'bad guy', Nik refrained from asking his father which of his wives had ever given him anything other than stomach ulcers and astronomical bills. Surely even he couldn't reframe his romantic past as anything other than a disaster.

'One day you will have a family, Lily.' Kostas Zervakis surveyed her with misty eyes and Nik observed this emotional interchange with something between disbelief and despair.

His father had known Lily for less than five minutes and already he was ready to leave her everything in his will. It was no wonder he'd made himself a target for every woman with a sob story.

Callie had spotted that vulnerability and dug her claws deep. No doubt Diandra was working on the same soft spot.

A dark, deeply buried memory stirred in the depths of his brain. His father, sitting alone in the bedroom among the wreckage of his wife's hasty packing, the image of wretched despair as she drove away without looking back.

Never, before or since, had Nik felt as powerless as he had that day. Even though he'd been a young child, he'd known he was witnessing pain beyond words.

The second time it had happened, he'd been a teenager and he remembered wondering why his father would have risked putting himself through such emotional agony a second time.

And then there had been Callie...

He'd known from the first moment that the relationship was doomed and had blamed himself later for not trying to save his father from that particular mistake.

And now here he was again, trapped in the unenviable position of having to make a choice between watching his father walk into another relationship disaster, or potentially damaging their relationship by trying to intervene.

Lily was right that his father was a grown man, able to make his own decisions. So why did he still have this urge to push his father out of the path of the oncoming train?

Emotions boiling inside him, he glanced across the table to his future stepmother, wondering if it was a coincidence that she'd picked the chair as far from his as possible.

She was either shy or she was harbouring a guilty conscience.

He'd promised he wouldn't interfere, but he was fast rethinking that decision.

He sat in silence, observing rather than participating, while staff discreetly served food and topped up glasses.

His father engaged Lily in conversation, encouraging her to talk about her life and her love of archaeology and Greece.

Forced to sit through a detailed chronology of Lily's life history, Nik learned that she'd had three boyfriends, worked numerous low-paid jobs to pay for college tuition, was allergic to cats, suffered from severe eczema as a child and had never lived in the same place for more than twelve months.

The more he discovered about her life, the more he realised how hard it had been. She'd made a joke about Cinderella, but Lily made Cinderella look like a slacker.

Learning far more than he'd ever wanted to know, he turned to his father. 'What is the "news" you have for me?'

'You will find out soon enough. First, I am enjoying having the company of my son. It's been too long. I have resorted to the Internet to find news of what is happening with you. You have been spending a great deal of time in San Francisco.'

Happy to talk about anything that shifted the focus from Lily, Nik relaxed slightly and talked broadly about some of the technology developments his company was spearheading and touched lightly on the deal he was about to close, but the diversion proved to be brief.

Kostas spooned olives onto Lily's plate. 'You must persuade Nik to take you to the far side of the island to see the Minoan remains. You will need to go early in the day, before it is too hot. At this time of year everything is very dry. If you love flowers, then you will love Crete in the spring. In April and May the island is covered in poppies, daisies, camomile, iris.' He beamed at her. 'You must come back here then and visit.'

'I'd like that.' Lily tucked into her food. 'These olives are delicious.'

'They come from our own olive groves and the lemonade in your fridge came from lemons grown on our own trees. Diandra made it. She is a genius in the kitchen. You wait until you taste her lamb.' Kostas leaned across and took Diandra's hand. 'I took one mouthful and fell in love.'

Losing his appetite, Nik gave her a direct look. 'Tell me about yourself, Diandra. Where were you brought up?' He caught Lily's urgent glance and ignored it, instead listening to Diandra's stammered response.

From that he learned that she was one of six children and had never been married.

'She never met the right person, and that is lucky for me,' his father said indulgently.

Nik opened his mouth to speak, but Lily got there first.

'You're so lucky having been born in Greece,' she said quickly. 'I've travelled extensively in the islands but living here must be wonderful. I've spent three summers on Crete and one on Corfu. Where else do you think I should visit?'

Giving her a grateful look, Diandra made several suggestions, but Nik refused to be deflected from his path.

'Who did you work for before my father?'

'Ignore him,' Lily said lightly. 'He makes every conversation feel like a job interview. The first time I met him I wanted to hand over my résumé. This lamb is *delicious* by the way. You're so clever. It's even better than the lamb Nik and I ate last week and that was a top restaurant.' She went on to describe what they'd eaten in minute detail and Diandra offered a few observations of her own about the best way to cook lamb.

Deprived of the opportunity to question his future stepmother further, Nik was wondering once again what 'news' his father was preparing to announce, when he heard the sound of a child crying inside the house.

Diandra shot to her feet and exchanged a brief look with his father before scurrying from the table.

Nik narrowed his eyes. 'Who,' he said slowly, 'is that?'

'That's the news I was telling you about.' His father turned his head and watched as Diandra returned to the table carrying a toddler whose tangled blonde curls and sleepy expression announced that she'd recently awoken from a nap. 'Callie has given me full custody of Chloe as a wedding present. Niklaus, meet your half-sister.'

CHAPTER SEVEN

Lily sat on the sunlounger in the shade, listening to the rhythmic splash from the infinity pool. Nik had been swimming for the past half an hour, with no break in the relentless laps back and forth across the pool.

Whatever had possessed her to agree to come for this wedding?

It had been like falling straight into the middle of a bad soap opera.

Diandra had been so intimidated by Nik she'd barely opened her mouth and he, it seemed, had taken that as a sign that she had nothing worth saying. Lunch had been a tense affair and the moment his father had produced his little half-sister Nik had gone from being coolly civil to remote and intimidating. Lily had worked so hard to compensate for his frozen silence she'd virtually performed cartwheels on the terrace.

And she couldn't comprehend his reaction.

He was too old to care about sharing the affections of his father, and too independently wealthy to care about the impact on his inheritance. The toddler was adorable, a cherub with golden curls and a ready smile, and his father and Diandra had been so obviously thrilled by the new addition to the family Lily couldn't understand the problem.

On the walk back from lunch she'd tentatively broached

the subject but Nik had cut her off and made straight for his office where he'd proceeded to work without interruption.

Trying to cure her headache, Lily had drunk plenty of water and then read her book in the shade but she'd been unable to concentrate on the words.

She knew it was none of her business, but still she couldn't keep her mouth shut and when Nik finally vaulted from the pool in an athletic movement that displayed every muscle in his powerful frame, she slid off her sunlounger and blocked his path.

'You were horrible to Diandra at lunch and if you want to heal the rift with your father, that isn't the way. She is *not* a gold-digger.'

His face was an uncompromising mask. 'And you know this on less than a few minutes' acquaintance?'

'I'm a good judge of character.'

'This from a woman who didn't know a man was married?'

She felt herself flush. 'I was wrong about him, but I'm not wrong about Diandra, and you have to stop giving her the evil eye.'

Droplets of water clung to his bronzed shoulders. 'I was not giving her the evil eye.'

'Nik, you virtually grilled her at the table. I was waiting for you to throw her on the barbecue along with the lamb. You were terrifying.'

'*Theé mou,* that is *not* true. She behaved like a woman with a guilty conscience.'

'She behaved like a woman who was terrified of you! How can you be so *blind*?' And then she realised in a flash of comprehension that she was the one who was blind. He wasn't being small-minded, or prejudiced. That wasn't what was happening. She saw now that he was afraid for his father. His actions all stemmed from a desire to protect him. In his own way he was displaying the exact loyalty she valued so highly. Like a gazelle approaching a sleeping lion, she tiptoed carefully. 'I think your perspective may be a little skewed because of what happened with your father's other relationships. Do you want to talk about it?'

'Unlike you, I don't have the desire to verbalise every thought that enters my head.'

Lily stiffened. 'That was a little harsh given that I'm trying to help, but I'm going to forgive you because I can see you're very upset. And I think I know why.'

'Don't forgive me. If you're angry, say so.'

'You told me not to verbalise every thought that enters my head.'

Nik wiped his face with the towel and sent her a look that would have frozen molten lava. 'I don't need help.'

Lily tried a different approach. 'I can see that this situation has the potential for all sorts of complications, not least that Diandra has been given another woman's child to raise as her own just a few days before the wedding, but she seemed thrilled. Your father is clearly delighted. They're happy, Nik.'

'For how long?' His mouth tightened. 'How long until it all falls apart and his heart is broken again? What if this time he doesn't heal?' His words confirmed her suspicions and she felt a rush of compassion.

'This isn't about Diandra, it's about you. You love your father deeply and you're trying to protect him.' It was ironic, she thought, that Nik Zervakis, who was supposedly so cold and aloof, turned out to have stronger family values than David Ashurst, who on the surface had seemed like perfect partner material. It was something that her checklist would never have shown up. 'I love that you care so much about him, but has it occurred to you that you might be trying to save him from the best thing that has ever happened in his life?'

'Why will this time be different from the others?'

'Because he loves her and she loves him. Of course having a toddler thrown into the mix will make for a challenging start to the relationship, but—' She frowned as she examined that fact in greater depth. 'Why did Callie choose to do this now? A child is a person, not a wedding present. You think she was hoping to derail your father's relationship with Diandra?'

'The thought had occurred to me but no, that isn't what she is trying to do.' He hesitated. 'Callie is marrying again and she doesn't want the child.'

He delivered that news in a flat monotone devoid of emotion, but this time Lily was too caught up in her own emotions to think about his.

Callie didn't want the child?

She felt as if she'd been punched in the gut. All the air had been sucked from her lungs and suddenly she couldn't breathe.

'Right.' Her voice was croaky. 'So she gives her up as if she's a dress that's gone out of fashion? I'm not surprised you didn't like her. She doesn't sound like a very likeable person.' Horrified by the intensity of her response and aware he was watching her closely, she moved past him. 'If you're sure you don't want to talk then I think I'm going to have a rest before dinner. The heat makes me sleepy.'

He frowned. 'Lily—'

'Dinner is at eight? I'll be ready by then.' She steered her shaky legs towards her bedroom and closed the door behind her.

What was the matter with her?

This wasn't her family.

It wasn't her life.

Why did she have to take everything so *personally*?

Why was she worrying about how little Chloe would feel when she was old enough to ask about her mother when it wasn't really any of her business? Why did she care about all the potential threats she could see to his family unit?

The door behind her opened and she stiffened but kept her back to him. 'I'm about to lie down.'

'I upset you,' he said quietly, 'and that was not my intention. You were generous enough to come here with me, the least I can do is respond to your questions in a civil tone. I apologise.'

'I'm not upset because you didn't want to talk. I understand you don't find it helpful.'

'Then what's wrong?' When she didn't reply he cursed softly. 'Talk to me, Lily.'

'No. I'm having lots of feelings of my own and you hate talking about feelings. And no doubt you'll find some way to interpret what I'm feeling in a bad way, because that seems to be your special gift. You twist everything beautiful into something dark and ugly. You really should leave now. I need to self-soothe.'

She expected to hear the pounding of feet and the sound of a door closing behind him, but instead felt the warm strength of his hands curve over her shoulders.

'I do not twist things.'

'Yes, you do. But that's your problem. I can't deal with it right now.'

'I don't want you to self-soothe.' The words sounded as if they were dragged from him. 'I want you to tell me what's wrong. My father asked you a lot of personal questions over lunch.'

'I don't mind that.'

'Then what? Is this about Chloe?'

She took a juddering breath. 'It's a little upsetting when adults don't consider how a child might feel. It's lovely that she has a loving father, but one day that little girl is going to wonder why her mother gave her away. She's going to ask herself whether she cried too much or did something wrong. Not that I expect you to understand.'

There was a long pulsing silence and his grip on her arms tightened. 'I do understand.' His voice was low. 'I was nine when my mother left and I asked myself all those questions and more.'

She stood still, absorbing both the enormity and the implications of that revelation. 'I didn't know.'

'I don't talk about it.'

But he'd talked about it now, with her. Warmth spread through her. 'Did seeing Chloe stir it all up for you?'

'This whole place stirs it up,' he said wearily. 'Let's hope Chloe doesn't ask herself those same questions when she's older.'

'I was a baby and I still ask myself those questions.' And she had questions for him, so many questions, but she knew they wouldn't be welcome.

'I appreciate you listening to me, but I know you don't really want to talk about this so you should probably leave now.'

'Seeing as I am indirectly responsible for the fact you're upset by bringing you here in the first place, I have no intention of leaving.'

'You should.' Her voice was thickened. 'It's the situation, not you. You've never even met your half-sister so you can't be expected to love her and your father is obviously pleased, but a toddler is a lot of work and he's about to be married. What if he decides he doesn't want Chloe either?'

'He won't decide that.' His hands firm, he turned her to face him. 'He has wanted her from the first day, but Callie did everything she could to keep the child from him. I have no idea what my father will say when Chloe is old enough to ask, but he is a sensitive man—much more sensitive than I am as you have discovered—and he will say the right thing, I'm sure.' His hands stroked her bare arms and she gave a little shiver.

She could see the droplets of water clinging to dark hair that shadowed his bare chest.

Unable to help herself, she lifted her hand to his chest and then caught herself and pulled back.

'Sorry—' She took a step backwards but he muttered something under his breath in Greek and hauled her back against him. Her brain blurred as she was flattened against the heat and power of his body, his arm holding her trapped. He used his other hand to tilt her face to his and she drowned in the heated burn of his eyes in the few seconds before he bent his head and kissed her. And then there was nothing but the hunger of his mouth and the erotic slide of his tongue and it felt every bit as good as it had the first time. So good that she forgot everything except the pounding of her pulse and the desperate squirming heat low in her pelvis.

Pressed against his hard, powerful chest she forgot about feeling miserable and unsettled.

She forgot all the reasons this wasn't a good idea.

She forgot everything except the breathtaking excitement he generated with his mouth and hands. His kiss was unmistakably sexual, his tongue tangling with hers, his gaze locked on hers as he silently challenged her.

'Yes, yes.' With a soft murmur of acquiescence, she wrapped her arms round his neck, feeling the damp ends of his hair brush her wrists.

The droplets of water on his chest dampened her thin sundress until it felt as if there were nothing between them.

She felt him pull her hard against him, felt his hand slide down her back and cup her bottom so that she was pressed against the heavy thrust of his erection.

'I promised myself I wasn't going to do this but I want you.' He spoke in a thickened tone, and she gave a sob of relief.

'I want you, too. You have no idea how much. Right through lunch I wanted to rip your clothes off and remove that severe look from your face.'

He lifted his mouth from hers, his breathing uneven, the smouldering glitter of his eyes telling her everything she needed to know about his feelings. 'Do I look severe now?'

'No. You look incredible. This has been the longest week of my life.' She backed towards the bed, pulling him with her. If he changed his mind she was sure she'd explode. 'Don't have second thoughts. I know this is about sex and nothing else. I don't love you, but I'd love a repeat of all those things you did to me the other night.'

With sure hands, he dispensed with her sundress. 'All of them?'

'Yes.' She wanted him so badly it was almost indecent and when he lowered his head and trailed his mouth along her neck she almost sobbed aloud. 'Please. Right now. I want your whole repertoire. Don't hold anything back.'

'You're shy, it's still daylight,' he growled, 'and I don't have a blindfold.'

'I'm not shy. Shy has left the party. I don't care, I don't care.' Her hands moved over his chest and lower to his damp swimming shorts. She struggled to remove them over the thrusting force of his erection but finally her frantic fumbling proved successful and she covered him with the flat of her hand.

He groaned low in his throat and tipped her onto the bed, covering her body with his, telling her how much he wanted her, how hard she made him, until the excitement climbed to a point where she was a seething, writhing mass of desire. She tore at his shirt with desperate hands and he swore under his breath and wrenched it over his head, his fingers tangling with hers.

'Easy, slow down, there's no rush.'

'Yes, there is.' She rolled him onto his back and pressed her mouth to the hard planes of his chest and lower until she heard him groan. She tried to straddle him but he flipped her onto her back and caught her shifting hips in his hands, anchoring her there.

Despite the simmering tension, there was laughter in his eyes. 'It would be a criminal waste to rush this, *theé mou.*'

'No, it wouldn't.' She slid her hands over the silken muscles of his back. 'It might kill me if you don't.'

It was hard to know which of them was most aroused. She saw it in the glitter of his eyes and heard it in his uneven breathing. Felt it in the slight shake of his fingers as he un-hooked her bra and peeled it away from her, releasing her breasts, taking his time. Everything he did was slow, unhur-ried, designed to torture her and she wondered how he could exercise so much control, such brutal discipline, because if it had been up to her the whole thing would have been over by now. He kept her still with his weight, with soft words, with skilled kisses and the sensual slide of his hand that dictated both position and pace.

She felt the cool air from the ceiling fan brush the heated surface of her skin and then moaned aloud as he drew her into the dark heat of his mouth. Sensation was sweet and wild and she arched into him, only to find herself anchored firmly by the rough strength of his thigh. He worked his way down her body with slow exploratory kisses and she shivered as she felt the brush of his lips and the flick of his tongue. Lower, more intimate, his mouth wandered to the shadows between her thighs and she felt the slippery heat of his tongue opening her, tasting her until she could feel the pleasure thundering down on her. She was feverish, des-perate, everything in her body centred on this one moment.

'Nik—I need—'

'I know what you need.' A brief pause and then he eased over her and into her, each driving thrust taking him deeper until she didn't know where she ended and he began and then he paused, his hand in her hair and his mouth against hers, eyes half closed as he studied her face. She was dimly aware that he was saying something, soft intimate words that blurred in her head and melted over her skin. She felt the de-licious weight of him, the masculine invasion, the solidity of muscle, the scrape of his jaw against hers as he kissed her, murmured her name and told her all the things he wanted to do to her. And she moaned because she wanted him to do them, right now. He was controlling her but she didn't care because he knew things about her she didn't know herself.

How to touch her, where to touch her. All she wanted was more of this breath-stealing pleasure and then he started to move, slowly at first, and then building the rhythm with sure, skilled thrusts until she was aware of nothing but him, of hard muscle and slick skin, of the frenzy of sensation until it exploded and she clung to him, sobbing his name as her body tightened on his, her muscles rippling around the thrusting length of him drawing out his own response.

She heard him groan her name, felt him slide his hand into her hair and take her mouth again so that they kissed their way through the whole thing, sharing every throb, ripple and flutter in the most intimate way possible.

The force of it left her shaken and stunned and she lay, breathless, trying to bring herself slowly back to earth. And then he shifted his weight and gathered her close, murmuring something in Greek as he stroked her hair back from her face and kissed her mouth gently.

They lay for a moment and then he scooped her up and carried her into the shower where, under the soft patter of steamy water, he proceeded to expand her sexual education with infinite skill until her body no longer felt like her own and her legs felt like rubber.

'Nik?' She lay damp and sated on the tangled sheets, deliciously sleepy and barely able to keep her eyes open. 'Is that why you don't like coming back here? Because it reminds you of your childhood?'

He stared down at her with those fathomless black eyes, his expression inscrutable. 'Get some sleep.' His voice was even. 'I'll wake you in time to change for dinner.'

'Where are you going?'

'I have work to do.'

In other words she'd strayed into forbidden territory. Somewhere in the back of her mind there was another question she wanted to ask him, but her brain was already drifting into blissful unconsciousness and she slid into a luxurious sleep.

* * *

Nik returned to the terrace and made calls in the shade, one eye on the open doors of Lily's bedroom.

So much for his resolve not to touch her again.

And what had possessed him to tell her about his mother? It was something he rarely thought about himself, let alone spoke of to other people.

It was being back here that had stirred up memories long buried.

He ignored the part of him that said it was the prospect of another wedding that stirred up the memories, not the place.

To distract himself he worked until the blaze of the sun dimmed and he heard movement from the bedroom.

He ended the call he'd made and a few minutes later she wandered onto the terrace, sleepy eyed and deliciously disorientated. 'Have you been out here the whole time?'

'Yes.'

'You're not tired?'

'No.'

'Because you're stressed out about your father.' She sat down next to him and poured herself a glass of water. 'For what it's worth, I like Diandra.'

He studied the soft curve of her mouth and the kindness in her eyes. 'Is there anyone you don't like?'

'Yes!' She sipped her water. 'I have a deep aversion to Professor Ashurst, and if we're drawing up a list then I should confess I didn't totally fall in love with your girlfriend from the other night, but that might be because she called me fat. And I definitely didn't like you a few hours ago, but you redeemed yourself in the bedroom so I'm willing to overlook the offensive things you said on the journey.' A dimple appeared in the corner of her mouth and Nik felt the instant, powerful response of his body and wondered how he was going to make it through an evening of small talk with people that didn't interest him.

She, on the other hand, interested him extremely.

'We should get ready for the party. The guests will be arriving soon and my father wants us up there early to greet them.'

'Us? You, surely, not me.'

'He wants you, too. He likes you very much.'

'I like him, too, but I don't think I should be greeting his guests. I'm not family. We're not even together.' Her gaze slid to his and away again and he knew she was thinking about what they'd shared earlier.

He was, too. In fact he'd thought of little else but sex with Lily since she'd drenched herself in his shower a week earlier.

Sex had always been important to him, but since meeting her it had become an obsession.

'It would mean a lot to him if you were there.'

'Well, if you're sure that's what he wants. This all feels a bit surreal.'

'Which part feels surreal?'

'All of it. The whole rich-lifestyle thing. Living with you could turn a girl's head. You can snap your fingers and have anything you want.'

Relieved by the lightening of the atmosphere, he smiled. 'I will snap my fingers for you any time you like. Tell me what you want.'

She smiled. 'You can get me anything?'

'Anything.'

'So if I had a craving for lobster mousse, you'd find me one?'

'I would.' He reached for his phone and she covered his hand with hers, laughing.

'I wasn't serious! I don't want lobster mousse.' Her fingers were light on his hand. There was nothing suggestive about her touch. Nothing that warranted his extreme physical reaction.

'Then what?' His voice was husky. 'If you don't want lobster mousse, what can I get you?'

Her eyes met his and colour streaked across her cheeks.

'Nothing. I have everything I need.' She removed her hand quickly and said something, but her words were drowned out by the clacking of a helicopter.

Nik rose reluctantly to his feet. 'We need to move. The guests are arriving.'

'By helicopter?' Her eyes were round, as if it was only now dawning on her that this wasn't an ordinary wedding party. 'Is this party going to be glamorous?'

'Very. Lunch was an informal family affair, but tonight is for my father to show off his new wife.'

'How many guests?'

'A very select party. No more than two hundred, but they're arriving from all over Europe and the US.'

'Two *hundred*? That's a select party?' Her smile faltered. 'I'm a gatecrasher.'

'You are not a gatecrasher. You're my guest.'

She pushed her hair back from her face. 'I'm starting to panic that what I brought with me isn't dressy enough.'

'You look lovely in everything you wear, but I do have something if you'd like to take a look at it.'

'Something you bought for someone else?'

'No. For you.'

'I told you I didn't want anything.'

'I didn't listen.'

'So you bought me something anyway. In case I embarrassed you?'

'No. In case you had a panic that what you'd brought wasn't dressy enough.'

'I should probably be angry that you're calling me predictable, but as we don't have time to be angry I'm going to overlook it. Can I see?' She stood up at the same time he did and her body brushed against his.

'Lily...' He breathed her name, steadied her with his hands and she gave a low moan.

'No.' Her eyes were clouded. 'Seriously, Nik, if we do it again I'll fall asleep and never wake up. The Prince is supposed to wake Sleeping Beauty, not put her to sleep with endless sex.'

He lifted his hand to her flushed cheek and gently stroked her hair back from her face. It took all his will power not to power her back against the wall. 'We could skip the party. Better still, we could grab a couple of bottles of champagne and have our own party here by the pool.'

'No way! Not only would that upset your father and Diandra, but I wouldn't get to ogle all those famous people. Brittany will grill me later so I need to have details. Am I allowed to take photographs?'

'Of course.' With a huge effort of will he let his hand drop. 'You'd better try the dress.'

The dress was exquisite. A long sheath of shimmering turquoise silk with delicate beads hand-sewn around the neckline. It fitted her perfectly.

She picked up her phone, took a quick selfie and sent it to Brittany with a text saying Rebound sex is my new favourite thing.

People were wrong when they thought rebound sex didn't involve any emotion, she mused. Yes, the sex was spectacular, but even though she wasn't in love that didn't mean two people couldn't care about each other. She cared about making this wedding as easy as possible for Nik, and he'd cared enough not to leave her alone when she was upset.

Somewhere deep inside a small part of her wondered if perhaps that wasn't how she was supposed to be feeling, but she dismissed it, picked up her purse and walked through to the living room.

'I could be a little freaked out by how well you're able to guess my size.'

He turned, sleek and handsome in a dinner suit.

Despite the undisputable elegance and sophistication, formal dress did nothing to disguise the lethal power of the man beneath.

Testosterone in a tux, she thought as he reached into his pocket and handed her something.

'What's this?' She took the slim, elegant box and opened it cautiously. There, nestled in deep blue velvet, was a necklace of silver and sapphire she immediately recognised. 'It's one of Skylar's. I admired the picture.'

'And now you can admire the real thing. I thought it would look better on your neck than in a catalogue.' He took it from her and fastened it round her neck while she pressed her fingers to her throat self-consciously.

'When did you buy this?'

'I had it flown in after you admired her pot.'

'You had it *flown in*? From New York? There wasn't time.'

'This piece was in a gallery in London.'

'Unbelievable. So extravagant.'

'Then why are you smiling?'

'Because I like pretty things and Skylar makes the prettiest things.' Smiling, she pulled her phone out of her purse again. 'I need to capture the moment so when I'm sitting in my pyjamas in a cramped apartment in rainy London I can relive this moment. It's a loan, obviously, because I could never accept a gift this generous.' She took a couple of photos and then made him pose with her. 'I promise not to sell these to the newspapers. Can I send it to Sky? I can say *Look what I'm wearing.*'

A smile touched the corners of his mouth. 'It's your photo. You can do anything you like with it.'

'Skylar will be over the moon. I'm going to make sure everyone sees this necklace tonight. Now, tell me how you're feeling.' She'd asked herself over and over again if his earlier confession was something she should mention or not. But how could she ignore it when it was clearly the source of his stress?

His expression shifted from amused to guarded. 'How I'm feeling?'

'This is a party to celebrate your father's impending wedding, which you didn't want to attend. Is it hard to be here thinking about your mother and watching your father marry again? It must make marriage seem like a disposable object.'

'I appreciate your concern, but I'm fine.'

'Nik, I know you're not fine, but if you'd rather not talk about it—'

'I'd rather not talk about it.'

She kept her thoughts on that to herself. 'Then let's go.' She slipped her hand into his. 'I guess everyone will be trying to work out whether you're pleased or not, so for Diandra's sake make sure you smile.'

'Thank you for your counsel.'

'Ouch, that was quite a put-down. I presume that was your way of telling me to stop talking.'

'If I want to stop you talking, I have more effective methods than a verbal put-down.'

She caught his eye. 'If you feel like testing out one of those methods, go right ahead.'

'Don't tempt me.'

She was shocked by how badly she wanted to tempt him. She considered dragging him back inside, but a car was waiting outside the villa for them. 'I didn't realise there were cars on the island. How do they get across here?'

'There is a ferry, but my father usually takes a helicopter to the mainland if he is travelling.'

'We could have walked tonight.'

'There is no way you'd be able to walk that far in those shoes, let alone dance.'

'Who says I'll be dancing?'

His gaze slid to hers. 'I do.'

'You seem very sure of that.'

'I am, because you'll be dancing with me.'

She felt a shiver of excitement, excitement that grew as they drew up outside the imposing main entrance. The villa was situated on the far side of the island, out of sight of the mainland. 'This is a mansion, not a villa. Normal people don't live like this.'

'You think I'm not a normal person?'

'I *know* you're not.' She took his arm as they walked past a large fountain to the floodlit entrance of the villa. 'Normal people don't own five homes and a private jet.'

'The jet is owned by the company.'

'And you own the company.' It was hard not to feel overwhelmed as she walked through the door into the palatial entrance of his father's home. Towering ceilings gave a feeling of space and light and through open doors she caught a glimpse of rooms tastefully furnished with antiques and fine art. 'Tell me again what your father does?'

Nik smiled. 'He ran a very successful company, which he sold for a large sum of money.'

'But not to you.'

'Our interests are different.'

There was no opportunity for him to elaborate because Diandra was hovering and Lily noticed the nervous look she gave Nik.

To break the ice, she enthused over the other woman's dress and hair and then asked after Chloe.

'She's sleeping. My niece is watching her while we greet everyone, then I'm going to check on her. It's been a very unsettling time.' Diandra kept her voice low. 'I wanted to postpone the wedding but Kostas won't hear of it.'

'You're right, I won't.' Kostas took Diandra's hand. 'Nothing is going to stop me marrying you. You worry too much. She will soon settle and in the meantime we have an army of staff to attend to her happiness.'

'She doesn't need an army,' Diandra murmured. 'She needs the security of a few people she knows and trusts.'

'We'll discuss this later.' Kostas drew her closer. 'Our guests are arriving. Lily, you look beautiful. You will stand with us and greet everyone.'

'Oh, but I—'

'I insist.'

Lily quickly discovered that Nik's father was as skilled at getting his own way as his son.

Unable to extract herself, she stood and greeted the guests, feeling as if she were on a movie set as a wave of shimmering, glittering guests flowed past her.

'This isn't my life,' she whispered to Nik but he simply smiled and exchanged a few words with each guest, somehow managing to make everyone feel as if they'd had his full attention.

She discovered that even among this group of influential people everyone wanted a piece of him, especially the women.

It gave her a brief but illuminating insight into his life and she saw how it must be for him, surrounded by people whose motives in wanting to know him were as mixed up and murky as the bottom of the ocean.

She was beginning to understand both his reserve and his cynicism.

The evening was like something out of a dream, except that none of her dreams had ever featured an evening as glittering and extravagant as this.

What would it be like, she wondered, if this really *were* her life?

She pushed that thought aside quickly, preferring not to linger in fantasyland. Wanting a family was one thing, this was something else altogether.

Candles flickered, silverware gleamed and the air was filled with the heady scent of expensive perfume and fresh flowers. The food, a celebration of all things Greek, was served on the terrace so that the guests could enjoy the magnificent sight of the sun setting over the Aegean.

By the time Nik finally swung her onto the dance floor Lily was dizzy with it.

'I talked to a few people while you were in conversation

with those men in suits. I didn't mention the fact I'm a penniless archaeologist.'

'Are you enjoying yourself?'

'What do you think?'

'I think you look stunning in that dress.' He eased her closer. 'I also think you are better at mindless small talk than I am.'

'Are you calling me mindless?' She rested her hand lightly on his chest. 'Did you know that the very good-looking man over there with the lovely wife owns upmarket hotels all over the world? He's Sicilian.'

He glanced over her shoulder. 'Cristiano Ferrara? You think he's good-looking?'

'Yes. And his wife is beautiful. They seem like a happy family.'

He smiled. 'Her name is Laurel.'

'Do you know everyone? She was very down-to-earth. She admired my necklace and he pulled me to one side to ask me for the details. He's going to surprise her for her birthday.'

'If Skylar sells a piece of jewellery to a Ferrara I can assure you she's made. They move in the highest circles.'

'Laurel wants an invitation to her exhibition in London. I have plugged Skylar's jewellery to at least ten *very* wealthy people. I hope you're not angry.'

He curved her against him in a possessive gesture. 'You are welcome to be as shameless as you wish. In fact I'm willing to make a few specific suggestions about how you could direct that shameless behaviour.'

A few heads turned in their direction.

'Thank you for telling this room full of strangers that I'm a sex maniac. Are you sure you don't want to dance with someone else?'

His eyes were half shut, his gaze focused entirely on her. 'Why would I want to dance with anyone else?'

'Because there are a lot of women in this room and they're

looking at you hopefully. Me, they look as if they'd like to kill. They're wondering why you're with me.'

'None of the men are wondering that,' he drawled. 'Trust me on that.'

'Can I tell you something?'

'That depends. Is it going to be a deeply emotional confession that is going to send me running from the room?'

'You can't run anywhere because your father is about to make a speech and—oh—' she frowned '—Diandra looks stressed.' Taking his hand, she tugged him across the crowded dance floor towards Diandra, who appeared to be arguing with Kostas.

'Wait five minutes,' Kostas urged in a low tone. 'You cannot abandon our guests.'

'But she needs me,' Diandra said firmly and Lily intervened.

'Is this about Chloe?'

'She's woken up. I can't bear to think of her upset with people she doesn't know. It's already hard enough on her to have been left here by her mother.'

'Nik and I will go to her,' Lily said immediately and saw Nik frown.

'I don't think—'

'We'll be fine. Make your speech and then come and find us.' Without letting go of Nik's hand, Lily made for the stairs. 'I assume you know where the nursery is or should we use GPS?'

'I really don't think—'

'Cut the excuses, Zervakis. Your little sister needs you.'

'She doesn't know me. I don't see how my sudden appearance in her life can do anything but make things a thousand times worse.'

'Children are sometimes reassured by a strong presence. But stop glaring.' She paused at the top of the stairs. 'Which way?'

He sighed and led the way up another flight of stairs to a suite of rooms and pushed open the door.

A young girl stood there jiggling a red-faced crying toddler. Relief spread across her features when she saw reinforcements.

'She's been like this for twenty minutes. I can't stop her crying.'

Nik took one look at the abject misery on his half-sister's face and took her from the girl, but, instead of her being comforted by the reassuring strength in those arms, Chloe's howls intensified.

Sending Lily a look that said 'I told you so', he immediately handed her over.

'Perhaps you can do a better job than I can.'

She was about to point out that he was a stranger and that Chloe's response was no reflection on him when the toddler flopped onto her shoulder, exhausted.

'You poor thing,' Lily soothed. 'Did you wake and not know where you were? Was it noisy downstairs?' She continued to talk, murmuring soothing nothings and stroking the child's back until the child's eyelids drifted closed. She felt blonde curls tickle her chin. 'There, that's better, you must be exhausted. Are you thirsty? Would you like a drink?' She glanced across the room and saw Nik watching her, his expression inscrutable. 'Say something.'

'What do you want me to say?'

'Something. Anything. You look as if someone has released a tiger from a cage and you're expected to bag it single-handed.'

There was a tension in his shoulders that hadn't been there a few moments earlier and suddenly she wondered if his response to the child was mixed up with his feelings for Callie.

It was obvious he'd disliked his father's third wife, but surely he wouldn't allow those feelings to extend to the child?

And then she realised he wasn't looking at Chloe, he was looking at her.

He lifted his hand and loosened his tie with a few flicks of those long, bronzed fingers. 'You love children.'

'Well I don't love *all* children, obviously, but at this age they're pretty easy to love.' She waited for him to walk across the room and take his sister from her, but he didn't move. Instead he leaned against the doorway, watching her, and then finally eased himself upright.

'You seem to have this under control.' His voice was level. 'I'll see you downstairs when you're ready.'

'No! Nik, wait—' She shifted Chloe onto her other hip and walked across to him, intending to hand over the wriggling toddler so that he could form a bond with her, but he took a step back, his face a frozen mask.

'I'll send Diandra up as soon as she's finished with the speeches.' With that he turned and strode out of the room leaving her holding the baby.

CHAPTER EIGHT

NIK MADE HIS way through the guests, out onto the terrace and down past the cascading water feature that ended in a beautiful pool. Children cried for a million reasons, he knew that, but that didn't stop him wondering if deep down Chloe knew her mother had abandoned her. The fact that he'd been unable to offer comfort had done nothing for his elevated stress levels, but the real source of his tension had been the look on Lily's face.

He could see now he'd made a huge mistake bringing her here. *Cristos*, who was he kidding? The mistake had been taking her back to his place from the restaurant that night, instead of dropping her safely at her apartment and telling her to lock the door behind her.

She was completely, totally wrong for him and he was completely, totally wrong for her.

Cursing under his breath, he yanked off his tie and ran his hand over his jaw.

'Nik?'

Her voice came from behind him and he turned to find her standing there, her sapphire eyes gleaming bright in the romantic light of the pool area. The turquoise dress hugged the lush lines of her body and her blonde hair, twisted into Grecian braids, glowed like a halo. The jewel he'd given her sat at the base of her throat and suddenly all he wanted to do was rip it off and replace it with his mouth. There wasn't a man in the room who hadn't taken a second glance at her and he was willing to bet she hadn't noticed. He'd always considered jealousy to be a pointless and ugly emotion but tonight he'd experienced it in spades. He should have given her a dress of shapeless black, although he had a feeling that would have made no difference to the way he felt. It was a shock to discover that will power alone wasn't enough to hold back the brutal arousal.

'I thought you were with Chloe. Is she asleep?'

'Diandra came to take over. And you shouldn't have walked away from her.' She was stiff. Furious, displaying none of the softness and gentleness he'd witnessed in the nursery.

The wind had picked up and he frowned as he saw her shiver and run her hands over her arms. 'Are you cold? Crete often experiences high winds.'

'I'm not cold. I'm being heated from the inside out because I'm boiling mad, Nik. I don't think it's exactly fair of you to take your feelings for her mother out on a child, that's all.'

Nik took a deep breath, wondering how honest to be. 'That is not what is happening here.'

'No? Well there has to be some reason why you looked at Chloe as if she was a dangerous animal.'

'This is not about Chloe.'

'What then?'

There was a long, throbbing pause. 'It's about you.'

'Me?' She stared at him blankly and he cursed under his breath.

'You are the sort of woman who cannot pass a baby without wanting to pick it up. You see sunshine in a thunderstorm, happy endings everywhere you look and you believe family is the answer to every problem in the world.'

She stared at him with a total lack of comprehension. 'I do like babies, that's true, and I don't see any reason to apologise for the fact I'd like a family one day. I don't see sunshine in every thunderstorm, but I do try and see the positive rather than the negative because that's how I prefer to live my life. I put up an umbrella instead of standing there and getting wet. Sometimes life can be crap, I know that but I've learned not to focus on the crap and I won't apologise for that. But I don't see what that has to do with the situation. None of that explains why you behaved the way you did in that room. You looked as if you'd been hit round the head with a plank of wood and then you walked out. And you say it was about me, but how can it possibly—?'

Her expression changed, the shards of anger in her eyes changing to wariness. 'Oh. I get it. You're worried that because I want a family one day, that because I like babies, it makes me a dangerous person to have sex with, is that right?' She spoke slowly, feeling it out, watching his face the whole time and she must have seen something there that confirmed her suspicions because she made a derisive sound and turned away.

'Lily—'

'No! Don't make excuses or find a tactful way to express how you feel. It's sprayed over you like graffiti.' She hitched up her dress and started to walk away from him and he gritted his teeth because he could see she was truly upset.

'Wait. You can't walk back in those shoes—'

'Of course I can. What do you think I usually do when I'm out? I'd never been in a limo in my life before I met you. I walk everywhere because it's cheaper.' She hurled the words over her shoulder and he strode after her, wondering how to intervene and prevent a broken ankle without stoking her wrath.

'We should talk about this—'

'There is nothing to talk about.' She didn't slacken her pace. 'I cuddled your baby sister and you're afraid that somehow changed our relationship. You're worried that this isn't about sex any more, and that I've suddenly fallen in love with you. Your arrogance is shocking.'

He kept pace with her, ready to catch her if she twisted her ankle in those shoes. 'It is not arrogance. But that incident upstairs reinforced how different we are.'

'Yes, we're different. That's why I picked you for my rebound guy. It's true I want children one day, but believe me you're the last man on earth I'd want to share that with. I don't want a guy who describes a crying child as an "incident".'

'That is not—*Cristos*, will you *stop* for a moment?' He caught her arm and she shrugged him off, turning to face him.

'Believe me, Nik, I have never been *less* likely to fall in love with you than I am right at this moment. A little girl was distressed and all you could think about was how to extract yourself from a relationship you're not even having! That doesn't make you a great catch in my eyes so you're perfectly safe. I understand now why you have emotionless relationships. You're brilliant at the mechanics of sex, but that's it. I'd get as much emotional comfort from a laptop. Seriously, you should stick to your technology, or your investments or whatever it is you do—' She tugged her arm from his grip and carried on walking down the path, her distress evident in each furious tap of her heels.

He stared after her, stunned into silence by her unexpected attack and shaken by his own feelings. In emotional terms, he kept women at a distance. He'd never aspired to a deeper attachment and when his relationships ended he invariably felt nothing. He had no interest in marriage and didn't care about long-term commitment.

But he really, really cared that Lily was upset.

The feeling was uncomfortable, like having a stone in his shoe.

He followed at a safe distance, relieved when she reached the terrace and ripped off her shoes. She dumped them unceremoniously on a sunlounger and carried on walking. The braids of her Grecian goddess hairstyle had been loosened by the wind, and her hair slithered in tumbled curls over her bare shoulders.

A man with a sense of self-preservation would have left her to cool down.

Nik carried on walking. He walked right into the bedroom, narrowly avoiding a black eye as she swung the door closed behind her.

He caught it on the flat of his hand, strode through and slammed it shut behind him.

She turned, her eyes a furious blaze of blue. 'Get out, Nik.'

He shrugged off his jacket and slung it over the nearest chair. 'No.'

'You should, because the way I feel right now I might punch you. No, wait a minute, I know exactly how to make you back out of that door.' She tilted her head and her mouth curved into a smile that didn't reach her eyes. 'You should leave, Nik, because I'm—oh, seconds away from falling in love with your irresistible self.' Her sarcasm made him smile and that smile was like throwing petrol on flame. 'Are you laughing at me?'

'No, I'm smiling because you're cute when you're angry.'

'I'm not cute. I'm fearsome and terrifying.'

What was fearsome and terrifying was how much he wanted her but he kept that thought to himself as he strolled towards her. 'Can we start this conversation again?'

'There is nothing more to say. Stop right there, Nik. Don't take another step.'

He kept walking. 'I should not have left you with Chloe. I behaved like an idiot, I admit it,' he breathed, 'but I'm not used to having a relationship with a woman like you.'

'And you're afraid I don't understand the rules? Trust me, I not only understand them but I applaud them. I wouldn't *want* to fall in love with someone like you. You make Neanderthal man look progressive and I've studied Neanderthal man. And stop looking at me like that because there is no way I can have sex with you when I'm this angry. It's not happening, Nik. Forget it.'

He stopped toe to toe with her, slid his hand into her hair and tilted her face to his. 'You've never had angry sex?'

'Of course not! Until you, I've only ever had "in love" sex. Angry sex sounds horrible. Sex should be loving and gentle. Who on earth would want to—?' Her words died as he silenced her with his mouth.

He cupped her face, feeling the softness of her skin beneath his fingers and the frantic beat of her pulse. He took her mouth with a hunger bordering on aggression and felt her melt against him. Her arms sneaked round his neck and he explored the sweet heat of her mouth, so aroused he was ready to rip off her dress and play out any one of the explicit scenarios running through his brain.

He had no idea what it was about her that attracted him so much, but right now he wouldn't have cared if she was holding an armful of babies and singing the wedding march, he still would have wanted to get her naked.

Without lifting his mouth from hers, he hauled her dress up to her waist and slid his fingers inside the lace of her panties. He heard her moan, felt her slippery hot and ready for him, and then her hands were on his zip, fumbling as she tried desperately to free him. As her cool fingers closed around him his mind blanked. He powered her back against the wall, slid his hands under her thighs and lifted her easily, wrapping her legs around his hips.

'Nik—' She sobbed his name against his mouth, dug her nails into his shoulders and he anchored her writhing hips with his hands and thrust deep. Gripped by tight, velvet softness, he felt his vision blur. Control was so far from his reach he abandoned hope of ever meeting up again and simply surrendered to the out-of-control desire that seemed to happen whenever he was near this woman.

He withdrew and thrust again, bringing thick waves of pleasure cascading down on both of them. From that moment on there was nothing but the wildness of it. He felt her nails digging into his shoulders and the frantic shifting of her hips. He tried to slow things down, to still those sensuous movements, but they were both out of control and he felt the first powerful ripples of her body clenching his shaft.

'*Cristo*—' He gave a deep, throaty groan and tried to hold back but there was no holding back and he surrendered to a raw explosive climax that wiped his mind of everything except this woman.

It was only when he lowered her unsteadily to the floor that he realised he was still dressed.

He couldn't remember when he'd last had sex fully clothed.

Usually he had more finesse, but finesse hadn't been invited to this party.

He felt her sway slightly and curved a protective arm around her, supporting her against him. His cheek was on her hair and he could feel the rise and fall of her chest as she struggled for air.

Finally she locked her hand in the front of his shirt and lifted her head. Her mouth was softly swollen and pink from his kisses, her eyes dazed. 'That was angry sex?'

Nik was too stunned to answer and she gave a faint smile and gingerly let go of the front of his shirt, as if testing her ability to stand unsupported.

'Angry sex is good. I don't feel angry any more. You've taught me a whole new way of solving a row.' She swayed like Bambi and he caught her before she could slide to the floor.

'*Theé mou*, you are *not* going to use sex to solve a row.' The thought of her doing with anyone else what she'd done with him sent his stress levels soaring.

'You did. It worked. I'm not saying I like you, but all my adrenaline was channelled in a different direction so I'm feeling a lot calmer. My karma is calmer.'

Nik was far from calm. 'Lily—'

'I know this whole thing is difficult for you,' she said, 'and you don't need to make the situation more difficult by worrying about me falling in love with you. That is never going to happen. And next time your little sister is upset, don't hand her to someone else. I know you don't like tears, but I think you could make an exception for a distressed two-year-old. Man up.'

Nik, who had never before in his life had his manhood questioned, struggled for a response. 'She needed comfort and I have zero experience with babies.' He spoke through his teeth. 'My approach to all problems is to delegate tasks to whichever person has the superior qualifications—in this instance it was you. She liked you. She was calmer with you. With me, she cried.'

She gave him a look that was blisteringly unsympathetic. 'Every expert started as a beginner. Get over yourself. Next time, pick her up and learn how to comfort her. Who knows, one day you might even be able to extend those skills to grown-ups. If you didn't find it so hard to communicate you might not have gone so long without seeing your father. He adores you, Nik, and he's so proud of you. I know you didn't like Callie, but couldn't you have swallowed your dislike of her for the occasional visit? Would that really have been so hard?'

Nik froze. 'You know nothing about the situation.' Unaccustomed to explaining his actions to anyone, he took a deep breath. 'I did *not* stay away from my father because of my feelings about Callie.'

'What then?'

He was silent for a long moment because it was a topic he had never discussed with anyone. 'I stayed away from him because of her feelings for me.'

'That's what I'm saying! Because the two of you didn't get along, he suffered.'

'Not because I didn't like her. Because she liked me—a little too much.' He spoke with raw emphasis and saw the moment her expression changed and understanding dawned. 'That's right. My stepmother took her desire to be "close" to me to disturbing extremes.'

Lily's expression moved through a spectrum encompassing confusion, disbelief and finally horror. 'Oh, *no*, your poor father—does he know?'

'I sincerely hope not. I stayed away to avoid there ever being any chance he would witness something that might cause him distress. Despite my personal views on Callie I did not wish to see his marriage ended and I certainly didn't want to be considered the cause of it, because that would have created a rift that never would have healed.'

'So you stayed away to prevent a rift between you, but it caused a rift anyway and he doesn't even know the reason. Do you think you should have told him?'

'I asked myself that question over and over again, but I decided not to.' He hesitated. 'She was unfaithful several times during their short marriage and my father knew. There was nothing to be gained by revealing the truth and I didn't want to add to my father's pain.'

'Of course you didn't.' Lily's eyes filled. 'And all this time I was thinking it was because of your stubborn pride, because you didn't like the woman and were determined to punish him. I was *so wrong*. I'm sorry. Please forgive me.'

More unsettled by the tears than he was by her anger, Nik backed away. 'Don't cry. And there is nothing to forgive you for.'

'I misjudged you. I leaped to conclusions and I try never to do that.'

'It doesn't matter.'

'It does to me. You said that she had affairs—' Her eyes widened. 'Do you think that Chloe might not be—?'

He tensed because it was a possibility that had crossed his mind. 'I don't know, but it makes no difference now. My father's lawyers are taking steps to make sure it's a legal adoption.'

'But if she isn't and your father ever finds out—'

'It would make no difference to the way he feels about Chloe. Despite everything, I actually do believe she is my father's child. For a start she has certain physical characteristics that are particular to my family, and then there is the fact that Callie did everything in her power to keep her from him.'

'You really think she used her child as currency?'

'Yes.' Nik didn't hesitate and he saw the distress in her eyes.

'I think I dislike her almost as much as you do.'

'I doubt that.'

'I'm starting to see why you were worried about your father marrying again. Is Callie the reason you don't believe love exists?'

'No.' His voice didn't sound like his own. 'I formed that conclusion long before Callie.'

He waited for her to question him further but instead she leaned forward and hugged him tightly.

Unaccustomed to any physical contact that wasn't sexual, he tensed. 'What's that for?'

'Because you were put in a hideous, *horrible* position with Callie and the only choice you had was to stay away from your father. I think you're a very honourable person.'

He breathed deeply. 'Lily—'

'And because you were let down by a woman at a very vulnerable age. But I know you don't want to talk about that so I won't mention it again. And now why don't we go to bed and have apology sex? That's one we haven't tried before, but I'm willing to give it my all.'

Hours later they lay on top of the bed, wrapped around each other while the night breeze cooled their heated flesh.

Lily thought he was asleep, but then he stirred and tightened his grip.

'Thank you for helping with Chloe. You were very good with her.'

'One day I'd love to have children of my own, but it isn't something I usually admit to out loud. When people ask about your aspirations, they want to hear about your career. Wanting a family isn't a valid life choice. And I'm happy and interested in my job, but I don't want it to be all there is in my life.'

'Why did you choose archaeology?'

'I suppose I'm fascinated by the way people lived in the past. It tells us a lot about where we come from. Maybe it's because I don't know where I come from that it always interested me.'

There was a long silence. 'You know nothing about your mother?'

'Very little. I like to think she loved me, but she wasn't able to care for me. We assume she was a teenager. What I always wonder is why no one helped her. She obviously didn't feel she could even tell anyone she was pregnant. I think about that more than anything and I feel horrible that there wasn't anyone special in her life she could trust. She must have been so lonely and frightened.'

'Have you tried to trace her?'

'The police tried to trace her at the time but they had no success. They thought she was probably from somewhere outside London.' It was something she hadn't discussed with anyone before and she wondered why she was doing so now, with him. Maybe because he, too, had been abandoned by his mother, even though the circumstances were different. Or maybe because his honesty made him surprisingly easy to talk to. He didn't sugar coat his views on life, nor did he lie. After the brutal shock of discovering how wrong she'd been about David Ashurst, it was a relief to be with someone who was exactly who he seemed to be. And although she'd accused Nik of arrogance, part of her could understand how watching her with Chloe might have unsettled him. That moment had highlighted their basic differences and the truth was that his extreme reaction to her 'baby moment' had been driven more by his reluctance to mislead her, than arrogance.

It was obvious that his issues with love and marriage had been cemented early in life.

What psychological damage had his mother caused when she'd walked out leaving her young son watching from the hallway?

What message had that sent to him? That relationships didn't last? If a mother could leave her child, what did that say to a young boy about the enduring quality of love?

He'd been let down by the one person he should have been able to depend on, his childhood rocked by insecurity and lack of trust. Everything that had followed had cemented his belief that relationships were a transitory thing with no substance.

'We're not so different, you and I, Nik Zervakis.' She spoke softly. 'We're each a product of our pasts, except that it sent us in different directions. You ceased to believe true love existed, whereas I was determined to find it. It's why we're both bad at relationships.'

'I'm not bad at relationships.'

'You don't have relationships, Nik. You have sex.'

'Sex is a type of relationship.'

'Not really. It's superficial.'

'Why are we talking about me? Tell me why you think you're bad at relationships.'

'Because I care too much. I try too hard.'

'You want the fairy tale.'

'Not really. When you describe it that way it makes it sound silly and unachievable and I don't think what I want is unrealistic.'

'What do you want?'

There was a faint splash from beyond the open doors as a tiny bird skimmed across the pool.

'I want to be special to someone.' She spoke softly, saying the words aloud for the first time in her life. 'Not just special. I'm going to tell you something, and if you laugh you will be sorry—'

'I promise not to laugh.'

'I want to be someone's favourite person.'

There was a long silence and then his arms tightened. 'I'm sure you're special to a lot of people.'

'Not really.' She felt the hot sting of tears and was relieved it was dark. 'My life has been like a car park. People come and go. No one stays around for long. I have friends. Good friends, but it's not the same as being someone's favourite person. I want to be someone's dream come true. I want to be the person they call when they're happy or sad. The one they want to wake up next to and grow old with.' She wondered why she was telling him this, when his ambitions were diametrically opposed to hers. 'You think I'm crazy.'

'That isn't what I think.' His voice was husky and she turned her head to look at him but his features were indistinct in the darkness.

'Thank you for listening.' She felt sleep descend and suppressed a yawn. 'I know you don't think love exists, but I hope that one day you find a favourite person.'

'In bed, you are definitely my favourite person. Does that count?' He pulled the sheet up over her body, but didn't release her. 'Now get some sleep.'

The next couple of days passed in a whirl of social events. Helicopters and boats came and went, although tucked away on the far side of the idyllic island Lily was barely aware of the existence of other people. For her, it was all about Nik.

There had been a subtle shift in their relationship, although she had a feeling that the shift was all on her side. Now, instead of believing him to be cold and aloof, she saw that he was guarded. Instead of controlling, she saw him as someone determined to be in charge of his own destiny.

In between socialising, she lounged by the pool and spent time on the small private beach next to Camomile Villa.

She loved swimming in the sea and more than once Nik had to extract her with minutes to spare before she was expected to accompany him to another lunch or dinner.

He was absent a lot of the time and she was aware that he'd been spending that time with his father and, judging from the more harmonious atmosphere, that time had been well spent.

After that first awkward lunch, he'd stopped firing questions at Diandra and if he wasn't completely warm in his interactions with her, he was at least civil.

To avoid the madness of the wedding preparations, Nik was determined to show Lily the island.

The day before the wedding he pulled her from bed just before sunrise.

'What time do you call this?' Sleepy and fuzzy-headed after a night that had consisted of more sex than sleep, she grumbled her way to the bathroom and whimpered a protest when he thrust her under cold water. 'You're a sadist.'

'You are going to thank me. Wear sturdy shoes.'

'The Prince never said that to Cinderella and I am never going to thank you for anything.' But she dragged on her shorts and a pair of running shoes, smothering a yawn as she followed him out of the villa. She stopped when she saw the vintage Vespa by the gates. 'I hate to be the one to tell you this but something weird happened to your limo overnight.'

'When I was a teenager this was my favourite way of getting round the island.' He swung his leg over the bike with fluid predatory grace and she laughed.

'You are too tall for this thing.' But her heart gave a little bump as she slid behind him and wrapped her arms round hard male muscle. 'Shouldn't I have a helmet or a seat belt or something?'

'Hold onto me.'

They wound their way along dusty roads, past rocky coves

and beautiful beaches and up to the crumbling ruins of the
Venetian fort where they abandoned the scooter and walked
the rest of the way. He took her hand and they scrambled to
the top as dawn was breaking.

The view was breathtaking, and she sat next to him, her
thigh brushing his as they watched the sun slowly wake
and stretch out fingers of dazzling light across the surface
of the sea.

'I could live here,' she said simply. 'There's something
about the light, the warmth, the people—London seems so
grey in comparison. I can't believe you grew up here. You're
so lucky. Not that you know that of course—you take it all
for granted.'

'Not all.'

He'd brought a flask of strong Greek coffee and some of
the sweet pastries she adored and she nibbled the corner and
licked her fingers.

'I don't believe you made those.'

'Diandra made both the coffee and the pastries.'

'Diandra.' She grinned and nudged him with her shoulder. 'Confess. You're starting to like her.'

'She is an excellent cook.'

'And a good person. You're starting to like her.'

'I admit that what I took for a guilty conscience appears
to be shyness.'

'You like her.'

His eyes gleamed. 'Maybe. A little.'

'There, you said it and it didn't kill you. I'll make a romantic of you yet.' She finished the pastry, contemplated another
and decided she wouldn't get into the dress she'd brought to
wear at the wedding. 'That was the perfect start to the day.'

'Worth waking up for?' His voice was husky and she
turned her head, met his sleepy, sexy gaze and felt her tummy
tumble.

'Yes. Of course, it would be easier to wake up if you'd let
me sleep at night.'

He lowered his forehead to hers. 'Do you want to sleep, *erota mou*?' He curved his hand behind her head and kissed her with lingering purpose. 'I could take you back to bed right now if that is what you want.'

Her heart was pounding. She had to keep telling herself that this was about sex and nothing else. 'What's the alternative?'

'There are Minoan remains west of here if you want to extend the trip.'

'There are Minoan remains all over Crete,' she said weakly, telling herself that she could spend the rest of her life digging around in Minoan remains, but after this trip was over she'd never again get the chance to spend time with Nik Zervakis. 'Bed sounds good to me.'

CHAPTER NINE

THE CREAM OF Europe's great and good turned up to witness the wedding of Kostas Zervakis and Diandra.

'It's busier than Paris in fashion week,' Lily observed as they gathered for the actual wedding.

Nik was looking supremely handsome in a dark suit and whatever reservations he had about witnessing yet another marriage of his parent he managed to hide behind layers of sophisticated charm.

'You're doing well,' Lily murmured, reaching down to rescue the small posy of flowers that Chloe had managed to drop twice already. 'I'm proud of you. No frowning. All you have to do is keep it up for another few hours and you're done.'

He curved his arm round her waist. 'What's my reward for not frowning?'

'Angry sex.'

There was laughter in his eyes. 'Angry sex?'

'Yes. I like that sort. It's good to see you out of control.'

'I'm never out of control.'

'You were totally out of control, Mr Zervakis, and you hate that.' She hooked her finger into the front of his shirt and saw his eyes darken. 'You are used to being in control of everything. The people around you, your work environment, your emotions—angry sex is the only time I've ever seen you lose it. It felt good knowing I was the one responsible for breaking down that iron self-control of yours. Now, stop talking and focus. This is Diandra's moment.'

The wedding went perfectly, Chloe managed to hold onto the posy and after witnessing the ceremony Lily was left in no doubt that the love between Kostas and Diandra was genuine.

'She's his favourite person,' she whispered in a choked voice and Nik turned to her, wry humour in his eyes.

'Of course she is. She cooks for him, takes care of his child and generally makes his life run smoothly.'

'That isn't what makes this special. He could pay someone to do that.'

'He *is* paying her.'

'Don't start.' She refused to let him spoil the moment. 'Have you seen the way he looks at her? He doesn't see anyone else, Nik. The rest of us could all disappear.'

'That's the best idea I've heard in a long time. Let's do it.'

'No. I don't go to many weddings and this one is perfect.' Teasing him, she leaned closer. 'One day that is going to be you.'

He gave her a warning look. 'Lily—'

'I know, I know.' She shrugged. 'It's a wedding. Everyone dreams at weddings. Today, I want everyone to be happy.'

'Good. Let's sneak away and make each other happy.' His eyes dropped to her mouth. 'Wait here. There's one thing I have to do before we leave.' Leaving Lily standing in the shade, he walked across to his new stepmother and took her hands in his.

Lily watched, a lump in her throat, as he drew her to one side.

She couldn't hear what was said but she saw Diandra visibly relax as they talked and laughed together. And then they were joined by Kostas, who evidently didn't want to be parted from his new bride.

The whole event left Lily with a warm feeling and a genuine belief that this family really might live happily. Oh, there would be challenges of course, but a strong family weathered those together and she was sure that, no matter what had gone before, Kostas and Diandra were a strong family.

Just one dark cloud hovered on the horizon, shadowing her happiness. Now that the wedding was over, they'd both be returning to the reality of their lives.

And Nik Zervakis had no place in the reality of her life.

Still, they had one more night and she wasn't going to spoil today by worrying about tomorrow. She was lost in a private and very erotic fantasy about what the night might bring when Kostas drew her to one side.

'I have an enormous favour to ask of you.'

'Of course.' Her mind elsewhere, Lily wondered if it was time to be a bit more bold and inventive in the bedroom. Nik brought a seemingly never-ending source of energy, creativity and sexual expertise to every encounter and she wondered if it was time she took the initiative. Planning ways to give him a night he'd never forget, she remembered Kostas was talking and forced herself to concentrate.

'Would you take Chloe for us tonight? I am thrilled she is with us, but I want this one night with Diandra. Chloe likes you. You have a way with children.'

Lily's plans for an erotic night that Nik would remember for ever evaporated.

How could she refuse when her relationship with Nik was a transitory thing and this one was for ever?

'Of course.' She hid her disappointment beneath a smile, and decided that the news that they were sharing Camomile Villa with a toddler was probably best broken when it was too late for Nik to do anything about it, so instead of enlisting his help to transport Chloe's gear across to the villa, she did it herself, sending a message via Diandra to tell him she was tired and to meet her back there when he was ready.

She'd settled a sleepy Chloe into her bed at the villa when she heard his footsteps on the terrace.

'You should have waited for me.' Nik stopped in the doorway as she put her finger to her lips.

'Shh—she's sleeping.'

'*Who* is sleeping?'

'Chloe.' She pointed to where Chloe lay, splayed like a starfish in the middle of the bed. 'It's their wedding night, Nik. They don't want to have to think about getting up to a toddler. And in case you're thinking you don't want to get up to a toddler either, you don't have to. I'll do it.'

He removed his tie and disposed of his jacket. 'She is going to sleep in the bed?'

'Yes. I thought we could babysit her together.' She eyed him, unsure how he'd react. 'I know this is going to ruin our last night. Are you angry?'

'No.' He undid the buttons on his shirt and sighed. 'It was the right thing to do. I should have thought of it.'

'She might keep us awake all night.'

His eyes gleamed with faint mockery. 'We've had plenty of practice.' He looked at the child on the bed. 'Tell me what you want me to do. This should be my responsibility, not yours. And I want to do the right thing. It's important to me that she feels secure and loved.'

Her insides melted. 'You don't have to "do" anything. And if you'd rather go to bed, that's fine.'

'I have a better idea. We have a drink on the terrace. Open the doors. That way we'll hear her if she wakes up and she won't be able to escape without us seeing.'

'She's a child, not a wild animal.' But his determination to give his half-sister the security she deserved touched her, and Lily stood on tiptoe and kissed him on the cheek. 'And a drink is a good idea. I didn't drink anything at the wedding because I was so nervous that something might go wrong.'

'I know the feeling.' He slid his hand behind her head and tilted her face to his. 'Thank you for coming with me. I have no doubt at all that the wedding was a happier experience for everyone involved because you were there.' His gaze dropped to her mouth and lingered there and her heart started to pound.

All day, she'd been aware of him. Of the leashed power concealed beneath the perfect cut of his suit, of the raw sexuality framed by spectacular good looks.

A cry from the bedroom shattered the moment and she eased away regretfully. 'Could you pick her up while I fetch her a drink? Diandra says she usually has a drink of warm milk before she goes to sleep and I'm sure today was unsettling for her.'

'It was unsettling for all of us,' he drawled and she smiled.

'Do you want warm milk, too? Because I could fix that.'

'I was thinking more of chilled champagne.' He glanced towards the bedroom and gave a resigned sigh. 'I will go to her, but don't blame me when I make it a thousand times worse.'

Perhaps because he was so blisteringly self-assured in every other aspect of his life, she found his lack of confidence strangely endearing. 'You won't make it worse.'

She walked quickly through to the kitchen and warmed milk, tension spreading across her shoulders as she heard Chloe's cries. Knowing that all that howling would simply ensure that Nik didn't offer to help a second time, she moved as quickly as she could. As she left the kitchen, the cries ceased and she paused in the doorway of the bedroom, transfixed by the sight of Nik holding his little sister against his shoulder, one strong, bronzed hand against her back as he supported her on his arm. As she watched, she saw the little girl lift her hand and rub the roughness of his jaw.

He caught that hand in his fingers, speaking to her in Greek, his voice deep and soothing.

Lily had no idea what he was saying, but whatever it was seemed to be working because Chloe's eyes drifted shut and her head thudded onto his broad shoulder as she fell asleep, her blonde curls a livid contrast to the dark shadow of his strong jaw.

Nik stood still, as if he wasn't sure what to do now, and then caught sight of Lily in the doorway. He gave her a rueful smile at his own expense and she smiled.

'Try putting her back down on the bed.'

As careful as if he'd been handling delicate Venetian glass, Nik lowered the child to the bed but instantly she whimpered and tightened her grip around his neck like a barnacle refusing to be chipped away from a rock.

He kept his hand securely on her back and cast Lily a questioning look. 'Now what?'

'Er—sit down in the chair with her in your lap and give her some milk,' Lily suggested, and he strolled onto the terrace, sat on one of the comfortable sunloungers and let the toddler snuggle against him.

'When I said I wanted to spend the evening on the terrace with a woman this wasn't exactly what I had in mind.'

'Two women.' Laughing, she sat down next to him and offered Chloe the milk. 'Here you go, sweetheart. Cow juice.'

Nik raised his eyebrows. 'Cow juice?'

'One of my friends used to call it that because whenever she said "milk" her child used to go demented.' Seeing that the child was sleepy, Lily tried to keep her hold on the cup but small fingers grabbed it, sloshing a fair proportion of the contents over Nik's trousers.

To give him his due, he didn't shift. Simply looked at her with an expression that told her she was going to pay later.

'Thanks to you I now have "cow juice" on my suit.'

'Sorry.' She was trying not to laugh because she didn't want to rouse the sleepy, milk-guzzling toddler. 'I'll have it cleaned.'

'Let me.' He covered Chloe's small fingers with his large hand, holding the cup while she drank.

Lily swallowed. 'You see? You have a natural talent.'

His gaze flickered to hers. 'Take that look off your face. This is a one-time crisis-management situation, never to be repeated.'

'Right. Because she isn't the most adorable thing you've ever seen.'

Nik glanced down at the blonde curls rioting against the crisp white of his shirt. 'I have a fair amount of experience with women and I can tell you that this one is going to be high maintenance.'

'What gave you that idea? The fact that she wouldn't stay in her bed or the fact that she spilled her drink over you?'

'For my father's sake I hope that isn't a foreshadowing of her teenage years.' Gently, he removed the empty cup from Chloe's limp fingers and handed it back to Lily. 'She's fast asleep. Now it's my turn. Champagne. Ice. You.' His gaze met hers and she saw humour and promise under layers of potent sex appeal.

Her stomach dropped and she reached and took Chloe from him. 'I'll tuck her in.'

He rose to his feet, dwarfing her. 'I'll get the champagne.'

Wondering if the intense sexual charge ever diminished when you were with a man like him, Lily tiptoed through to the bedroom and tucked Chloe carefully into the middle of the enormous bed.

This time the child didn't stir.

Lily brushed her hand lightly over those blonde curls and stared down at her for a long moment, a lump in her throat. When she grew up was she going to wonder about her mother? Did Callie intend to be in her life or had she moved on to the next thing?

Closing the doors of the bedroom, Lily took the cup back to the kitchen. By the time she returned Nik was standing on the terrace wearing casual trousers and a shirt.

'You changed.'

'It didn't feel right to be drinking champagne in wet trousers.' He handed her a glass. 'She's asleep?'

'For now. I don't think she'll wake up. She's exhausted.' She sipped the champagne. 'It was a lovely wedding. For what it's worth, I like Diandra a lot.'

'So do I.'

She lowered the glass. 'Do you believe she loves him?'

'I'm not qualified to judge emotions, but they seem happy together. And I'm impressed by how willingly she has welcomed Chloe.'

She slipped off her shoes and sat on the sunlounger. 'I think Chloe will have a loving and stable home.'

He sat down next to her, his thigh brushing against hers. 'You didn't have that.'

She stared at the floodlit pool. 'No. I was a really sickly child. Trust me, you don't want the details, but as a result of that I moved from foster home to foster home because I was a lot of trouble to take care of. When you face the possibility of having to spend half the night in a hospital with a sick kid when you already have others at home, you take the easier option. I was never the easy option.'

He covered her hand with his. 'Was adoption never considered?'

'Older children aren't easy to place. Especially not sickly older children. Every time I arrived somewhere new I used to hope this might be permanent, but it never was. Anyway, enough of that. I've already told you far more than you ever wanted to know about me. You hate talking about family and personal things.'

'With you I do things I don't do with other people. Like attend weddings.' He turned her face to his and kissed her. 'You had a very unstable, unpredictable childhood and yet still you believe that something else is possible.'

'Because you haven't experienced something personally, doesn't mean it doesn't exist. I've never been to the moon but I know it's there.'

'So despite your disastrous relationships you still believe there is an elusive happy ending waiting for you somewhere.'

'Being happy doesn't have to be about relationships. I'm happy now. I've had a great time.' She gave a faint smile. 'Have I scared you?'

He didn't answer. Instead he lowered his head to hers again and she melted under the heat of his kiss, wishing she could freeze time and make this moment last for ever.

When she finally pulled away, she felt shaky. 'I've never met anyone like you before.'

'Cold and ruthlessly detached? Wasn't that what you said to me on that first night?'

'I was wrong.'

'You weren't wrong.'

'You reserve that side of you for the people you don't know very well and people who are trying to take advantage. I wish I were more like you. You're very analytical. There's another side of you that you don't often show to the world, but don't worry—it's our secret.'

His expression shifted from amused to guarded. 'Lily—'

'Don't panic. I still don't love you or anything. But I don't think you're quite the cold-hearted machine I did a week ago.'

I still don't love you.

She'd said the words so many times during their short relationship and they'd always been a joke. It was a code that acted as a reminder that this relationship was all about fun and sex and nothing deeper. Until now. She realised with a lurch of horror that it was no longer true.

She wasn't sure at what point her feelings had changed, but she knew they had and the irony of it was painful.

She'd conducted all her relationships with the same careful, studied approach to compatibility. David Ashurst had seemed perfect on the surface but had proved to be disturbingly imperfect on closer inspection whereas Nik, who had failed to score a single point on her checklist at first glance, had turned out to be perfect in every way when she'd got to know him better.

He'd proved himself to be both honest and unwaveringly loyal to his family.

It was that honesty that had made him hesitate before

finally agreeing to take her home that night and that honesty was part of the reason she loved him.

She wanted to stay here with him for ever, breathing in the sea breeze and the scent of wild thyme, living this life of barefoot bliss.

But he didn't want that and he never would.

The following morning, Nik left Lily to pack while he returned Chloe to his father and Diandra, who were enjoying breakfast on the sunny terrace overlooking the sea.

Diandra took Chloe indoors for a change of clothes and Nik joined his father.

'I was wrong,' he said softly. 'I like Diandra. I like her a great deal.'

'And she likes you. I'm glad you came to the wedding. It's been wonderful having you here. I hope you visit again soon.' His father paused. 'We both love Lily. She's a ray of sunshine.'

Nik usually had no interest in the long-term aspirations of the women he dated, but in this case he couldn't stop thinking about what she'd told him.

I want to be someone's favourite person.

She said she didn't want a fairy tale, but in his opinion expecting a relationship to last for a lifetime was the biggest fairy tale of all. His mouth tightened as he contemplated the brutal wake-up call that awaited her. He doubted there was a man out there who was capable of fulfilling Lily's shiny dream and the thought of the severe bruising that awaited her made him want to string safety nets between the trees to cushion her fall.

'She is ridiculously idealistic.'

'You think so?' His father poured honey onto a bowl of fresh yoghurt. 'I disagree. I think she is remarkably clear-sighted about many things. She's a smart young woman.'

Nik frowned. 'She is smart, but when it comes to relationships she has poor judgement just like—' He broke off and his father glanced at him with a smile.

'Just like me. Wasn't that what you were going to say?' He poured Nik a cup of coffee and pushed it towards him. 'You think I haven't learned my lesson, but every relationship I've had has taught me something. The one thing it hasn't taught me is to give up on love. Which is good, because this twisty, turning, sometimes stony path led me to Diandra. Without those other relationships, I wouldn't be here now.' He sat back, relaxed and visibly happy while Nik stared at him.

'You're seriously trying to convince me that if you could put the clock back, you wouldn't change things? Try and undo the mistakes?'

'I wouldn't change anything. And I don't see them as mistakes. Life is full of ups and downs. All the decisions I made were right at the time and each one of them led to other things, some good, some bad.'

Nik looked at him in disbelief. 'When my mother left you were a broken man. I was scared you wouldn't recover. How can you say you don't regret it?'

'Because for a while we were happy, and even when it fell apart I had you.' His father sipped his coffee. 'I wish I'd understood at the time how badly you were scarred by it all and I certainly wish I could undo some of the damage it did to you.'

'So if you had your time again, you'd still marry her?'

'Without hesitation.'

'And Maria and Callie?'

'The same. There are no guarantees with love, that's true, but it's the one thing in life worth striving to find.'

'I don't see it that way.'

His father gave him a long look. 'When you were building your business from the ground and you hit a stumbling block, did you give up?'

'No, but—'

'When you lost a deal, did you think to yourself that there was no point in going after the next one?'

Nik sighed. 'It is *not* the same. In my business I never make decisions based on emotions.'

'And that,' his father said softly, 'is your problem, Niklaus.'

CHAPTER TEN

THE JOURNEY BACK to Crete was torture. As the boat sped across the waves, Lily looked over her shoulder at Camomile Villa, knowing she'd never see it again.

Nik was unusually quiet.

She wondered if he'd had enough of being with her.

No doubt he was ready to move on to someone else. Another woman with whom he could share a satisfying physical relationship, never dipping deeper. The thought of him with another woman made her feel ill and Lily gripped the side of the boat, a gesture that earned her a concerned frown.

'Are you sea sick?'

She was about to deny that, but realised to do so would mean providing an alternative explanation for her inertia so she gave a little nod and instantly he slowed the boat.

That demonstration of thoughtfulness simply made everything worse.

It had been so much easier to stay detached when she'd thought he was the selfish, ruthless money-making machine everyone else believed him to be.

Now she knew differently.

The drive between the little jetty and his villa should have been blissful. The sun beamed down on them and the scent of lavender and thyme filled the air, but as they grew closer to their destination she grew more and more miserable.

She was lost in her own deep pit of gloom, and it was only

when he stopped at the large iron gates that sealed his villa off from the rest of the world that she realised his mistake.

She stirred. 'You forgot to drop me home.'

'I didn't forget.' He turned to look at her. 'I'll take you home if that's what you want, or you can spend the night here with me.'

Her heart started to pound. 'I thought—' She'd assumed he'd drop her home and that would be the end of it. 'I'd like to stay.'

The look in his eyes made everything inside her tighten in delicious anticipation.

He muttered something under his breath in Greek and then turned his head and focused on the driving, a task that seemed to cost him in terms of effort.

She knew he was aroused and her mood lifted and flew. He might not love her, but he wanted her. That was enough for now.

It wasn't one night.

They'd already had so much more than that.

He shifted gears and then reached across and took her hand and she looked down, at those long, strong fingers holding tightly to hers.

Her body felt hot and heavy and she stole a glance at his taut profile and knew he was as aroused as she was. In the short time they'd been together she'd learned to recognise the signs. The darkening of his eyes, the tightening of his mouth and the brief sideways glance loaded with sexual promise.

He wore a casual shirt that exposed the bronzed skin at the base of his throat and she had an almost overwhelming temptation to lean across and trace that part of him with her tongue. To tease when he wasn't in a position to retaliate.

'Don't you dare.' He spoke through his teeth. 'I'll crash the car.'

'How did you know what I was thinking?'

'Because I was thinking the same thing.'

It amazed her that they could be so in tune with each other, when they were so fundamentally different in every way.

'You need a villa with a shorter drive.'

He gave a laugh that was entirely at his own expense, and then cursed as his phone rang as he pulled up in front of the villa.

'Answer it.' She said it lightly, somehow managing to keep the swell of disappointment hidden inside.

'I'll get rid of them.' He spoke with his usual arrogant assurance before hitting a button on his phone and taking the call.

He switched between Greek and English and Lily was lost in a dream world, imagining the night that lay ahead, when she heard him talking about taking the private jet to New York.

He was flying to New York?

The phone call woke her up from her dream.

What was she doing?

Why was she hanging around like stale fish when this relationship was only ever going to be something transitory?

Was part of her really hoping that she might be the one that changed his mind?

The happiness drained out of her like air from an inflatable mattress.

She never should have come back here. She should have asked him to drop her at her flat and made her exit with dignity.

Taking advantage of the fact he was still on the phone, she grabbed her small bag and slid out of the car.

'Thanks for the lift, Nik,' she whispered. 'See you soon.'

Except she knew she wouldn't.

She wouldn't see him ever again.

He turned his head and frowned. 'Wait—'

'Carry on with your call—I'll grab a cab,' she said hastily, and then proceeded to walk as fast as she could back up his drive in the baking heat.

Why did his drive have to be so *long*?

She told herself it was for the best. It wasn't his fault that her feelings had changed, and his hadn't. Their deal had been rebound sex without emotion. She was the one who'd brought emotion into it. And she'd take those emotions home with her, as she always did, and heal them herself.

Her eyes stung. She told herself it was because the sun was bright and scrabbled in her bag for sunglasses as a car came towards her down the drive. She recognised the sleek lines of the car that had driven her and Nik to the museum opening that night. It slowed down and Vassilis rolled down the window.

He took one look at her face and the suitcase and his mouth tightened. 'It's too hot to walk in this heat, *kyria*. Get in the car. I'll take you home.'

Too choked to argue, Lily slid into the back of the car. The air conditioning cooled her heated skin and she tried not to think about the last time she'd been in this car.

She was about to give Vassilis the address of her apartment, when her phone beeped.

It was a text from Brittany.

Fell on site, broke my stupid wrist and knocked myself out. In hospital. Can you bring clothes?

Horrified, Lily leaned forward. 'Vassilis, could you take me straight to the hospital please? It's urgent.'

Without asking questions, he turned the car and drove fast in the direction of the hospital, glancing at her in his mirror.

'Can I do anything?'

She gave him a watery smile and shook her head. At least worrying about Brittany gave her something else to think about. 'You're already doing it, thank you.'

'Where do you want me to drop you?'

'Emergency Department.'

'Does the boss know you're here?'

'No. And he doesn't need to.' She was glad she'd kept the sunglasses on. 'It was a bit of fun, Vassilis, that's all.' Impulsively she leaned forward and kissed him on the cheek. 'Thank you for the lift. You're a sweetheart.'

Scarlet, he handed her a card. 'My number. Call me when you're ready for a lift home.'

Lily located Brittany in a ward attached to the emergency department. She was sitting, pale and disconsolate, in a room where she was the only occupant. Her face was bruised and her wrist was in plaster and she had a smear of mud on her cheek.

Putting aside her own misery, Lily gave a murmur of sympathy. 'Can I hug you?'

'No, because I'm dangerous. I'm in a filthy mood. It's my right hand, Lil! The hand I dig with, type with, write with, feed myself with, punch with— Ugh. I'm so *mad* with myself. And I'm mad with Spy.'

'Why? What did he do?'

'He made me laugh! I was laughing so hard I wasn't looking where I was putting my feet. I tripped and fell down the damn hole, put my hand out to save myself and smashed my head on a pot we'd dug up earlier. It would be funny if it wasn't so tragic.'

'Why isn't Spy here with you?'

'He was. I sent him away.' Brittany slumped. 'I'm not good company and I couldn't exactly send him to pack my underwear.'

'What's going to happen? Are they keeping you in?'

'Yes, because I banged my head and they're worried my brain might be damaged.' Brittany looked so frustrated Lily almost felt like smiling.

'Your brain seems fine to me, but I'm glad they're treating you with care.'

'I want to go home!'

'To our cramped, airless apartment? Brittany, it will be horribly uncomfortable.'

'I don't mean home to the apartment. I mean home to Puffin Island. There is no point in being here now I can't dig. If I've got to sit and brood somewhere, I'd rather do it at Castaway Cottage.'

'I thought you said a friend was using the cottage.'

'Emily is there, but there's room for two. In fact it will be three, because—' She broke off and shook her head dismissively, as if realising she'd said something she shouldn't. 'Long story. My friends and I lurch from one crisis to another and it looks as if it's my turn. Can you do me a favour, Lil?'

'Anything.'

'Can you book me a flight to Boston? I'll sort out the transfer from there, but if you could get me back home, that would be great. The doctor said I can fly tomorrow if I feel well enough. My credit card is back in the apartment.' She lay back and closed her eyes, her cheeks pale against the polished oak of her hair.

'Have they given you something for the pain?'

'Yes, but it didn't do much. I don't suppose you have a bottle of tequila on your person? That would do it. Crap, I am so selfish—I haven't even asked about you.' She opened her eyes. 'You look terrible. What happened? How was the wedding?'

'It was great.' She made a huge effort to be cheerful. 'I had a wonderful time.'

Brittany's eyes narrowed. 'How wonderful?'

'Blissful. Mind-blowing.' She told herself that all the damage was internal. No one was going to guess that she was stumbling round with a haemorrhaging wound inside her.

'I want details. Lots of them.' Brittany's eyes widened as she saw the necklace at Lily's throat. 'Wow. That's—'

'It's one of Skylar's, from her *Mediterranean Sky* collection.'

'I know. I'm drooling with envy. He *bought* you that?'

'Yes.' She touched her fingers to the smooth stone, knowing she'd always remember the night he'd given it to her.

'He had one of her pots in his villa—do you remember the large blue one? She called it *Modern Minoan* I think. I recognised it and when he found out I knew Skylar, he thought I might like this.'

'So just like that he bought it for you? How the other half lives. That necklace you're wearing cost—'

'Don't tell me,' Lily said quickly, 'or I'll feel I have to give it back.' She'd intended to, but it was all she had to remind her of her time with him.

'Don't you dare give it back. You're supporting Sky. Her business is really taking off. It's thrilling for her. In my opinion she needs to ditch the guy she's dating because he can't handle her success, but apart from that she has a glittering future. That is one serious gift you're wearing, Lily. So when are you seeing him again?'

'I'm not. This was rebound sex, remember?' She said it in a light-hearted tone but Brittany's smile turned to a scowl.

'He hurt you, didn't he? I'm going to kill him. Right after I put a deep gouge in his Ferrari, I'm going to dig out his damn heart.'

Lily gave up the exhausting pretence that everything was fine. 'It's my fault. Everything I did was my choice. It's not his fault I fell in love. I still don't understand how it happened because he is *so* wrong for me.' She sank onto the edge of the bed. 'I thought he didn't fit any of the criteria on my list, and then after a while I realised he did. That's the worst thing about it. I've realised there are no rules I can follow.'

'You're in love with him? Lily—' Brittany groaned '—a man like that doesn't *do* love.'

'Actually you're wrong. He loves his father deeply. He doesn't show it in a touchy-feely way, but the bond between them is very strong. It's romantic love he doesn't believe in. He doesn't trust the emotion.' And she understood why. He'd been deeply hurt and that hurt had bedded itself deep inside him and influenced the way he lived his life. His security had been wrenched away from him at an age when it should have been the one thing he could depend on, so he'd chosen a different sort of security—one he could control. He'd made sure he could never be hurt again.

She ached for him.

And she ached for herself.

Brittany took her hand. 'Forget him. He's a rat bastard.'

'No.' Lily sprang to his defence. 'He isn't. He's honest about what he wants. He would never mislead someone the way David did.'

'Not good enough. He should have seen what sort of person you were on that very first night and driven you home.'

'He did see, and he tried to.' Lily swallowed painfully. 'He spelled out exactly what he was offering but I didn't listen. I made my choice.'

'Do you regret it, Lil?'

'No! It was the most perfect time of my life. I can't stop wishing the ending was different, but—' She took a deep breath and pressed her hand to her heart. 'I'm going to stop doing that fairy-tale thing and be a bit more realistic about life. I'm going to "wise up" as you'd say, and try and be a bit more like Nik. Protect myself, as he does. That way when someone like David comes into my life, I'll be less likely to make a mistake.'

'What about your checklist?'

'I'm throwing it out. In the end it didn't prove very reliable.' And deep down she knew there was no chance of her making a mistake again. No chance of her falling in love again.

'Does he know how you feel?'

'I hope not. That would be truly embarrassing. Now let's forget that. You're the important one.' Summoning the last threads of her will power, Lily stood up and picked up her bag. 'I'm going to go back to our apartment, pack you a case of clothes and book you on the first flight out of here.'

'Come with me. You'd love Puffin Island. Sea, sand and sailing. It's a gorgeous place. There's nothing keeping you here, Lily. Your project is finished and you can't spend August travelling Greece on your own.'

Right now she couldn't imagine travelling anywhere.

She wanted to lie down in a dark room until she stopped hurting.

Brittany reached out and took her hand. 'Castaway Cottage is the most special place on earth. We may not have Greek weather, but right now living here is like being in a range cooker so you might be grateful for that. When I'm home, I sleep with the windows open and I can hear the birds and the crash of the sea. I wake up and look out of the window and the sea is smooth and flat as a mirror. You have to come. My grandmother thought the cottage had healing properties, remember? And it looks as if you need to heal.'

Was healing possible? 'Thanks. I'll think about it.' She gave her friend a gentle hug. 'Don't laugh at any jokes while I'm gone.'

She took a cab home and tried not to think about Nik.

Sweltering in their tiny, airless bedroom, she hunted for a top or a dress that could easily be pulled over a plaster cast.

It was ridiculous to feel this low. Right from the start, there had only been one ending.

She'd be fine as long as she kept busy.

But would he?

The next woman he dated wouldn't know about his past, because he didn't share it.

They wouldn't understand him.

They wouldn't be able to find a way through the steely layers of protection he put between himself and the world and they'd retreat, leaving him alone.

And he didn't deserve to be alone.

He deserved to be loved.

Through the window of her apartment she could see couples walking hand in hand along the street on their way to the nearest beach. Families with small children, the nice gay couple who owned Brittany's favourite bar. Everyone was in pairs. It was like living in Noah's ark, she thought gloomily, two by two.

She resisted the urge to lie down on the narrow bed and sob until her head ached. Brittany needed her. She didn't have time for self-indulgent misery, especially when this whole thing was her own fault.

She found a shirt that buttoned down the front and was folding it carefully when she heard a commotion in the street outside.

Lily felt a flicker of panic. The cab couldn't be here already, surely?

She was about to lean out of the window and ask him to wait when someone pounded on the door.

'Lily?' Nik's voice thundered through the woodwork. 'Open the door.'

The ground shifted beneath her feet and for a moment she thought there had been a minor earthquake. Then she realised it was her knees that were trembling, not the floor.

What was he doing here?

Dragging herself to the door, she opened it cautiously. 'Stop banging. These apartments aren't very well built. A cupboard fell off the wall last week.' She took in his rumpled appearance and the tension in his handsome face and felt a stab of concern. 'Is something the matter? You look terrible. Was your phone call bad news?'

'Are you ill?' He spoke in a roughened tone and she looked at him in astonishment.

'What makes you think I'm ill?'

'Vassilis told me he took you to the emergency department. You *were* very pale on the boat. You should have told me you were feeling so unwell.'

He thought she'd gone to the hospital for herself? 'Brittany is the one in hospital. She had a fall. I'm on my way there now with some stuff. I really need to finish packing. The cab will be here soon.' Knowing she couldn't keep this up for much longer, she turned away but he caught her arm in a tight grip.

'Why did you walk away from me? I thought we agreed you were going to stay another night.'

'I didn't walk. I bounded. That's what happens after rebound sex. You bound.' She kept it light and heard him curse softly under his breath.

'You didn't need to leave.'

'Yes, I did.' Aware that her neighbours were probably enjoying the show, she reached past him and closed the door. 'I shouldn't have agreed to stay in the first place. I wasn't playing by the rules. And as it happened Brittany needed me, so your phone call was perfect timing.'

'It was terrible timing.'

Discovering that being in the same room as him was even harder than not being in the same room as him, Lily walked back to the bedroom and finished packing. 'So you're flying back to New York? That sounds exciting.'

'Business demands I fly back to the US, but I have things to settle here first.'

She wondered if she was one of the things he had to settle.

He was trying to find a tactful way of reminding her their relationship hadn't been serious.

The ache inside grew worse. She tried to think of something to say that would make it easy for him. 'I have to get to the hospital. Brittany fell on site and fractured her wrist. She's waiting for me to bring her clothes and things and then I have to arrange a flight for her back to Maine because she can't stay here. She has invited me to spend August with her. I'm going to say yes.'

'Is that what you want?'

Of course it wasn't what she wanted. 'It will be fantastic.' Her control was close to snapping. 'Did you want something, Nik? Because I have to ring a cab, take some clothes to Brittany at the hospital and then battle with the stupid Wi-Fi to book a ticket and it's a nightmare. I did some research before

the Internet crashed and at best it's a nineteen-hour journey
with two changes. She's going to have to fly to Athens, then
to Munich where she can get a direct flight to Boston. I still
have to research how she gets from Boston to Puffin Island,
but I can guarantee that by the time she arrives home she'll
be half dead. I'm going to fly with her because she can't do
it on her own, but I hadn't exactly budgeted for a ticket to the
US so I'm having to do a bit of financial juggling.'

'What if I want to change the rules?'

'Sorry?'

'You said you weren't playing by the rules.' His gaze was
steady on her face. 'What if I want to change the rules?'

'The way I feel right now, I'd have to say no.'

'How do you feel?'

She was absolutely sure that was one question he didn't
want answered. 'My cab is going to be here in a minute and
I have to book flights—'

'I'll give you a lift to the hospital and arrange for her to
use the Gulfstream. We can fly direct to Boston and she can
lie down all the way if she wants to,' he said. 'And I know a
commercial pilot who flies between the islands, so that problem is also solved. Now tell me how you feel.'

'Wait a minute.' Lily looked at him, dazed. 'You're offering to transport Brittany home on a private jet? You can't do
that. When I told you I was going to have to do some financial juggling I wasn't fishing for a donation.'

'I know. It sounds as if Brittany's in trouble and I'm always happy to help a friend in trouble.'

It confirmed everything she already knew about him but
instead of cheering her up, it made her feel worse. 'But she's
my friend, not yours.'

He drew in a breath. 'I'm hoping your friends will soon
be my friends. And on that topic, *please* can we focus on
us for a moment?'

Her heart gave an uneven bump and she looked at him
warily. 'Us?'

'If you won't talk about your feelings then I'll talk about mine. Before we left the island this morning, I had a long conversation with my father.'

Lily softened. 'I'm pleased.'

'I'd always believed his three marriages were mistakes, something he regretted, and it wasn't until today that I realised he regretted nothing. Far from seeing them as mistakes, he sees them as a normal part of life, which delivers a mix of good and bad to everyone. Yes, there was pain and hurt, but he never once faltered in his belief that love existed. I confess that came as a surprise to me. I'd assumed if he could have put the clock back and done things differently, he would have done.'

Lily gave a murmur of sympathy. 'Perhaps it was worse for you being on the outside. You only had half the story.'

'When my mother left I saw what it did to him, how vulnerable he was, and it terrified me.' His honesty touched her but she resisted the temptation to fling her arms round him and hug him until he begged for mercy.

'You don't have to tell me this. I know you hate talking about it.'

'I want to. It's important that you understand.'

'I do understand. Your mother walked away from you. That was the one relationship you should have been able to depend on. It's not surprising you didn't believe in love. Why would you? You had no evidence that it existed.'

'Neither did you,' he breathed, 'and yet you never ceased to believe in it.'

She gave a half-smile. 'Maybe I'm stupid.'

'No. You are the brightest, funniest, sexiest woman I've met in my whole life and there is no way, *no way*,' he said in a raw tone, 'I am letting you walk out of my life.'

'Nik—'

'You asked me why I was here. I'm here because I want to renegotiate the terms of our relationship.'

She almost smiled at that. Only Nik could make it sound

like a business deal. 'Is this because you know I have feelings for you and you feel sorry for me? Because, honestly, I'm going to be fine. I'll get over you, Nik. At some point I'll get out there again.' She hoped she sounded more convincing than she felt.

'I don't want you to get over me. And I don't want to think of you "out there", a pushover for anyone who decides to take advantage of you.'

'I can take care of myself. I've learned a lot from you. I'm Kevlar.'

'You are marshmallow-coated sunshine,' he drawled, 'and you need someone with a less shiny view on life to watch out for you. I don't want this to be a rebound relationship, Lily. I want more.'

Suddenly she found it difficult to breathe. 'What exactly are we talking about here? How much more?'

'All of it.' He stroked her hair back from her face with gentle hands. 'You've made me believe in something I never thought existed.'

'Fairy tales?'

'Love,' he said softly. 'You've made me believe in love.'

'Nik—'

'I love you.' He paused and drew breath. 'And unless my reading of this situation is completely wrong, I believe you love me back. Which is probably more than I deserve, but I'm selfish enough not to care about that. When it comes to you, I'll take whatever I can get.'

'Oh.' She felt a constriction in her chest. Her eyes filled and she covered her mouth with her hand. 'I'm going to cry, and you hate that. I'm really sorry. You'd better run.'

'I hate it when you cry, that's true. I don't ever want to see you cry. But I'm not running. Why would I run when the one thing in life that is special to me is right here?'

A lump wedged itself in her throat. She was so afraid of misinterpreting what he said, she was afraid to speak. 'You love me. So y-you're saying you'd like to see me again? Date?'

'No, that's not what I'm saying.' Usually so articulate, this time he stumbled over the words. 'I'm saying that you're my favourite person, Lily. And I apologise for proposing to you in a cramped airless room with no air conditioning but, as you know, I'm very goal orientated and as my goal is to persuade you to marry me then the first step is to ask you.' He reached into his pocket and pulled out a box. 'Skylar doesn't make engagement rings but I hope you'll like this.'

'You want to marry me?' Feeling as if she were running to catch up, she stared at the box. 'I'm your favourite person?'

'Yes. And when you find your favourite person it's important to hold onto them and not let them go.'

'You love me? You're sure?' She blinked as he opened the box and removed a diamond ring. 'Nik, that's *huge*.'

'I thought it would slow you down and make it harder for you to escape from me.' He slid it onto her finger and she stared at it, dazzled as the diamond caught the sun's rays.

'I'm starting to believe in fairy tales after all. I love you, too.' It was her turn to stumble. 'I knew I was in love with you, but I wasn't going to tell you. It didn't seem fair on you. You were clear about the rules right from the beginning and I broke them. That was my fault.'

With a groan, he pulled her against him. 'I knew how you felt. I was going to force you to talk to me, but then I had to take that phone call and you vanished.'

'I didn't want to make it awkward for you by hanging around,' she muttered and he said something in Greek and eased her away from him.

'What about you?' His expression was serious. 'This isn't a first for you. You've fallen in love before.'

'That's the weird thing—' she lifted her hand to take another look at her ring, just to make sure she hadn't imagined it '—I thought I had, but then I spent time with you and told you all those things and I realised that with you it was different. I think I was in love with the idea of love. I thought I knew exactly what qualities I wanted in a person. But you can't use a checklist to fall in love. With you, I wasn't trying and it happened anyway. I need to change. I need to find a new way to protect myself.'

'I don't want you to change. I want you to stay exactly the way you are. And I can be that layer of protection that you don't seem to be able to cultivate for yourself.'

'You're volunteering to be my armour?'

'If that means spending the rest of my life plastered against you that sounds good to me.' His mouth was on hers, his hands in her hair and it occurred to her that this level of happiness was something she'd dreamed about.

'I was going to spend August on Puffin Island with Brittany.'

'Spend it with me. I have to go to New York next week, but we can fly Brittany to Maine first. I have friends in Bar Harbor. That's close to Puffin Island. While I'm at my meeting in New York you could visit Skylar. Then we can fly to San Francisco and take some time to plan our life together. I can't promise you a fairy tale, but I can promise the best version of reality I can give you.'

'You want me to go with you to San Francisco? What job would I do there?'

'Well, they have museums, but I was thinking about that.' He brushed away salty tears from her cheeks. 'How would you feel about spending more time on your ceramics?'

'I can't afford it.'

'You can now, because what's mine is yours.'

'I couldn't do that. I don't ever want our relationship to be about money.' She flushed awkwardly. 'It's important I keep custody of my rusty bike so I'm going to need you to sign one of those pre-nuptial agreement things so I'm protected in case you try and snatch everything I own.'

He was smiling. 'Pre-nuptial agreements are for people whose relationships aren't going to last and ours will last, *theé mou.*' Those words and the sincerity in his voice finally convinced her that he meant it, but even that wasn't enough to convince her this was really happening.

'But seriously, what do I bring to this relationship?'

'You bring optimism and a sunny outlook on life that no amount of money can buy. You're an inspiration, Lily. You're willing to trust, despite having been hurt. You have never known a stable family, and yet that hasn't stopped you believing that such a thing is possible for you. You live the life you believe in and I want to live that life with you.'

'So I bring a smile and you bring a private jet? I'm not sure that's an equitable deal. Not that I know much about deals. That's your area of expertise.'

'It is, and I can tell you I'm definitely the winner in this particular deal.' He kissed her again. 'The money is going to mean I can spoil you, and I intend to do that so you'd better get used to it. I thought being an artist would fit nicely round having babies. We'll split our time between the US and Greece. Several times a year we'll come back here and stay in Camomile Villa so we can see Diandra and Chloe and you can have your fill of Minoan remains.'

'Wait. You're moving too quickly for me. You have to understand I'm still getting used to the idea that I've gone from owning a bicycle, to having part ownership of a private jet.'

'And five homes.'

'I have real-estate whiplash. But at least I know how to clean them!' But it was something else he'd said that had really caught her attention. 'A moment ago—did you mention babies?'

'Have I misunderstood what you want? Am I sounding too traditional? Right now my Greek DNA is winning out,' he groaned, 'but what I'm trying to say is you can do anything you like. Make any choices you like, as long as I'm one of them.'

'You'd want babies?' She flung her arms round him. 'You haven't misunderstood. Having babies is my dream.'

His mouth was on hers. 'How do you feel about starting

SARAH MORGAN   187

right away? I used to consider myself progressive, but all I
can think about is how cute you're going to look when you're
pregnant so I have a feeling I may have regressed to Neanderthal man. Does that bother you?'

'I've already told you I studied *homo neanderthalensis*,'
Lily said happily. 'I'm an expert.'

'You have no idea how relieved I am to hear that.' Ignoring the heat, the size of the room and the width of the bed,
he pulled her into his arms and Lily discovered it was possible to kiss and cry at the same time.

'We've had fun sex, athletic sex and angry sex—what
sort of sex is this? Baby sex?'

'Love sex,' he said against her mouth. 'This is love sex.
And it's going to be better than anything that's gone before.'

* * * * *

CHANGING
CONSTANTINOU'S
GAME

JENNIFER HAYWARD

For the Watermill Writers – Alison, Helene, Jo, Lesa, Louise, Pippa, Rachael, Sharon and Suzie. My week with you all in Tuscany listening to stories of rhinestone-studded cat collars, peach thongs and lines like 'flattered but not tempted' puts a smile on my face, always. I love you all.

And thank you to Mike, the elevator repair technician who took away some of my drama, but who also educated me on how very, very safe elevators are! I think I'll take the less dramatic ride for the rest of my life. :)

CHAPTER ONE

AS FAR AS luck went, Manhattan-based reporter Isabel Peters had been enjoying more than her fair share of it lately. She'd managed to nab a cute little one-bedroom on the Upper East Side she could actually afford, she'd won a free membership to the local gym, which might actually enable her to keep off the fifteen pounds she'd recently lost, and because she'd been in the right place at the right time, she'd landed a juicy story about the New York mayoral race that was putting her name on the map at the network.

But as she raced through the doors of Sophoros's London offices, slapped her card down on the mahogany reception desk in front of the immaculately dressed receptionist and blurted out her request to see Leandros Constantinou, the look on the blonde's face suggested her lucky streak might finally have run out.

"I'm afraid you've missed him, Ms. Peters," the receptionist said in that perfectly accented English that never failed to make Izzie feel totally unworthy. "Mr. Constantinou is already on his way back to the States."

Damn. The adrenaline that had been rocketing through her ever since her boss had texted her as she was about to board her flight home from Italy this morning and sent her on a wild-goose chase across London came to a screeching, sputtering halt, piling up inside her like a three-car collision. She'd done everything she could to make it here before Sophoros's billionaire CEO left. But midday traffic hadn't been on her side. Neither had her poky cab driver, who hadn't seemed to recognize the urgency of her mission.

She struggled to control the frustration that was no doubt writing its way across her face, reminding herself that this woman could still be useful. "Thank you," she murmured, wrapping her fingers around the card and sliding it back into her purse. "Would you happen to know which office he's headed for?"

"You would have to ask his PA that," the blonde said with a pointed look. "She's in the New York headquarters. Would you like her number?"

"Thanks, I have it." Izzie chewed on her bottom lip. "How long ago did he leave?"

"Hours," the other woman drawled. "So sorry it was a wasted trip."

Something about the gleam in the gatekeeper's eyes made Izzie give her a second look. Was the elusive Leandros Constantinou holed up in his office avoiding her? She wouldn't put it past him from what her boss had said about his magic disappearing acts when it came to the press, but she didn't have time to flush him out. Her flight back to New York left in exactly three and a half hours, and she intended to be on it.

She gave the other woman a nod, zipped up her purse and turned away from the desk. James, her boss, wasn't going to be happy about this. From what he'd said in his texts, the scandal rocking Constantinou's gaming software company was about to go public. And if NYC-TV didn't get to him before it did and persuade him to do the interview, every media outlet in the country was going to be knocking on his door. At that point, their chances of landing the feature would be slim to none.

She swung her purse over her shoulder with a heavy sigh and made her way out the heavy glass doors to the bank of elevators. A glance at the bored, restless expressions of those in the packed reception area told her she'd walked right into the middle of the midday caffeine and nicotine exodus. Which wasn't to say she herself didn't have bad habits. Hers were just more of the "shoving food she didn't need in her mouth" variety. Or obsessing over a story when she should be at the gym sweating off a few extra pounds. But what was a girl to do when her mother was a famous Hollywood diva and her sister sashayed down runways for a living? Perfection was never going to be all that attainable.

The ping of an elevator arriving pulled her gaze to the row of silver-coated death traps. A group of people crammed themselves inside like a pack of sardines, and she should have gone with them, really, given her hurry. But her heart, which hadn't quite recovered from the trip up, started pounding like a jackhammer. Just looking at the claustrophobic eight-by-eight-foot box made her mouth go dry and her legs turn to mush.

She glanced at the fire exit door, wondering how bad, exactly, walking down fifty flights of stairs would be. *Bad,* she decided. Three-inch heels did not lend themselves to such activity and besides, she *had* to catch that flight. Better to slay her demons and get on with it. Except, she reasoned, taking a step back as the thick steel doors slammed shut on the dozen people inside, having a whole contingent bear witness to her incapacitating fear of elevators wasn't going to happen.

Telling herself she was a rational, levelheaded woman with what many would call a heck of a lot of responsibility on her shoulders every day, she looked desperately around the lobby at the crowd that was left in search of a diversion. She could do this. She wasn't a total head case.

She took in the drop-dead perfect figure of the woman to her right, covered in a body-hugging dress that screamed haute couture. *Stunning. Were these women everywhere? And weren't those designer heels? So not fair.* The only pair of designer shoes she owned were a ruby-red marked-down find she'd fallen in love with, then spent a quarter of a month's salary on. Which had seen her eating cereal for dinner for weeks.

She kept her gaze moving. Over a man who looked as if he indulged in one too many pastries at tea every day to the distinctly *not* middle-aged specimen leaning against the wall beside him typing on his smartphone. Her jaw dropped. How could she have missed *him*? He was distraction with a capital *D*. And even that didn't begin to describe the six-foot-something-inches of pure testosterone in the designer suit. He was distraction in all caps. And then some...

Wow. She took in every magnificent inch of him. She'd never seen a guy wear a suit *that* well. Not even the full-of-themselves peacocks who liked to show off in the financial district bars of Manhattan. Because the way the tailored dark gray creation molded this man's tall, lean frame to perfection? Should be illegal. Particularly the way it hugged his muscular, to-die-for thighs like a glove.

Damn but he was hot. Like "her body temperature ratcheted up about ten degrees" hot. She dragged her gaze northward to check out his swarthy, sexy Mediterranean profile. And froze. Somewhere along the way he'd looked up from his phone...*at her.* Lord. That dimple, indentation, or whatever you called it in the middle of his chin— it was just so...*yum.*

She held her breath as he embarked on a perusal that bore little resemblance to her guilty ogling. No—this was a fully adult, ultra-confident assessment of her assets by a man who'd surely had his pick of those he'd bestowed it upon in the past. She twitched, pushing her feet into the floor, wanting to squirm like a six-year-old. But her training as a reporter had taught her that was the last thing she should do when cornered. By the time his gaze moved back to her face, unleashing a full blast of heady dark blue on her, she was sure her cheeks weren't the only thing that were beet-red.

A long moment passed—which surely had to be the most excruciating of her life. Then he broke the contact with a deliberate downward tilt of his chin, his attention moving back to his phone.

Dismissed.

Her cheeks flamed hotter. *Honestly, Izzie, what were you expecting? That he would ogle you back? This has been happening your entire life. With men who weren't that far out of your league.*

A Latin tune filled the air. Grew louder. Adonis lifted his head; frowned. *Her phone. Dammit.* She fumbled in her bag and pulled it out.

"So…?" Her boss barked. "What happened?"

"He was already gone, James, sorry. Traffic was bad."

Her boss let out a short, emphatic expletive. "I'd heard he was uncatchable but I thought that was only for the female population."

Izzie had no idea what Leandros Constantinou looked like—or anything about him for that matter. She'd never heard of the gaming company he ran, nor its wildly popular racing title, *Behemoth*, before this morning when she'd gotten James's text on the way home from her girls' trip to Tuscany and he'd ordered her to make this pit stop. His text had said Constantinou's former head of software development, Frank Messer, who'd been pushed out of the company years ago, had walked into NYC-TV today claiming he was the brains behind *Behemoth*. Determined to get his due, he'd launched a court case against the company.

And offered an exclusive interview to her boss to tell his side of the story.

She pursed her lips. "I asked the receptionist which office he was headed for, but she wouldn't tell me."

"My source says it's New York." Her boss sighed. "No worries, Iz, we'll get him here. He can't avoid us forever."

We? She frowned. "Are you going to let me work on this?"

There was silence on the other end of the line. "So I wasn't going to tell you until you got back, given that you get yourself all worked up about stuff like this, but since the timing's changed I better let you know now. Catherine Willouby is retiring. The network execs have been impressed with your work of late and they want you to try out to replace her."

Her breath caught in her lungs, her stomach doing a loop-to-loop. She took an unsteady step backward. Catherine Willouby, NYC-TV's much-loved matriarch and weekend anchor, was retiring? And they wanted *her*, a lowly community reporter with a handful of years of experience to audition to replace her?

"But I'm two decades younger than her," she sputtered. "Don't they want someone with more experience?" And wasn't she an idiot for even mentioning that fact?

"We're getting killed with the younger demographic," James said flatly. "They think you can bring in some of that age group, plus you already have a great relationship with the community."

Her head spun. She wiped a clammy palm against her skirt. She should be over the moon that they thought that highly of her. But her stomach was too busy tying itself up in knots. "So what does this have to do with the Constantinou story?"

"The execs think your weak spot is a lack of hard news experience…something your competition has tons of. So

I'm going to hand you this story and you're going to knock it out of the park."

Oh. She swallowed hard. Pressed her phone tighter against her ear and rocked back on her heels. The Constantinou story was going to make headlines across the country. *Was she ready for this?*

"You still there?" James demanded.

"Yes," she responded, her voice coming out a high-pitched squeak. She closed her eyes. "Yes," she repeated firmly.

"Stop freaking out," he admonished. "It's an interview—that's all. You might not get any further than that."

An interview in the biggest media market in the world, likely in front of a panel of stiff-suited network execs who would analyze her down to her panty hose brand...

The knot in her stomach grew bigger. "When?"

"Ten a.m. tomorrow, here at the station."

Tomorrow? She shot a glance at an arriving elevator. "James, I—"

"I gotta go, Iz. I've emailed you some prep questions. Rehearse them inside out and you'll be fine. Ten a.m. Don't be late."

The line went dead. She stood there dumbfounded. *What had just happened?*

The tall, dark-haired hunk picked up his bag and moved toward the empty elevator. A quick scan of the lobby told her they were the only two left. She tossed her phone in her purse and made herself follow. Except five feet from the doors, her feet glued to the spot and refused to move. She stood there staring at the empty metal cube, her pulse rate skyrocketing. The hunk pushed his hand courteously against the door as it started to close, impatience playing around the edges of his mouth. "You coming?"

She nodded, momentarily distracted by the New York

accent mixed with the sexy faint flavoring of something foreign. Greek, maybe?

Move, she told herself, managing a couple of tentative steps toward the terrifying little box. But the closer she got, the harder it was to drag oxygen into her constricted lungs. She came to a skittering halt a foot away.

His gaze narrowed on her face. "You okay?"

She inclined her head. "Slight fear of elevators."

His brow furrowed. "Millions of people travel in them every day…they're unbelievably safe."

"It's the unbelievable part I worry about," she muttered, staying where she was.

He rolled his eyes. "How do you get to work every day?"

"I take the stairs."

His mouth tightened. "Look, I have to get to the airport. You can take this one or the next…your choice."

She swallowed. "Me too…have to get to the airport, I mean."

He gave her a steady look, visibly controlling his impatience. "Get on, then."

A vision of her and her sister curled up in a dark elevator yelling for help flashed through her head. Like it always did when she had to make herself do this. She remembered the utter silence of the heavy metal box as they'd sat there shivering against the wall for hours, their knees drawn up to their chins, terrified it was going to drop. Her absolute conviction that nobody was ever going to find them and they were going to spend the night in the cold, silent darkness.

He let out an oath. "I have to go."

She stared at him blankly as he jabbed his finger against the button, his words bouncing off the terror freezing her brain. The heavy metal doors started to close.

She could not miss that flight.

Dragging in a deep breath, she dived forward, shoving her bag between the closing doors, then throwing her body through after it. Adonis cursed, jamming his hand into the opening. "What the hell?" he ground out as she landed against the back of the elevator, palms pressed to the metal to steady herself. "What kind of a stupid maneuver was that?"

She jumped as the doors slammed shut. "I have a job interview tomorrow...I can't miss my flight."

"So you thought that getting there in multiple pieces was a better idea?" He shook his head and looked at her as though she was a crazy person.

"Slight fear of elevators...remember?" She wrapped her fingers around the smooth metal bar that surrounded the elevator and held on for dear life.

He lifted a brow. "Slight fear?"

She nodded, leaning back against the bar in as casual a pose as she could manage with her shaking knees threatening to topple her. "Don't mind me. I'm good."

He didn't look convinced, but transferred his attention to the television screen running a ticker recap of the day's news. A couple of minutes tops, she told herself. Then she'd be back on solid ground and on her way to the airport.

The elevator moved smoothly downward, whizzing through the floors. She started to think she *was* a little crazy. This wasn't so bad... She took a couple of deep, steadying breaths and relaxed her fingers around the bar. She could do this, she repeated like a mantra in her head, glancing up at the numbers as they lit up. Just thirty-four more floors...

A couple of businessmen immersed in a politically incorrect joke joined them on the thirty-third floor, their deep voices booming in the echoing confines of the elevator. By the time they got off on the thirty-second floor,

Izzie was smiling. Perhaps not socially acceptable, but the joke *was* funny.

The elevator picked up speed again. And more speed. She whipped her gaze up to the LCD panel. Thirty-one, thirty, twenty-nine... Was it her imagination, or were the floors whizzing by faster than before? Her heartbeat accelerated. She *must* be imagining it because elevators didn't change speed, did they? The numbers whizzed by faster. She flicked an alarmed look at the hunk. He was staring at the numbers too. Twenty-eight, twenty-seven, twenty-six...*they were definitely accelerating.*

"Wh-what's happening?" she croaked, clutching the bar behind her.

He swung around, his mouth set in a grim line. "I don't—"

The rest of his words were ripped from his mouth as the elevator slammed to a sudden, screeching halt. She shrieked as the force of the impact tore her hands from the bar and sent her careering forward. The stranger lunged for her, but the bouncing elevator threw him off balance and he slammed into her. The floor came up to meet them, the heavy weight of his body crashing down on hers. The sound of her head hitting the tile reverberated in her ears. Then everything went silent.

Alex lay on top of the girl, fighting to pull air into his lungs. The car swayed and creaked — seemed to be making up its mind whether to stay put or not. He froze, not daring to move, until several seconds had passed and the elevator remained where it was. An eerie silence consumed the space. *The emergency brakes must have deployed.* Thank. God.

The sound of frantic, staccato breathing filled his ear. His face was buried in a sea of thick, silky hair, the weight of his body crushing the woman's smaller, slighter frame.

He cursed inwardly, wondering how badly he'd hurt her. In trying to catch her, he'd taken her out hard—like an outside linebacker on a mission.

He pressed his hands against the tile and levered himself gingerly off her. She was lying facedown on the floor, motionless except for her frantic breathing. He curved a hand around her shoulder. "Are you okay?"

She didn't respond, her breath coming in gasping mouthfuls. He slid an arm underneath her and gently turned her over. Her glassy eyes and paper-white face made his heart pound. *Christós.* The nasty purple bump beginning to form on the left side of her forehead made it accelerate even faster.

He trained his gaze on hers until she focused on him. "Are you okay?"

Her lips parted. "The—the elevator… Are w-we stopped?"

He let out a long breath. "Yes. The emergency brakes kicked in."

Relief filled her glazed eyes. But it didn't last long. Her gaze darted, bouncing like a tennis ball off the metal walls, her quick, gasping breaths increasing in speed as her fingers dug into the tile floor and she tried to push herself into a sitting position. "I— I can't—I don't—"

He gripped her shoulders and pushed her back to the floor. "You need to calm down or we're going to be in even more trouble here," he ordered. "Deep breaths, in and out."

She stared at him, chest heaving, eyes huge.

"*Now.*" He slid his fingers under her chin and held her immobile. "Breathe. In and out."

She pulled in a breath. Then another. They were quick, shallow pulls of air, but more than before and gradually, her breathing slowed. "Good," he nodded approvingly. "Keep it up."

He kept her breathing in and out until the panic receded from her eyes and her face regained some color.

"Better?" he asked softly.

"Yes, thank you." She pulled in another deep breath, blinked and looked around. "I can't see...my glasses," she murmured. "I must have lost them in the fall."

He stood and searched for them. Found them in the corner of the elevator, miraculously intact. He carried them back to her, knelt down and slid them on her face. "You hit your head. Are you dizzy at all?"

She sat up slowly. Twisted her head to the left and right. "Not unless I think about the fact that I'm in here."

"Then don't." He stood up and moved toward the control panel. Pulled the phone from behind a metal door and barked a greeting. The line crackled and a young male voice responded. "Everybody okay in there?"

"Yes," Alex said grimly. "Are we stable?"

"Yes, sir. We had an issue with the generator, but the emergency brakes deployed."

His heartbeat slowed, his grip on the receiver relaxing. "How long until you get us out?"

"We're working on getting a crew over there as soon as we can. But by the time we do that and assess how we're going to get you out of there, it may be a few hours."

He flicked a glance at the white-faced woman on the floor. "By that you mean...?"

"The car you're in is stuck between floors. In that situation, we either try to move the car manually from the control room and pry the doors open or we take you out the top. Obviously we'd prefer to do the former, but with the generator out that may not be possible."

He moved his gaze over the bump on the woman's face, the fact that he was going to miss his flight a far lower priority than her potential injuries. "The sooner the better...."

The other passenger in here with me—she hit her head when we stopped."

"We'll go as fast as we can," the technician promised. "Anything else I can do for you?"

"Hurry up," Alex muttered roughly and hung up. Telling the guy he owned half the building wasn't going to make it happen any faster.

The woman watched him with those big brown eyes of hers, her tense expression only this side of full-on panic.

"When are they going to get us out of here?"

He walked back over to her and sank down on his haunches. "They have to get a technician here and see what's happening. It may take a while."

Her gaze sharpened on his face. "Don't they just pry the doors open?"

He hesitated, wondering whether or not to tell her the truth. "We're stuck between floors," he said finally. "A generator's out, which means they can't move us."

Her eyes widened, her hands flailing as she sat up and stared at him. "*What*?"

"Calm down," he ordered. "They'll find a way, but panicking isn't going to help."

Her throat convulsed. "How long did they say?"

"A few hours."

"*I can't be in here that long.*" She fixed her gaze on his. "I really, really don't do elevators."

He took her hands in his. They were clammy and she was shaking like a leaf. "Look—" he said, arching a brow at her. "What's your name?"

"Izzie."

"*Izzie?*"

"Short for Isabel," she elaborated, distractedly. "But most people call me Izzie."

"Isabel," he elected to use instead, his tone firm but reassuring, "I promise you everything's going to be fine.

These guys handle situations like this all the time. They're going to get a crew over here, figure out how to get us out and in a few hours you'll be laughing this off."

She looked at him as though he had two heads.

"Okay," he conceded. "But you know what I mean. It's going to be fine, I promise."

She stared at him for a long moment, her teeth worrying her lip. "You're sure? We aren't going to drop again?"

"I'm sure."

She lifted her chin. "All right. I can do this."

"Good girl."

She pressed her lips together. "Since you're the only thing keeping me sane, you could tell me *your* name."

"Alex." He let go of her hands and pushed to his feet. Located her discarded bag and picked it up. "Anything in here we can use to get the swelling down on your head?"

She shook her head. "I'm not sure."

"Can I look?"

She nodded.

He sat down beside her and riffled through it. The bag was a modern marvel of how much a woman could shove into a few cubic inches of leather. Chocolate, water, books, a brush, a *full bottle of aspirin*…

"Is there anything you *don't* have in here?" he questioned drily. "I'll never understand why you women feel you have to carry half your lives around with you. There is a drugstore on every corner, you know.…"

She wrinkled her nose at him. "That's a bit of an exaggeration."

He pulled out a lint brush. "Really? You need to carry a lint brush with you?"

A pink stain filled her cheeks. "Have you ever sat on a cat-infested sofa in a black wool skirt?"

"Can't say that I have," he drawled. "You've got me

on that one." He pulled out a can of still-cold soda. "How about this? It could work."

"Wait," she gasped, sitting up. "My flight takes off in a few hours."

"So does mine," he returned grimly. "I think we can safely assume we're not making it."

"But I have to…" she burst out. "I have that interview in Manhattan tomorrow morning."

"You're going to have to reschedule your flight," he told her, handing her the can of soda. "And hope you can get another tonight."

She sliced a panicked look at her watch. He glanced at his. Two forty-five. There wasn't a hope in hell he was making his flight to New York. Which was a problem; with Frank Messer trying to rip his company apart, he was putting out fires left, right and center, and the Sophoros jet was under maintenance at Heathrow, necessitating a commercial flight.

"Ouch." She winced as she held the can to the now robin's egg-sized lump on her forehead. He leaned over, tipped her chin up with his fingers and inspected the bump. "You're going to be black and blue for a while, but hopefully that's all it'll be."

She stared at him with a deer-in-the-headlights expression that should have warned him off, but didn't. He was far too busy noticing how the lashes on her almond-shaped, exotic eyes were a mile long and how those full lips of hers could take him to the moon and back should she choose to apply them correctly…

And what the hell was he thinking? He let go of her chin and shifted away from her. She was attracted to him. She'd made that clear upstairs in the lobby. And of course he'd noticed her. It had been hard not to. Disheveled, distracted, she'd been jabbering into her mobile phone in a husky, breathless voice that had made it easy to envision her in his bed. That and that body… The kind of curves that would look even better without clothes.

He shook his head and looked in the opposite direction. Not the kind of thinking that boded well for hours in close proximity.

"Alex?"

She was holding out a bottle of water, her cheeks even pinker than before. "Want one?"

He took it, if only to cool down his overheated libido. A paperback spilled out of her bag, a half-dressed woman in the arms of a bare-chested male emblazoned on the cover.

He picked it up. "Do you actually read this stuff?" he demanded incredulously.

"I do," she said stiffly. "Can I please have it back?"

He ignored her outstretched hand. Turned the book over. "Looks smutty…is that why you women like it?"

"I suppose you have *Othello* in your bag," she came back tartly, reaching for it.

He pulled it away. "Actually, *Great Expectations*. Want to have a browse?"

She gave him a long look. "You've got to be kidding."

He braced his hands on the floor to roll to his feet. She waved him off. "Okay, I believe you. You've had your laugh…can I have my book back, please?"

He gave her a considering look. "It *is* smutty, isn't it?"

She glared at him. Watched as he flipped pages, stopped to read one, then moved on. He halted at a particularly juicy section. "Oh this is good." He quoted out loud, deepening his voice to add an over-the-top commentary. "He ran his finger over her erect nipple, making her groan in response…Ellie—" he flicked a glance at her, "who calls their characters Ellie, by the way? Anyway," he looked back at the book, "Ellie arched her back and—"

"*Alex,*" she pleaded, dropping the can and lunging for the book. "Give it to me."

He held it away from her. "I just want to know. What's the appeal? That a guy's going to charge in on a white steed and carry you off, and you'll live happily ever after?"

"I don't need a man to rescue me," she muttered, sitting back and wrapping her arms around herself. "I can do my own rescuing."

"That," he stated drily, "is up for debate." He handed the book back to her.

She shoved it in her bag with a decisive movement. He decided to be a humanitarian and move on. "So what are you doing in London? Work or play?"

"I'm doing a favor for my boss." She grimaced and pressed the can tighter to her head. "It was supposed to be a quick in and out on my way home from Italy."

"Just your luck," he grinned. "You picked the one faulty elevator in London."

"Please don't remind me."

"What line of work are you in?"

She took a sip of her water. "Communications... You?"

"I own an entertainment company, based in New York." He leaned back against the wall, keeping up the small talk he abhorred as it seemed to be putting a bit of color back into her cheeks. "Was Italy work too?"

She shook her head. "I was doing a cooking course with my girlfriends in Tuscany. We rented a villa on the coast, chilled out and learned how to make a mean bruschetta."

"That will make your man very happy."

"I didn't do it for a man, I did it for myself."

He noted the defensive edge to her voice. "No man in your life, then?"

She set her jaw. "No."

He wondered why he liked that idea. "How many of you were in Italy?"

"Eight of us, including me."

He smiled. "The Italian men must not have known what hit them."

She shot him a sideways look. "Meaning?"

"Meaning I can only imagine the impression eight of you made on the locals…Tuscany will never be the same, I'm sure."

Her mouth curved. "My friend Jo was a big hit with the Italian men. She's a bit of a one-woman wrecking crew."

He gave her a considering look. "I'm sure she wasn't the only one."

She blinked. Looked away. *Shy,* he registered in astonishment. Were there actually any of those women left in Manhattan? It had been so long since he'd met one he'd thought they were extinct.

A loud creak split the air. He dropped the water, his heart slamming into his chest as he braced his hands on the floor. Isabel launched herself at him, wrapping her limbs around him. He held her close as the elevator swayed and groaned beneath them, his breath coming hard and fast.

What the hell?

CHAPTER TWO

"WHAT WAS THAT?"

Isabel screeched the words in his ear, wrapping her arms around his neck in a chokehold. The car rocked beneath them, but this time more gently, without the blood-curdling creak. He sucked in a breath. "It's just shifting," he told her, hoping that's all it was. "You're okay."

Her chest rose and fell rapidly against him. Seconds ticked by. The swaying slowed and then stopped. "Isabel, we're fine," he murmured, his heartbeat regulating as he brought his head down to hers. "I promise you, those cables don't break."

She drew in a deep breath, then another, stayed pressed against him. As his cortisol levels came down, his awareness of her skyrocketed. Her fingers were dug into his thigh, her light floral scent filling his nostrils. Her thoroughly touchable curves were plastered against him. And God help him, it was making him think improper thoughts. Like how much he'd appreciate those slender fingers wrapped around another part of his anatomy...

She drew back, her face chalk-white. Exhaled a long, agitated breath. Realized where her hand was. He struggled to wipe his expression clean as she lifted her horrified gaze to his, but he was pretty sure from the way her eyes widened and the speed with which she snatched her hand away, she'd known exactly where his head was at.

"I am so sorry," she murmured. But she was still in his lap, clutching his shoulder for dear life, and he was in severe danger of getting extremely turned on. Worse when she caught her plump bottom lip in her teeth and hell, he wished she wouldn't do that. He wanted to kiss her, and not the "Sunday walk in the park" variety.

Her pupils dilated, but she didn't go anywhere. He cleared his throat. "If this was your book," he drawled mockingly, "this'd be the part where I ravish you in the elevator, no?"

She was off his lap in a flash. She sat back against the wall, her shoulders pressed against the paneling. "Yes, well, that's why they have security cameras in elevators, don't they?" she pronounced stiffly. "To prevent that sort of behavior."

He had to stop himself from laughing out loud. "That sort of behavior? How very Victorian of you."

She fixed her eyes on the wall opposite her. "I think this elevator's getting to me."

She wasn't the only one. He waved a hand at her. "Think of it as extreme exposure therapy. After this you'll definitely be cured."

"Or I'll never set foot in an elevator again."

"Let's work toward the former." He gestured toward the can that had rolled to the corner of the elevator. "Put that on again."

She lifted it to her forehead. Stayed plastered against the wall like a modern painting, her white, pinched face a halo against the dark paneling. He cursed inwardly. He needed a distraction or this wasn't going to be pretty. *What in the world would he say to his sister Gabby, who was severely claustrophobic?*

"I have an idea," he suggested. "Let's play a game."

"A *game?*"

"You tell me something no one knows about you and I'll do the same."

She lifted a brow. "I'm channeling my sisters here," he offered grimly. "Humor me. If you go all panicky, it's not a good thing."

"Okay." She closed her eyes and leaned her head back against the wall. "In seventh grade, when Steven Thompson asked me to dance at the school mixer, I told him I'd sprained my ankle."

"You didn't like him?"

"I *adored* him." She opened her eyes. "I'd idolized him for years. But I thought my sister had put him up to it, like I was some kind of charity case, so I turned him down." She grimaced. "Turns out she hadn't."

"Ouch. So the poor guy got rejected for no good reason?"

She nodded. "I was persona non grata after that."

"And you females wonder why men aren't gallant anymore. We stick our necks out for *that*."

She gave him a wry look. "I hope you're using the royal 'we,' because I can't imagine you have ever been rejected in your entire life."

And that's where she was wrong. The one time he had been, the only time it had *mattered,* he'd been left for dead by the woman who'd meant everything to him.

"Nobody goes through life unscathed," he said roughly. "You should have given the guy a chance. Maybe you scarred him for life."

"Since he was dating Katy Fielding by the next Monday, I highly doubt it." Cynicism tainted her voice. "Okay, your turn."

He thought about it. And for some strange reason, he was dead honest. "I wish I'd made different decisions at times."

Her gaze sharpened on him. "Is that a general observation or something you'd care to elaborate on?"

Most definitely not. He'd shut the door on that part of his life a long time ago. Never to be opened again. "A general observation." He rested his gaze on her face. "Sometimes in life you're only given one shot. Use it wisely."

Her eyes stayed on his, assessing, inquisitive. Then she let it go with a sigh. "This interview I have tomorrow? I don't even know if I want the job. But it's a once-in-a-life-time kind of thing."

He frowned. "Why don't you want it? I assume it's a step up?"

"Fear," she said simply. "I'm afraid of what happens *if* I get it."

"Take it from me," he counseled, "fearing the unknown is far worse than facing it. I have no doubt you'll knock them dead, Isabel. Just be your quirky self."

She looked insulted. "Quirky?"

"Tell me it doesn't fit."

"Well…maybe just a bit."

She jumped as the phone rang. He pushed to his feet, walked over and picked up the receiver. But the news wasn't what he wanted to hear. *Two and a half hours.*

He hung up. "We have to sit tight for another couple of hours."

Isabel's face fell.

"Think on the bright side," he said, sliding down beside her and giving her a wicked look. "You can read me excerpts from your book. It was just getting good."

Exactly two and a quarter hours later, at about the time Izzie's flight was scheduled to take off from Heathrow, a rescue team arrived.

She and Alex stood to one side as the crew unscrewed a panel from the top of the car and dropped a ladder down, a burly, safety-cable-laden rescuer climbing in moments later with two harnesses slung over his shoulder.

"Ready to get out of here?" he asked them, a wide grin splitting his face.

"You've no idea," Izzie murmured, flashing a sideways look at Alex. She really wasn't sure what she would have done without him. She had a sneaking suspicion she would have lost it completely.

"All right then," the technician said, strapping one of the harnesses around Izzie. "The next floor is about eight feet above us. We're going to climb up the ladder, out the top of the elevator and up onto the lobby floor." He snapped the harness into place and stepped back. "Keep moving, don't look down and you'll be fine."

Every limb in her body went ice cold. *They wanted her to climb through an elevator shaft?*

"I'll be right behind you," Alex said quietly. "It's mind over matter, Isabel."

Yes, but she didn't have a mind left! Her legs started to shake; her breath came in short, frantic bursts. "But what if—"

Alex took her hands in his, wrapping his fingers around hers. "There *is* no 'what if.' We're going to climb out of here and it's all going to be over, okay?"

She took a deep breath and let it out slowly, absorbing the quiet confidence in his voice, the warmth of his hands around hers. "You'll stay right behind me?"

He nodded.

"Okay." She pulled in another big breath and let go of his hands with a decisive movement. "Let's do it."

The technician strapped the other harness around Alex. Then they started up the ladder, Alex following Izzie. Her legs were shaking so hard she had to inject every bit of concentration she possessed into each step, her hands clutching the side of the ladder for balance.

"One step at a time," Alex murmured, anchoring his

hands firmly around her hips to steady her. "You're doing great."

She didn't *feel* great. Her heart was in her mouth, acid stung the back of her throat in the very real threat she might throw up, and she felt as if she was going to collapse in a puddle.

She forced herself to keep moving, her slow climb taking her up to where the ladder emerged from the car. She looked down. Gasped at the endless plunge into darkness.

"Don't look down," the technician said, turning around. "Keep going."

But her legs wouldn't move. "I can't," she whispered. "My legs, they—they're shaking so much I'm afraid I'll—"

Alex stepped up on the ladder behind her, his hands digging into her waist. "You can do this," he insisted firmly. "I'm right here and I'm not letting go. Just put one foot in front of the other and we'll be out of here in a minute."

The heat of his hands penetrated the thin cotton of her dress. Sank into her skin, warming her. Grounding her. "Mind over matter, Isabel," he whispered, his hands tightening. "Move with me."

She gritted her teeth and forced herself to focus on the strength of his hands around her waist. *He would not let her fall. He would keep her safe...*

She started climbing again, focusing only on putting one foot in front of the other as they emerged from the elevator, walked across the top of it and climbed the ladder toward the floor above. Step up, make sure her foot was securely on the rung, bring the other foot up. Repeat. She said it over and over again in her head as she did it, Alex's hands never leaving her waist. And then, someone was reaching down and grasping her by the arms and lifting her to solid ground.

Alex stepped up behind her, the look of grim relief on his face making her knees go weak. "You okay?"

She nodded. Swayed as her shaking knees turned to mush. He closed his arms around her and pulled her close, his chin coming down on top of her head. "It's okay," he murmured into her hair. "It's over."

Izzie had the strange feeling that once here, she might never want to leave. She buried her face in the rock-solid wall of his chest, her limbs shaking so hard she wondered if they'd ever stop.

"The paramedics are downstairs in the lobby, waiting to check you out," the burly rescuer said. "Sorry to say, the generator's still out, so you'll have to take the stairs."

Since Izzie never intended to get on another elevator in her life, that was just fine with her. But by the time they'd descended twenty-three flights of stairs and she'd gotten thoroughly poked and prodded by a young medic she was done.

"How many fingers am I holding up?" the medic asked, sticking up four.

She waved her hand at him. "I'm good, really. I hardly bumped it at all."

"It was a hard knock," Alex interjected, holding his cell phone away from his ear. "Let him do his job."

Izzie made a face. "Four," she sighed. "And I'm not seeing double…no halos, nothing…"

"Any dizziness?" he asked patiently.

"No."

"Okay, I think you're fine." He started packing up his kit. "But you should be watched for the next twenty-four hours to make sure you haven't suffered any kind of internal issues."

Izzie nodded. "No problem. I'm going to rebook myself on another flight to the States tonight so there'll be a whole planeload full of people ready to catch me if I keel over."

The medic frowned. "Flying isn't the best idea after an injury like that."

She shrugged. "I have no choice."

He gave her a long look. "Do you have someone in London you can stay with if that flight doesn't happen? Otherwise we can admit you to the hospital overnight for observation."

She blanched. Spending the night in the hospital wasn't an option. She *had* to get a flight. "I do," she lied. "Thanks so much for your help."

Alex was still on the phone when she picked up her bag and walked over to him. He held the phone to one side. "We can't get a flight to the States tonight. Give me your ticket and I'll have my assistant rebook you on something tomorrow morning."

Tomorrow? "There must be a flight tonight…a red-eye? I'll take a red-eye…"

He scowled. "By no flights, I mean no flights, Isabel."

Oh. She bit her lip, frantically sifting through the alternatives, but coming up with none. "Can you see if she can make it as early as possible tomorrow?" she asked, dragging her ticket out of her purse and handing it to him. "I have that interview in the morning."

He nodded, took the ticket and started rattling off the information into the phone. She left him to it, collapsing into one of the sterile-looking leather lobby chairs. If she caught a super early flight tomorrow she had a shot at making the interview, given the time difference. But she wasn't even sure overseas flights left that early in the morning. In fact she was pretty sure they didn't.

She swallowed hard and removed her fingernail from her mouth before she mangled it. This was a once-in-a-lifetime opportunity. What she'd been obsessively working toward for the past four years, coming into the studio at eight when most reporters didn't amble in until their 10:00 a.m. editorial meeting and working well past when most had left. She, a single girl in New York, had no personal life. Her job *was* her life. Which was fine, because dating was like some type of ancient torture for her, and in ten years she'd have a flourishing career to point to rather than a series of America's worst matchmaking stories.

Her stomach dropped. She just hadn't expected to be taking her big leap *now*.

An audition for an anchor job in the most high-pressure media market in the country was a daunting task for even the most experienced reporter. Ten times so for someone like Izzie, who tended to burn out like the brightest star when the stakes were the highest.

Been there, done that. She squeezed her eyes shut. She was not that Izzie anymore—the terrified, unsure eighteen-year-old who'd walked into that audition and blown the biggest opportunity of her life. She would not go back there. *Ever.* Particularly not when today, facing her mortality, she'd suddenly had a crystal-clear vision of how short life could be.

A shaky sigh escaped her as she leaned back into the smooth leather. What was she doing, anyway? If those emergency brakes hadn't deployed, she and Alex would have been smashed to smithereens. Worrying about a job was just nuts! But to be fair, she'd spent her whole life worrying. On a low, chronic level that couldn't be good for a person. About keeping her job. About how she looked. About what the future held. And right now, that seemed like a very, very stupid way to live.

Alex dropped down in the chair beside her. "You okay?"

She nodded, her brain settling into an oddly lucid state. "Actually," she said slowly, "I am."

He gave her a long look as if he was trying to decide if she'd lost it. Then handed her ticket back with some scribbles on it. "The best Grace could do was an eleven-thirty tomorrow morning."

She did the calculation in her head. If she left here at

eleven-thirty, she'd land in New York around one-thirty. Maybe, just maybe, James could get the execs to stay later.

"Thank you," she murmured, sliding the ticket into her purse.

"No problem." His gaze sharpened on her face. "What did the paramedic say?"

"He says I'm fine…just to keep an eye on my head."

"You mean have someone keep an eye *on you*," he corrected. "For at least twenty-four hours probably. Any of those girlfriends of yours live in London?"

She shook her head. "I'm sure I'm fine. I'll just book a hotel, get a good night's sleep and it'll all be good."

His dark brows slanted together. "You don't fool around with a head injury, Isabel. It's serious stuff."

"I don't *have* a head injury. I have a bump on my head."

He gave her a dark look and raked his hand through his hair. "Give me a second. I'm going to see if I can find a nurse or someone who can keep an eye on you."

"*No* way I—*dammit*—" she cursed as he turned on his heel and strode off, already talking into his phone. She didn't need a nurse. She needed to get back to New York.

He came back five minutes later, his frown deeper. "My assistant couldn't find someone on such short notice."

"Well, that's it, then," she said, trying not to look relieved. "I'll make sure I keep an eye on myself and if I feel the slightest bit strange, I'll go to the hospital."

"No, you won't." His eyes darkened to a forbidding cobalt-blue. "I have plenty of space at my place in Canary Wharf. You can stay with me."

Her jaw dropped open. *Her stay with him at his place? Umm…no.* "That's very nice of you," she said, "but I can't impose like that."

"You need to be watched." He reached down and picked up her bag. "I don't know about you but I need a hot shower and something to eat. Let's go."

She shook her head. "Alex, I—"

"*Isabel.* I had a friend suffer a massive hemorrhage after he hit his head. We all thought he was fine. He died that night, at home *alone.*"

"Oh." She stared at him, scared silly.

"*Exactly.* You've had a brutally traumatic day, you look like you're going to pass out, and I'm the one responsible for you whacking your head. So do me a favor and stay at my place so I don't have to spend the night worrying about you expiring in a hotel room."

And what was she supposed to say to that? Suddenly, staying alone in a hotel room seemed the height of stupidity. The thing was…despite how she knew instinctively she could trust him, despite how he'd taken care of her in that elevator, she didn't *know* him. He could be an ax murderer for all she knew. On the other hand, she knew *that* was ridiculous. As a reporter she lived by her instincts, and her instincts told her she could trust Alex.

"Just say yes," he muttered. "I'm out of patience."

She chewed on her lip. "All right. If you're sure it's not too much trouble…"

A rueful smile curved his mouth. "I have a feeling *you* are trouble, Isabel Peters. Having you stay with me is not."

But Izzie wasn't at all sure that was the truth. Seated in the low, sleek sports car Alex had parked in the underground lot, her pulse raced as fast as the high-performance engine rippling beneath her. It might have been the way she couldn't look at his muscular thighs on the low bucket seat beside her without remembering how that hard, male muscle had felt under her hands. Or the fact that despite his abrupt dismissal in the lobby earlier, there *had* been a spark between them in that elevator. Unless she was totally deluded…which had been known to happen when it came to her and men.

Tired of watching Izzie sit on the sidelines in Italy,

her girlfriend Jo had finally staged an intervention. "You have to engage with men to catch them," she'd advised caustically. "We aren't participating in immaculate conception here."

Izzie was clear on *that*. She just happened to be very, very bad at engaging.

She darted a sideways glance at the hard profile of the drop-dead-gorgeous man beside her. Could he actually be attracted to her? Or was she just kidding herself about that chemistry in the elevator? A man like that could have any woman he wanted. Why would he want vanilla when he could undoubtedly savor crème brûlée any day of the week?

The left and right sides of her brain warred with each other. Suddenly she was very, very tired of being Izzie the responsible. The girl who never took a risk. And it occurred to her that until she did, she might never know who she really was.

A flock of butterflies swooped through her stomach on a wild roller-coaster ride. Did she have the courage to find out tonight whether vanilla cut it? And if so, would it go down as the single most stupid thing she'd ever done? Or the best?

CHAPTER THREE

LEANDROS ALEXIOS CONSTANTINOU, Alex to all who knew him, stood on the terrace of his Canary Wharf penthouse at sunset, drinking in the spectacular light that blazed a golden path across the Thames. It never failed to take his breath away, this 270-degree panoramic vista of the city skyline and the river. Especially on a night like this, one of those warm, sultry summer evenings in London that made you think you'd be nuts to live anywhere else.

Worth every penny of the £2.5 million he'd paid for it, the peace and relaxation it brought him at the end of a fourteen-hour workday was usually foolproof. But not tonight. Not when all hell was breaking loose with his company back in New York, he was 3,500 miles away and his partner was an engineering genius, not a business brain. Not when a woman he was undoubtedly attracted to was showering in his guest room. The type of woman he'd vowed he wouldn't touch with a ten-foot pole after Jess had walked out on him.

He stared at the sky as its deep burnt-gold hue darkened into an exotic orange, then pink, streaks of color floating across the darkening horizon. He was more thrown by that free fall that could have plunged him and Izzie into oblivion than he'd care to admit. He supposed he wouldn't be human if he wasn't. But he didn't like where it was sending his mind. The uncharacteristic, impulsive things it was making him do. Like bringing a chaotic bundle of nerves named Isabel Peters home with him.

Truthfully, though, he hadn't had much choice. It was his fault she'd hit her head. He couldn't let her stay alone in a hotel room—not after losing his former teammate Cash as he had. And without a nurse to look after her, responsibility fell squarely in his lap.

Speaking of which... He turned and cocked his head toward the open windows. Izzie had been in that shower forever. All he needed was for her to collapse and drown. She'd certainly been pale enough.

Hell. He strode inside, stopped outside the bedroom he'd put her in and opened the door. "Are you okay in there?" he yelled.

"I'm good," she called back over the sound of running water. "Getting out now."

He shut the door, *firmly,* as his head went directly to an image of her naked and slippery under his hands, foam highlighting those curves.

He went back outside and switched on the lights. A whisper-soft breeze picked up as he walked to the edge of the terrace and rested his forearms on the top of the concrete wall. At least she was keeping his mind off Taylor Bayne, who'd taken his European expansion plans and dismantled them with a flick of his Rolex-clad wrist this morning.

Christós. His gut twisted in a discomforting reminder of that disaster of a boardroom this morning at Blue Light Interactive. He'd known something was up the minute he'd shaken the normally gregarious CEO's hand and the other man had studiously avoided his gaze. Waved him to the massive dark-stained table, where the fractures in the deal had started to appear, one by one. All of a sudden things that hadn't been issues before became major sticking points and Bayne was backpedaling faster than a quarterback who'd run out of room.

He let out a string of curses. What had made Bayne do a complete 180 like that? And how had he misread him so badly? For a man whose life had been a series of carefully orchestrated steps to take him where he was going, it was disconcerting to say the least. For Alex, there were no missteps. No deviations. No distractions. Only the master plan.

When he was six, growing up in sports-obsessed New York City, he'd decided he was going to be a famous football player. Never mind his father's plans for him to take over C-Star Shipping as the family's only male heir. For Alex it had only ever been about football. From the first time he'd held that piece of rawhide in his hands playing in the backyard with the neighborhood boys, he'd known it was the only thing he ever wanted to do.

A successful high school career and a brilliant Hail Mary pass to win his college team a national championship made his dream of playing professional football a reality. He got an offer from a New York team. Had been touted as the next big thing. That was when his father had hit the roof...this "hobby" of Alex's had to stop. It was time for him to be a man and join the ranks of tough, brilliant Constantinou businessmen.

His hands tightened around the railing, the dusky, early-evening sky transforming into the dark Boston bar where his father had sat him down with a bottle of whiskey and hell in his eyes. Tonight they were going to hash this out, he'd told Alex. Didn't he realize the shame he was bringing on the Constantinou name by abandoning his birthright for a frivolous career like American football?

Thud. Thud. Thud. The sound of the bottle hitting the worn wooden table was indelibly imprinted in his head. The bitter taste of the whiskey he'd never liked lingered in his mouth even now. His father's harsh, nicotine-stained voice as he brushed aside Alex's quietly issued plea. *You've achieved your dream. Let me go after mine.* Hristo's reply, sharp as a knife. *Sign that contract, Alexios, and you are no longer a part of this family.*

His heart contracted, his knuckles shining white against the concrete barrier. He'd been so hurt, so angry, he'd signed the three-year contract the next day. And true to his word, his father had disowned him—had never come to another game.

He'd played incredibly well—become a superstar. He'd made an insane amount of money. But he'd never earned his father's respect. And then, on one fateful evening, in the third year of his career, it had all been taken away from him. He'd had to learn what it was like to be a survivor. To hit rock bottom, claw his way out and start all over again.

Sophoros had been the result of that single-minded determination. Alongside his best buddy from college, brilliant software programmer Mark Isaacs, he'd built America's most successful computer gaming company.

His mouth tightened, his fingers flexing around the concrete. It would be over his dead body that he'd watch Sophoros fail because of a greedy, lazy, half-talented former employee out for a free ride.

He stared up at the night sky, Venus making her first sparkling appearance. Calling to him like a signpost. *No deviations. No distractions.* He should be thinking about the mess that was waiting for him back in New York. Figuring out his game plan. Not worrying about what the hell Isabel Peters was still doing in the shower when she'd said ten minutes ago she was getting out.

"Alex—this is unbelievable!"

He turned around to find Isabel standing barefoot behind him, wearing the dress of his sister's he'd found in the spare bedroom.

His first reaction was that his sister didn't look like that in that dress. His second was that he was a dead man. Still far too pale, her dark hair and eyes shone in the early evening light, set off by the cappuccino-colored dress. She'd put her hair up in a ponytail, her face bare of makeup except for a berry-colored gloss on her lips. Innocent. Harmless enough. The dress that hugged every inch of her curvy figure, emphasizing high breasts, a narrow waist and gently rounded hips, was not. She had the kind of body that made a man want to put his hands all over her, he thought distractedly. In no particular order.

Her blush as he raised his gaze to hers wasn't something he'd seen on a woman in a long time. "I think I might be a size bigger than your sister."

Deciding there was no appropriate response to that question he could verbalize, he cleared his throat and kept his eyes firmly focused on her face. "You're white as a ghost."

She pressed her hands to her cheeks. "I feel much better after the shower."

"You need a stiff drink." *Theos*, he needed a stiff drink.

She followed him inside, perching herself on a stool at the solid mahogany bar while he searched for and found a bottle of brandy.

"Wow. This place is fabulous."

He turned around and studied her. It was an observation. An appreciation of the luxury they were standing in rather than the typical "I want this place to be mine" expression he'd seen on the faces of the few women he'd brought up here.

"Thanks," he nodded, uncorking the bottle and pouring an inch in one glass and double in the other. He handed her the smaller one. "It was a good investment given the London real estate market."

She wrapped her fingers around the crystal tumbler, their slim grace and perfectly manicured nails drawing his eye. "Alex— I—" She stopped, looking hesitant. "I don't know how to say thank you for everything you've done for me today."

"Don't." He screwed the lid back on the bottle and returned it to the shelf. "It was nothing."

"It *was*," she insisted, those big brown eyes of hers sweeping hesitantly over him as he turned back to her. "I think I would have completely lost it if it wasn't for you."

He shrugged. "Phobias are powerful things."

"Still," she said, lifting her chin and holding his gaze. "Thank you."

"You're welcome." He nodded toward her glass. "Drink up. The brandy will help."

She took a sip. Made a face. "Must be an acquired taste."

He shot her an amused look. "Are you calling me old, Isabel?"

Twin dots of pink stained her cheeks. "Hardly. You're what…thirty?"

"Thirty-two. And you?"

"Twenty-five." She lifted her shoulders in an attempt at a sophisticated shrug. "Seven years…that's not so much of a difference."

"You'd be surprised what you can pack into those seven years," he said drily. He sat his drink on the bar and walked to the shelf of CDs in the living room. "I've ordered some dinner from the restaurant downstairs. I thought we could have it on the terrace."

"I'd love that. The view's amazing."

"Then I'm putting you to bed." *Unfortunately not his.*

"I'm so wired I'm not sure I can sleep."

He turned to face her. She seemed incredibly vulnerable sitting there, a restless energy emanating from her he found mirrored in himself. It had been one hell of a day. "The brandy and a good meal will solve that. You're probably running on adrenaline now."

"I think I am."

He turned back to the CDs and scanned the titles. "Any preference in music?"

"I listen to everything."

"Classical?"

"Yes." She smiled as he looked over at her. "My dad's a music professor at Stanford. I was brought up listening to that stuff."

"Did he make you play every instrument known to man?"

"Yes, until he discovered I had absolutely no artistic talent whatsoever."

His lips curved. "He must have been crushed."

"I hated it," she said, shaking her head. "I'm all thumbs when it comes to anything creative."

Did that include the bedroom? he wondered. He wasn't so caught up with creativity. But natural passion was a must.

Christós He forced his gaze back to the music in front of him. He really had to get his mind out of the gutter. Away from the fact that every time she swung those slim legs on that stool, he wondered what they would feel like wrapped around him. Whether she'd dig her heels into his back while he took her slow and deep and—

Whoa. He slapped the CD he was looking at back on the shelf and raked a hand through his hair. Had it been too long since he'd had a woman? Was that what this was all about? What had it been? Two, three months? He'd been so buried in the Blue Light Interactive deal he hadn't had two seconds to even think about a woman, let alone bed one.

Or maybe it had just been three hours stuck in an elevator fighting an attraction that seemed to be growing by the minute?

He stared at the CDs. Spanish…he was going with Spanish. He grabbed a compilation of adagios and slid it into the player. The haunting strains of a lone guitar filled the room.

"I wouldn't have pegged you as the classical guitar type," she said as he walked back over to join her at the bar.

He aimed a reproving glance at her. "Stereotyping me, Isabel? You were questioning my reading taste earlier…"

Her mouth twisted. "You're right. My mistake. You're just a bit of a closed book, unlike me and my big mouth."

He shrugged and picked up his drink. "You know the basics. I'm a native New Yorker, run my own company…"

"The details are overwhelming," she said drily. "The accent is Greek?"

He nodded. "I was born in the US to Greek parents. But I spent my summers in the islands."

"Where'd you go to school?"

"Boston College."

"Why Boston when you had all those schools in New York?"

"Sports and their business program." She didn't need to know he'd gone on full scholarship. That as far as the university brass had been concerned, he'd been the closest thing to a savior their football program had ever seen.

"Ah, a typical male," she teased. "The sports bug."

"The natural order of things," he agreed with a lazy smile, tilting his glass toward her. "Where did you go to school?"

"Columbia."

"But you aren't from New York." He lifted a brow. "I can hear the faint traces of a Southern drawl."

She shook her head. "California. Palo Alto. I moved to New York to go to school."

"Are your family still out West?"

"Just my dad. My parents are separated. My mom lives in New York and my sister—" her lips curved "—well, she's a nomad. She models all over the world. I never know what city I'm calling her in."

He took a sip of his drink, feeling the smooth brandy burn its way down his throat. "How old were you when your parents separated?"

A rueful glint lit her eyes. "It's kind of like the divorce that never happened."

Sounded like hell to him. At least his mother had made up her mind and gotten out. He folded his arms and tucked his drink against his chest, resting his gaze on her face. "How so?"

She shrugged. "My mother's an actress. Used to the bright lights and the big city. She was always leaving for shoots, for extended appearances in London in the theater...and eventually she just stopped coming home. I think she decided one day that we and Palo Alto just weren't exciting enough for her."

He frowned. "Would I know her?"

She hesitated, looked as if this was the last thing she wanted to talk about. "Her name is Dayla St. James."

A vague recollection of a dark-haired bombshell floated into his head. "Was she in a wartime movie? Played a woman whose husband never came back from the front?"

She nodded. "That's her. Kind of ironic, isn't it?"

"Kind of." He studied her face. "You don't look much like her."

"So she likes to tell me."

He drew his brows together. "I didn't mean you aren't beautiful, Isabel. Surely many men have told you that you are."

Her gaze dropped to her brandy. She swirled it around the glass. "You don't need to humor me. My mother is a gorgeous movie star...my sister is a glamorous international model. I get it. I've been living with it my whole life."

He held his tongue and counted to five. Anything he said here could and would be used against him. He had three sisters. He knew how their minds worked. "You should have more confidence in yourself," he said flatly. "You're a beautiful girl."

She pressed her lips shut. Stared at him.

His phone rang. *Thank the Lord for small favors.*

"Can you set the table while I take this?" He pulled his phone out of his pocket. "Plates are in the cupboard beside the sink."

His partner Mark's cheerful voice boomed over the line. "Grace told me what happened. You okay, man? That must have been one hell of a ride."

"This whole day's been one hell of a ride." Alex elbowed his way through the door to his study. "But yes, I'm fine."

"Blue Light wasn't good?"

He sank down on the corner of his desk. "Something happened between our last meeting and today. Bayne was backing off left, right and center."

"I think I have the explanation for you," Mark drawled. "And you aren't going to like it."

An uneasy feeling snaked its way up his spine. "What?"

"Taylor Bayne met with Frank Messer last week in London."

Alex uttered a low curse. "How do you know?"

"Do you really want me to answer that?"

He grimaced. "No." His partner, who had seen him through the darkest of times when his career ended and was still his only close confidant, was a programming genius. Which, translated, meant he was a hacker who could crack anything. "So what were they talking about?"

"Don't know." He heard his partner take a sip of something, which was undoubtedly coffee. He was addicted to it. "But you can be damn sure it had something to do with today."

"He's laying the groundwork for the court case." It was all starting to fall into place. Having watched Sophoros's stock value skyrocket, his ex-director of software, Frank Messer, was getting greedy, figuring he'd let them off far too lightly when they'd parted ways seven years ago. So now he was taking them to court claiming he should have been given a much bigger settlement the first time around. And apparently was trying to alienate the people Sophoros did business with.

He slammed his fist against the desk. "*Christós,* Mark, we should have buried him while we had the chance."

"Truer words have never been said. The lawyers think we have a hell of a fight on our hands."

Great. Just what he needed to hear after this fiasco of a day. "I need the jet, Mark. I've got to get out of here."

"Way ahead of you, buddy. Grace has them working on it tonight. She'll give you a call in the morning with an update."

"Good." His twenty-three-year-old PA was a formidable force way beyond her years. She'd have that jet in the air tomorrow morning if it was humanly possible.

"Alex…" Isabel's voice rang out, a panicked, shrill sound that made him stiffen.

"Is that a woman's voice?" His partner's tone deepened to one of incredulity. "Seriously, Alex, I don't know how you do it. You're grounded in London for a few hours and you have a woman there already?"

"It's a long story," Alex said shortly, the hairs on the back of his neck standing up as he beat it toward the kitchen. "I gotta go. I'll talk to you in the morning."

"I can't wait to hear it." His partner's voice dripped with amusement. "Enjoy yourself, buddy."

He disconnected the call, arriving in the kitchen just in time to see Isabel standing on top of the counter, her hands pressed against a row of wineglasses that had toppled over and threatened to crash to the floor.

"What *are* you doing?" He hoisted himself up beside her and grabbed a handful of the glasses.

She pushed the rest back onto the shelf. "I'm sorry. I—I just thought we'd want the wineglasses. You had that bottle of wine on the counter and then I got a little dizzy and knocked one over and there was this chain reaction and—"

Visions of an exhausted Isabel falling and cracking her head open on the hard tile let loose a string of curses from Alex. He jumped down to the floor, reached up, wrapped his hands around her waist and lifted her down, setting her bottom on the counter. "Did you really think this was a good idea?"

She pushed some stray curls out of her face, her cheeks turning a bright red. "I didn't feel dizzy before I went up there."

He shook his head. "You need to eat." And if he were a smart man he would back away right now. Back away from the eye-level temptation staring back at him.

"Alex…?" She sank her teeth into her lower lip and gave him one of those wide-eyed looks.

"What?" he asked roughly.

"Am I a total idiot or do you want to kiss me?"

He blinked. Closed his eyes. He never lied. *Ever.* But right about now it seemed like a good idea. "Can I pass on that one?"

"Alex."

He opened his eyes.

"My friend Jo told me I never engage." She bit down harder into her lip. "With men, I mean. Which is why I'm asking the question. To see if I'm seriously deluded or not."

He bit out a curse he hadn't uttered since his college days. "I'm not the right guy for you, Isabel."

She gave him a determined look. "I'm talking about a kiss. Not the rest of our lives."

He shook his head. "Same answer."

She hesitated, swallowed hard. "You said in the elevator that it's better to face the unknown than fear it. What if you're my modern-day Steven Thompson?"

"This time you *should* walk away," he muttered.

"Please answer the question," she pleaded. "Otherwise I'm going to feel like a total idiot. Good or bad, I can take it."

He pressed his hands to his temples. It'd taken a lot of nerve to ask that question. And it had been *his* mistake in ever admitting he found her attractive. "Yes," he conceded finally, "I want to kiss you but—"

"Alex." The tension in her face slid away. "Get on with it, will you?"

"This is an insanely bad idea," he groaned. But he was already stepping into her and lowering his mouth to the lush temptation in front of him. Because really, how much would one kiss hurt? "You just about passed out up there," he murmured against her lips.

"I'm fine," she said, tilting her chin up so their lips touched more firmly. Then the insanity of the day took over and he brought his mouth down on hers in a sensual tasting that explored every centimeter of her undeniably sweet lips.

His brain told him this was a bad idea even as he reached up and cupped the back of her head to change the angle of the kiss. Deeper, harder it went until she sighed and melted into him, curling her hands into his shirt. He was not unaware of how easy it would be to slip her panties off, wrap her legs around his waist, release himself and take her right there, right now. Exactly as he'd imagined it a few minutes ago...

Except he was a sane man. She hadn't eaten. She was dizzy. And she most definitely did not know the score.

He lifted his mouth from hers and gently pushed her away from him. "You need to eat," he said roughly. "This has been quite a day."

Myriad emotions flickered through those dark eyes of hers. "Alex, I—"

He put a finger to her mouth. "No more talking. Not one word until we eat."

"But—" The doorbell interrupted her.

"That's dinner." He ran his hands through his hair and straightened his clothing. "Go outside and sit down. I'll bring everything out."

She gave him one last, long look, then pressed her lips together and slid off the counter. He cursed under his breath as he watched her walk out of the room. He'd been right. He was a dead man.

Izzie focused on forking the small amount of food she thought she could consume into her mouth at the small candlelit table Alex had set on the terrace. The herbed pasta was delicious, but it was hard to eat when her heart was still pounding and her hands trembling so much negotiating a fork seemed like a new and highly complex activity. And why wouldn't it when she had literally jumped into the deep end and invited the most spectacularly good-looking man she'd ever met to kiss her—and he had! Not to mention the fact that the kiss had been the most incredible of her life and all she could think about was experiencing more of the bone-meltingly delicious heat that had coursed through her veins. It was as if every nerve ending in her body had been switched on for the first time and she wasn't sure whether to revel in it or be completely terrified of what she was feeling.

She swallowed hard, forced down the food. The fact that

she'd been right—that Alex was attracted to her—made her head feel as though it was going to explode. Maybe Jo was right. Maybe it had been her defensive attitude that had turned men off in the past and not the few extra pounds she'd been carrying. Which had always been her excuse.

She took another sip of the rich, full cabernet that was going a long way to mellowing her out. But the wine didn't seem to be having the same effect on Alex, who'd glowered at her throughout the entire meal—as if she'd committed a crime rather than simply kissed him.

She risked a quick glance at him. He was still watching her with that same implacable frown on his face, that penetrating blue gaze of his impossible to read. And it occurred to her she hadn't fully thought through her plan. She had the mind-numbing confirmation that he was attracted to her. The question now was what was she going to do about it?

Her heart pounding in her chest, she set her fork down with an abrupt movement, and the sound of metal clattering against fine china echoed in the still night air.

He gave her half-empty plate a narrowed glance. "That's all you're going to eat?"

"It was delicious, thank you. I think that's about all I can handle."

"All right." He laid his fork down with a deliberate movement and pushed his plate away. "Let's talk about what happened."

Gladly. She took another sip of her wine to fortify herself and set the glass down.

"That kiss shouldn't have happened."

She was ready for that one. "Why not?"

"I'm much more experienced than you, Isabel. I'm not interested in relationships—in fact, mine never last longer than a few months, and the women I date are well aware of that."

"So?"

He did a double take at the belligerent note in her voice. "You're also probably still in shock from what happened today."

"I'm absolutely fine," she countered. "In fact, I feel like I have more clarity right now than I've ever had in my life."

He sat back in his chair, his gaze on her face. "What kind of clarity?"

She twisted the stem of her wineglass on the table, watching the bloodred liquid shimmer in the candlelight. "That was my worst fear today. Facing it—getting through it—" she paused, looking up at him "—it's made me realize how much of my life I've lived in fear...how many times I've not gone after what I wanted because I was afraid I wouldn't get it or it would explode in my face."

He gave a wary nod. "That's a good realization."

She shook her head. "I'm not looking for a relationship, Alex." A husky laugh escaped her. "In fact, that's the last thing I need right now."

His eyes narrowed. "Then what *are* you looking for?"

"I don't want to live with any more regrets."

He shook his head, a wry smile curving his lips. "You're twenty-five, Isabel. How many regrets can you have?"

She took a deep breath, meeting his gaze head-on. "I will regret it if I walk away from tonight without exploring the attraction that's between us."

A muscle jumped in his jaw. He sat there completely silent, staring at her. "I'm not sure you know what you're doing."

She shook her head. "I know exactly what I'm doing."

A long moment passed; it might have been four, five seconds, she wasn't sure. All she knew was that she was holding her breath, sure at one point he was going to reject her. The warm night air pressed so heavily against her lungs she thought they would burst. And then something shifted, morphed on the air between them. And she got her answer in the darkening of his eyes.

He stood up and held out a hand. "Let's go enjoy the view, then."

CHAPTER FOUR

THE SULTRY NIGHT AIR, so quiet and still as they stood at the railing and took in the cityscape, seemed to envelop Izzie in a world so far removed from her normal life that she could almost believe that it was. That it was just the two of them who existed and this incredible panoramic view of London with its lights twinkling across the water had been created for them and them alone.

That what felt like a defining moment in her life was utterly, absolutely the right thing to do.

"You must spend so much time out here," she said to Alex, shaking her head. "It's breathtaking."

A wry smile curved his mouth. "It's my second office when I'm in London. When the weather is good…"

Izzie tried to focus as he pointed out the London landmarks to her, stopping to give her a bit of history on each, but the anticipation coursing through her veins made her feel weak-kneed. Light-headed.

"What's that?" She pointed at a series of small structures stretching across the water on either side of a bridge.

"That's the Thames barrier."

"Those white things that look like little Sydney Opera Houses?"

He moved behind her and directed her fingers toward the circular structures she'd been looking at. "Those."

Her temperature spiked dramatically as the hard, warm length of him brushed against her back. "Right," she murmured. "That's what I thought."

He didn't move away, but dropped his hands to the railing instead, resting them on either side of her. Her heartbeat sped up.

"Flooding has become an issue for London over the years. Water levels have been continuously rising and threatening the city. In one of the big floods, many years back, hundreds of people died."

"Really?" She could barely breathe, so distracted was she by the pulses of electricity his big, warm body was sending through hers.

"Are you listening?" He moved his lips closer to her ear. "There's going to be a quiz later, you know."

"Later?" She gave up all pretext of paying attention when his hand brushed the weight of her hair aside and he set his lips to the sensitive skin at the nape of her neck.

"Mmm...one kiss was not nearly enough, Isabel."

Her legs felt as though she'd been through one too many Spin classes. Weaker still when he pressed his mouth to the sensitive junction between her neck and shoulder. The question was, did she have the guts to go through with this? For all her bravado, she'd only ever had one lover—and not a good one at that—in her college boyfriend. What if she disappointed Alex with her lack of experience?

"I can see the smoke coming out of your ears," he murmured against her skin. "Stop thinking so much."

Which was exactly what she needed to do. She'd been thinking so much her entire life she felt as though she'd been watching it from the sidelines. And if there was anything this crazy day had taught her, it was that life was tenuous. Fragile. And it could be taken from you at any moment. So best to jump in and take your chances.

Taking a deep breath, she turned around and met the

questioning intensity of his deep blue gaze. Felt the heat—oh dear Lord—the heat of those sizzling good looks up close. The hard planes of his face that made him look formidable…until he smiled. That square jaw with its delicious indentation that made a woman want to put her lips to it. The sensuous, full mouth… It was all a bit heart-stopping.

And incredibly difficult to find her voice. In the end, she didn't try. Just went up on tiptoes, lifted her chin, and brought her lips a hairbreadth away from his in silent invitation.

Something flickered in his eyes. "Can I ask you a question?"

She nodded.

"Are those glasses for distance?"

She blinked. "Yes."

He reached up and plucked them from her face. "Then I guess you won't be needing them." Her breath caught, strangled in her throat as he set the glasses down on the railing beside them. "This is about to get up close and *very* personal."

Oh God. Her heart raced in her chest as he reached up and captured her jaw in his palm, his gaze following his thumb as it swept across her cheek and over the surface of her bottom lip. "You have the most amazing mouth," he murmured, exerting a slight downward pressure so she opened for him. "It's the kind of mouth a man couldn't resist even if he wanted to."

Which was good because if he didn't kiss her right now, she was going to die. Transfixed, she watched as he lowered his head, her lashes fluttering down as he angled his mouth over hers in a caress so light, so sensuous, it made her whole body go weak. Her hands came up to balance her against the hard wall of his chest, a sigh escaping her throat as he explored, tasted every centimeter of her lips, getting intimately acquainted in a way that made her toes curl.

The kiss seemed to go on forever and ever, a leisurely tasting that neither of them seemed inclined to end. "This needs to go," he muttered, reaching up to unclasp her hair so it fell in a heavy swath down her back.

He drew back and raked his gaze over her. "You also have the most sensational hair."

"I almost cut it all off recently." She'd thought it might look more professional on-camera.

He reached out to twist one of her curls around his finger. "Don't ever, *ever* do that."

She smiled. "What is it about men and hair?"

He wound the curl tight, then let it go. "It's great fodder for fantasies…I've been imagining what it would look like spread across the white satin sheets of that big lonely bed of mine in there."

Words. She knew there were words in the English language. But the thought of him fantasizing about them in bed together wiped them clean from her head.

It didn't matter, though, because he was lifting her up on her tiptoes again, tunneling his hands in her hair to cup the back of her head, his sinful expression as his mouth came down on hers telling her he intended to indulge every minute of that fantasy in short order.

This time his kisses were of the hot, openmouthed variety that left her gasping. He made her give back everything he was offering her, hotter and hotter until she felt as though she were going to combust.

By the time his tongue traced the trembling fullness of her bottom lip, dipping inside and tangling erotically with hers, she wanted all he had to offer and more. She tipped her head back and took him in, giving him full access to her mouth. The intimacy of the kiss set her blood on fire.

He nudged her backward against the cool, hard concrete of the wall, his muscular thigh sliding between hers at the same time he dragged his lips down to explore the sensitive skin at the base of her throat. "Your pulse is racing…" he murmured against her skin.

She fought to control a shiver than ran through her as he trailed his lips across her collarbone to the soft skin of her shoulder. "I'm a little—"

"Excited?" he finished, a wicked smile curving his lips as he raised his blue gaze to hers. "But we're only just getting started, sweetheart."

Izzie squeezed her eyes shut, heat flooding her cheeks. Alex's low laughter danced across the night air as he bent to press his lips to her shoulder, his teeth nipping lightly at the tender skin as he slid his fingers under the strap of her dress and eased it off her shoulder. Izzie grabbed hold of the wall on either side of her as his lips worked their way over to her other shoulder and dispensed with the other strap.

Her eyes flew open as he eased the material of her dress away from her skin, pushing it down over the swell of her breasts to reveal the lacy bra she wore underneath. His soft curse made her cheeks burn anew. She lifted her hands to cover herself, a bout of extreme self-consciousness overwhelming her.

"Isabel…" He slid his fingers under her chin and brought her gaze back up to meet his. "You are so gorgeous you blow my mind."

She let her hands fall away then, the heat in his gaze holding her, drawing her back in. He lowered his head until his mouth brushed against hers. Took her lips in a hard kiss that wiped every last insecurity from her head. Her bones went liquid as he demonstrated how much he wanted her, demanding her response as he took her deeper. And she gave herself up to the sensations he was creating, gasping as his big hands came up to cup the weight of her breasts.

"Beautiful," he murmured, skating his thumbs over her nipples and bringing them to instant, hard, aching erectness under the lace of her bra. She squeezed her eyes shut at the erotic image, digging her nails harder into the concrete. He bent to take a lace-covered peak in his mouth, while his fingers continued to tease the other. The liquid heat invading her body sped to her core. Melted her from the inside out. His tongue flicked and teased her nipple, the sensation so exquisitely good she forgot where she was, everything but how good what he was doing to her felt.

He stopped playing then, taking her lace-covered nipple deep inside his mouth, sucking and tugging on it with his teeth until a slow, dull ache started deep inside her. An ache she'd never felt before.

"Alex," she murmured helplessly, not knowing what was happening to her, unsure of what to do with this extreme pleasure he was giving her.

He shifted his attention to her other breast. "Good?" he murmured, taking the hard peak inside his mouth.

"Mmm…" Her case of no words was rapidly getting worse. She shifted restlessly against his hard thigh, searching for some kind of relief. Sucking deeply on her nipple, he ran his hands down over her hips, found the hem of her dress and dragged it up, so he could settle his thigh between her bare legs. *Oh…* Izzie gasped at the sensation of his cloth-covered thigh rasping against her skin. It felt unbearably intimate and oh so good pressed against the damp heat of her. And she realized exactly what he'd given her. His hard muscles were the perfect antidote to the burning ache building inside of her. More so when she rocked against them and tiny sparks of electricity zigzagged through her.

"*Theos*, you're going to be the end of me," he muttered, lifting his head from her breast to stare at her, hot color staining his cheekbones.

The fact that he was as aroused as she was made every nerve ending quiver. Gave her a confidence she'd never known she had as she met his gaze, letting him see exactly how much she wanted him. He slid his thigh from between hers, pulled her against him, and bent slightly to run his hands up the back of her thighs. She drew in a breath as he cupped her bottom, arching her into him until she could feel his hard arousal. *Good Lord.* Her throat went dry. He felt big and hard and…intimidating. Very intimidating.

Biting down her apprehension, she held her breath as he traced the edge of her panties over the curve of her bottom. "A thong," he muttered huskily in her ear. "You really are trying to be the ultimate male fantasy, aren't you?"

Her cheeks burned as he brought his hands around to the front of her, pushing her back so he could trail his fingers teasingly along the front edge of her panties until he reached the damp warmth between her thighs.

His gaze speared hers. "Tell me what you want."

Her legendary ability to talk failed her. How was she supposed to tell him that when she didn't even *know* what she wanted? Her ex had never been into touching her *there*. Had never been interested in anything more than his own pleasure.

Alex saved her, his eyes darkening with amusement. "How about this?" he murmured, sliding his fingers against her through the thin material, pushing it into her so he could feel the damp evidence of her arousal.

Izzie closed her eyes.

He laughed softly, his thumb moving up to rotate against the hard nub at the center of her. "I love that I can turn you on like this."

The wicked things he was doing with his thumb wiped her embarrassment clean from her head. She gripped the concrete wall harder with her hands, head thrown back, eyes closed as she gave herself in to the sensations he was administering.

"Alex," she murmured, the need in her voice shocking her.

"Tell me what you want," he encouraged softly.

"Anyone could see us here…"

"They'd have to have a telescope."

What if they did? She stopped caring when he pressed his lips to her neck and increased the pressure of his thumb against her. "Touch me," she pleaded desperately, her hips rotating against his hand.

"But I am…"

"You know what I mean."

The first slide of his fingers against her hot, swollen flesh was the single most pleasurable thing she'd felt in her adult life. Her knees went weak and she leaned against the wall for support. "*Theos,* you are so turned on," he groaned, moving his thumb up to the hard button of her arousal, this time without any barrier. "This what you want, Iz?" he murmured, beginning that maddening set of circles against her that was building an unbearable tension in her body. Izzie bit back the moan that rose in her throat, convinced she wasn't going to make it through this. Every nerve in her body felt as if it was centered under his fingers, and it felt so good she was crazy with it.

"*Yes.*" Twisting restlessly against him, she begged him for more, faster, anything that would help her deal with the insane ache he was building in her.

"And this?" There was a raspy edge to his voice as he slid one of his long fingers inside her. Izzie sank her teeth into her lip, feeling her body accommodate the intrusion. Then the incredible feeling of him stroking her, stretching her, sent her to a whole other stratosphere.

"Alex," she heard herself say brokenly, no longer in control of anything she was doing or feeling.

"More?" he asked, sliding another of those pleasure-inducing fingers into her, waiting while she accepted him. This time her gasp rang out on the night air as he set a rhythm that was taking her somewhere she knew she wanted to go. *Now*. Before she shattered into a million little pieces.

"Please," she begged him, not knowing what to do, what to ask for to make it happen.

He bent his head to hers, dragging his mouth across her swollen lips. "Go with it, Iz," he urged in a soft, husky voice that inflamed her senses. "Let yourself go."

"I don't— *Oh*," she breathed against his lips as he slid his thumb against the center of her while his fingers continued to slide in and out of her, increasing their rhythm now until there was such an unbearable tension focused between her legs she thought she would scream.

Then, with one last maddening press of his thumb against her, he took her over the edge, the most exquisite wave of pleasure washing over her, stiffening her limbs and focusing every nerve in her body on the white-hot pleasure radiating out from the center of her. She shoved a fist into her mouth, terrified she *would* scream out as he kept his fingers pressed to her to extract every last second of her orgasm.

Her first. The mind-shattering pleasure soaked her senses as she came slowly back to reality and found Alex watching her, the intent look on his face telling her he'd guessed it had been exactly that.

"That's never happened to you before."

"No."

"Are you a virgin?"

She shook her head.

The tension in the hard set of his jaw slackened.

"Would it have mattered?"

"Of course it would have. I told you I don't get complicated with women, Isabel."

"And a virgin is more complicated?" She didn't get it. She was one step removed from being one herself, and it didn't feel complicated.

He shrugged. "Of course they are. Women always want to romanticize their first sexual experience. Didn't you?"

She shook her head. "My ex-boyfriend was more interested in satisfying himself than me. Not that we want to dredge up stories of past lovers," she added lightly, desperately afraid he might ask her exactly how many men she'd slept with.

"No, we don't," he agreed, bending down to slide an arm under her knees so he could swing her up into his arms. "I can think of much better things to do with the time."

Izzie had never been carried by a man. Which was a shame, really, because she felt so delicate and feminine in Alex's arms as he carried her inside she decided it was an experience every woman should have at least once in her life.

He set her down on the cool hardwood floor of the utterly masculine master bedroom he'd shown her on the tour earlier. The bedroom featured the same floor-to-ceiling views the rest of the penthouse had, decorated in rich, muted tones that perfectly reflected the man himself.

She looked around as he flicked on some lamps. "No curtains."

He gave her an amused look. "You can't see in the glass, only out."

Which made it the perfect venue for an incredibly erotic sexual experience, she decided, trying not to jump out of her skin as he moved behind her and set his teeth to her shoulder. "Was that your idea or the builder's?"

He laughed softly. "The builder's. Were you imagining me creating some sort of seduction pad?"

She shrugged, jealousy flaring inside her despite the fact that she had absolutely no claim on him. "I'm sure you've brought more than a few women up here."

His fingers moved to the clasp of her bra. "Are you asking?"

She made herself shake her head. Except when he unhooked it with extreme ease and flipped it to the floor, she thought maybe she should.

He slid his arms around her and cupped her breasts. "I'm a pretty choosy guy when it comes to female companionship."

She gasped as his thumbs brought her nipples back to erectness. She was sure he could afford to be.

The soft rasp of her zipper came next. Cool air hit her skin as he pushed the dress over her hips and it fell to the floor, leaving her clad only in her thong. She swallowed hard as he turned her around and surveyed her from head to toe. "Beautiful," he said softly, his gaze catching and holding hers. "You take my breath away, Isabel."

She felt breathless, unable to pull even the tiniest bit of air into her lungs. He picked up her hand and placed it over the top button of his shirt. "I think I'm a bit overdressed, don't you?"

The thought of exposing all that hard, tanned flesh had her hands shaking as she worked on the first button. It slipped frustratingly out of her grasp.

"Relax." He captured her hand and lifted it to his mouth. "We're in no hurry here."

The calm, sexy assurance in his gaze grounded her, made her heart flip over in anticipation. Returning her fingers to the buttons, she managed to get the first one undone. Then the second and third, exposing a mouthwatering expanse of olive-skinned torso. *Dear heavens*, he had one of those six-packs, what looked like the consummate athlete's body. *Insane.*

She pushed the shirt off his shoulders, her mouth dry as she took him in. Alex groaned. "*Christós,* Izzie, touch me. I'm going a little nuts here…."

Emboldened by the want in his eyes, she lifted her hand to trace his pecs, feathering her palms down over his nipples. His quick intake of breath spurred her on, sending her hands down over the taut muscles of his washboard stomach. He was all hard male and nothing but. It thrilled and intimidated her at the same time.

Forcing herself not to think, she moved her hands to his belt, her unsteady but determined fingers pulling the leather from the buckle. His zipper was next, her hands brushing against his arousal as she pulled it down. He let out a tortured groan.

She lifted her gaze to his. "Should I stop?"

A harsh bark of laughter escaped him. "I would say that's the last thing you should do."

She kept going, unsure exactly about what she was supposed to be doing because with her ex there had never been any foreplay. Letting her instincts guide her, she slid her hands inside the waistband of his pants and pushed them down over his hips to the floor. He stepped out of them, clad only in a pair of sexy, body-hugging black boxers that did little to disguise the thick, hard length of him. At that moment, looking at his size, she wasn't at all sure this was going to work.

He must have seen the uncertainty in her face. Sliding his fingers under her jaw, he brought her gaze back up to his. "I'm big, Izzie, I know, but I promise I won't hurt you. We'll take this as slow as we need to, okay?"

She nodded, wondering why she trusted this man she hadn't even known for twenty-four hours more than she'd trusted anyone in her life. He lifted her up and carried her over to the huge king-size bed, the soft satin sheets and comforter of which were indeed white. Her head landed in the fluffy pillows, a smile curving her lips. "How's the hair?"

He ran his gaze lazily over her, his mouth quirking up on one side. "Better than I could have imagined."

Resting a knee on the bed, he looked every bit the part of an incredibly sexy Greek god, and her heart tripped over itself. Then went into freefall as he laid another one of those lazy, never-ending kisses on her that brought her body firing back to life in a heated rush. His hand slid down between her legs to caress her sensitized flesh, stroking her gently until she was once again writhing under his touch.

"Alex..." She wanted more this time. Wanted that incredible hard length of him she'd touched inside her.

He rose in a swift movement and stripped off his boxers, sheathing a condom over the jutting evidence of his arousal. She stared dry-mouthed at the size of his erection as he came back to her, his powerful thighs nudging hers apart. It had been two years since she'd been with her ex. Did your body go back to a virginal state after that amount of time? She supposed she was about to find out.

He read her expression easily. A corner of his mouth lifted in a teasing smile. "Sweetheart, you're so ready for me I can guarantee this isn't going to be an issue."

Her heart skipped a beat. And then his hands were sliding under her hips, lifting her as he moistened the tip of his erection with her wetness. Izzie closed her eyes, his erotic foreplay much too much for her to meet head-on.

The first couple of inches as he took her made her gasp and open her eyes. "Alex," she breathed, "I can't—"

"Shh." He set a finger against her lips, holding himself completely still. "Wait..."

She closed her eyes and tried to force herself to relax. And felt her body slowly loosen, stretch to accommodate him, until the discomfort she was feeling turned into something very different.

"Okay?"

She nodded her head up and down, opening her eyes. "More."

His gaze darkened, the iron control he was holding over himself evident in the tense set of his jaw as he slid another couple of inches into her. Pure pleasure sliced through her at the incredible feeling of him filling her, but still he held back. She arched her hips in invitation. "Alex," she murmured. "I'm good."

A muscle jumped in his jaw. "You sure?"

"Yes."

His thrust, as he took her completely, stole her breath. Had her digging her nails into the sheets at the feeling of him everywhere inside her, knowing she couldn't have taken another inch…another centimeter even.

He tightened his hands around her hips, withdrew ever so slowly, then eased into her again, making her feel it all over.

"Theos, Izzie, you feel so good," he gritted out, taking her again and again until she was half-crazy for him. Built a slow-burning fire he fanned with every rhythmic slide inside her.

"Wrap your legs around me," he encouraged huskily, her gasp of pleasure as she did so and felt him even deeper echoing throughout the room. And then there was no longer self-control, holding back. Now there was only his fierce, deep strokes as he buried himself inside her, his throaty words of encouragement as she took him deeper and deeper the most potent aphrodisiac. Her gaze met his as he slid his hands out from under her hips and braced them on either side of her, his muscular biceps holding him above her. Higher and higher, watching her the entire time, he took her ever closer to that insanely good release she now knew was right around the corner.

"Hell, Izzie," he ground out, a sheen of perspiration breaking out on his brow. "I can't stand this much longer."

She wrapped her legs tighter around his hips, her gaze locking onto his. "Now, Alex...I'm so close."

With a muttered curse, he drove into her then, faster, harder, until a burst of pleasure tightened her body around him and send her spiraling off into a wave of sensation that seemed to go on forever. He groaned as she contracted around him, swelled inside of her and found his own release, his hoarse cry the sexiest thing she thought she'd ever heard.

She lay there, his big body on top of her, limbs entangled with hers, their ragged breathing slowing on the night air. And knew that what had just happened was something incredibly unusual—that intense connection that had fueled everything between them today. She wasn't so naive she didn't realize that.

"Okay?" Alex lifted himself up on his forearms to study her face.

A smile she couldn't hide curved her lips. "More than okay."

"I'd have to agree with that," he said softly, shifting onto one arm so he could run a finger down her cheek. "That was incredible."

The heat that bloomed under his fingers must have been visible because he laughed softly and pulled her close. "A little late for shyness, *agape*. You blew me away."

Which was such a switch from what her ex had told her afterward. It was like wiping away the past in one fell, satisfying swoop. "The Greek is...very sexy," she murmured. "I think I'm a sucker for it."

He threw back his head and laughed. "I fall into it sometimes when I'm passionate about something." He brushed his thumb across her lower lip in a caress that gave her goose bumps, his voice deepening to a husky whisper. "I would demonstrate more but it's late and you look exhausted."

She *was* exhausted. And although she wanted to stay awake, to enjoy as much of this amazing night with Alex as she could, she didn't protest when he shifted onto his side and tucked her against his warm, hard frame. Exhaustion overtook her, settling her lashes down on her cheeks.

Her last thought was that this entire day had been meant to happen for a reason. She had been meant to face up to her biggest fear once and for all. Meant to enjoy this one amazing night with this incredible man. The problem was, she thought sleepily, she couldn't see any other man ever living up to it.

CHAPTER FIVE

"YOU'RE GOING TO love me as usual."

Alex held his phone to his ear as he eased away from the warmth of Izzie's body and out of bed, his PA's comment making him smile. "I already love you for being up at—" he glanced at his watch as he walked out into the living room "—midnight working."

"You know I'm a control freak," she returned drily. "The plane and pilot are ready for you."

"You are amazing." He ran his fingers through his hair. "Remind me what the red tape is for flying someone else back on the jet…? Gerry just needs to add them to the manifest, right?"

"Yup. And they need their documentation." Papers rustled in the background. "Oh, and a producer from NYC-TV has been trying to get a hold of you. Is this something about the Messer case?"

He grimaced. "Yes. Tell them I'm in Maui."

"Is this going to turn into a circus?"

"Very possibly." But he was going to do his damnedest to shut Frank Messer down before it got to that. "Get some sleep. Come in a bit later if you like."

She yawned. "As if, with the amount of work on my plate. See you tomorrow."

He stepped into the shower while Izzie slept, letting the

hot sting of the spray ease the tension in his shoulders. As amazing as last night had been, it now seemed like an ill-advised foray into a complication he didn't need. Every second he spent doing anything other than figuring out how to beat Frank Messer was time he couldn't afford to lose. He needed to get back to New York, meet with his lawyers and put together a game plan.

He did not need the distraction of Izzie on a transatlantic flight with him. The odds of him keeping his hands off of her were slim to none, and that just couldn't happen. Last night had been an agreed-upon one-night stand. An opportunity to enjoy each other as two consenting adults.

Also unbelievably hot… The look on Izzie's face when she'd come apart in his arms on the terrace made his body stir to life under the pounding, hot spray. The extreme pleasure of driving into that tight, welcoming warmth of hers a seriously tempting invitation to put his pilot off a half hour longer and wake her up. But he needed to get out of here, Izzie needed to sleep and she already had a flight booked. The better idea would be to send a car for her and get out.

He shut off the shower, dried himself and slung a towel around his hips. It was better for both of them to end it now. Clean. Neat.

He headed into the bedroom and pulled on a pair of boxers and a T-shirt.

"What time is it?"

A still half-asleep Izzie sat up and rubbed her eyes. A gorgeous Izzie, he might add, her long dark hair falling over her edible shoulders as she struggled to focus. His gaze dropped to her pink-tipped, perfectly shaped breasts where the sheet had slipped and he got hard all over again.

She flushed and dragged the sheet up to her collarbone. "It feels early."

"It's five-thirty," he said briefly, pulling on a pair of

jeans. "I have to go, but you should sleep. I'll send a car for 8:30 to take you to the airport…"

She pushed her hair back, a confused look spreading across her face. "I—er, aren't we on the same flight?"

He walked over and sat down beside her on the bed. "The jet's been fixed. I need to get out of here."

"Oh." The wounded look in her eyes made him feel like a total cad.

"I have an emergency to take care of," he explained, unable to stop himself from sliding a hand under the sheet and cupping one of her gorgeous breasts, the tip hardening immediately under the caress of his thumb. He watched her eyes darken to that same chocolate-brown, almost-black color they had last night when he'd made love to her. "It's better you rest and take the later flight."

She nodded, but the slight wobble in her chin near killed him. He bent his head and brushed his lips over hers. "Thank you for last night."

But what was meant to serve as a brief kiss that would have secured him an appropriate exit was quickly revealed for the mistake it was, her mouth softening and parting underneath his, the attraction that was electric between them sparking to life. He groaned, unable to help himself from enjoying one more taste of her, it had just been so incredibly sweet last night. Tunneling his hands in her hair, he took the kiss deeper until she curled her hands in his T-shirt and this was only going in one direction…

He pulled back before he lost his head completely. "I have to go."

Her teeth sank into her bottom lip and she nodded. Brushing a chunk of her thick hair out of her face, he tucked it behind her ear. "I left some clothes for you on the chair. They're too big for you, but they're clean."

"Thanks."

He held her gaze, refusing to issue false promises. "Keep jumping, Iz. It's the only way to live."

She said nothing, those big eyes on him. He finished dressing and grabbed his wallet and watch before he changed his mind. It wasn't until he was halfway through the door that he stopped and turned around.

"No regrets?"

A wry smile curved her mouth. "No regrets."

"Good." He turned around and made himself leave, wondering why it was so hard to walk away. He'd done it a million times. This time felt different.

Izzie took a deep breath as she heard the front door of the penthouse click shut. Took another, tried to calm herself, and when that didn't work, picked up the nearest missile, which happened to be Alex's pillow, and chucked it against the wall, pretending it was him. Had he actually just left her here like that? When he knew she needed to get back to New York? *Really*? She sank back against the pillows, her breath coming out in a long *whoosh*. How hard would it have been for him to wait? He could have woken her up and she'd have been ready in five minutes flat, much happier to go with him now than wait for her flight.

Unbelievable. She stared at the pink dawn creeping across the London sky through the floor-to-ceiling windows. She'd just been unceremoniously dropped like a hot potato by a man who couldn't seem to get out of here fast enough. As if he'd thought she'd make a scene.

Scowling, she hugged her arms around herself. Maybe some of his women did that. But not her. She'd said one night and she'd meant one night. The last thing she needed to do was complicate her life right now. Not when she had a seven-hour flight and a panel of network executives to face on the other end of it, if James did indeed manage to persuade them to stay.

Not when she'd promised herself she'd never let a man rule her emotions the way her mother had her father's.

But heavens, it'd been worth it. The image of Alex on a dartboard faded to one of him naked on this bed, his beautiful body giving her more pleasure than she'd ever dreamed possible. Warmth flooded her cheeks. How she'd let him do those things to her on the terrace in full view of anyone who'd have cared to look… His husky encouragements to tell him what she wanted releasing a completely wanton side of her she hadn't even known existed…*God.* That *I'd be incredible in bed* tattoo he wore across his chest? Definitely not false advertising.

She threw the covers off, swung her legs over the side of the bed and headed for the shower. There was no way she was going to be able to go back to sleep after that last kiss, which had made her want to turn her one-night plan into a whole lot more. But since he had now *dumped* her, that wouldn't be a problem.

She pulled on the huge Boston College athletics T-shirt he'd left her, obviously his, and the pair of jeans that necessitated three roll-ups so she didn't trip over them. It wasn't fashionable, but it was necessary with her suitcase in New York without her.

Padding her way into the kitchen, she told herself she was going to be the smart girl she was and relegate Alex to her good—make that hot—memory book. The thing that had made her realize how completely she hadn't been living her life.

Mouth firm, she settled down on a kitchen bar stool with a cup of coffee she managed to wring out of the high-tech espresso machine, and went over the interview questions James had sent. She was going to give this interview her best shot. Forget about the past, know she'd worked hard and had grown so much, and put her demons aside.

This was the new Izzie. Time to unleash her on the world.

Sixteen hours later, Izzie exited her interview with the network execs in NYC-TV's Rockefeller Plaza offices so physically and mentally exhausted she could hardly put one foot in front of the other. A transatlantic flight, a whirlwind cab trip to the studios, and an hour and a half of nonstop grilling by the execs could do that to a person.

Visions of a bergamot-scented bath filled her head. She tucked her portfolio under her arm and stumbled her way through the newsroom, ignoring the envious, almost spiteful, look on Katy Phillip's face as she passed the entertainment desk. *So not going there.* She'd had a lot of that since she'd walked in this afternoon as the emerging star and she didn't have the strength to process it.

She sat down at her desk, thankful she hadn't been out on assignment today, with a story to edit ahead of her. Tomorrow was soon enough to catch up on email and everything else waiting for her. She yanked off her pumps, pulled her sneakers out of her bottom drawer and had just about laced them up when her boss's shiny loafers appeared in front of her.

Damn. She'd been so close...

"I heard it went well."

"I think so." She finished tying her sneaker and straightened up. "Given I was pretty much comatose."

James plopped down on the corner of her desk and crossed his arms over his chest. "They loved you. They think you have the young, fresh look that will appeal to the demographic we're going after."

She grinned. "Really?"

"Really." His face lit up. "They think you're very talented."

Her stomach muscles relaxed, a wave of relief flooding through her. "And the bad?"

"They're worried you're not experienced enough to handle the pressure."

Go figure. So was *she*.

"I told them any daughter of Dayla St. James is more than up to it."

Her mouth dropped open, dismay spreading through her. "What did you do that for?"

He scowled. "We're in it to win it, Iz. Get with the program."

The program didn't include her mother. *Ever*. "James, you know I want to do this on my own."

He waved a hand at her. "You want to make it in this business, you use the weapons at your disposal. This is a once-in-a-lifetime shot. Nobody's going to play nice."

She nodded. "I know that, I do. And I appreciate the opportunity. I'd just rather keep her out of it."

"You know that's never going to happen."

It would if she had anything to do with it. "What next, then?"

"They're putting together a short list. I'm pretty sure you'll be on it. Then they'll do trial weekends with each of the candidates. Meanwhile," he said, dumping a file on her desk, "we amp up your star potential with the Constantinou story. This," he said, pointing to the file, "is the real reason I want this interview."

She frowned. "I thought it was the juicy court case."

"That's good stuff." He flipped the file open and pointed at a magazine cover. "This is better."

She looked down at the glossy sports magazine. Squinted at the photo of the lone figure dressed in a football uniform, kneeling on a dusty field, helmet in hand. Felt the blood drain from her face. It couldn't be.... There was just no way. Her gaze flew to the headline. The Next King of Football? Is College Quarterback Sensation Alexios Constantinou the Player Who Will Revive Pro Football in New York?

Her head spun; the lights of the busy newsroom blurred around her. The football player in the photo was undoubtedly Alex, the man she'd just spent the night with.

"I thought his name was *Leandros,*" she croaked.

"Goes by his middle name," James dismissed. "Something about his father disowning him."

Oh my God. Alex was Alexios. Alexios Constantinou. *Who'd supposedly been long gone by the time she'd gotten to Sophoros's London offices*, according to his receptionist. Her mind flashed back to the blonde's expression when she'd asked how long *Leandro* had been gone. The challenging look on the receptionist's face. *She'd been right.* She'd had Leandros Constantinou, *Alex,* under her fingertips the entire time. Had been stuck in an elevator with him for hours...and what had she done? She'd *slept with him.*

OMG.

"Izzie?"

Her boss was staring at her. She shook her head, trying desperately to contain her horror. "Why does it matter that he was a football player? This is about Frank Messer's offer to tell all."

James settled himself more comfortably on her desk. "Alexios Constantinou was one of the best quarterbacks to ever come out of the college system. Charismatic, smart, he was a born leader...a real golden boy. Led his team to a national championship and was drafted first overall by the New York Crusaders. He was touted as the player who would put football back on the map in the Big Apple. The problem is—" her boss grimaced "—we can't leave a player like that alone in this city. We have to pile the pressure on him until he cracks and we have a self-fulfilling prophecy."

Her gaze slid to the photo, her brain still trying to catch up. Alex had been a star football player?

"So what happened?" she asked warily.

"The press was all over him like he was the second coming. Expected him to turn the team around way too fast." His mouth twisted. "He almost did it, too, in his third year. Then he blew his rotator cuff in a qualifying game for the playoffs and ended his career for good. Twenty-four years old and his career was over. One of the true tragic stories in professional sports."

Her stomach twisted in a sea of knots. *Sometimes in life you're only given one shot,* Alex had said in the elevator. *Use it wisely.*

She cleared her throat. "Okay, so all very dramatic, but isn't it ancient history now? And what does this have to do with Frank Messer?"

An intense, self-satisfied smile curved her boss's lips. "The night Alex Constantinou was injured, he disappeared, never did another interview. Then he resurfaces a few years later with this red-hot software company he's created with his college buddy and they launch this title, *Behemoth,* that sets the gaming world on fire. The man's probably made a hundred times more money on it than he would ever have made in football, but he still never talks to media. Ever." His gaze locked on hers. "I want that story. *His* story."

Her brain whirled, tried to keep up. "So you want to land the exclusive story on Alexios Constantinou and use Frank Messer as leverage."

"Exactly. And you'll be the one to convince him. Everyone knows Constantinou has an eye for the ladies."

Izzie almost choked on that. *Dear Lord.* She waved her hand at him. "If he hates the press that much, James, he isn't going to do it. He'll say to hell with public opinion and let the courts decide."

Her boss shrugged. "I think we can convince him it's better to tell his side of the story than let Messer do it for him."

"*If* the lawyers let him…."

He lifted a brow. "CEOs are mavericks. Especially this guy. He'll do what he wants. You just need to convince him."

Right. Her stomach lurched. What would Alex think of her when he realized what she did for a living? It wasn't as if she'd deliberately tried to mislead him about her profession. After a few nasty encounters with people who weren't fans of the media, including a guy who'd verbally assaulted her in a bar, she didn't advertise what she did upon first meeting. It just made life easier to say she was in communications.

Until now.

Every muscle in her body screamed out that she couldn't do this. But how was she supposed to tell her boss that? And *why*.

James looked at her expectantly. "Well?"

Her brain spit out a desperate solution. She'd find a way to discredit Messer so the story never became an issue. So they had nothing to strong-arm Alex with. Her boss could find her another juicy assignment that *didn't* involve the man she'd just devoured last night and everyone would be happy.

"Okay," she said, nodding. "I'll call Messer in the morning and schedule a background interview."

He nodded. "And *find* Constantinou. He's back in the country. I don't care if you have to camp out in front of his office building."

She was so never doing that. James slid off her desk and did his usual pre-news-hour circuit of the room. Izzie shoved her phone in her purse and stared at the lucky silver charm dangling from the strap. How could this have happened to her? Of all the men she could have chosen to have a one-night stand with, it had to have been *Alexios Constantinou*?

Inconceivable. She stood up, deciding she'd do a better job figuring this out in the bathtub. A commotion near the entrance to the newsroom made her look up. A petite brunette stood court in the middle of a group of reporters, her megawatt smile on full display. *Her mother.* Good Lord. She was back in town.

Dayla St. James chatted for a few minutes with the crowd, reveling in the attention they heaped on her, then blew them a kiss and made her way over to Izzie's desk with that same shoulders-back, confident strut she'd been using her entire life. Izzie blew out a long breath and steeled herself for the hurricane that was her mother.

"I'm back," Dayla announced unnecessarily, arriving in a flurry of floral perfume to press a kiss to both of Izzie's cheeks. Her mother's violet eyes took her in, the heart-shaped face that had sent a billion men's hearts fluttering still so absolutely perfect at fifty-one she made Izzie feel like an awkward, overblown offshoot. "I've come to whisk you off for a drink."

Izzie sat down on the edge of her desk. She needed to process, not go for a drink. This was what little white lies were for. "I have plans with the girls."

Her mother frowned. "Surely you can have a quick drink with me first? I'm going to get all tangled up in this play tomorrow and I haven't seen you in weeks."

She groaned inwardly. "How long is your engagement?"

"Three months," her mother said with satisfaction. "Perfect timing for me to help you with your anchor run."

Izzie stared at her. "How could you possibly know about that already? *I* just found out."

"The network is one big gossip machine, Iz. You know that."

She hadn't thought it worked *that* fast. She sighed. "Look, Mother, we both know what happened last time you tried to give me advice. I need to do this on my own."

Her mother's ultrasharp gaze softened. "Izzie, you were so young. I never should have pushed you into that audition. You weren't ready."

No kidding. She winced, remembering that stiflingly hot day in L.A. as if it were yesterday. Her mother had pulled strings to get her a trial for an entertainment reporter position with a national news show at the network she'd been doing a television sitcom for at the time. Fresh out of school and nervous as hell, Izzie had been up against competition with five times her experience, and known the only reason she was in the room was because the producer was half in love with her mother.

"It was a disaster," Izzie muttered. "I completely fell apart."

"You were terrified. It was wrong of me to do that."

Had it been? Or had she just choked? Izzie cringed, remembering how she'd forgotten first one line, then another, her mother's face getting redder and redder as her daughter blew it over and over again. Until finally the producer, a sympathetic look on his face, had suggested that they call it a day.

Her jaw tightened as she remembered how silent her mother had been on the drive home. As if to say, *I knew you were the ordinary, less spectacular daughter, but did you have to embarrass me that badly?*

She wrapped her arms around herself. "I've made my way here, Mother. My career has been all me. You need to respect that."

Her mother nodded. "I respect the fact that you want to do this on your own. In fact," she lifted a brow, "I applaud that. But you need to start letting me in. I've been trying for months to make things right between us and all you keep doing is pushing me away."

Izzie gave her mother a disbelieving look as Dayla delivered the line as though she was on a set with a live audience of hundreds. How could she think a few months of sporadic attempts to connect with her daughter was going to make up for a lifetime of not caring? "You need to earn that right, Mother."

"I'm trying to. But you aren't budging an inch."

Izzie's mouth flattened. "Unlike you, I'm not good at command performances."

Her mother's frown deepened. Izzie watched her mentally check herself and pull her mouth out of its twist. Frowns were bad for business. Frowns took years off your career. "Sometimes I think you're the one who has the drama degree, Izzie."

She got pointedly to her feet. "How about Wednesday for dinner?"

Her mother nodded, halfway across the room before she tossed her parting barb. "I'll have Clara make reservations for sushi. We have to keep you in anchor shape."

Oh my God. Izzie balled her hands into fists. "I hate sushi!"

"Oh that's right…" Her mother disappeared through the double glass doors leaving devastation behind in her wake. As usual.

Izzie picked up her phone and called Jo, deciding a bottle of wine at her best friend's place superseded the need for a bath. She tossed the Messer file into her bag; she'd read it on the subway ride over to Jo's. There had to be *something* in that file that would discredit Frank Messer. Because interviewing Alex was not an option. Ever.

CHAPTER SIX

"YOU NEED TO stop looking like you're being dragged to your execution," Jo chided, pushing Izzie through the tuxedo- and ball gown-clad crowd toward the bar. "It's just an interview. Ask him to do it and get it over with."

"Easy for you to say," Izzie muttered. "You're not the one who told a half truth, then had a ridiculously hot one-night stand with the man you're supposed to be interviewing."

"Oh come on, Iz." Jo slid onto a stool at the gleaming ebony bar and lifted a brow at her. "How many scrapes did we get ourselves out of in J school? Where is your adventurous spirit?"

"This is not creative ways to explain covering a high-end escort service as our final project," Izzie retorted, sliding onto the stool beside her. "Why couldn't you have lectured me *after* Italy?"

"Then you wouldn't have had the big night with the stud." Jo's smile was ear to ear. "Which was the best thing that's ever happened to you, by the way."

Izzie made a face at her. The bartender came over, leaned his palms on the rich dark wood and gave Jo a long look. "What'll you have?"

"Two dirty martinis," Jo said with a flirtatious smile. "Heavy on the olives."

"You got it." He gave her friend one last admiring look before grabbing a shaker.

Izzie groaned. "You are something else. It's like every man in the world is programmed to love you."

Jo lifted a brow. "I send out pheromones, Iz. *Phare-o-moans*. As in I give guys a chance. You're so caught up in your 'up at six for a run, eight to eight caffeine-induced endurance race' you wouldn't know fun if it hit you in the butt."

Izzie glared at her. "That is so unfair. I have a career. I'm climbing the ladder…"

"You need some fun in your life. Desperately."

"I *do* have fun."

"You think putting purple nail polish on your toes is a walk on the wild side. I'm talking *fun*."

"Yes, well, look where all the wildness has gotten me." She'd spent the last two days trying to discredit Frank Messer in a desperate attempt *not* to do this, but the more she'd spoken with him and researched, the more credible he'd become. He'd played an awfully significant role in the creation of *Behemoth* and everyone in the industry knew it. So here she was, stuck in the vomit-inducing position of having to approach Alex at this gala event for the Met that NYC-TV was sponsoring, to ask him for the interview.

The gala was hosted in the museum's breathtaking Temple of Dendur with its exotic ambient lighting and ancient temples lit by a mystical, otherworldly glow, and the organizers had perfectly captured the spirit and ambience of ancient Egyptian times. But instead of enjoying the atmosphere, Izzie had spent the whole evening searching for Alex's tall, dark figure, her heart in her mouth.

She'd twisted back around on her stool to watch Jo bestow another high-wattage smile on the flirtatious bartender, when her friend's eyes sharpened on the crowd. "Tall, black hair, blue eyes, you said?"

Izzie froze, a fist tightening in her chest. "Yes, why, do you see him?"

"Killer body?"

"Yes," she croaked, her throat dry as the Sahara.

"This could be him. He's with another guy—blond, nerdy in a cute kinda way."

"His business partner, Mark," Izzie said weakly. She'd done her research.

A low whistle escaped her friend. "Wow, Iz. He is *smoking*."

Not helping. The crowded room seemed to close in on her as she turned ever so slowly and followed Jo's gaze. Suddenly it was terribly, impossibly hard to breathe. Alex was standing talking to the Met's PR person, not fifty feet away, the black Armani tux he wore drool-inducing on his tall, powerful frame.

She whipped her head around before he could see her, pressed clammy hands against her thighs. What was she supposed to do now? Walk up to him, say hi and unload her bombshell? She'd spent so much time trying to discredit Messer she didn't have a plan. And suddenly that seemed very stupid indeed.

"Drink," Jo said, shoving the martini at her. "A bit of liquid courage is all you need."

Alex smiled at whatever the PR woman for the Met was saying, hearing none of it. He detested the inane small talk these occasions required. Yes, she was glad Sophoros had sponsored the evening. Yes, he understood his checkbook was important to the organization's continued success. He got it. Enough.

He was tired. His temper was short. Pretty much bottom of the barrel since his lawyers had told him Frank Messer was going to be a big, huge pain in his behind. He needed to figure a way out of this mess with the least damage to Sophoros and he wasn't doing that here making small talk.

The PR person finally took the hint and moved on to

schmooze another of the sponsors. Alex shot a glance at Mark. "Ready to get out of here?"

His partner nodded. "Except you might want to check out the blonde at the bar near the fountain. She's been staring at you for a few minutes now and she's a looker."

Normally all about the blondes, Alex found himself bored by the thought. He'd been annoyingly, persistently consumed by thoughts of a particular voluptuous brunette all week. And even though he'd told himself Izzie was all wrong for him, that he didn't need a woman distracting him when being on his game was all that mattered, he couldn't get her out of his head.

Hell. He glanced in the direction Mark was looking. His partner was right. The blonde *was* stunning. The kind of leggy, sophisticated beauty he'd normally be all over. And she *was* staring at him. But it was the brunette beside her who caught his eye. Her back to him, she had the same long, thick chestnut hair and curvaceous body Izzie had. And the dress she had on was fantastic, a body-hugging number that left her back completely bare...

"Something else, isn't she?" Mark muttered.

"So is the woman beside her." His gaze sharpened on the brunette. Something in the way she held herself, in the tilt of her head, reminded him of Izzie. And now he was losing his mind, because in a city of eight million, the chances of Izzie being here were slim to none.

He was just about to turn away when the brunette twisted slightly in her seat to look at them. He stiffened, his gaze locking onto her face. *It was Izzie.* Minus the dark-rimmed glasses he'd removed before taking her to bed. He took in how the gown molded her delectable figure, her wide-eyed stare as she sat frozen on the stool. And wondered how fate had put her in his path twice in one week.

His gaze narrowed as she slid off the stool and walked quickly toward the opposite end of the ballroom. *She was running away from him?* He stared incredulously as she hightailed it through the crowd as fast as those ridiculously high shoes she was wearing allowed.

"I'll be right back," he muttered to Mark, clenching his teeth. Women didn't walk away from him. And certainly not this one.

Izzie knew the minute Alex started to follow her. It was like a centrifugal force that pulled on her steps, threatened to drag her back toward him, but she kept going, determined to face him when she had her wits about her. And that was not now.

She twisted her way through the crowd, as fast as she could go in her prize possession four-inch designer heels. Trained her gaze on the ladies' room doors.

"Izzie." It was a command, not an address. She kept walking. She was almost there, just a few more steps and—

"Izzie." Alex clamped a hand down on her shoulder and swung her around. "What are you doing?"

She swallowed hard, her high heels bringing her face-to-face with his furious glare. "I—I needed to use the ladies' room."

"At the exact moment you saw me?" The scathing disbelief in his voice made her cringe. "Try again."

Heat filled her cheeks. She shifted her weight to the other foot, her gaze dropping away from his. "Believe what you like. I need to pee."

The look on his face told her he didn't believe her for a second. But he dropped his hand and took a step back. "Fine. I'll be here." He propped himself up against the wall near the entrance to the ladies' room, arms crossed over his chest. Izzie lowered her gaze and stalked past him.

She took an extraordinarily long time while she collected herself. Debated how to approach what she had to do. When she came out, he was standing in exactly the same place, arms crossed over his chest, looking indolently, indecently gorgeous. She made an attempt at casual, but a lacing of bitterness edged her voice. "How was your flight?"

His dark brows drew together. "I had to leave, Izzie. I told you I had an emergency."

Frank Messer. She reminded herself what this night was all about. Business. Not acting like a girl. She waved a hand at him. "It's fine. I'm over it."

"Then why walk away like that?"

She shook her head. "I told you I—"

"Needed to use the washroom." He gave her a grim look. "Okay, let's try this another way." Taking her arm, he walked her toward the exit. Her pulse accelerated at the thought of being alone with him again and that was just silly, because what she should be focusing on was convincing him to do this interview.

"That was your friend Jo, I assume." He stood back while she preceded him through the French doors to the outdoor terrace, deserted except for a couple of men smoking. "She looks like a man slayer."

"The poor bartender was drooling all over her."

"She's attractive."

Izzie blinked at the understatement. "You don't think she's gorgeous?"

"I think *you're* gorgeous." He stopped at the far end of the terrace that overlooked the gardens and leaned back against the wall that separated the two, his gaze moving over her in a leisurely inspection that lingered on every curve.

"Alex," she muttered. "Stop looking at me like that."

"Why should I when you look so sensational in that dress?" A mocking glint entered his eyes. "When I saw you I thought it couldn't be you—it's such a crazy coincidence that we'd both be here."

Her cheeks heated to boiling. *Tell him now, Izzie.*

He shrugged his broad shoulders. "Then I convinced myself I must have conjured you up. I've been thinking about you, Iz. A lot…"

The world came to a grinding halt. "You have?"

"Mmm." He nodded. "I was wondering how you made out in the interview."

Oh. Her heart dropped. Of course he hadn't *really* been thinking about her.

"Izzie." His low, husky laughter wrapped itself around her. "I'm teasing you."

He stepped in close, picked up her hand and brought it to his lips, pressing an openmouthed kiss to her palm. "What are you doing?" she asked in a strangled tone.

"Checking to see if you taste as good as I remember."

Oh, God. "Alex, I—"

"Ssh—" He lifted his lips from her hand and pressed his thumb against her mouth.

Her stomach did a loop-to-loop. A wry smile curved his lips. "As hard as I try not to, all I keep thinking about is you in my bed, Iz…"

His deep, velvet tone made her heart race. Her lower lip trembled as his thumb dropped away from her mouth and he bent his head to hers. "Have you?"

"Have I what?" she asked helplessly.

"Have you thought about me?"

One last shred of self-preservation kicked in as she remembered how he'd left her in London. "I thought we agreed it was only one night."

"Does it *feel* like it's over?" he growled, dragging her closer so she could feel his heart pounding against hers.

No. No, it didn't. She braced herself as he brought his mouth firmly down on hers, staking his claim. A wild flurry of excitement at being in his arms again rushed through her. With a helpless sigh, she wound her arms around his neck and kissed him back. Just one kiss…

"I like this dress," he muttered against her lips, his hands burning into her bare skin as he swept them down her back. "Hell, Izzie, I have no self-control when it comes to you."

His words thrilled her, sent a shiver of excitement down her spine. She lost herself in the feeling of his hands on her again. The sensuous slant of his mouth as he nudged hers open and took the kiss deeper. She arched her neck, welcoming the sweep of his tongue as it slid against hers. He groaned and dragged her against the hard length of his body. Started an ache deep inside her she wanted desperately to assuage the same way they had the last time.

"Come home with me," he urged raggedly.

Her body said yes. But her brain… She yanked herself out of his arms and took an unsteady step backward. Sucked in a breath. "I have something I need to tell you…"

He frowned, running a distracted hand through his hair as his gaze tracked her. "Okay…"

She swallowed hard. "When I told you that night in London I was in communications I didn't tell you the—"

"There you two are."

She looked up, horrified, as James walked across the terrace toward them, his eyes glittering with the satisfaction of a hunter who'd cornered his prey. "You're a hard man to find, Constantinou."

Alex drew his brows together. "Do I know you?"

James stopped in front of him, sticking out his hand. "Izzie's boss, James Curry, from NYC-TV."

Alex froze. Kept his hands by his sides. "The James Curry who's been calling my office every day for a week?"

"The very same," her boss acknowledged, unperturbed. "Has Izzie gotten around to explaining what we want to do with the exclusive?"

Alex's voice was icy cold as he turned to her. "You're a reporter."

Izzie blanched, every ounce of blood in her body seeming to flee to her feet. "I was just about to explain."

Her boss's gaze swung to Izzie, then back to Alex. "Do you two know each other?"

Alex's mouth tightened. "Nice try, Curry. Wasn't half a dozen unreturned phone calls enough to convince you I'm not interested?"

Her boss shrugged. "Messer's going to kill you in the court of public opinion."

"Messer doesn't have a leg to stand on."

James lifted his shoulders. "Do you really want to take a chance on that?"

Alex's gaze flicked to Izzie, moving scathingly over her. "So you sent Isabel to *persuade* me? Don't you think that's going a bit far?"

"I thought some female persuasion might help, yes."

Izzie felt herself sink into the depths of hell. "James," she interjected, "why don't you let Alex and I finish our conversation? We can—"

"Actually," Alex interrupted, "I'd like to know…do you often ask your reporters to go to the lengths Izzie did for this story? Or was I a special case?"

Her boss frowned. "I have no idea what you're talking about."

Alex's fists clenched by his sides. "You really are scum of the earth, aren't you?" He took a step closer to James, his six-feet-plus, wide-shouldered frame dwarfing her boss's slighter one. James stood toe to toe with him, unfazed, his chin jutting out belligerently.

"What are you talk—"

"*James.*" Izzie stepped between the two men, heart pounding. "Please go inside. I'll handle this."

Her boss shook his head. "I don't think I should—"

"That's an excellent suggestion, Curry," Alex broke in, a dangerous glimmer lighting his eyes. "Why don't you follow it before I do what my fists are itching to do."

Her boss looked from Alex to Izzie and back. "I think you should ex—"

"James," Izzie broke in desperately. "Alex and I have something we need to discuss. Please go. I'll find you afterward."

Her boss gave her an uncertain look. Izzie pleaded with him with her eyes. "All right," he said finally. "Think about it, Constantinou. It's the smart thing to do."

Izzie watched him go, sucking in a deep breath. Alex looked her over, his voice so cold, it sent a shiver down her spine. "You should have been an actress like your mother," he drawled. "Your performance was utterly brilliant, Iz. I bought the naive young thing hook, line and sinker."

She shook her head. "It isn't anything like that. I was coming to track you down that day, yes, but I had no idea who you were when we got stuck in that elevator. Your receptionist said you'd left hours earlier and I was looking for Leandros, not Alex."

His lip curled. "You expect me to believe that? You forget I have a hell of a lot of experience dealing with the media. I know exactly what lengths reporters will go to for a story, although I have to admit prostituting yourself is above and beyond."

"Prostituting myself?" She stared at him, horrified. "I would never do that, Alex, I—"

"How did you manage it?" A disdainful glitter shone in his eyes. "My schedule was all over the place that day."

She shook her head, knowing this was getting way out of control. "I didn't manage anything. I went into reception, asked for *Leandros*, they told me you had gone back to the U.S. and I left. You were very closemouthed about yourself that night."

"You wonder why," he came back savagely. "So you just *happened* to get stuck in that elevator with me. Are you even afraid of them by the way?"

"Yes." She took a deep breath. "Alex, be reasonable here."

"Given what's going on in my head, I think I'm being exceedingly reasonable."

He *looked* like he wanted to put his hands around her neck and strangle her. She took a step backward. "I swear to you I had no idea who you were until I came back to work and James showed me a picture of you. Everything that happened between us was real."

"You expect me to believe *that*?" His blue eyes gleamed with leashed fury. "How much of a fool do you think I am?"

"You heard James," she said desperately. "He had no idea what you were talking about. This wasn't a setup, it was—"

"Enough." He ground the word out with such force she stopped in her tracks. She backed up until she met the hard concrete of the wall. He followed her, pinning her against it. "No more lies."

She willed herself not to flinch as he took her jaw in his hand. "What if I'd been an overweight, unattractive has-been, Iz? Would you still have had the guts to seduce me?"

She raised her chin in defiance. "I went to bed with you for exactly the reasons I told you in London."

Disbelief flared in his eyes. "What was that—oh yes, I remember now," he jeered, his gaze raking over her. "You didn't want to have any regrets. For once in your life you wanted to go after what you wanted. Well, you sure did, Iz. Too bad it was a wasted effort."

Tears stung the back of her eyes. How dare he dismantle their wildly romantic night and make it into something dirty and disgraceful. "It wasn't—"

"Tell me something, Iz." He slid his thumb across her trembling lower lip. "Did you enjoy yourself while you did your duty? Or were those little moans all an act?"

She lifted her hand to slap him, but he caught it easily in his own before she got it halfway to his face. "Save it," he bit out grimly. "I've had enough."

He took a step back, his face hard as stone. "Tell your boss he has a snowball's chance in hell of getting this story." Then he turned and strode back inside, his long, furious steps eating up the length of the terrace. She stared blindly at the entrance, at the lights and laughter of a party still in full swing. Sank back against the wall, palms sweaty, heart racing. How had it all gone so horribly wrong? How could she have predicted Alex would drag her out here and kiss her after walking out on her in London? That he would want a repeat performance of that night as much as she did?

She pressed her fingers to her lips, still stinging from the intensity of his kiss. A kiss that had thrown her off her game completely...made her believe they might have something together. *Stupid*, she berated herself. Stupid, stupid, stupid. How could she have made such a mess of this? How could Alex think she had set him up like that? *Slept with him to get an interview?* It was inconceivable.

A wave of perspiration broke out on her brow. How was she going to convince Alex it had all been a huge, crazy coincidence?

What was she going to tell her boss?

She found him inside, talking to a producer from a rival station. He blew off the conversation and cornered her in a quiet spot behind the exhibits. "What is going on, Izzie?"

She took a deep breath and squared her shoulders. "I will fix this, James."

"You sure as hell will. What in God's name was Constantinou talking about? What setup?"

Her stomach lurched. "It's complicated. He's just…misinterpreted something."

His gaze narrowed. "Misinterpreted what?"

She pressed her lips together. "This has nothing to do with work, James, we—I— It's personal."

"I can see that. When were you going to tell me you knew him?"

"He's just an acquaintance. He's misunderstood something. Give me a chance to make this right and I will."

Her boss sighed. Seemed to run out of anger. "Look, Izzie, I know you wouldn't do anything unethical. It's just not you. So whatever's going on…fix it and get that interview."

She nodded. That's exactly what she was going to do. She just had no idea *how* she was going to do it. What exactly did the odds of a "snowball's chance in hell" equate to?

CHAPTER SEVEN

ALEX COULD COUNT on one hand the times in his life he'd made a decision that went against his instincts. It had made him difficult to coach on the football field. He'd been dubbed the Rebel Quarterback for his penchant for changing a play late in the game, giving his coaches a virtual heart attack. But nine times out of ten he'd won the game. Because his instincts, his feel for the field, had always been dead-on.

But standing here, looking out at the Manhattan skyline from Sophoros's fiftieth-floor offices, he was about to act against them. After an epic battle between him and the PR team, he had conceded they had to be proactive about the way the Messer case was framed in the media. The interview with NYC-TV, his director of PR had insisted, was the perfect contained opportunity to do so. Isabel Peters was anything but a hard-edged reporter, they could play it as they liked, and the network would syndicate it across the country, allowing him then to go underground, his version of the story out there.

He blew out a long breath and pressed a hand against the glass. Laura Reed was one of the best PR people in the country. The lawyers were okay with the strategy, with certain ground rules. It was the right thing to do. Except every bone in his body was telling him not to do it. He'd spent eight years avoiding the media. Eight years avoiding any chance that some fame-seeking reporter would smell something wrong about the night his career had ended and expose his biggest mistake. And *now* he was going to jeopardize that?

His stomach twisted, contracted as though it was being put through a sieve. Laura Reed had called this a contained story. There was only one person on the planet who knew about his biggest lapse in judgment, and that person would never talk. He had to do this. Had to contain Frank Messer in the only way possible. But to give the interview to Izzie after she'd deceived him like that? It made his soul burn.

He slammed his palm against the glass. That he'd fallen into James Curry's trap so easily was downright embarrassing. How had his radar not picked up on what Izzie was? Because of course she'd been staking him out. He'd deliberately waited until the crowds were gone to get on that elevator, and she'd stood there jabbering on her phone until exactly the right moment to jump on with him.

What he wanted to know was why she hadn't asked him about the interview that night in London while she'd had the chance. Why had she waited until the charity event to ambush him? Had she been trying to soften him up first? Then make the ask?

He rubbed his hand over his face, fatigue attacking every cell of his body. If he were to be honest, the disappointment was the worst. Yes, he'd lusted after her that night as any red-blooded male would have. But it had been more than that. He'd liked Izzie. She'd seemed different from the jaded, ambitious women who filled his social circles. And when he'd seen her again that night, he couldn't stay away. Hadn't wanted to.

His mouth tightened as he looked down at the midday

traffic jamming Lexington Avenue. He'd broken his iron-clad rule not to trust another female after one night of potently good sex. Crazy, when there couldn't be a man alive who'd received such a clear demonstration of the untrustworthiness of women than him, not once but twice in his life. First with his mother, who'd walked out on his family for another man. Then with his own blind faith in the fiancée he'd been so madly in love with he hadn't seen her betrayal coming until she'd set her engagement ring down on the kitchen table and told him she was leaving him for his biggest competition—the man who'd taken his job and his dream along with it.

He would never trust a woman again. *Ever.* So why had Izzie gotten to him so?

Why did he *still* want her?

He let out a curse and levered himself away from the window. Even after everything she'd done, he still burned for her. Maybe it was the desire for revenge...maybe he just couldn't get enough. Whatever it was, it was still insistently *there*.

He walked to his desk and picked up his espresso. The plan he'd devised would rid him of both problems. He would handle Isabel Peters far more deftly than she'd tried to handle him. He would take what he wanted and walk away. And he was going to enjoy every minute of it.

A knock sounded on the door. Grace slipped in, set a pile of papers on his desk and turned her curious gaze on him. "Isabel Peters is here."

"Thanks. Show her in."

He leaned against the front of his solid wooden desk as Izzie appeared in the doorway, wearing a simple green dress that hugged her lush figure. He zeroed in on the stiff set of her face and shoulders. She was nervous. Good.

He gestured toward the sitting area by the windows. "Have a seat."

She walked past him and perched on the corner of one of the matching leather chairs. He sauntered over and sat opposite her, deliberately letting silence reign until she squirmed in her seat.

"What made you change your mind?"

"My management team thinks we need the public on our side."

"You'll do the interview then?"

He nodded. "With a few conditions."

A guarded look replaced the relieved glimmer in her eyes. "Which are?"

"We have complete control over the final edit."

"That'll never happen."

"Then you won't get the interview."

She frowned. "What else?"

"You'll be the reporter."

"James assigned the story to me. It's mine."

He sat back and crossed his arms over his chest. "That part I don't understand. The community reporter doing an investigative feature? Working your way up the ladder Hollywood-style, Iz?"

She clenched her hands in her lap, fire flashing in her dark eyes. "What's it going to take for you to believe the truth? I didn't know it was you, Alex."

"Give it up," he encouraged in a bored tone. "We're wasting time here. What I am interested in," he said deliberately, "is if you're still part of the package?"

Her face turned the exact color of his fire-engine-red Ferrari. "That was way over the line."

"Too bad," he gibed. "I'm in the driver's seat now. You *need* me."

She looked down at her hands, twisted them together in her lap. "You said a few conditions…"

He nodded. "I'm assuming you want to get started on the interview right away?"

She inclined her head.

"I have business in California this week," he drawled. "You'll need to come with me."

Her mouth fell open. "I—we—I can't do that. We can do the pre-interviews by phone."

He shook his head. "We do it in person or we don't do it at all."

She chewed on her lip, uncertainty glittering in those big brown eyes. "What's the matter?" he goaded. "You were all over me that night in London."

"That was real," she hissed. "This has to be strictly business now."

He moved his gaze leisurely over her curves in the sexy, understated dress. "Why, when we clearly mix business and pleasure so well?"

Her back went ramrod straight. "That's enough."

A slow smile stretched his lips. "I recognize ambition, Iz. I get it. I'm ruthless too. Why not scratch the itch? Get it out of our systems?"

She flashed him a heated look. "If we do this it's business."

He crossed one leg over the other in an indolent gesture. "Does your boss know we've slept together? How far you decided to take it? Or was that just because you were enjoying it and you made the call?"

She stood up. "I'm done with this conversation."

"Get your bag packed, Iz." He rolled to his feet. "We leave tomorrow morning."

"I can't do that." She gaped at him. "I have stories I'm working on."

"Hand them off," he ordered, striding over to his desk. "Grace will call you with the details. Oh," he added, sitting down in his chair. "Don't forget your bathing suit. The pool is spectacular."

Her mouth tightened. She walked out without a backward glance. He smiled and pulled a file toward him. He'd bet his Ferrari Izzie looked amazing in a bikini. He couldn't wait to find out.

CHAPTER EIGHT

SHE REALLY SHOULD get out of the sun, Izzie thought lazily, staring up at the perfect, clear blue California sky. Except after the stress of the past couple of days, heaven right now was floating on her back in Alex's infinity pool and escaping the heat.

She sighed and trailed her hands through the water. It was one of those sweat-inducing, steaming-hot summer California days that made everyone go a little crazy. So she'd done what any self-respecting native Californian would have done while Alex was in San Francisco in meetings and the ever-present tension between them was gone for a few hours. She'd headed outside to the pool, armed with a pitcher of cold lemonade and a book.

She should get out of the sun. And she would soon. It was just that the infinity pool with its gasp-inducing, hundred-foot drop to the Pacific was like teetering on the edge of heaven. In fact, everything about Alex's excessively private Spanish-style home perched over the wildly beautiful golden beaches of Malibu was heavenly. Acres of tropical gardens swamped the grounds with color, its expansive outdoor living spaces encouraging one to spend all their time outside. And then there was the house, with the works of the great Impressionists on the walls.

She flicked her hand through the water and sent an arc

of diamond-shaped drops through the air. It was a privileged, luxurious slice of paradise, as elusive to most as the man she'd been interviewing all week. Four days into their stay, three days into their background interviews, and she still knew so little about the man behind the trophies she was afraid to pick up James's calls. That night in London hadn't been an outlier. Alex didn't talk about himself. Had given one-line answers to every question she'd asked and nothing more.

She shut her eyes against the blinding rays of the sun, sweat dripping down her forehead and beneath her lashes. Alex was hosting a party for business associates tomorrow, after which she was headed back to New York, with or without the story. Which meant today she had to get him to talk. A near impossible task when your interview subject had zero trust in you.

She waved her arms and pushed herself back to the center of the pool. She'd done everything she could to convince Alex she was telling the truth but it was like talking to a wall. The man she'd met in London was gone. And the aloof stranger who'd replaced him unnerved her. So did the ever-present heat between them. He might hate her for what she'd done, but he still wanted her. That hadn't gone away. It'd made her flee dinner on the intimate little terrace last night like a woman possessed.

Twenty-four hours, she told herself. Twenty-four hours and she'd be out of danger. But she needed him to talk first.

"You researching cloud formations?"

The sardonic observation from a deep, amused male voice had her yanking herself upright and feeling for the bottom. But the water was too deep and she plunged, her arms and legs flailing. Kicking back to the surface, she pulled in a breath, coughing and sputtering.

"Do you always sneak up on people like that?"

"I thought you said you were a champion swimmer..."

"That doesn't help when you scare the life out of me." She pushed her soaking hair out of her face and took in yet another of the gorgeous designer suits that molded every lean muscle of his body into a work of art.

His gaze slid over her. She'd put her minuscule bikini on while he was out. *What had possessed her to do that?*

He shrugged out of his jacket and threw it on a lounger. "Don't you have piles of research to do? Five miles to run? Fifty laps to swim?"

She eyed him. "You're one to talk. You never stay still either."

"Yes, but I do know how to relax." He sank down on his haunches beside the edge of the pool. "This," he said, nodding his head toward her, "gives me hope for the control freak in you."

"I am not a control freak."

"Sure you are." He whipped off his tie and threw it on top of his jacket. "You even eat with everything perfectly segmented. Meat first, potatoes next, vegetables last."

Her cheeks, already warm from the heat of the sun, got about five degrees hotter. "That's because I like the vegetables the least. That doesn't equal a control freak."

"Says a lot about a person." His gaze sharpened on her. "In London, you said you've always been afraid of things blowing up in your face." He tipped his head to one side. "What are you afraid of now, Izzie? That you'll give in to this heat between us?"

Yes, she thought desperately. She pulled her gaze resolutely away from his. "I was just about to get out. Can we start early then? We have a lot of ground to cover."

"Sure." He held out a hand.

She shook her head. "I'll get out in a sec. You go change first."

He gave her a thoughtful look. "You don't want to get out of the pool in that bikini, do you?"

Damn right she didn't.

"Coward," he mocked. "I've seen you naked. What's a bikini?"

She surveyed the distance between her and the stairs at the other end of the pool.

"You'll never make it."

She looked back at him. He was *laughing* at her. "Okay, you've had your fun. Go inside, change and we'll meet back here."

"Nicely asked but no. I can't leave you unattended in the pool. I could be sued if anything happens to you."

"That's ridiculous," she sputtered. "I've been out here for ho—"

He grabbed her arm and hauled her dripping up onto the pool deck. "Problem solved."

Problem started. Heat flared between them, her soaking-wet body dripping all over his designer suit as he kept a firm grip on her wrist. "Alex—"

"All week you've been sending out these mixed signals, Iz." He released her wrist to slide a hand around her waist and pull her closer. "Which is it—you want me or you don't?"

"Don't." She pressed a hand hard against his chest and shoved him away. "You are the most egocentric—" She stopped in her tracks as he rocked back on his heels to steady himself, sidestepped to keep his balance, missed the concrete entirely and fell into the pool.

Her hands flew to her mouth as he came to the surface, biting out some choice swear words. "Oh my God, I'm so sorry, I didn't mean to do that."

He swiped the water from his face, slicking his dark hair back. "Somehow I find that hard to believe."

She shoved her hands on her hips. "It's your fault. I'm trying to keep things business between us…"

"Liar," he muttered, wading toward the steps, his wet

clothes weighing him down. "You've been wondering as much as I have what it would be like to do it again."

"Doesn't mean I'm going to," she growled. She picked up her towel, threw it on the pool deck for him and stalked inside past the flabbergasted-looking housekeeper who was standing with a tray of drinks in her hands watching Alex climb out of the pool.

A much calmer, pulled-together Izzie returned to the terrace ten minutes later, showered and composed. Alex had changed into a similar outfit to hers—shorts and a T-shirt that did a whole lot for his tanned, muscular legs and washboard abs. She resolutely removed her gaze from him. *No more mixed signals.* "Ready?"

He nodded and led the way down the steep set of stairs to the beach. She'd suggested a walk instead of their usual session on the terrace, thinking maybe if she wasn't sitting across from him with a pad of paper and a tape recorder, he'd open up.

At the bottom of the old wooden stairs, she kicked off her shoes and sank her toes into the sand. Alex did the same and they started walking.

"Did you manage to meet your dad for lunch?"

She nodded.

"How is he?"

"He's…fine. Better than I've seen him for a while."

"Did he ever find someone else? After your mother left?"

She shook her head. "I wish he would."

"Why do you think he hasn't?"

"I think he's still in love with my mother."

"After all this time?"

"Crazy, huh?"

His gaze sharpened on her face. "You think he's a fool?"

She threw him a sideways look. "She destroyed him when she walked out. She never deserved him. So yes, I do."

Her sweet, loving father had worshipped the ground her mother had walked on. He'd been doing the music for one of her films when they'd met and fallen head over heels for the beautiful, charismatic actress. Unfortunately, he'd idealized her as the silver screen legend she was rather than the flawed woman he'd married. Had never wanted to see how unhappy she was with small-town life in Palo Alto until the day she'd walked out the door. Her stomach twisted. The sight of their father falling apart wasn't one two teenage girls should have had to deal with. And yet they had.

"The blame is rarely one-sided." Alex kicked a sharp seashell out of the way, the still-scorching hot sun pouring down on them. "Marry two people long enough and they'll find a way to hate each other."

"Wow. I thought I was cynical."

"If you've done your homework you'll know my parents' marriage was disastrous."

She had. Knew Hristo and Adelphe Constantinou had separated when Alex was a teenager and his mother had married another very rich man in a scandal that had rocked New York society.

"It was not a nice divorce," she commented.

"It was not. Are we on the record now?"

"Yes."

She watched the now-familiar shield come down over his face, wiping his expression clean of emotion. As it did every time things turned personal.

"Tell me about your relationship with your father."

"That has nothing to do with this story."

"I disagree." She shot him a sideways look. "You need

to start talking to me, Alex, or we'll go with Messer's story and leave you out."

He lifted his shoulders. "That might be tough when your boss wants my story, not Messer's."

True. But he still needed to talk. She pressed her lips together. "I get that your PR person wants you to stay on message. But you have to give me something. You know we want to highlight your football background and for that I need to understand your beginnings."

A frown creased his brow. "My father was a workaholic who spent every waking hour of his life building C-Star Shipping. He didn't care about anyone or anything that didn't involve his company. End of story."

Ouch. So the rumors about Alex and Hristo Constanti-nou's relationship were true. "What caused the falling-out between you and your father?"

"We had a philosophical disagreement about whether or not I would run C-Star Shipping," he said flatly. "We parted ways after that."

"What do you mean, parted ways?"

His expression went from blank to ice-cold. "I mean we parted ways."

The rumor was that Hristo had disowned him. She'd thought it was just some crazy angle the press had blown up, but apparently it was true. Wow. She was speechless for a moment, the black-and-white of it all blowing her away. When she'd been a teenager, she would have died for the talent and charisma to follow in her mother's footsteps. The heir apparent to run C-Star Shipping, Alex had chosen to follow his own path and his father had disowned him for it. It was as though you couldn't win no matter what you did. Or maybe that was just when you had megalomaniac parents like theirs? Hristo Constantinou was an autocrat who ruled his empire with an iron fist. Had Alex's insub-ordination simply been too much for him to take?

"What did your mother think of all this? Didn't she have any say in it?"

"She was out of the picture by then. She'd married Jack Sinclair and my father never gave her any true power in the company despite all the family money she sank into it."

"What about your sisters? Why couldn't they have taken the reins?"

His mouth curled. "My father would never have put a woman at the helm."

"What are they like, your sisters?" She asked the question more out of curiosity than a need to know.

His face took on a decidedly softer edge. "They're all completely different. Agape, whose dress you wore, she's the oldest, an event planner in New York. Bubbly, always talking too much. Gabby is a librarian, has middle-child syndrome. Always trying to please everyone. And Arty—" his mouth curved as Izzie gave him a curious look "—short for Artemis, and yes my mother really called her that, and yes we teased her about it and called her a goddess her entire life, is finishing up her final year at law school. Whip smart."

She smiled. "They sound completely different. Which one are you closest to?"

He shrugged. "All of them, really. They came to live with me when I turned pro. Agape and I are the most alike, I guess."

"Agape is the one coming tomorrow night?"

"Yes. She helped me plan the party."

Which reminded her that her time to get him to talk was running out. She dug in. "Back to Frank Messer then. You've said Mark created *Behemoth*. Messer claims he did. How do you reconcile that?"

"Developing a game like *Behemoth* involves hundreds of people. Come take a tour of our development facility. It's mind-boggling how much work goes into a title. For *years*. Messer played a key role, yes, but so did dozens of other designers. The platform, the *starting point*, was Mark's vision. The patents rightfully belong to Sophoros."

"Then why did you pay him off?"

He scowled. "We were rewarding him for everything he'd put into the company. He deserved it for his tenure."

"He says you took unfair advantage of him. Bullied him into it."

"Funny he should be saying that now when the game is a raging success." Sarcasm dripped from his voice. "He was fine enough with the money before."

"He says he has proof *he* created the platform."

"Then let him bring it forward. It doesn't exist."

Fine. She was starting to get that feeling the more unforthcoming Messer became on that point. She took a deep breath. "I need to ask you about the night your career ended."

A wary expression slid over his face. "What's there to ask? I came back too soon, tore my rotator cuff and it was over."

She bit down on her lip. Forced herself to go on. "I talked to your coach, Brian Sellers. And to Dr. Forsyth. They both said you weren't supposed to play that night, Alex. Dr. Forsyth had given you strict orders to stay on the bench for at least another month. And Sellers had backed him up."

His jaw tightened. "I felt fine so I decided to play."

She struggled to keep up with him as his strides lengthened. "But why would you do that? You'd told Coach Sellers you weren't going to play. Why risk your career?"

He stopped in his tracks, the hint of a storm brewing in his blue eyes. "I thought I was fine. I made a mistake. That's all there is to it."

She pressed sweaty palms to her thighs, telling herself to just get it over with. "But Gerry Thompson was already starting. You didn't have to go out there. Surely your career was more important than one game?"

"What the hell would you know about it?" he roared, his sudden explosion making her take a step back in the sand. His eyes blazed, skin stretched taut across his cheekbones. "How could you have any idea about the pressure I was under? About what I was risking by *not* playing? The media—*you*," he said, pointing a finger at her, "you wanted my head on a platter."

Izzie's heart was pounding as if it were going to jump out of her chest, but she pressed on. "You needed to prove to your father you could be a success. You played because failure was not an option."

"I didn't care what the hell my father thought," he ground out. "*Christós,* Izzie, have you listened to a word I've said? I thought I was fine so I played. That's it."

"I know about the illegal painkillers." She forced the words past her constricted throat. "I know you had someone supply you with a street-level narcotic that allowed you to play that night…that allowed you to mask your injury. That there were some who worried you might have become…*dependent* on it."

His tanned face turned ashen. "Who told you that?"

"I can't reveal my source."

He stood there utterly silent, feet spread apart, fists clenched at his sides, the absolute devastation on his face shaking her to the core. But it was nothing compared to the look of white-hot rage that was spreading across it now, making her breath catch in her throat, making her take another step backward.

When he finally spoke, it was in a voice so lethally quiet she had to strain to hear it over the crash of the waves.

"We are done with this conversation. I will answer the question about why I played on camera next week, at which time I'll give the answer I just did. And that will be the last

time it's mentioned, *ever*, or this story will not happen."
He trained his gaze on her face. *"Do you understand?"*

She nodded, hands, knees, everything shaking as he
stalked down the beach away from her. Her brain spun.
How could one night have possibly been more important
than an entire golden career? Brian Sellers had charac-
terized Alex as a man who'd never taken an unsure step
in his life. So what had happened that night to push him
over the edge? To make him play when there was no way
he should have ever taken a step onto that field?

CHAPTER NINE

THIRTY LAPS OF his fifty-metre pool was generally pretty cathartic for Alex. But after spending the last twenty-four hours ruminating over yesterday's conversation with Izzie and facing demons he'd thought long ago put to bed, it wasn't having the desired effect.

Biceps crying out from the vicious workout, he stepped out of the shower, toweled himself off and stalked into the bedroom where he rifled through his closet for his tuxedo shirt. He should have listened to his instincts and never agreed to do the interview. Because those questions Izzie had asked yesterday, the pieces of his past she was digging up, were nobody's business but his own. She and James Curry were clearly taking this interview in a whole different direction from what they'd agreed upon, and the private life he'd guarded so closely for so long was in danger of being blown wide open by a woman he had severely conflicting feelings about.

He jammed his hand against the closet door, dropped his head and let out a string of curses. *How had Izzie found out about the illegal painkillers?* The only person who knew he'd taken them was his former teammate, Xavier Jones. And Xavier wouldn't have talked to a reporter. No way.

But then again, he thought, agitation rocketing through him, what did it really matter now? His football career was history. He'd paid for his mistake in the worst way possible. And he'd moved on. He didn't *need* football anymore.

So why did he feel gutted? As if someone had sliced him wide open? *Because the only thing worse than reliving it all over*, a little voice in his head said, *would be to be made into a pity party all over again*. To have the whole world know his shame. He'd worked too hard building Sophoros into an international powerhouse to let the media make a tragedy of him a second time. To overshadow everything he'd done since.

He would not let it happen. *Could not*.

He yanked his shirt out of the closet, found some boxers, and pulled them on. He would do exactly as he'd said. He'd do this interview, he'd draw the lines, then he'd never talk about it again. No one could prove anything. And as for Izzie? He grimaced as he did up the finicky little pearl buttons on the shirt. He was at a loss. Ever since she'd walked into his life, she'd been driving him slowly, surely mad. And it wasn't getting any better. When he should be thinking about Frank Messer and the case his lawyers were mounting against him, he was wondering instead how to get her into bed. How to satisfy the craving in him that ached for another taste of her.

His shirt finally done up, he located his tuxedo trousers, pulled them on and went searching for his bow tie. He should hate Izzie for setting him up. For digging into his painful past. But the satisfaction of harboring that against her was being called into question after the conversation he'd had with Laura Reed this morning. He and his head of PR had been covering some items that couldn't wait until he was back in New York when Laura's tone had changed into that serious, "you need to listen to me" one she reserved for the most important points. "Alex," she'd censured. "I met James Curry at an industry breakfast this morning. He asked me what the deal was with you.

Said you tore into him at the Met fund-raiser about him setting you up…and he still couldn't figure out what you were talking about."

"The guy's an underhanded son of a bitch," he'd replied. "Let's leave it at that."

"He's an important son of a bitch," Laura had reminded him drily. "He's the news director at one of New York's most influential television stations. You want him on your side. I don't know what issue you have with him, but he's a straight shooter, Alex. In my ten years of working with him I've never seen him do anything unethical. Set anyone up. So whatever you're thinking, you're wrong. Kiss and make up and play nice."

He'd muttered something to pacify her, then moved on. But the conversation had been playing over in his head ever since. Izzie had steadfastly stuck to her story that their meeting in the elevator had been a coincidence. His receptionist in London had confirmed she'd lied to Izzie about his whereabouts to get rid of her per his standing instructions to do so. Which left him wondering if maybe their elevator meeting *had* just been a bizarre coincidence.

He located his shoes and jammed his feet into them without care for the supple Italian leather. Izzie was up for a big promotion at NYC-TV. It explained why she'd been so desperate to land this story on Sophoros. And made the heavy weight sitting in his chest sink even deeper. *What if his paranoia about the media had led him to a completely wrong judgment of Izzie?* What if she *was* the woman he'd thought he'd met that night in London? And if she was, what did that mean?

His mind buzzing, he recalled the look of complete incomprehension on Curry's face that night at the Met when he'd accused him of setting him up. Izzie's frantic attempts to hide the fact that they'd slept together. *Curry hadn't known.*

He picked up his watch and strapped it around his wrist. Had that night in London been so intense, so real for him that he'd been willing to believe the worst about Izzie to avoid making the same mistake twice? A search for any reason not to fall for another woman as hard as he had Jess?

He glanced at the clock and gave his head a shake. He had a black-tie party for a hundred people to get through on a night when he'd rather do anything but. But his bigger problem by far was Isabel Peters. And what the hell he was going to do with her.

If there was anything she *should* be good at, it was the fine art of negotiating a cocktail party. Izzie plucked a glass of champagne off a passing waiter's tray and perched herself against a tree in the lantern-lit gardens of Alex's Malibu hideaway. Years of reluctantly attending her mother's premieres and engagements, not to mention the local events the station sponsored, *should* make this all second nature to her. Instead she tended to feel like a fish out of water, always the gauche, awkward daughter of Dayla St. James who did not thrive in the spotlight.

She took a sip of the bubbly, dry vintage, taking in Agape's party planning genius. Alex's sister had done an amazing job transforming the pool and garden area into a lush, exotic oasis—as if you'd entered the Garden of Eden on a particularly electric, sensual night. Flaming torches glowed around the outskirts of the gardens, and floral-shaped candles floated on the pool, casting a muted glow across its surface. And the breezy, lazy music coming from the hip-looking DJ in the corner was typical laid-back California cool.

She frowned. She might actually have enjoyed a party for a change if she weren't wound so tight she felt as though she was going to snap in half. Her confrontation with Alex yesterday had left her shaken—utterly unsure what to do.

She had the true story about what had happened on the last night of his career. At least *most* of it. Had an explosive angle that would ensure a headline story. But she wasn't sure she could do it. Wasn't sure she could blow Alex's life apart like that.

Letting out a long breath, she leaned back against the pillar and scanned the crowd for him. Long, lean and outrageously handsome in a perfectly tailored tux, he was chatting with a group of people in the center of the buzzing, affluent crowd that, according to Agape, consisted of everything from film directors to financiers to every type of entertainment industry professional in between.

She studied the tension written across his strongly carved features. Brooding, tunnel-visioned since their confrontation yesterday, he'd avoided her completely. And she wondered why she just couldn't stay immune to him. Why her pulse, even now, raced in a zigzag of confusion.

What was it about a brooding, fabulously good-looking man that made you want him to turn all that intensity on you? Even if you knew it was a *bad, bad* idea?

He turned his head, their gazes meeting and holding. Her breath caught in her throat as an emotion other than anger flickered in his eyes. Desire? Confusion? She'd been expecting hatred. Antagonism. Not this.

Her mouth went dry as he worked his way down over the sexy spaghetti-strap dress she'd bought in Malibu today to fit the occasion. To catch his attention if she was honest. And why do that? Why play with fire *now,* when she was so close to escape?

She swallowed hard. It was *irresistible.*

He moved the heated intensity of his gaze back up to her face. Electricity arced between them, along with thoughts of a career-ending variety. How much damage would one more night do if no one ever knew? And how could she even be *thinking* that, now of all times?

And then it came to her. What she should have known from the beginning…she had never been nor would she ever be objective when it came to Alex Constantinou. She could not turn his personal tragedy into the most-watched interview of the year. Whatever had made him play that night, take those drugs, it didn't belong in her story. It didn't belong in anyone's story.

Someone grabbed a hold of Alex's arm and commanded his attention. She exhaled a long, shaky breath. And suddenly knew exactly what she was going to do. She was going to bury the information. Tell James he was going to have to go with a different angle. And in doing so throw away her best chance at landing this anchor job. At making her career.

Her trembling fingers bit into her glass to keep it from falling to the ground. A cold knot formed in her stomach. She was risking her job. Her vow to tell the truth no matter what. For a man who thought she was a cold-hearted opportunist. *Nice one, Izzie.*

She made it through the next couple of hours in a muted haze as the party wound down and the crowd began thinning out. Agape was witty and charming and they hit it off. Debated the merits of some of the eligible men in the crowd. She was at her side when the last few guests made their way toward the driveway and Agape declared herself done.

"Walk me out?" she said to Izzie. "We'll have to do drinks when we're back in New York."

She said goodbye to Agape. Found herself standing beside Alex as he waved her off and finished chatting with the last remaining guest, the CEO of an offshore drilling company that operated off the coast of California. The sideways look he gave her as the taillights of Agape's bright red convertible zigzagged down the driveway had her stepping backward.

The weight of his hand came down on her shoulder. "Don't even think about it," he muttered under his breath. She stood there while he shook the CEO's hand, her heartbeat accelerating in a painful mixture of fear and anticipation. The tall Southerner clapped Alex on the back, folded himself into his sports car and drove off.

She cleared her throat. "Alex, I'm really tired. Maybe we can—"

He squared to face her. "If you don't think we're settling this tonight, you *are seriously* deluded, Izzie."

Her breath caught in her throat. The heat of his palm burned into the bare skin of her shoulder as he marched her toward the house.

"Stay put," he instructed, when they reached the legions of catering staff packing up in the pool area. He disappeared, then came back with a bottle of champagne and two glasses. Her heart beat like a snare drum as he propelled her toward the back of the house.

"Where are we going?"

He gave her a sideways look. "I thought you'd prefer doing this in private rather than broadcasting it to every gossip magazine in L.A."

Good point. She picked up her pace to keep up as he turned the corner of the house and headed for the terrace off his master suite. The sheer drop to the Pacific was gobsmackingly gorgeous. Her stomach felt as though it was going down along with it.

Alex deposited the bottle and glasses on the table and stripped off his jacket. The lump in her stomach increased to the size of a grapefruit. He shot her a sideways look. "Why don't you open the champagne?"

His quietly spoken words struck her as glaringly symbolic. She went completely still, studying the expression on his face. Searching for the softening she'd seen earlier.

"I know you didn't set me up, Izzie."

Her eyes widened. "How?"

"I talked to Laura Reed this morning and she gave me an earful. Said James was the type who plays by the rules. That setting me up wasn't something he would do."

"But you didn't believe that before," she said slowly. "Why now?"

He shrugged and loosened his tie. "I'm a little—a lot," he corrected, "paranoid about the media. They've made my life hell with their lies and speculation. And sometimes I get a little crazy about it." He pulled off the tie and slung it over a chair. "After I talked to Laura, I remembered how desperately you tried to get James to leave that night at the Met, and I realized he had no idea about us. Then my rational brain finally kicked in. It isn't you, Izzie."

She caught her lip between her teeth. "You really believe me?"

"Yes."

Bewildered, she let it sink in. Felt a warm feeling spread through her, relief mixed with something else. It had *killed* her to think he believed her capable of that after what they'd shared. She swallowed hard and lifted her gaze to his. "I'm giving up the story."

His brows pulled together. "Why?"

"I'm not objective about you, Alex, I never have been."

His mouth twisted. "You've been doing a pretty good job of giving Frank Messer a fair shake."

She shook her head. "It's not that. I— I'm burying the information about the illegal drugs. You don't need to worry about it."

He stared at her. "Why?"

Because I fell for you so hard that night in London I can't see straight. She lifted her chin and said instead, "Because I can't do that to you."

"You're up for a promotion. You need this story."

She shrugged. "Some things in life are more important than a story."

"Your boss would disagree."

Her stomach twisted. "He would disagree with just about everything I've done thus far. I think I have a bit of soul-searching to do."

He undid his cuff and rolled it back. "An anchor job is going to be a hell of a lot of pressure, Izzie. Cutthroat competition."

"You did it, being a quarterback."

"I thrive on pressure. It's in my DNA. I don't think you're built like that."

No, she wasn't. What she loved was working in the community every day, telling people's stories. But an anchor job was a once-in-a-lifetime opportunity. And a lot could be done to better the community from that position as well. Maybe more.

She absorbed the roar of the Pacific beneath them. Suddenly everything seemed very, very out of control.

She reached for the champagne, pulled the foil off and worked the cork out with shaking fingers. Amber liquid sloshed over the side of the glass as she poured.

"Izzie." Alex moved behind her and pried the bottle from her fingers. "What's going on?"

Inhaling deeply, she breathed in the sexy, spicy smell of him, the undertone of musky male that was all Alex. And knew she hadn't truly thought of anything but being back in his arms for weeks.

He turned her around. Watched her with that all-seeing gaze of his until she shook her head and gave him an uncertain smile. "Do you know what's funny? I promised myself I would never, *ever* let a man get in the way of my career. And now not only am I doing that," she said, her voice holding more than a trace of irony, "but I'm doing it at the most important moment of my career."

He reached up and ran his thumb across her cheek. "Don't you know control is a myth? None of us are in control of anything, Iz. Not over that elevator we were in and not over this thing between you and me."

His words hit her with soul-destroying precision. Knocked down every last barrier she had. Because he was right. And believing any less made a mockery of the promise she'd made to herself that night in London.

She tipped her head back to look up at him, the fog in her brain clearing. "We still have the issue that I'm a reporter and you hate them."

"I'm willing to suspend judgment on that." He dragged his thumb down over the soft skin of her throat to the throbbing pulse at the base of her neck. "Because this particular reporter," he said softly, "I like very much."

"Alex—" She pressed a hand against his chest. "That night in London the rules were clear-cut. We said it was one night and I— I could handle that. But this—" she shook her head "—I'm pretty sure I'm out of my league right about now…"

He reached up and laced his fingers through the hand she had pressed against his chest. "I'm pretty sure I am too."

She stared at him. "What do you mean?"

He released her hand and drew her to him. She pulled in a shaky breath as he cupped her face in his palm. "I told myself I shouldn't touch you that night in London because I knew with you it was going to be different. That I wasn't going to be able to walk away afterward like I always do."

"But you did."

He nodded. "That morning when I left, I was *running*, Iz. I thought if I ran fast enough I could ignore what I was feeling. But it didn't work. I almost picked up the phone a dozen times before I saw you that night at the Met."

She tried to keep her wits about her as he slid a hand

into her hair and tipped her head back. "How about we start over?" he suggested softly, this stripped-down, open version of Alex doing crazy things to her common sense. "A blank slate. No expiration dates. No rules. And see where it goes."

It was…crazily, frantically tempting. "But you don't do 'let's see where this goes.'"

"I don't have a choice with you," he admitted huskily, lowering his head until his mouth brushed against hers. "I think that's pretty clear."

For the second time in little more than two weeks Izzie Peters went with her gut and made a massive decision with major repercussions. But this time she was hoping it was going to last more than one night.

She lifted up on tiptoes, swayed into him and let him take her mouth in a hot, sensuous kiss that pulled her into a deep, dark vortex she never wanted to emerge from. She reached up and cupped his jaw with her fingertips, her lips clinging to his as he changed angles, tasted her as if he couldn't get enough.

And when that wasn't enough, she indulged her need to touch the rock-hard body that had been far too temptingly on display this past week. Sank her fingertips into the hard, thick muscles of his shoulders. Slid them down over his pecs, those washboard abs.

Alex groaned. Dragged her closer. "Izzie," he said thickly, "let me take you to bed."

She tipped her head back to look up at him. "Yes," she agreed, the smoky, seductive tone of her voice sounding completely foreign to her.

Fire burned in his eyes. He picked her up and carried her inside, striding through the sitting room and into the bedroom. "One second," he murmured, setting her down on the huge king-size bed. He disappeared, then came back with the champagne bottle.

"I *really* don't need any of that," she said, pressing damp palms against her thighs as she knelt on the bed in front of him.

"Who said we were going to drink it?"

Heat raced to her cheeks. Her body trembled like a violin. She was *so* not prepared for this. She gulped in a breath as he set the bottle on the floor beside the bed and sank his knee down between her thighs. Then moved her fingers to the buttons of his shirt. "Take it off," he invited, his voice dropping to that of a sensually charged invitation. "And I'll show you."

She followed his command, doing only a marginally better job than she had that night in London, but finally it was off, exposing his magnificent abs. Her heart skittered in her chest as he leaned down and took her mouth in a slow, hard kiss, a vision of him as a conquering lord flashing through her head as he arched her neck back and showed no mercy. Except this wasn't one of her paperback novels…this was full-on reality.

His teeth nipped at her bottom lip, demanding entry at the same time he slid his palms down over the small of her back, over her hips and thighs, then brought them back up, sliding underneath her dress to close over the rounded curve of her bare bottom.

"Theos." He lifted his gaze to hers, color staining his cheekbones. "I spent the whole night wondering if you were wearing anything under this."

"I couldn't."

His hands tightened on her hips, lifted her so she was straddling him. She shivered as he settled her against his hard erection, her brain shutting down completely. The need to move against him, to press her sensitized flesh against the hard ridge of him, was undeniable. He felt amazing.

"Izzie," he said hoarsely, "you need to stop that or this is going to happen way too fast."

But she was drunk on how he was making her feel, how she was making *him* feel, and she didn't want to slow down. She wanted fast, wanted to ride the tidal wave of lust sweeping her forward. Sliding back, she moved her hands to his belt and yanked it open. His swift intake of breath as she undid the button of his pants and slid the zipper down emboldened her. His curse as her fingers brushed against the hard length of him made her smile.

She reached into his boxers and freed him. *"Izzie,"* he groaned. "You need to be ready for me. I'm too big for you to—"

She put her fingers to his mouth. "Shut up."

His eyes darkened to that deep cobalt-blue she could drown herself in. He sat back, braced his arms on the bed and watched as she lifted her dress and brought the aroused, hard length of him against her hot, aching flesh. *God.* She closed her eyes. He was so big. How exactly was she going to accomplish this?

Alex caught her hand in his, brought it to his mouth and pressed a kiss against her palm. Her eyes fluttered open, telegraphed her fear. His lips curved in a tortured smile. "Slowly, sweetheart. Take me slowly and it'll be fine."

The fact that Izzie had never been in love before didn't stop her from thinking she might be falling madly in love with Alex rather than just *seeing where this went,* such was the soul-destroying tenderness of that gesture. Taking a deep breath, refusing to go *there*, she reached down and guided him inside her, taking him inch by inch as she'd done before. But in this position, he felt bigger, thicker. And the sensation as she sank down on him was incredible.

She let out a sigh of pleasure. He gave her a strained look. "Good?"

She nodded, finding it almost unbearably intimate to be joined with him like this while he watched her with a heavy-lidded desire that made her insides quiver. Squeezing her eyes shut, she started to move, rotate her hips, taking him deep inside her, then shallower, establishing a rhythm that made him groan. He caught her chin in his fingers. "Look at me, Iz. I want to see your face."

She did. Because something in him grounded her. Always had. She let the heat, the focus in his gaze as she rode him, excite her unbearably. Make her experiment. The thick muscles of his biceps flexed against the bed. "*Theos,*" he bit out in a raw voice. "You feel so good...I'm not sure how long I can stand this."

"Let go," she whispered. Rode him harder, faster, until his breath was coming in short, shallow spurts and his dark lashes swept down over his eyes. She wanted to make him come apart for her. To feel that control. She pressed down on him hard, taking him even deeper inside of her, the friction as she took him again and again so delicious she was getting close...so close...

"Izzie," he groaned, his hips driving up into her now, setting the pace. "I need to— I can't—"

She sank her fingers into the hard muscles of his shoulders, felt his body swell inside her, shake against her, come apart, his face dropping into the curve of her neck. She held him to her, reveling in how uncontrolled, how complete his release was.

His ragged breathing slowed. He pushed back so he could see her face. "That wasn't how it was supposed to be," he growled, a dark frown slanting its way across his face. "I don't lose control like that."

She bit her lip, dropped her gaze to the dark hair dusting his chest. "I wanted it to be good for you."

He tipped her chin up with his fingers. "You were incredible," he assured her, a gravelly edge to his voice. "You were close?"

She nodded.

He slid his fingers under the straps of her dress and

pushed it off her shoulders with a deliberate movement. "Then let's get things back on course."

Her heart galloped like a high-strung racehorse anticipating extreme excitement. He moved his hands to her thighs and urged her up onto her knees. "Put your hands over your head," he ordered. She obeyed and he yanked her dress off, leaving her clad only in her lacy bra.

He set his palm to her chest and pushed, sending her back into the duvet with a soft *swoosh*. Then he picked up the bottle.

A protest rose in her throat. He wasn't actually going to—

"You're going to ruin your duvet," she breathed as he straddled her, bottle in hand.

"To hell with the duvet," he murmured, tipping the bottle upside down and spilling the amber liquid over her heated flesh. "I always thought Cristal couldn't get any better, but this might change my mind."

"Alex," she protested, raising herself up on her elbows. "I don't think—"

He pushed her back down with a flick of his wrist. "Relax."

Oh. Her stomach churned with anticipation as he put his lips to the curve of her breast where the champagne trail began. Took a lace-covered, champagne-soaked nipple into his mouth and sucked deeply. Her insides twisted, heat flaring in the moist, aroused part of her that had been left unfinished. He lavished the same pleasure on her other breast, driving her higher, making her squirm against the whisper-soft down beneath her.

She bolted upward as he pressed his mouth against the trembling skin of her stomach. "I've never—"

His mouth stilled on her inflamed skin. "Don't tell me that selfish boyfriend of yours didn't indulge you in this either."

She shook her head. He pressed a kiss against the tense muscles of her abdomen. "You are so beautiful, Iz. I want to see, taste every part of you…"

She melted. Completely. Released her anxious grip on her muscles, let him part her thighs and arrange her to his satisfaction…follow the trail of liquid downward to her most sensitive flesh. "Oh," she gasped as he parted her, tasted her, the act so soul-baringly intimate she dug her fingers into the bedding and squeezed her eyes shut. But then the hypersensitivity turned to white-hot pleasure as his tongue began a slow, hot torture that made her hips buck off the bed.

"Easy." He held her down with firm hands as he pleasured her with long, slow strokes of his tongue.

"I can't…I don't—*oh*—" Digging her nails harder into the sheets, she willed herself to accept the pleasure he was offering her. But she was too far gone and when his tongue moved against the hard nub that was the center of her pleasure, she couldn't take any more.

"Alex, please—"

"Shh." He slid a hand under her bottom and lifted her to him. "I know."

And then he was sliding a long finger inside her, stroking deep, adding a whole new layer to her pleasure, and she was jerking in to his hands, begging him to give her release. He did, the magic slide of his fingers tipping her over the edge into an orgasm so intense her entire body shook, her head flinging back against the pillows.

Shivers snaking through her, feeling as though she'd been hit by a ten-ton truck, she lay there trying to catch her breath. Alex slid up her body, rested his elbows on either side of her and ran a finger down her cheek.

"You are full of surprises, Isabel Peters," he drawled softly.

Her cheeks heated fifty shades of red. "You don't do so badly yourself."

He dug his hands under her and scooped her up into his arms and carried her to the en suite bathroom. "We need to shower this off you or you'll be a sticky mess."

We?

He flicked on the taps, ran the water hot and pulled her into the huge walk-in shower with him. She closed her eyes as he washed her with an erotic thoroughness that made her want him all over again. Then he carried her back to his bed and made her wish come true.

Izzie let her head drift to his shoulder, absorbing the feeling of rightness she always felt with this man. How utterly complete and protected he made her feel.

Tomorrow she might wonder if she'd made a huge mistake. Tonight, she didn't care.

CHAPTER TEN

THREE THOUGHTS OCCURRED to Izzie as she woke up in Alex's bed, the vibrant blue of the Pacific sparkling beyond the French doors. She was sprawled on top of him as if she *owned* him. She'd made a huge decision with wide-ranging career implications last night, and she had a flight to catch in a few hours.

The last thought, in particular, had her gingerly detaching herself from him and rolling onto her side to look at the clock on the bedside table. Ten o'clock. She needed to leave in a couple of hours. Plenty of time.

Plenty of time to ruminate over what she'd done.

A glance at the man who was normally out of bed by six confirmed he was still asleep. He looked so sexy with a dusting of early-morning stubble covering his jaw, his long, dark lashes swept down over his cheeks; her heart tripped over itself. *Oh my.*

She collapsed back against the pillows and let out the quietest of sighs. In the space of twenty-four hours, she'd slept with her interview subject, agreed to give up the story of a lifetime and committed to starting over with a man who could and surely would break her heart.

Awesome. Way to go, Izzie. You definitely have your priorities in order.

The cold light of day literally and figuratively crowding in on her, she covered her face with her hands. James was going to flip his lid. But what choice had she had? Ethically, she couldn't have continued to work on a story on a man she was now sure she was head-over-heels infatuated with.

She grimaced. Fingered the fine silk sheet draped over her. James wouldn't see it that way. He'd see it as a foolish, shortsighted decision. A wasted opportunity few ever got. Which brought up the question, what *was* she doing? How had she gone from being an ultra-independent woman who knew the value of providing for herself to a blithering idiot when it came to this man?

Was she in love with Alex?

"That's a pensive look if I've ever seen one."

She jumped at the mockingly spoken words, her gaze flicking to a now fully alert Alex. His slow smile melted her insides. "I'm thinking about my boss's reaction on Monday morning."

"He'll get over it."

She twisted the sheet around her finger. "Everything depends on my anchor appearance now."

He captured her hand in his. "You'll be great."

She stared at her tiny hand wrapped in his much larger one. "I have a history of blowing these things when they matter most."

He lifted a brow.

"My mother set up a big interview for me with a national news show when I was fresh out of school. I blew it badly. It's been my Achilles' heel ever since."

He shook his head. "You're beating yourself up over something that happened when you were still wet behind the ears?"

"It's hard not to when nothing you've ever done lives up to your mother's expectations."

He frowned. "Why do you care so much about what

she thinks? You could spend your whole life looking for parental approval and never get it."

He should know. She retrieved her hand from his. "I'm doing this for myself. *I* need to prove I can do this."

He looked at her for a long moment, then nodded and held out his hand. "Come here."

The dark glitter in his eyes made her pulse quicken. "I have a flight to catch."

"Stay. Fly back on Monday with me."

She shook her head. "I need to get back to New York and talk to James."

"One day isn't going to make a difference. Call him. Tell him I'm being difficult."

"You *are* difficult."

"Then it's the perfect excuse, isn't it?" He rolled her beneath him, his muscular thighs pinning her to the mattress. And then she didn't care about James, her flight or anything but the hedonistic side of her that seemed to have taken over.

Hedonism seemed less than a solid choice on Tuesday morning as Izzie stood in front of her boss in his office, her romantic, off-the-charts-hot weekend with Alex a distant memory in the frantic buzz of the newsroom.

"Tell me you have an update for me," he prompted impatiently, from behind his paper-cup-strewn desk.

Her stomach rolled as though she was on the high seas. "I need you to give the Constantinou story to someone else."

He screwed up his face. "Sorry?"

She picked a spot on the wall several centimeters to the right of his face and kept her eyes glued there. "I need you to give the story to someone else."

He sat up straight. "Why?"

She swallowed hard. "Because Alex and I are involved."

"Define involved."

"Involved."

"You're sleeping with him?"

She nodded.

He raked his hands through his hair and threw her a disbelieving look. "Since when? Was this going on that night at the Met?"

"No." Which was the truth. Technically. She gave him an imploring look. "We confronted our feelings this weekend and I—"

"Dammit, Iz." He slammed his hand on his desk so hard brownish liquid from an old coffee sloshed over a pile of papers. He cursed and shoved them out of the way. "You were *screwing* him while you were supposed to be getting the story?"

She felt the blood drain from her face. "That is *not* what happened. I didn't intend on having anything to do with him and then things—things just happened."

"While you're working on the most important story of your career?" he roared. "How could you be so stupid? You of all people, Iz. You've always put your career first—been clear on your priorities."

Apparently not anymore. She pushed her hair out of her face with a shaky hand. "We have something, James."

Her boss snorted. "He's a man. A goddamned shark. You think you're going to be any different than any of the other woman in this town he's gone through?"

Her chest tightened. "It's done. I can't take it back."

He pressed his hands to his temples and pushed out of his chair, pacing to the other side of the room. "You've been off ever since you came back from Italy. Did you actually get concussed in that elevator? What is wrong with you?"

She wasn't actually sure.

"My God, Izzie." He looked at her disbelievingly. "This story would have given you exactly what you needed to win this anchor job."

She bit her lip. "I'll have to prove myself in the audition."

"That would be the understatement of the year." He let out a long breath. "Did you at least get anything good out of him?"

"Not much," she lied, her insides twisting. "The man is a closed book."

His mouth tightened. "I could make a crude remark right about now but I'm going to abstain."

She wrapped her arms around herself. "Would you rather I'd kept my mouth shut?"

"I'd prefer it if I had my smart, rational reporter back."

Bile climbed the back of her throat. "James—"

He waved her out of his office with a dismissive hand. "I need to figure this out. Go out there and do your job. *If you can.*"

Humiliation and confusion mixed to form a potent cocktail as she left, tail between her legs. She went out, shot her story on a heroic mutt who'd saved an elderly lady from having her purse snatched, filed it on autopilot and escaped home before James could give her one more pained look, as though she was his deviant teenager.

Alex had flown her home this morning, then left immediately on business to Toronto, which left her alone in her cozy little apartment with only her mad actions to keep her company. She poured herself a glass of the emergency chardonnay she kept in the fridge for girlfriend visits, stepped over her still-unpacked suitcase and collapsed on the sofa. She'd done the right thing. She knew she had. She was just going to have to put her head down, knock this audition out of the park, and everything would work out.

Wouldn't it?

Alex Constantinou is a shark. She flinched at James's depiction of the man she'd just thrown a piece of her career away for. Was she was a total idiot? Had her near miss in that elevator spurred deviant behavior rather than the courageous sort she was aiming for? Because right now the shark was out wining and dining a client who could be a six-foot amazon for all she knew. And could she really compete with that?

She groaned and covered her face with a pillow. Those two days in Malibu had made her feel things she'd never even knew existed—mad, unexplainable feelings for a man who was as interesting and smart as he was sexy and gorgeous. When they hadn't been in bed together, they'd spent the day on the beach, gone out to dinner and barbecued on the housekeeper's night off. Their discussions, ranging from politics to classic literature to the science of a good run had proved that their natural chemistry together was just as strong out of bed as in it. But even if they had that, was it enough that she should think she *was* any different? Or was James right and she was risking everything she'd ever wanted for a man who would move on when the wind turned?

An image of her mother walking out the front door of their little bungalow flashed through her head. She'd stood there crying, certain she was leaving for good this time, her father's blank face as he'd tried to fight back tears forever imprinted on her mind.

Her throat ached; her eyes burned at the memory. After that had come the seemingly endless amount of tears her father hadn't been able to hide. His complete and utter dissolution. Her and Ella's attempts to make everything right when nothing was.

She reached for her wine and took a big gulp. *A blank slate. No expiration dates. No rules.* Alex hadn't promised her anything. So where was she getting her carte blanche to throw her master plan away? Her "take care of yourself at all costs" plan that had been suiting her just fine. Depend on nothing. Then no one could hurt you.

She clenched her jaw. Told herself she needed to re-focus and refocus fast on what was going to sustain her. *Her career.* Alex might be in her life, but that didn't mean abandoning all common sense. And now was the perfect time to reset the speedometer—when Mr. Testosterone was out of town.

CHAPTER ELEVEN

Izzie sat in the chair in the makeup room of the studios a week later, her stomach rolling like a ride on the deadliest of roller coasters. Where the week had gone leading up to her anchor appearance, she didn't know. She just knew she didn't feel ready. Didn't know if she'd ever feel ready.

Her gaze flicked to the clock on the wall. Thirty minutes. Actually, to be accurate, twenty-nine minutes, thirty-two seconds, before the fate of her career was decided. Her hand shook as she took a sip of water. No pressure there…

"I'm going light on this, Iz," Macy, NYC-TV's makeup artist, said, sweeping powder over Izzie's nose and forehead. "That mother of yours gave you some perfect skin."

Izzie wished her mother had passed along some of her arrogant self-confidence, too. She could have used some of that right about now. Sixty minutes, she told herself. It was like one measly yoga class. Surely she could do that?

Macy twirled a fluffy brush into some rose-colored powder and ran it along Izzie's cheekbone. She drew back, added some more color to the brush, and eyed her subject. "You look different. Alive…you got a new man or something?"

"Of course it's a man," James grumbled, striding into the makeup room, a bouquet of flowers in his hands. "What else would fry her brain into giving up the story of the year?"

Izzie made a face at him. "Are those from you?"

"Nope. Was on my way over here and said I'd bring them."

She looked up at him. After his initial fury, he'd moved on and put all his energy into prepping her for tonight. She was lucky to have him.

"Thank you for all your support the past few weeks."

The cynicism faded from his face. He deposited the flowers on the counter and rested his elbow on it. "You're going to rock this tonight," he said quietly. "Believe in yourself and do what I know you can do."

A lump grew in her throat. He squeezed her arm and took off to shout something at one of the producers. She looked at the huge bouquet of calla lilies to distract herself. Alex was out of town. Had he remembered what tonight was and sent them? She pulled out the card, her skin going all tingly as she recognized his distinctive scrawl.

"Man's got taste," Macy mused.

"Man's got everything," Izzie muttered. "It's a problem."

"Only if you make it one," Macy drawled.

Izzie slid the card out of the envelope. *Game day is all about adrenaline and how you use it. Channel it. Focus it. And...break a leg. —A.*

She sank her teeth into her bottom lip and stared at the flowers. Now he was showing his sensitive side. *Dammit.*

David Lake, the weekend producer, poked his head into the room. "You just about ready to go?"

Macy swept a neutral color over Izzie's lips. "She's good."

Izzie stood up, her legs feeling like spaghetti, her stomach rolling even worse now.

It's all about adrenaline and how you use it. Channel it. Focus it.

She nodded and swallowed hard. Sixty minutes. She could do this.

* * *

James Curry walked Alex to a back corner of the set. "Izzie's on edge," he murmured. "Whatever you do, don't let her see you."

Alex nodded. "Got it."

Curry gave him a wary look. "Listen, Constantinou—"

"I talked to Laura," Alex cut him off. "I owe you an apology. I was barking up the wrong tree."

"You sure as hell were." James dug his hands in his pockets and fixed his gaze on the monitor. "Glad we got that straight."

The producer counted down to air. Izzie's face was pinched and pale, her hands clasped nervously in front of her as she looked into the camera.

"Come on, Iz," James said quietly. "Let's nail this."

Izzie's cohost, Andrew Michaels, greeted the viewers and introduced Izzie. She smiled and returned the greeting, but her demeanor was stilted, completely unlike her. His stomach tightened. *Come on, Izzie. Relax. Breathe… channel it.*

She started reading the headlines, her voice high and rushed, her gaze fixed on the teleprompter. They rolled a clip. He watched her give herself a mental shake. *That's it. Shrug it off.* She started on another story. This time she spoke slower, more evenly. She still looked tense, but a steadiness had come over her. Curry gave an audible sigh. By the time they went to break she was bantering with Michaels, her usual animated expression on display.

Alex's lips curved. She was going to be okay. Good girl.

He leaned back against the wall and crossed his arms over his chest, wondering what the hell he was doing here anyway. A few hours ago, he'd been in an excruciatingly boring meeting in Boston, trying to focus on the stack of numbers the gray-haired CFO of a consumer electronics retailer was throwing at him, and failing miserably. All he could think about was Izzie and being here for her.

After all, he'd rationalized, who knew better than him what it was like to have your career hang in the balance? To have everything you'd worked for come down to four quarters that flew by in the blink of an eye? So he'd called his old friend he'd had dinner plans with, canceled and hightailed it home.

What he didn't know was what he was actually doing. When two weeks of satisfying your lust with a woman didn't inspire the "it's been fun" speech, a smart man walked.

He wasn't walking.

"And that's a wrap. Thanks, everyone…"

Izzie sat at the anchor desk in a daze as David bounded up onto the set and unclipped her mic. "Great job," he beamed. "It was a really good show."

"Except for the rocky start."

"Nothing you wouldn't have extracted yourself from given a little more experience." Andrew, her cohost, clapped her on the back. "Nice job, Izzie."

Relief swept over her like a tidal wave, her hands and feet tingling under the bright lights. The sweet buzz of victory raced through her veins. It had either been channeling her fear or allowing it to consume her for the rest of her life.

She had done it.

She stood up, walked into James's bear hug. He drew back, a grin on his face. "Lester Davies called me five minutes ago raving about you."

The head of the network?

James grinned. "He apparently missed the first five minutes…"

Her stomach knotted. "It was bad, wasn't it?"

"You loosened up." He jerked his head over his shoulder. "I'd say let's go celebrate but I'm figuring you're gonna choose him over us."

Him? She squinted into the darkness. A tall figure straightened away from the wall. *Alex.*

"We can do our drinks another night," James said gruffly. "Get out of here."

Izzie didn't hesitate, her legs wobbling as she walked toward Alex, but this time for a totally different reason. She stopped in front of him, tipped her head back and looked up at him. "You're supposed to be in Boston."

"I managed to get home early." His mouth tipped up at the sides. "You were great, Iz."

"I got better as I went."

His gaze swept over her. "You look sexy in a suit."

Heat spread through her. "The words on the card were perfect. Thank you."

He nodded toward the crew. "I know I'm barging in on your night, but I have some champagne in the fridge I thought we could...drink."

Her pulse raced. "I'm getting my jacket."

Her feet couldn't seem to move fast enough as she sped back to her desk, switched off her computer and gathered her things. She was turning to leave when she noticed the folded tabloid on her desk. Frowning, she picked it up and flipped it open. And suddenly felt winded. A photo of Alex and a stunningly beautiful brunette coming out of a restaurant together was emblazoned on the front page.

She glanced at the date. Thursday. When he'd said he couldn't see her.

She dragged the paper closer to read the caption.

Former football star and sexy CEO Alex Constantinou had dinner with his former fiancée at Miro's on Thursday night. He and the soon-to-be ex-wife of

Flames quarterback Gerry Thompson looked ultra-cozy together, making us wonder if things are back on.

The warm glow inside her chilled. She stood there, her heart shriveling up into a tiny ball. The sound of hushed voices penetrated her haze. She looked over at the two reporters at the entertainment desk, watching her. *They'd left it for her.*

She turned her back on them. And searched for an explanation. Alex wasn't the type of guy to cheat. He was brutally honest in everything he did.

So why was he having dinner with his ex?

She took a deep breath, shoved the paper in her bag and walked toward the exit. She'd ask him. As a rational woman who wasn't crazy with jealousy would. That was her, right?

"All right, out with it. What's wrong?" Alex threw his keys on the hall table at his penthouse and shut the door.

"I think I've hit the wall," Izzie murmured, no closer to knowing how to bring up the photo than she'd been a half hour ago.

He lifted a brow. "*Now*, Iz."

She walked over to where her bag lay on the floor. "Someone left this on my desk," she said quietly, pulling the tabloid out and handing it to him.

He scanned the story, his mouth tightening as he read. Then he tossed it down on the hall table. "She's going through a tough time with her divorce," he said flatly. "That's *you* people blowing a simple dinner up into something it isn't."

She bit her lip. "Why didn't you tell me it was her that night?"

"Because I thought you'd have the same insecure reaction you're having right now," he bit out. "It was nothing."

She swallowed hard, pressed her damp palms against her thighs. If it was nothing why hadn't he told her? Wasn't she allowed a *little* insecurity over a dinner he'd deliberately kept secret from her? With his *ex?*

"She's obviously still in love with you," she said quietly. "One look at that photo and it's as plain as day."

"There's nothing between Jess and me, Iz. You have to trust me or this is never going to work."

She clenched her hands at her sides, frustration bubbling over. "You can't blame me for asking. Alex, you almost married the woman, then you go out for dinner with her and I find out about it in the tabloids."

He let out a harsh breath. "You of all people should know what they print in those rags is complete crap."

"I do—I just—" She floundered helplessly. "I just wish you'd told me."

He jammed his hands in his pockets. "This is my life, Iz. This is what *you* people have been doing to me my entire life, spinning lies and painting them as truth."

"I am not *you people*. I'm the woman who gave up the story of a lifetime to protect you."

Color stained his high cheekbones. "This is never going to end. It's who I am. What you signed up for by agreeing to be with me. The press love to dish the dirt on my relationships. There'll undoubtedly be more telling their story when the money's right. So if you can't handle it maybe you should get out now."

His words rang out, stark and unrelenting in the quiet stillness of the penthouse. The silence between them stretched to deafening. He spun on his heel and stalked toward the kitchen.

Alex pulled two champagne flutes out of the cupboard, set them on the counter and leaned his forehead against the cool wood. What was he doing? Izzie hadn't deserved that.

But that tabloid had set him off. On the heels of everything else he was dealing with, after that unexpected phone call from Jess this week, it was just too much.

Jess's voice had been raw, thick with tears when she'd caught him on his way out of a meeting. Her marriage to Gerry was falling apart. She needed him. And fool that he was, he'd canceled on Izzie and agreed to meet her for dinner, because no matter what she'd done to him, he'd loved her once and she needed him.

Pressure built in his head, the kind before a thunderstorm that held you in its vise. Once he would have died to hear Jess tell him she still loved him. That she'd made a mistake. Instead it had seemed like some cruel joke that was ten years too late. Because he'd stopped missing her, *needing* her a long time ago.

Because he was falling for another woman. Hard.

He pressed his palms against the wood and levered himself away from the counter. Pulled the chilled champagne out of the wine fridge and started unpeeling the foil. Anything to avoid the truth. That he was terrified of falling so hard again, of putting that power in another person's hands that it was almost blinding.

He worked the cork out of the bottle. The thing was, Izzie wasn't anything like Jess. Sitting across from his ex it had become crystal clear for him. With Izzie, honesty was like a truth serum she'd drunk at birth. Whereas Jess had spun lie after lie, abandoned him when he needed her most, Izzie had given up that story for him. She was strong and she was courageous. And yes, a little neurotic and insecure at the same time. But weren't they all human? Didn't they all have their weaknesses?

The cork hit the ceiling with a resounding thump. The question was, could he offer Izzie more than a brief, few-month affair? Had Jess's betrayal rendered him incapable of trust again?

He picked up the bottle and poured the champagne. His overwhelming instinct was to walk in there and finish what he'd started so she'd call it quits for him. Yet something told him if he messed things up with Izzie, it would be the biggest regret of his life.

Which left him exactly where?

Scooping up the bottle and glasses, he found her on the terrace, looking out at the floodlit 843-acre New York landmark that was Central Park. Her shoulders were straight as a board, her hands curled into fists at her sides.

She turned around. "Alex, I—"

He waved her off. Handed her a glass. "I need to tell you about Jess. About that night…"

Her eyes widened. He walked to the railing, turned and leaned back against it. Started talking before he changed his mind. "I met Jess in high school. She was smart, strong, working two jobs to keep her family going after her mother walked out on them and her dad fell apart and started drinking. I was from a wealthy family. I could help them, so I did. She was determined to keep her brothers and sisters together and not let the family get split up by social services."

"And trying to get through school at the same time," Izzie added quietly. "That must have been tough."

He nodded. "When I finished college and went to play in New York, Jess came to live with me and my sisters. At first things were great. She loved New York, she loved living the life of a professional football player's girlfriend, and I loved indulging her. But then I got injured."

He pulled in a breath at the sudden tightness in his chest. "It's never a good thing when a quarterback tears his rotator cuff, but my physical therapy was going well and there was every indication I'd recover. Jess, on the other hand, wasn't handling it so well. She couldn't handle any kind of uncertainty in her life and the thought of me losing my career made her nuts."

"Because of her past."

He nodded. "She'd heard they were worried about my arm. There was speculation in the press they were grooming Gerry Thompson, the backup quarterback, to take my job. We had a big fight the night before a qualifying game for the playoffs. She said I was being naive. That I didn't see how management was writing me off."

He pulled the top buttons of his shirt open and paced across the terrace. "I went out and had a few too many drinks...wondered if she was right about Gerry."

Izzie pressed her fingers to her temples. "And you decided to play."

He nodded. "I'd been so nervous about my arm and trying to speed my recovery, but I was hurting. A friend told me about this guy who had high-level street painkillers that had helped him through an injury. They worked well, too well for me, and I started to take them regularly, telling myself I could stop when I needed to. That night, when I decided to play, I double dosed. I felt amazing. I was so high by the third quarter I felt invincible. And then I threw that pass."

"I saw the tapes," Izzie said huskily. "It was so perfect."

It had been perfect. It had also been his last. His throat constricted, threatened to cut off the air he so desperately needed. The memory of the ball leaving his hand, sailing through the air in a perfect arc and landing in Xavier's outstretched arms would forever be burned into his mind. The roar of the crowd, the glare of the lights as Xavier dove into the end zone for the touchdown. *He was back.* They were winning. And that was all that had mattered.

The illegal hit, long after the play, had been unexpected. The weight of the defender crashing into him, taking him to the ground until all he could feel was the searing pain in his right arm. *His throwing arm.* The indescribable white-hot burn that had pushed him to his knees. The hush that had fallen over 60,000 fans…the most eerie sound he'd heard in his life.

He blinked hard. The humiliation of being lifted off the field in a stretcher had been the most helpless feeling he'd ever experienced. The knowledge that that night had been the last time he would ever lead his team onto the field excruciating. Because he'd known. *He'd known.*

The weight of Izzie's hand on his forearm brought his gaze up. "There was nothing the doctors could do?"

He shook his head. Each surgeon's diagnosis had been the same. *It's damaged too badly, Alex. Your career is over.*

He ran his fingers through his hair. "I wouldn't go to my father and plead for a job. Jess left me and married Gerry a few months later."

Izzie's fingers tightened around his arm. "She wasn't worth half of you, Alex."

He'd felt as if he wasn't worth anything in those months afterward. His body broken, his future in tatters, it had taken him a year to pull himself together.

He shrugged her fingers off. "I didn't tell you this for your pity. I told you because I need you to understand what happened between Jess and me. I can't be with someone with those types of insecurities."

"How could you not want her back?" She said it as if she couldn't help herself. "She's so stunning. You have so much history together."

"Because I want you," he said quietly. "And if you'd ever stop comparing yourself to that mother and sister of yours, you might actually see why."

A dull red color stained her cheeks. "I know, it's just—hard to break old habits."

"You're going to have to or this isn't going to work." He

stepped closer and ran his thumb over her cheek. "There's a part of me that doesn't believe it has to be the same as it was for our parents.. They made choices. *We* create our own destiny. But, I am only one-half of this equation, Iz. I need you with me."

Her gaze darkened. "I can, I promise you I can. I just may not always be perfect about it. You've got to cut me some slack."

He let out the breath he hadn't even realized he was holding. Hadn't realized how important her answer was to him. He dragged his thumb down over the soft flesh of her bottom lip. "Prove it."

Her eyes widened as she registered what he was asking of her. She pressed her lips shut and took a step backward and he wasn't sure if she was going to run or stay. Then she deposited her glass on the table and moved her fingers to the buttons of her blouse.

She was shaking, her hands fumbling with the tiny pearl buttons. But he held himself back. This had to be all Izzie.

She released the second, the third button; exposed the rounded curves of her breasts. The dusty blue of the silk that encased her flesh made his throat go dry. Down her hands went, dispensing with the rest of the buttons. She pulled the shirt from the waistband of her skirt, shrugged out of it and dropped it to the ground. The dusky imprint of her nipples protruding through the silk made him pull in a breath.

Kill me now. Except he'd asked for this. Some strange, demented part of him needed to see that she had the self-confidence to be with him.

Her hands slid to the zipper of her skirt. She undid it and pushed it down over her hips. Her curves in the almost-there underwear were pure perfection, the dark shadow of her feminine curls drawing his eye. He ached to bury himself in her. *Now.*

Any semblance of self-control vanished. "You can let me know when I'm allowed to put my hands on you," he rasped, his body so hard it was painful. "I'm thoroughly convinced."

She arched a brow at him. "That quick?"

"That quick," he said, taking a step toward her.

She stepped back, giving him a considering look. "I'm not sure I'm done."

He took two steps forward, sank his hands into her waist and slung her over his shoulder. "I am."

The bedroom had been his destination, but his aching body had him diverting to the flat surface of the pool table. He set her down on the edge, stepped between her legs and took her mouth in a kiss that told her this would be no slow seduction. Tonight he needed to take her hard and fast. To exorcise the demons raging in his head.

She moved against him, her low whimper as she wrapped her legs around him and ground the hard ridge of his arousal against her setting his blood on fire. "I can't make this slow tonight," he groaned, burying his face in her throat.

"I don't want it slow," she gasped, clutching his hair. He pressed his mouth to the racing pulse at the base of her throat. Spread her silky thighs with his hand and sought out her slick, wet heat. Her low moan as he sank his middle finger into her almost undid him. When he was sure she was ready, he stepped back, tore at his clothes with his hands. His belt, the button on his pants, his zipper; he didn't stop until he'd freed his rock-hard erection and ripped off the barely there wisps of lace covering her hips. The sight of her wet, glistening flesh as she parted her legs to him was the biggest turn-on he'd ever experienced.

He moved forward, brushed the pulsing, aching length of him against her. She dug her fingers into his forearms. "Please, I need—"

"Look at me."

She opened her eyes, her gaze locking onto his. He reached down and took her hips in his hands, filling her with a thrust that made her gasp and clamp her eyes shut. He paused while her tight body adjusted to him. And when she relaxed, pleaded for more in a desperate, husky voice that made him crazy, he began to move in deep, cathartic strokes that drove everything from his mind but how right it always was with this woman. How easily she made him forget everything but being with her.

The sound of their lovemaking filled the air—the slick push and pull of him sliding into her, the soft little moans she made at the back of her throat when she took him deep, the sound of his raspy breath rapidly losing control...

But still he held back, afraid to unleash that last part of him that took him into the darkness. Afraid of what might happen if he totally lost control.

"Alex," Izzie murmured, watching him. Reading him. "It's okay...please—I want you so much."

His low curse rang out on the night air as he drove into her harder, faster, rougher than he'd ever taken a woman, a primitive part of him reveling in the pain of her fingernails as they dug into the hard flesh of his shoulders. He felt her body tighten around him, clench at him. He slid his fingers under her hips and took more of her weight, arched her higher against him, taking their lovemaking even deeper until he lost himself somewhere along the way. Izzie cried out and convulsed around him, the intense spasms of her body sending him over the edge along with her.

The red-hot pleasure that flashed through him as he came almost brought him to his knees. He held her there, wrapped around him, until his legs felt steady enough to carry her to bed. Then he turned out the lights and they slept.

For the first time in a week he did not dream. There

were no sweat-drenched nightmares of the night everything had ended. Sweet, sweet Izzie wrapped around him was like an angel sent to rescue him from a place he could no longer go.

CHAPTER TWELVE

COULD YOUR LIFE actually be this perfect?

Izzie balanced her latte on her knee while James made mincemeat of the entertainment reporter in their morning editorial meeting. And contemplated the question. She was a front-runner for an anchor job currently being hashed out by the execs, she was starting to deal with her insecurities on a fundamental level and she had the man of her dreams at her side to help her do it.

A tiny smile curved her lips. Perhaps it was possible. Maybe Alex was right. Maybe all you had to do was believe it could be different.

She picked up her pen and started doodling as James droned on. It helped to know why Alex was who he was. The demons that haunted him... She knew where she had to bend. When she had to be strong. It was never going to be easy to be with a man like Alex whom everyone wanted a piece of. But she was getting there.

James lit into another reporter, working his way through the room like a raging bull. Izzie put her head down and focused on her doodles. Even her relationship with her mother was showing signs of life. They'd had dinner and coffee a couple of times without actually wanting to tear each other's hair out. And somehow, deep down, it felt as if this time her mother was actually trying. That she wanted to be a part of her life.

She sketched a big question mark on her pad. Opening herself up so completely was life affirming, but it was also terrifying. Because she knew realistically, her mother and Alex could walk away tomorrow and there was nothing she could do about it.

It was a risk she had to take.

"Can someone *please* give me some uplifting news?" James's sarcastically drawled entreaty brought her head up.

"I'll have a rough cut of the Constantinou story ready for you this afternoon," Bart Forsyth piped up. "Right on time."

"A half a day late," her boss ripped back. "How's it going?"

Bart shrugged. "Pretty much ready to go. Messer's refused to do a follow-up interview now that he knows we're positioning Isaacs as the guy behind *Behemoth*. So I'm just polishing it off." He flicked a glance at Izzie. "Did you forget to give me some of your notes?"

She froze, her heart skipping a beat.

"I can't find anything on his Boston College days," Bart continued, frowning. "I thought you said you had that stuff."

Her breath came out in a long whoosh. "Let me check. Maybe I missed something."

James wrapped the meeting up. She was halfway out of her chair when he waved her to a halt. "Give me a minute."

Damn. She hugged her notebook to her chest while the others fled the room. Her heart started to pound. She hadn't done anything to earn a one-on-one berating, had she? *Except bury crucial information.*

Her boss hitched his thigh onto the end of the table and crossed his arms over his chest. "I need you to anchor the news tonight. Gillian's sick."

Her stomach dropped. Anchoring on the weekend was one thing. Anchoring the nightly news, home to multimillions of viewers, was entirely another. "Of course," she made herself respond calmly. "I'd love to."

"It's good timing," he nodded. "The execs are going to make their decision any day. One more chance for you to make an impression."

She forced a bright smile to her lips. "Absolutely."

He went off to unleash his fury on the rest of the staff. Izzie ran clammy palms over her skirt and took a deep breath. She could do this. A bigger audience didn't change anything. And that tricky political panel Gillian hosted every Wednesday night? Maybe they'd have Chris, Gillian's coanchor, do it.

She went back to her desk, dug the notes out for Bart and handed the folder over. Tried to work. But the words blurred on her computer screen and her brain kept bouncing forward to tonight. *Focus. Channel it.*

Another ten minutes went by and she hadn't read a word. She called Alex. He picked up on the third ring, his voice distracted. "What's up?"

She pushed her pencil against her cheek. "You sound busy."

"I'm about to go into a meeting. You okay?"

"Yes, I just—" She stopped as she heard voices in the background. Someone call Alex's name. "It's no biggie. You go. We'll talk later."

"Okay. Look, Iz…" His voice softened. "Jess is having a really rough day and she's asked me for some advice. I'm going to have a drink with her after work, make sure she's okay, then I'll meet you back at the penthouse."

Jealousy clawed at her insides. Weighted down the phone line. "Fine," she said slowly, keeping her voice neutral. "I'm going to be late anyway."

He signed off. She put the phone down and pushed her hands through her hair. *Focus on the things you can control, Iz.* Like tonight.

* * *

When Izzie stepped onto the set that night, her mind was not in the right place. She was jittery, edgy and not on her game. By the time she hosted the political panel on the mayoral race, she was thoroughly shaken by her performance. So was the producer. He started prepping her with cues in her earpiece, but the panel tore her apart, her distraction too great to keep on top of the verbal zings ripping back and forth. They went to break and the producer tried to talk her through it. But it was as if her brain were frozen with fear. As if she were navigating a dark tunnel and couldn't find her way out.

When the red recording light on the camera flicked off, so did what was left of her composure. She unclipped her mic, murmured a robotic thanks to her cohost and walked off the set.

Somehow she found her way to her desk, grabbed her purse and stumbled outside before anyone could approach her. Sucked in the cool night air. She hadn't just been bad. She'd been a complete disaster.

She rode the subway home to her apartment. It felt too small, too claustrophobic after Alex's penthouse, so she yanked on sweats and sneakers and went outside for a run. Her footsteps hit the pavement with a rhythmical *thump, thump* that normally calmed her immediately. Not tonight. She ran down the side streets toward the park as if the devil were on her heels. And thought how amazing it was that life went on as usual when it felt as though yours was falling apart.

Through the park she ran, until her knees threatened to buckle. When she got back to her street, her steps slowed to a walk to cool off. She saw a male figure sitting on the front steps of her brownstone. *Alex.*

"Your boss is worried about you," he said grimly when she stopped in front of him.

She pulled her phone out of her pocket. Three missed calls. "I'll text him. I'm sorry, I didn't mean to alarm you."

He lifted a brow. Banked anger glimmered in his eyes. "I was waiting for you at home."

The hot tears she'd been fighting her entire run slipped down her cheeks. "I'm sorry."

He muttered an oath, stood and gathered her in his arms. "It's okay," he murmured into her hair. "One bad performance isn't going to kill you."

"This one will."

He shook his head. "No one judges you on one performance. You'll do it again. Kill it next time."

"I am not you," she yelled at him, pulling out of his arms with a panicked rage. "I do not thrive on game day. I choke, Alex. *I choked*. There is no way they're giving me another chance."

He frowned. "You don't know that."

"I do." She swiped the tears from her cheeks. "It's done."

His expression softened. "Go get your stuff. We'll talk at my place."

She stood there staring at him, wanting desperately to run into his arms and have him make everything right. But she was afraid to want him that much. To *need* him that much.

She lifted her chin. "I think I should stay here tonight."

"Why?" His response was low and shot through with challenge.

She looked away. "I just think it's a good idea given everything that's happened tonight."

Antagonism flared in his eyes. "You think something happened between Jess and me?"

"No…" She shook her head, but his penetrating gaze read her uncertainty.

"*Christós*, Izzie." He clenched his hands by his sides. "I was home worried sick about you, terrified something might have happened, when it finally occurred to me you might be here. I drive over here like a maniac, putting the lives of myself and others in danger, you're not here, and I'm dying." Fury shimmered in his eyes. "So don't act like you don't trust me when I'm obviously crazy about you."

Her heart slammed against her chest. *Crazy about her?* "I'm not doubting you," she summoned haltingly. "I just—"

"Exactly," he muttered. "You just are."

"Can you not see what she's doing?" she burst out. "She keeps asking for your help because she wants you back."

"And you need to trust me. That's what relationships are all about, Iz. Trusting the person you're with."

She locked her gaze with his. "Tell me she doesn't want you back, Alex."

Ruddy color dusted his cheekbones. "I've told you she means nothing to me anymore."

"Then tell her to find another shoulder to cry on," Izzie challenged.

"Because you can't *handle* it? I thought we'd been through this. You need to grow up."

She gave him a belligerent look. "Maybe you do, too, because that woman is only interested in one thing. *You.*"

A thunderous cloud fell over his face. "You're just about succeeding, you know that, Iz?"

She arched a brow at him. "Succeeding in what?"

"Pushing me away." He took a step toward her, picked her up and stalked to his car.

"What are you doing?" she demanded in a voice this side of shrill.

"Watching over you so you don't self-destruct," he muttered, tossing her in the car and demanding her keys. "Call your boss," he ordered. Then he marched up to her apartment, retrieved her purse and computer, slid back into the car, and drove her to his place.

Brushing aside her usual request to walk the twenty flights up to his penthouse with a roll of his eyes, he hustled her into the elevator. She sat numbly on the sofa while he made her an omelet, forced her to eat it, then put her under a hot shower. When she'd taken up second residence there, he ordered her out and to bed. She went willingly because her head was pounding, her body spent, and all she wanted to do was pretend this day had never happened.

Alex brought his laptop to bed and tucked her against his side while he worked. She burrowed into him, desperate for his warmth, for his ability to make everything better.

"I backslid badly today," she murmured. "I know it."

He brushed her hair away from her face, his expression softening. "I'll cut you some slack tonight."

"You're really crazy about me?"

His mouth tilted. "Unfortunately since I don't think you're going to make this easy on me, yes."

She curved her hand around his thigh. He gave her a wary look. "You need sleep, Iz."

"I need you," she corrected huskily, closing her fingers over the thick, hard length of him.

"Iz…"

She slid her hand inside his boxers and found his velvet heat. He ditched the laptop then. Flipped her over and started to explore her bare skin from the top down. "Does this feel like my interest is anywhere but right here?" he demanded, imprinting her with his considerable male assets.

"No," she gasped. But she let him prove it in a no-holds-barred exhibition of how he could make her forget her name. Down, down she went into the maelstrom that was Alex. Handed over that last piece of her heart she'd been holding back because if he wanted her like this, in her worst train-wreck moment of all time, she was already long, long gone. Had been, she feared, from that first night in London.

CHAPTER THIRTEEN

ALEX LEFT AT 5:30 a.m. to fly to Seattle after making her promise not to do anything rash. To think this through and talk to James before she drew any conclusions. She made the promise, slunk back into bed and slept for another couple of hours. Then she stumbled into Alex's big, bright walk-in steam shower and thought about putting her life back together.

She was obeying the eye-opening prompt of the eucalyptus body wash he favored when the bottle dropped from her fingers.

The notes.

Scenes from the night before flashed through her head. Her removing the Taylor Johnson transcript from Alex's file before handing it to Bart Forsyth. The scan through she'd done to make sure all other evidence of the illegal painkillers was removed. Her stomach lurched. What she had forgotten was the original set of notes from her interview with Taylor tucked in the front pocket.

She'd given Bart the evidence on the drugs.

Oh my God.

She fled the shower, threw on her pants from the night before and a spare shirt she kept in Alex's closet, then cabbed it to the station. It was quiet at eight-thirty, with only a few reporters at their desks. A frantic, covert search of Bart's desk for the folder was unsuccessful. She sat down at her own, rested her head in her shaking hands and drew in deep breaths. Bart either had the file at home with him, which meant he might have read it last night, or he'd locked it in his drawer.

Either way, she was in trouble. Her guts churned in sickening recognition of how much trouble. *Everything*, her job, Alex's reputation, was on the line if those interview notes were discovered. How could she have done it? Sure, she'd been stressed, but this was inconceivable.

She sat there, frozen to the spot, pretending to work until Bart came in an hour later. He gave her his usual whack on the shoulder and went off whistling to the kitchen to get his coffee. She rose and flew to his desk. There on the top was the blue folder. Heart slamming in her chest, she flicked it open, grabbed the notes and committed the most unrecoverable sin of her career. She hurried back to her desk and buried them in her purse for destruction at a later date. And hoped, *prayed* fate was on her side. Bart hadn't said anything about the notes, and surely he would have if he'd read such explosive testimony?

Maybe she'd slipped by by the skin of her teeth…

A fine sheen of perspiration broke out on her brow. James came in and she suffered through a horrendous debriefing of her performance the night before, during which he confirmed that she had indeed done her chances at the anchor job a great deal of damage. But he wouldn't know how much until he talked with management. Meanwhile, he told her, stay the course. Pull yourself together and see what happens.

She was only too happy to put her head down and do her job, but by the end of the day, her nerves were frayed beyond repair. Neither Bart nor James had said anything, she had no idea if they knew about Taylor Johnson or not, and she could barely prevent herself from lurching to the bathroom and throwing up what little lunch she'd consumed.

She was packing up her stuff when her phone buzzed. She looked down at it. *A reminder of dinner with her mother.* Oh God no. She could not do that tonight. She could not. Unfortunately, her mother didn't pick up when she called to cancel and was likely on her way to the restaurant.

Her mother had a bottle of Chianti on the table when she arrived at the elegant little Italian trattoria on Fifth Avenue that treated its Hollywood clientele with an understated attention to detail Dayla loved. Her mother gave her a long look, rose and kissed her on the cheek.

"We're drinking."

Izzie collapsed in the leather chair opposite her mother. "I might need more than a bottle."

Her mother gestured for the waiter to pour her some wine. "What happened?"

The same as before...except this time she'd fallen apart in front of millions of viewers.

Her mother sighed. "Everyone has bad performances, Izzie. Pick yourself up and move on."

"Maybe you were right that day in L.A." She fixed her mother with a belligerent stare. "Maybe I'm just not cut out for the spotlight."

Her mother took a sip of her wine and set it down. "What do you think?"

"I don't know," she returned in an antagonized tone. "I like being in front of the camera when I'm out on assignment. Anchoring...that's a whole other story."

Her mother sat back in her chair. "You don't thrive in the spotlight like your sister and I do. And you don't have the same thick skin. You thought I was being unnecessarily cruel guiding you away from acting, but I was trying to protect you, Izzie. The pressure to be always on, to always look perfect...to never be able to escape the public eye no matter how much you want to." She shook her head.

"It's unrelenting. I may have been a terrible mother, but I never wanted you to go through that. You're too smart. You have too much to give. Look at those stories you do out in the community. You were always one of those kids who was going to change the world." She gave her a penetrating look. "Maybe that's all you need."

Izzie stared at her, stunned into silence.

"If you get that anchor job," her mother continued, "it's always going to be about how good you look for how long. A glorified popularity contest. A political tug-of-war that will never end. Sure you can affect change in that role, you'll have the power, but it isn't going to be about the story anymore. It's going to be about your image."

Izzie twisted her hands in her lap, wondering where *this* mother had been all her life. "I don't even know if I want the job…or if it's even a possibility anymore."

Her mother frowned. "So why kill yourself trying to win a job that stresses you out this much?"

Because I've never stopped trying to win your approval. Because despite the fact that I told myself I didn't care what you thought anymore, I've spent my entire career trying to prove I'm good enough for you.

She blinked back the tears that threatened. Her mother reached across the table and wrapped her fingers around hers. "Live with it for a day or two, Iz. You'll know what the right decision is."

Izzie stared down at her mother's hand wrapped around hers and felt her chest constrict. "I can't have you walking in and out of my life," she said heavily. "It's too hard."

Her mother's fingers tightened around hers. "I'm not going anywhere. I promise you that, Iz. Not anymore."

Izzie's phone beeped. Releasing her mother's hand, she dug it out and saw that the message was from Alex. He had sent her another one of his quotes. Courage was not the absence of fear, but the triumph over it. Nelson Mandela. How are you?

Her mouth curved.

"Alex?" her mother asked.

"Yes."

Her mother's gaze sharpened on her. "You're crazy about him."

Her smile faded. "Yes."

"So why don't you look happier?"

She picked up a piece of bread and buttered it with elaborate precision. "We argued last night."

"About?"

"His ex-girlfriend." She abandoned any pretense of eating and laid the bread on her side plate. "His stunning ex-girlfriend he almost married who wants him back."

Her mother gave her a long look. "Do you trust him?"

"Yes."

"Then what's the problem?"

"I don't trust myself." She'd proven that last night, hadn't she? Her insecurities had cost her an anchor job and made Alex doubt her. Again.

"Maybe you should figure out why," her mother said softly. "It's clear you're madly in love with him, Iz."

She swallowed past the huge lump in her throat. "What if I'm not enough? What if he decides he's still in love with her?"

Her mother's mouth twisted. "Life is all about the chances we take. You can't reap the rewards if you don't put yourself out there."

And hadn't that night in London taught her that? Why was she having this huge regression? Was she determined to be a self-fulfilling prophecy? Or was her direction all wrong?

Her mother took a sip of wine and set it down. "You know how I remember you as a child? You were always the little daredevil, jumping off walls, falling off the balance beam, wild for roller coasters..." A smile lit her eyes. "Wild for trouble. You used to give us heart attacks. I swear I took you to the emergency room so many times when you were around six or seven they started to look at me funny."

Izzie smiled. "My right elbow still aches on rainy days."

"The monkey bar break." Her mother looked down at her wineglass and twisted the crystal stem between her fingers. "I remember talking to your father after I left, checking in on you guys. He told me Ella was her usual 'I don't care about anything' self, and that you were fine, doing great at school and raking in a bunch of athletic awards. But he knew you were hurting." She looked up at her daughter. "Then he said something that made me very sad."

Izzie felt her composure slipping, the memory of those awful first months trying to keep it all together, ones she never let herself revisit. Her mother's eyes grew suspiciously bright. "He said he'd been talking to your swimming coach about your progress and your coach had said it was a shame you didn't take risks anymore because you were good, but you could have been great."

Izzie drew in a breath, feeling as if she'd just been socked in the stomach. She dropped her gaze and found herself staring at her mother's shaking hands. *Please not now.* She couldn't do this now.

"What happened between your father and me was complex, Izzie." Her mother's voice held a lifetime of regret. "I know you think I destroyed him, but it's not that simple. Life isn't that simple. And not everyone's going to walk out on you. I promise you that. Take a chance on Alex. He seems like he's worth it."

Izzie thought about herself as that daredevil little girl. How that part of her had come out that night in London.

And wondered if she could channel it again. Because her mother was right. Alex *was* worth it. And she was madly, head-over-heels in love with him.

Alex leaned back against the elevator wall, his mouth curving. It seemed like forever ago he'd gotten stuck in that elevator with the whirling dervish who'd transformed his life, but in reality it had only been six weeks. Six weeks to him finding his penthouse empty without her. Six weeks to the man who never entertained the concept of long-term doing it on a regular basis.

He'd had plenty of time to think on his whirlwind twenty-four-hour trip to Seattle. And he'd come to the realization that Izzie had been right about Jess. He'd been so busy being self-righteous, he hadn't stopped to think how he would have felt if it had been her out to dinner with an ex she'd once been crazy about. No, he'd never given her any reason to doubt him, and she should trust him. But his ex did want him back. And that was different. He needed to tell Jess to find someone else to support her. He couldn't be that person. Not anymore.

He watched the skyline of Manhattan fly by as the glass-walled elevator slid upward. His need to prove himself to his father was the root cause of his biggest failures. The question was, could he alter that pattern for the future? Could he avoid being a chip off the old block in all the ways that mattered?

The doors opened on the fiftieth floor. He was so lost in thought it took him three tries to punch in the security code that bypassed the receptionist's desk through the back doors. There wasn't one minute since he'd met Isabel Peters that he hadn't known she was different. She made him a little insane—yes. But he was also starting to think she might be the one. That he might be in love with her.

His hand froze on the handle of the double glass doors

that led to the executive offices. He'd sworn he'd never utter those words again after Jess had left. Did he have it in him to be the man who stayed when Izzie seemed to want to run every time things got tough?

He thought, perhaps, yes.

Head spinning, he pushed through the doors and headed toward Grace to grab his messages. Tonight, according to the heads-up James Curry had given him, Frank Messer's accusations were going to die a slow death in front of America. Sophoros would finally be rid of him with the generous settlement Alex had put together to make Messer disappear *forever* this time, and things would be back to normal. *Then* he would deal with Izzie.

Mark was sitting on Grace's desk, which wasn't an unusual sight per se, but the dark look on his face was. "Alex," Grace greeted him, getting jerkily to her feet. "You're back."

His PA's face was pale, her hands flailing uselessly at her sides. His smile faded. "What's wrong?"

Grace's gaze darted to Mark, then back to him. "Izzie's been trying to reach you."

He fished his phone out of his pocket. It was still on airplane mode. He'd missed *five* calls from Izzie?

An uneasy feeling snaked up his spine. "Is she okay?"

"Yes, I think so—she—" His assistant darted another glance at Mark. "I told her you were on your way. She's coming over."

His gaze narrowed. "What is going on, you two?"

"NYC-TV just ran the preview of your story," Mark said quietly.

The hairs on the back of his neck stood up. "Curry told me the story sided with Sophoros…"

"I think they went in a dif—"

His name blared from the television. A picture of him in a New York Crusaders uniform flashed across the screen.

A headline ran in the ticker beneath it. Painkiller Addiction Destroyed Football Hero's Career.

Blood whooshed in his ears. His legs went weak. He clutched the side of Grace's desk and stared at the screen. *This couldn't be happening.* Izzie had buried that information.

A clip of his old teammate Taylor Johnson flashed up on the screen. The host previewed an exclusive interview with him that evening: an athlete from the inside on how drugs were destroying professional sports. His blood ran cold. How could Johnson know? He hadn't been in the locker room that night. Xavier had been the only one with him, telling him not to do it.

A mad feeling of unreality enveloped him. *This was impossible.*

The host moved on to preview the weather. Alex stared at the screen, hands clenched at his sides, fighting the urge to tear the television from the wall. The clatter of high heels tapping across the tile floor brought his head around. Izzie half ran the last few steps down the hallway. He took one look at her panicked expression and pointed at his office. "Go."

She put her head down and did as she was told. He sucked in a lungful of air, walked into his office and slammed the door. She jumped, her hand flying to her mouth.

"What the hell," he bit out, "was that? Xavier and I were the only ones in the locker room that night."

"Taylor said he saw you take the drugs." Her voice was low but steady. "He knew the dealer. Had an issue himself."

His insides felt as though they were on fire. "Who told Bart about this?"

The color drained from her face. "I didn't mean to, Alex. I gave him some notes and—"

"I don't care how," he roared. "Did you or did you not

give Bart Forsyth the information about the illegal pain-killers?"

"Yes," she choked out. "But I didn't mean to. I—"

"Stop," he thundered. *"Stop."*

He stood there, legs spread apart, her answer tearing him to pieces. He'd been dying, *begging* for her to say no, she hadn't done it. But she had.

"That's all I need to know." His voice was so low, hollow-sounding, he didn't even recognize it as his own. "Get out."

"Alex, please, you have to listen to me."

He shook his head. "That's been my stupidity all along, Iz. I did listen to you. I believed in you. And you were just playing me for a fool." A muscle jumped in his jaw. "What do they say, 'fool me once, shame on you; fool me twice, shame on me.'"

"Alex, no. I—"

He threw up a hand and stalked to the door, twisted the handle, and threw it open before he said or did something unforgivable. "Get out of my life, Izzie."

She didn't move. Just stood there staring at him, her face paper-white. She was a really good actress, he decided. How had he not figured that out?

"I'm so sorry," she said finally, as if she knew nothing she said could make it better. "I swear I never meant to hurt you."

He hardened his heart against the tears shimmering in those beautiful eyes of hers. "The cameras aren't running, Iz. You can turn off the waterworks."

Grace gasped behind her. He waited until Izzie had walked out, then slammed the door. If he never saw Isabel Peters again, it would be too soon.

CHAPTER FOURTEEN

IZZIE OPERATED LIKE a robot for days. She forced herself out of bed, into the shower, onto the subway and to work, but she was functioning at half capacity, if that. She ate when she remembered to, which wasn't often, she slept through an entire weekend and didn't bother to work out. Not even her girlfriends' attempts to get her out for a drink were successful. She felt like wallowing in her misery, so that's exactly what she did.

Her first day back to work after Alex's story aired, James called her into his office. He had been acting as though he hadn't known about the drugs, he'd said, so he and Bart could get the story to air without her tipping off Alex and his lawyers. But it didn't mean he wasn't furious. She'd never seen him so angry. He could hardly speak to her. So he banished her to her desk, told her to keep her head down, and he'd figure out her punishment. Which may or may not include firing her. The execs still hadn't made up their minds about an anchor and he wasn't sure he could support her even if they chose her.

She was happy to put her head down and focus on her job, because it allowed her not to think about the mess she'd made of her relationship with the man she loved and gave her a chance to think about the future. To think about what she really wanted. Because she'd spent too much time with her eye on a prize she wasn't sure was even for her.

Her mother came over one night with two bottles of wine, and they drank one each. It was, it seemed, the only part of her life that was going in the right direction.

A couple of weeks into her exile, James called her into his office. It was the first time he'd spoken to her one-on-one since that conversation about her future. She walked in, palms sweaty, heart hammering in her chest. *Please, God. Don't fire me.*

He looked up from his schedule and waved her into the chair opposite him. "You remember the story Bart did on the River City Collegiate Warriors—the high school football team that'd been pegged for the state finals this year until they lost their coach in the big accident on the turnpike?"

She nodded. It was a hard story to forget.

"They've been struggling, but they still have a chance at state. I want you to go out and do a follow-up story on them. Put together a nice rah-rah piece that makes everyone feel good."

She sat up. "James—"

His mouth hardened. "I'm giving you a second chance, Iz. Get out of my office and prove to me you're the professional I know you are."

She got jerkily to her feet. *He wasn't going to fire her. She was going to keep her job.* The fog that had enveloped her brain these past few weeks lifted as she made her way to her desk. She had a chance to turn this around. So football was Alex. So it might break her heart to do this. She needed to put her feelings aside and act like a professional. James was right. She might not know if she wanted that anchor job, but she did love her current one. And she was going to knock this story out of the park.

She went to the River City practice that afternoon. It

was impossible not to watch the tough young quarterback trying to rally a team that had lost its heart and not think of Alex. Of how terrifying it must have been for him to walk out onto that field that night knowing his career was hanging in the balance. How she, who'd wanted to be the one to prove to him he could trust again, had been the one to destroy him.

The ball of hurt that had permanently lodged itself in her chest expanded, making it hard to breathe. If she learned nothing else from this heartbreak, she needed to learn she was *enough*. Because that was all she had.

She pulled in a deep breath, waiting for the oxygen to remind her a broken heart couldn't actually physically hurt her. That someday she would get over Alex and move on. Because it *was* over. She hadn't heard from him since that awful scene in his office when he'd looked at her as if he hated her. She was pretty sure he did.

Her eyes blurred as she watched the quarterback throw a bullet down the field for a touchdown. His teammates swarmed around him, slapping him on the back. They were regrouping. It was time she did too.

Jim Carter, the River City assistant coach in charge of the team until they found a head coach replacement, waved at her to join them on the field. She plastered a smile on her face and went down. Carter, a harassed-looking guy in his early forties, flashed her a distracted smile. "Sorry 'bout that. We're still a little all over the place without a head coach."

Izzie frowned. "I heard there were lots of candidates."

"Haven't found the right fit. We're lookin' for someone with Division One experience, and that ain't easy to find."

Alex had Division One experience. She bit her lip. "Would you take someone part-time? Someone with a great deal of experience to help out?"

Carter hooked his thumbs into his belt loops. "Who were you thinking of?"

She pursed her lips. A team that needed a hero. A man who needed to be a hero again… During their time together, she'd seen how much it had hurt Alex to exile himself from football. Had seen the hollow look in his eyes every time she accidentally flicked on a game on the television. She twisted her ponytail, thinking hard. Would Alex even consider it? His schedule was nuts, yes, but word had it the Messer case was being settled out of court.

She gave Carter an even look. "Give Alex Constantinou a call."

His brow furrowed. "The way I heard it, the guy wants nothin' to do with football."

"Call him," she said firmly. "I think he might feel differently if he meets the team."

"And you know this how?"

A sharp pang sliced through her. "I know Alex," she said quietly. "Give it a shot."

When Jim Carter called her two days later to say Alex had agreed to stop by a practice, it was a bittersweet moment. Maybe something, *something* good would come out of all of this.

"Jim, don't tell him I had anything to do with this, okay?"

He sounded curious, but agreed. She hung up. Walked into James's office and took herself out of the running for the anchor job. And felt as if the weight of the world had been lifted off her shoulders.

The smell of fresh-cut grass hit Alex first. The earthy, pungent fragrance of the dirt underneath, turned up by the players' cleats, came next. They were smells he could have conjured just by closing his eyes. Recalling the hundreds of times he'd walked out onto a field just like this. But today as he did it for the first time in eight years, he knew why he'd never come back.

It felt as though someone was tearing his heart out.

Shoving his hands in his pockets, he climbed the bleachers. He would stay for a half hour to make Carter happy. Then he'd tell him he couldn't do it and leave. Because he couldn't.

He leaned his forearms on the railing of the first row and watched Carter put the team through drills. The players reminded him of the torn-up, patchy-looking field. They'd seen better days. But there was talent here. Lots of it. Belief was the issue. Vision.

His mouth twisted. He knew the feeling. In the weeks following the airing of his feature, his office had been flooded with phone calls from media outlets wanting a piece of him. Desperate for a new angle, desperate to get a piece of a story that was captivating the airwaves. Were athletes pushing it too far with drugs? Was the pressure on them too great?

He flexed his arms and pushed away from the railing. His faith in humanity had taken a beating. He'd gone underground, avoided the calls that came daily from his three sisters. Told Mark to mind his own business. Then his sisters had shown up at his office and dragged him out for a talking-to. "It's better that it's all out," Agape, the pragmatist, had said. "Now you can move on."

Surprisingly, she'd been right. He felt a strange sense of freedom in no longer having anything to hide. To put a period on a part of his life that was over. So what was he doing here dredging it up all over again? "Just come meet the team," Carter had said. "Take in a practice. If you're still not interested, no harm done."

Carter yelled some instructions to the offensive line

and hopped up into the bleachers beside him. "What do you think?"

He shrugged. "Lots of talent out there."

Carter nodded, slid him a sideways look. "They need a leader."

"That wouldn't be me." Alex kept his eyes on the field. "I haven't played football in eight years."

"I'd say it'd be a right fresh start for you then."

He stared at the field, at the crooked uprights, at the sport that was everything he'd once loved. Why the hell wasn't he telling Carter no? Getting out of here?

Because in the wake of his disillusionment over Frank Messer, walking out onto this field today had been the rightest thing he'd done in a long, long time. He needed to believe again. And this team had an amazing story.

He looked at the scrappy young quarterback out there. So full of promise. So full of doubt. And knew he could help him.

He looked over at Carter. "I have an insane travel schedule."

"We'll work around it." A wide grin split the coach's face. "You in?"

"Guess I am."

Alex spent every minute of his spare time working with the team over the next couple of weeks. He devoted one-on-one time to every player, finding out what made them tick. What would make them gel as a unit. And finally, he started to see some cohesion. Some of that old brilliance shine through. He pulled in some favors, took them on a field trip to see the New York Crusaders play, hoping the glitz and excitement of watching a pro game in a private box would fire them up.

And somewhere along the way, felt himself heal.

He worked until he was bone-weary at night, then he came home and strategized. Built his game book. But no matter how tired he got, no matter how much he told himself it was a good thing Izzie was out of his life after what she'd done to him, she was everywhere. In his head, in his bed when he finally gave in and crashed at night, on the sofa watching him work, reading his copy of *Great Expectations* and interrupting him to debate the merits of the book.

It was a problem.

A few days before the game that would determine whether the Warriors went to state, he came home late, took a long, hot shower and headed out to the terrace, a beer in his hand. He opened his playbook, started to scribble some notes from today's practice, then stopped. There was one thing, *one thing* he couldn't figure out. If Izzie had intended to betray him all along, why hadn't she kept the story for herself and taken all the credit? Lynched him and guaranteed herself the anchor job?

It didn't make sense. That story had made Bart Forsyth a household name.

He dropped his head in his hands. *I didn't mean to*, she'd said in his office. He'd been so angry, so blind with fury he hadn't been able to see past anything but the fact that she'd splashed his deepest humiliation across the national news. But now, now that he could actually think, he realized he'd done exactly the same thing he'd done to her in the beginning. He'd judged her without letting her explain. Convicted her without a trial instead of believing in the woman he knew she was.

He was afraid he'd made a horrendous mistake.

He picked up the phone and called James Curry. When he was done he felt ill. All that talk he'd fed Izzie about believing in him. When he was the biggest fool of all.

He'd thrown a Hail Mary pass to win that championship for Boston College, its first in too many years to count. A desperate, adrenaline-fueled prayer that had somehow come out right. Could he do it again with the woman who'd captured his heart?

CHAPTER FIFTEEN

THE NIGHT THE River City Warriors took the field in their first game at home with their new assistant coach, Alexios Constantinou—a berth in the state championship at stake—the crisp fall evening, clear and crackling with tension, was the kind that had new beginnings written all over it.

Jim Carter had stepped back and let Alex lead. The players clearly respected, *idolized* him. And he had pushed them hard. He'd demanded they grieve, honor their fallen mentor, then move on. Focus. And in doing so he'd found his own kind of peace. But as he finished his pregame pep talk and sent the players out onto the field, a frozen tension gripped his body. He could hear the roar of the crowd from the tunnel. Knew there were hundreds of people out there to watch the Warriors play. And just as many to witness his return to football.

The buzz was immense. For the second time in his life, he could feel the pressure of a whole city's pride winding its way around his throat, choking him.

"That's a different team goin' out there tonight," Jim Carter said quietly at his side.

Alex nodded. Because he could not speak.

"Ready?"

He started walking by way of reply, down the tunnel toward the field. The lights blinded him as he stepped outside. The noise swept over him like an untamed beast. He blinked as the past and present collided like the cold and hot air of a viciously powerful storm. And found he couldn't move.

Eight years slid away. Suddenly the field was so quiet you could hear a pin drop. The voices of his teammates echoed in his head, reassuring him as they carried him off the field on a stretcher. *"You're gonna be all right, Consty. Hang in there."*

But it hadn't been all right. It had been over.

The chanting started then, low at first, then louder. He lifted his head.

"Alllexx, Alllexx, Alllexx."

They were chanting his name.

"Check out the signs," Carter said.

He lifted his gaze to the big handmade poster boards littering the crowd.

The Bull Is Back
Welcome Back #45
We Love You Alexios

His throat seized. *How was he supposed to do this?*

Carter gave him a sideways look. Somehow he started moving, putting one foot in front of the other until it became an unconscious rhythm that carried him to the bench. *Focus*, he told himself, the lump in his throat so large he could hardly swallow. *Channel it. You have a job to do.*

That was when he saw her. Seated in the press section of the bleachers, Izzie looked beautiful in a soft blue dress, her hair loose around her shoulders.

She was fumbling—with her purse, with her notebook, looking anywhere but at the Warriors' bench. He clenched his hands at his sides. He'd gone into the station to find her on Monday only to be told she was in the Caribbean for a long weekend with her sister.

Her gaze flicked to him now, as if she couldn't help herself, as if she knew he was watching her. She had stayed away from every practice he'd been around for. Avoided him completely. And she didn't look good. Didn't look rested. She looked pale and thinner than he'd ever seen her.

Carter nudged him. "They're ready for the coin toss."

He nodded. Dragged his gaze away.

"You know she was the one who told me to call you."

"Who?"

"Izzie."

"Izzie?"

Carter nodded. "She asked me not to say anything. But I'm thinkin' you might want to know that."

His heart flipped over with an emotion he hadn't felt in many, many years. *She had known he needed this. Needed football back in his life.* And he wondered how he could ever have let the most courageous woman he knew go.

Carter nudged him. "We gotta go."

He put his head down and walked to the center of the field.

Izzie had been on edge the entire game, but with the Warriors down by one point with three seconds left, she was practically hyperventilating. The Warriors kicker lined up for the field goal, the lights glinting off his dark hair. If he made it, the Warriors went to state. If he missed it, they were out.

After spending weeks working on this story, getting to know each one of these players' personal histories—what they'd gone through—she *needed* for them to win.

Her gaze flicked to Alex, standing motionless on the sidelines. His feet were spread wide, his eyes glued to the kicker as one of the special teams players placed the ball on the tee. To see him in his element, to see how alive his face was, made her heart throb in her chest.

The kicker backed up, eyed the ball, then ran forward

and sent it flying through the air. She craned her neck, tracking the ball as it soared through the glare of the lights and headed for the uprights. It had the height, but it was veering to the right. Her breath caught in her throat. She angled her body to the left, willing it to straighten out. And almost as if it was obeying her command, the ball scraped through the upright by inches.

The crowd erupted. Somehow this bedraggled, courageous team had done the impossible.

The bench emptied as the clock ran out, the players heaping themselves on top of one another in a tangle of red jerseys at midfield. Alex remained where he was, hands planted on his hips, a solitary figure among the mayhem. The lump in her throat grew to gargantuan proportions. And something inside her became unhinged.

If only she hadn't been so stupid.

Nick, her cameraman, stood and nodded toward the scrum of reporters forming around Alex.

"Ready?"

No. But she forced herself to nod and follow Nick down to the field. "Start with Alex?" he suggested.

She shook her head. "Let's start with Danny."

She managed to force half a dozen wooden questions out of her mouth, which the beaming young quarterback attempted to answer around his teammates' whoops and back slaps. The fact that Alex was giving an interview to a *Times* reporter a couple of yards away didn't help. The ache in her chest increased until she felt that her heart would throb out of it. She took a step backward, wrapped her arms around herself and declared the interview done.

Nick started to move toward Alex.

"No."

He stared at her as she pulled her microphone off. "What do you mean no? We need a sound bite from Alex."

"I can't do it."

"What happened to the most courageous woman I know? You can't ask me a few questions?"

She spun around at the sound of Alex's deep, rich voice. His gaze burned into her, all hot blue intensity. "I'm ready."

"Awesome, let's do it." Nick moved forward and refastened her mic with a let's-get-this-over-with look on his face. She took a deep breath, willing some air into her lungs. *What was Alex doing?*

Nick secured a mic to Alex's shirt and stepped back to turn the camera on. The other reporters watched from the sidelines, waiting for their turn. Izzie's tongue was stuck to the roof of her mouth, her brain incapable of constructing a question.

"How did it feel out there tonight?" Nick hissed from behind her.

She blurted the question out.

Alex smiled, his relaxed half smile that made her toes curl. "It felt great. Really really great. I'd forgotten how much I love this game."

Silence.

"What did you think of the team tonight?" Nick prompted.

Izzie asked the question.

"They were everything I knew they could be. The talent was there, they just needed to believe in themselves."

"You're a former quarterback," she said, her brain kicking in. "What did you think of Danny out there?"

Anyone else would have missed the flicker of emotion in that dark blue gaze. The pain he couldn't quite hide. "He's going to be a force to be reckoned with. He directed that team tonight like a true leader. I could see him playing pro ball someday."

"And what do you think about your chances at state?"

"I think we'll take it one day at a time."

And that was a perfect ending. "Well, that's great," she

concluded, plastering a smile across her face. "Congratulations and thank you v—"

"Aren't you going to ask me what lessons *I've* learned?"

Her heart skipped a beat. No—no she wasn't. She reached for her mic, but Alex kept talking, his gaze pinning her to the spot. "I've learned from this team that the past is the past and at some point we all have to move on. That trust is imperative, yet even when we know that, sometimes we still manage to screw up."

This wasn't about football. "Alex…"

"I'm not done."

Two dozen sets of eyes latched onto them, the press scrum clueing in to a whole other story entirely. She yanked off her mic. "I think we are."

"I know you didn't mean to hand over those notes, Iz."

She froze, mic in hand. He took a step closer, until they were only inches apart. "James told me what happened. I'm so sorry. Here I was preaching trust, when I wasn't trusting you at all."

Confusion rained down over her, making her head spin. He *believed* her? She flicked a glance at the reporters surrounding them. "I'm not sure this is the time or pl—"

"I don't give a crap where we are," he growled. "I want to know what happened."

She pulled in a breath. "The night I filled in as the weekday anchor, I was stressed—it was so last-minute. I owed Bart some notes, so I took the file over to him, but I was so distracted, I forgot about my backup notes from Taylor's interview." The ache in her throat had her swallowing hard. "It was a mistake. I— I swear to God I never meant to hurt you."

"I know." He pulled off his mic and handed it to Nick. "I was so angry at first, I couldn't see straight. Having my past splashed across the nation, thinking you'd betrayed me. It was too much. Then, later when my mind cleared, none of it made any sense. Why would you give up the story if you were going to betray me? If it was all about your ambition…"

She felt whatever composure she had left start to crumble. "I turned the job down."

"You did *what*?"

"I'm learning to trust myself. I thought about what I really wanted. And funnily enough, I just want to do my job. I want to go out there every day and tell stories about the soup kitchen lady who feeds the neighborhood out of her own pocket every night. Or Joey the mutt who catches purse snatchers…" She turned to Nick. "Can you please stop filming?"

"Not on your life."

She cursed under her breath. "Where are you going with all this?" she asked Alex. "I know you hate me. You'll always hate me for putting you through that."

He slid his fingers under her chin and held her gaze captive. "I'm asking for your forgiveness," he said softly. "Everything you've ever done has been for me, Iz. From giving up that story, to burying the truth, to getting me back on this football field tonight. You are courage personified. But instead of seeing that, I let my trust issues get in the way. And I am sorry. So sorry."

Her heart melted. Along with her knees. *What was he trying to say?*

A fierce glint entered his eyes. "I want you back…and this time I'm not letting you go."

Her stomach dropped out of her. The tears that had been threatening rolled down her cheeks. "Alex—"

He ran his thumbs across her cheeks and wiped the tears away. "Why are you crying?"

"Because you're on a football field," she burst out, unable to hold it together any longer. "And you look so happy.

The team's won and everything's right with the world. How could I feel anything else when I—"

His mouth tipped up at the corners. He slid his fingers to her jaw and cradled her face in his hands. "Finish the sentence, Iz."

Her mind went full circle. Back to that night in London when a big risk had led her to him. To thinking that no other man would ever live up to him. Finding out she'd been right. And being sure she'd lost him for good. She knew who she was now. And even though she might not be perfect, even though she might screw up many more times in her life, she really didn't want to live with regrets.

"All right," she said, looking up at him. "I was going to say I love you. That I—"

His kiss, fierce and hard, silenced her. He kissed her until her arms wound their way around his neck, and she didn't care if the entire press corps, the *entire world* was watching, which they might be later since Nick was still filming.

Alex pulled back. "I've told Jess she needs to find someone else to talk to. I should have been more considerate of your feelings given my history with her."

She bit her lip. "I have to let it go. I know that. I won't ever be perfect but I know I can do better."

He shifted his weight to the other foot, the strangest look coming over his face.

"What's wrong? I promise I'll do better."

He dropped to one knee.

"You aren't actually doing this to me, are you?" she asked faintly.

He grinned. "You'd better believe it, sweetheart. And I'm sweating bullets right now, so stay with me."

Her heart beat like a jackhammer. Sped even faster when he reached into his jacket and took out a tiny box.

"You have a ring," she croaked.

His mouth twitched. "Brilliant deduction. Just one of the things I love about you—your incredibly sharp brain. Followed closely by your slight neuroticism, your incurable love of those trashy romance novels, your insatiable need for control and even the way you eat your food, which, by the way, I do think is very odd, but I love it anyway."

The tears started up again, sliding down her cheeks like runaway bandits.

"But what I love most about you," he added softly, his gaze holding hers, "is your courage. Because you are the most courageous woman I know, Isabel Peters."

The stream of tears turned into a flood.

He flipped opened the box to reveal a stunning square-cut pink diamond, surrounded by a row of sparkling white stones. He looked up at her and took her hand. "I know you said that night in London a commitment is the last thing you're looking for, but I'm really hoping you're going to make an exception for me."

She wanted him to put that ring on her finger so badly her whole body shook.

"Marry me," he rasped. "Marry me so I don't have to feel as awful as I've felt the past few weeks without you."

Her whole body went numb. She was trying to find her voice when a groan sounded behind her.

"Come on, Izzie, just say yes."

She turned around to find that the entire Warriors team had assembled beside the reporters, helmets in hand.

"I don't know," she managed to tease. "I was thinking of making him suffer." She turned back to Alex, so ridiculously hot on one knee, she knew this moment would be imprinted on her mind forever. "I guess my dream one-night stand really backfired on me, huh?"

"That depends on how you define 'backfire.'" The sexy glint in his eyes made her hot all over. "If that means a million more of those before we grow old and tired, I'm okay with it."

Nick coughed. "Still filming." Izzie shoved her hand forward. Alex slid the ring on her finger, steadying her shaking hands with his own. The outrageously beautiful ring sparkled like pink fire in the glare of the stadium lights.

It fit perfectly.

The team whooped and hollered their approval. Alex got to his feet and pulled her into his arms for a kiss that was apparently not fit for broadcast because she heard Nick call it a wrap and fade into the background. Izzie sighed and wrapped her arms around Alex's neck. Because never in a million years would she have thought she'd get her quarterback.

When Alex finally set her away from him with reluctant hands he had a scowl on his face. "The only problem with this grand plan of mine is I can't kiss you like I want to."

"Patience," she murmured. "How many celebratory drinks do you think will do it?"

"One," he said flatly. "I'm buying them one and we're done."

He tucked her into his side as they walked toward the players. Her heart was so full she thought it might burst. "We've just left one question unanswered," she mused.

He lifted a brow. "What?"

"Damion."

"Damion? Who's Damion?"

"The hero from my book," she reminded him. "You asked me if he was good in bed…"

He shot her an amused look. "*Now* you're going to tell me? What's the verdict?"

"You are way, *way* better."

His shout of laughter rang out. Pulling to a halt, he lifted her up on tiptoes and captured her mouth in another of those long, sweet kisses that promised forever. "Give me an hour to celebrate with the team," he said huskily, "and I promise to blow that out of the water."

* * * * *

FALLING FOR
DR DIMITRIOU

ANNE FRASER

To Rachel and Stewart – my personal on-call doctors – and to Megan Haslam my supportive, patient and all round fabulous editor.

PROLOGUE

IT WAS THAT moment before dawn, before the sky had begun to lighten and the moon seemed at its brightest, when Alexander saw her for the first time. On his way to the bay where he kept his boat, his attention was caught by a woman emerging like Aphrodite from the sea.

She paused, the waves lapping around her thighs, to squeeze the water from her tangled hair. As the sun rose, it bathed her in light adding to the mystical scene. He held his breath. He'd heard about her—in a village this size it would have been surprising if the arrival of a stranger wasn't commented on—and they hadn't exaggerated when they'd said she was beautiful.

The bay where she'd been swimming was below him, just beyond the wall that bordered the village square. If she looked up she would see him. But she didn't. She waded towards the shore, droplets clinging to her golden skin, her long hair still streaming with water. If the village hadn't been full of gossip about the woman who'd come to stay in the villa overlooking the bay, he could almost let himself believe that she was a mythical creature rising from the sea.

Almost. If he were a fanciful man. Which he wasn't.

CHAPTER ONE

KATHERINE PLACED HER pen on the table and leaned back in her chair. She picked up her glass of water, took a long sip and grimaced. It was tepid. Although she'd only poured it a short while ago, the ice cubes had already melted in the relentless midday Greek sun.

As it had done throughout the morning, her gaze drifted to the bay almost immediately below her veranda. The man was back. Over the last few evenings he'd come down to the little bay around five and stayed there, working on his boat until the sun began to set. He always worked with intense concentration, scraping away paint and sanding, stopping every so often to step back and evaluate his progress. But today, Saturday, he'd been there since early morning.

He was wearing jeans rolled up above his ankles and a white T-shirt that emphasised his golden skin, broad shoulders and well-developed biceps. She couldn't make out the colour of his eyes, but he had dark hair, curling on his forehead and slightly over his neckline. Despite what he was wearing, she couldn't help thinking of a Greek warrior—although there was nothing but gentleness in the way he treated his boat.

Who was he? she wondered idly. If her friend Sally were

here she would have found out everything about him, down to his star sign. Unfortunately Katherine wasn't as gorgeous as Sally, to whom men responded like flies around a honey pot and who had always had some man on the go—at least until she'd met Tom. Now, insanely happily married to him, her friend had made it her mission in life to find someone for Katherine. So far her efforts had been in vain. Katherine had had her share of romances—well, two apart from Ben—but the only fizz in those had been when they'd fizzled out, and she'd given up on finding Mr Right a long time ago. Besides, men like the one she was watching were always attached to some beautiful woman.

He must have felt her eyes on him because he glanced up and looked directly at her. She scraped her chair back a little so that it was in the shadows, hoping that the dark glasses she was wearing meant he couldn't be sure she had been staring at him.

Not that she was at all interested in him, she told herself. It was just that he was a diversion from the work she was doing on her thesis—albeit a very pleasing-to-the-eye diversion.

Everything about Greece was a feast for the senses. It was exactly as her mother had described it—blindingly white beaches, grey-green mountains and a translucent sea that changed colour depending on the tide and the time of day. She could fully grasp, now, why her mother had spoken of the country of her birth so often and with such longing.

Katherine's heart squeezed. Was it already four weeks since Mum had died? It felt like only yesterday. The month had passed in a haze of grief and Katherine had worked even longer hours in an attempt to keep herself from thinking too much, until Tim, her boss, had pulled her aside and told her gently, but firmly, that she needed to take time off—especially as she hadn't had a holiday in years. Although she'd protested, he'd dug his heels in. Six weeks, he'd told her, and if he saw her in the office during that time, he'd call Security. One look at his face had told her he meant it.

Then when a work colleague had told her that the Greek parents of a friend of hers were going to America for the birth of their first grandchild and needed someone to stay in their home while they were away—someone who would care for their cherished cat and water the garden—Katherine knew it was serendipity; her thesis had been put to one side when Mum had been ill, and despite what Tim said about taking a complete rest, this would be the perfect time to finish it.

It would also be a chance to fulfil the promise she'd made to her mother.

The little whitewashed house was built on the edge of the village, tucked against the side of a mountain. It had a tiny open-plan kitchen and sitting room, with stone steps hewn out of the rock snaking up to the south-facing balcony that overlooked the bay. The main bedroom was downstairs, its door leading onto a small terrace that, in turn, led directly onto the beach. The garden was filled with pomegranate, fig and ancient, gnarled olive trees that provided much-needed shade. Masses of red bougainvillea, jasmine and honeysuckle clung to the wall, scenting the air.

The cat, Hercules, was no problem to look after. Most of the time he lay sunbathing on the patio and all she had to do was make sure he had plenty of water and feed him. She'd developed a fondness for him and he for her. He'd taken to sleeping on her bed and while she knew it was a habit she shouldn't encourage, there was something comforting about the sound of his purring and the warmth of his body curled up next to hers. And with that thought, her gaze strayed once more to the man working on the boat.

He'd resumed his paint scraping. He had to be hot down there where there was no shade. She wondered about offering him a drink. It would be the neighbourly, the polite thing to do. But she wasn't here to get to know the neighbours, she was here to see some of her mother's country and, while keeping her boss happy, to finish her thesis. Habits of a lifetime were too hard to break, though, and four days into her six-week holiday she hadn't actually seen very much of Greece, apart from a brief visit to the village her mother had lived as a child. Still, there was plenty of time and if she kept up this pace, her thesis would be ready to submit within the month and then she'd take time off to relax and sightsee.

However, the heat was making it difficult to concentrate. She should give herself a break and it wouldn't take her a moment to fetch him a drink. As it was likely he came from the village, he probably couldn't speak English very well anyway. That would definitely curtail any attempt to strike up a conversation.

Just as she stood to move towards the kitchen, a little girl, around five or six, appeared from around the corner of the cliff. She was wearing a pair of frayed denim shorts and a bright red T-shirt. Her long, blonde hair, tied up in a ponytail, bobbed as she skipped towards the man. A small spaniel, ears flapping, chased after her, barking excitedly.

'Baba!' she cried, squealing with delight, her arms waving like the blades of a windmill.

An unexpected and unwelcome pang of disappointment washed over Katherine. So he *was* married.

He stopped what he was doing and grinned, his teeth white against his skin.

'Crystal!' he said, holding his arms wide for the little girl to jump into them. Katherine could only make out enough of the rest of the conversation to know it was in Greek.

He placed the little girl down as a woman, slim with short blonde hair, loped towards them. This had to be the wife. She was carrying a wicker basket, which she laid on the sand, and said something to the man that made him grin.

The child, the cocker spaniel close on her heels, ran around in circles, her laughter ringing through the still air.

There was something about the small family, their utter enjoyment of each other, the tableau they made, that looked so perfect it made Katherine's heart contract. This was what family life should be—might have been—but would likely never be. At least, not for her.

Which wasn't to say that she didn't love the life she did have. It was interesting, totally absorbing and worthwhile. Public health wasn't regarded as the sexiest speciality, but in terms of saving lives most other doctors agreed it was public-health doctors and preventive medicine that made the greatest difference. One only had to think about the Broad Street pump, for example. No one had been able to stop the spread of cholera that had raged through London in the 1800s until they'd found its source.

When she next looked up the woman had gone but the detritus of a picnic still remained on the blanket. The man was leaning against a rock, his long legs stretched out in front of him, the child, dwarfed by his size, snuggled into his side, gazing up at him with a rapt expression on her face as he read to her from a story book.

It was no use, she couldn't concentrate out here. Gathering up her papers, she went back inside. She'd work for another hour before stopping for lunch. Perhaps then she'd explore the village properly. Apart from the short trip to Mum's village—and what a disappointment that had turned out to be—she'd been too absorbed in her thesis to do more than go for a swim or a walk along the beach before breakfast and last thing at night. Besides, she needed to stock up on more provisions.

She'd been to the shop on the village square once to buy some tomatoes and milk and had had to endure the undisguised curiosity of the shopkeeper and her customers and she regretted not having learnt Greek properly when she'd had the chance to do so. Her mother had been a native Greek speaker but she had never spoken it at home and consequently Katherine knew little of the language.

However, she hated the way some tourists expected the locals to speak English, regardless of what country they found themselves in, and had made sure she'd learnt enough to ask for what she needed—at the very least, to say please, thank you and to greet people. In the store, she'd managed to ask for what she wanted through a combination of hand signals and her few words of Greek—the latter causing no small amount of amusement.

She glanced at her papers and pushed them away with a sigh. The warm family scene she'd witnessed had unsettled her, bringing back the familiar ache of loneliness and longing. Since her concentration was ruined, she may as well go to the village now. A quick freshen-up and then she'd be good to go. Walking into her bedroom, she hesitated. She crossed over to her bedside drawer and removed the photograph album she always kept with her. She flicked through the pages until she found a couple of photos of

Poppy when she was six—around the same age as the little girl in the bay.

This particular one had been taken on the beach—Brighton, if she remembered correctly. Poppy was kneeling in the sand, a bucket and spade next to her, a deep frown knotting her forehead as she sculpted what looked like a very wobbly sandcastle. She was in a bright one-piece costume, her hair tied up in bunches on either side of her head. Another, taken the same day, was of Poppy in Liz's arms, the remains of an ice cream still evident on her face, her head thrown back as if she'd been snapped right in the middle of a fit of giggles. Katherine could see the gap in the front of her mouth where her baby teeth had fallen out, yet to be replaced with permanent ones. She appeared happy, blissfully so. As happy as the child she'd seen earlier.

She closed the album, unable to bear looking further. Hadn't she told herself that it was useless to dwell on what might have been? Work. That was what always stopped her dwelling on the past. The trip to the village could wait.

Immersed in her writing, Katherine was startled by a small voice behind her.

'Yiássas.'

Katherine spun around in her chair. She hadn't heard anyone coming up the rock steps but she instantly recognised the little girl from the bay. 'Oh, hello.' What was she doing here? And on her own? 'You gave me a bit of a fright,' she added in English.

The child giggled. 'I did, didn't I? I saw you earlier when I was with Baba. You were on the balcony.' She pointed to it. 'I don't think you have any friends so I thought you might want a visitor. Me!' Her English was almost perfect, although heavily accented.

Katherine laughed but it didn't sound quite as carefree as she hoped. 'Some adults like their own company.' She gestured to the papers in front of her. 'Besides, I have lots of work to do while I'm here.'

The girl studied her doubtfully for a few moments. 'But you wouldn't mind if I come and see you sometimes?'

What could she say to that? 'No, of course not. But I'm afraid you wouldn't find me very good company. I'm not used to entertaining little girls.'

The child looked astounded. 'But you must have been a little girl once! Before you got old.'

This time Katherine's laugh was wholehearted. 'Exactly. I'm old. No fun. Should you be here? Your family might be worried about you.'

The child's eyes widened. 'Why?'

'Well, because you're very small still and most of the time parents like to know where their children are and what they're up to.' She winced inwardly, aware of the irony of what she'd said.

'But they do know where I am, silly. I'm in the village! Hello, Hercules.' The girl knelt and stroked the cat. Suddenly pandemonium broke out. It seemed her spaniel had come to look for her. He ran into the room and spotting the cat made a beeline for it. With a furious yowl Hercules leapt up and onto Katherine's desk, scattering her papers, pens and pencils onto the floor. She grabbed and held on to the struggling cat as the dog jumped up against her legs, barking excitedly.

'Kato! Galen! Kato!' A stern male voice cut through the chaos. It was the child's father—the boat man. God, how many other people and animals were going to appear uninvited in her living room?

The spaniel obediently ran over to the man and lay down at his feet, tail wagging and panting happily. Now the father's censorious gaze rested on his little girl. After speaking a few words in Greek, he turned to Katherine. 'I apologise for my daughter's intrusion. She knows she shouldn't wander off without letting me know first. I didn't notice she'd gone until I saw her footprints headed this way.' His English was impeccable with only a trace of an attractive accent. 'Please, let us help you gather your papers.'

Close up he was overwhelmingly good-looking, with thick-lashed sepia eyes, a straight nose, curving sensual mouth and sharp cheekbones. Katherine felt another stab of envy for the blonde-haired woman. She lowered the still protesting Hercules to the floor. With a final malevolent glance at the spaniel, he disappeared outside.

'Please, there's no need...'

But he was already picking up some of the strewn papers. 'It's the least we can do.'

Katherine darted forward and placed a hand on his arm. To her dismay, her fingertips tingled where they touched his warm skin and she quickly snatched it away. 'I'd rather you didn't—they might get even more muddled up.'

He straightened and studied her for a moment from beneath dark brows. He was so close she could smell his soap and almost feel waves of energy pulsating from him. Every nerve cell in her body seemed to be on alert, each small hair on her body standing to attention. Dear God, that she should be reacting like this to a married man! What the hell was wrong with her? She needed to get a grip. 'Accidents happen, there is no need for you to do anything, thank you,' she said. Thankfully her voice sounded normal.

'Yes, Baba! Accidents happen!' the little girl piped up in English.

His response to his daughter, although spoken softly in Greek, had her lowering her head again, but when he turned back to Katherine a smile lighted his eyes and played around the corners of his mouth. He raked a hand through his hair. 'Again I must apologise for my daughter. I'm afraid Crystal is too used to going in and out of all the villagers' homes here and doesn't quite understand that some people prefer to offer invitations.'

Crystal looked so woebegone that Katherine found herself smiling back at them. 'It's fine—I needed a break. So now I'm having one—a little earlier than planned, but that's okay.'

'In which case we'll leave you to enjoy it in peace.' He glanced at her ringless fingers. 'Miss…?'

'Burns. Katherine Burns.'

'Katherine.' The way he rolled her name around his mouth made it sound exotic. 'And I am Alexander Dimitriou. I've noticed you watching from your balcony.'

'Excuse me! I wasn't watching you! I was working on my laptop and you just happened to be directly in my line of sight whenever I lifted my head.' The arrogance of the man! To take it for granted that she'd been watching him— even if she had.

When he grinned she realised she'd let him know that she had noticed him. The way he was looking at her was disturbing. It was simply not right for a married man to look at a woman who wasn't his wife that way.

'Perhaps,' he continued, 'you'll consider joining my family one day for lunch, to make up for disrupting your day?'

She wasn't here to hang around divine-looking Greek men—particularly married ones! 'Thank you,' she responded tersely. 'I did say to Crystal that she could come and visit me again some time,' she added as she walked father and daughter outside, 'but perhaps you should remind her to let you know before she does?'

She stood on the balcony, watching as they ambled hand in hand across the beach towards the village square, Crystal chattering and swinging on her father's arm. Even from this distance she could hear his laughter. With a sigh she turned around and went back inside.

Later that evening, after Crystal was in bed, Alexander's thoughts returned to Katherine, as they had over the last few days—ever since the morning he'd seen her come out of the water. It was just his luck that the villa she was staying in overlooked the bay where he was working on his boat.

He couldn't help glancing her way as she sat on her balcony, her head bent over her laptop as she typed, pausing only to push stray locks from her eyes—and to watch him.

And she *had* been watching him. He'd looked up more than once to catch her looking in his direction. She'd caused quite a stir in the village, arriving here by herself. The villagers, his grandmother and cousin Helen included, continued to be fascinated by this woman who'd landed in their midst and who kept herself to herself, seldom venturing from her temporary home unless it was to have a quick dip in the sea or shop for groceries at the village store. They couldn't understand anyone coming on holiday by themselves and had speculated wildly about her.

To their disappointment she hadn't stopped for a coffee or a glass of wine in the village square or to try some of

Maria's—the owner of only taverna in the village—home-cooked food so there had been no opportunity to find out more about her. Helen especially would have loved to know more about her—his cousin was always on at him to start dating again.

But, despite the fact Katherine was undeniably gorgeous, he wasn't interested in long-term relationships and he had the distinct impression that Miss Burns didn't do short-term ones.

However, there was something about this particular woman that drew him. Perhaps, he thought, because he recognised the same sadness in her that was in him. All the more reason, then, for him to keep his distance.

CHAPTER TWO

THE NEXT MORNING, having decided to work inside and out of sight, Katherine only managed to resist for a couple of hours before finding herself drawn like a magnet to the balcony.

Gazing down at the beach, she saw that Alexander, stripped to the waist, his golden skin glistening with a sheen of perspiration, was back working on his boat again. Dragging her gaze away from him, she closed her eyes for a moment and listened to the sound of the waves licking the shore. The sweet smell of oranges from a nearby orchard wafted on the breeze. Being here in Greece was like a balm for her soul.

A sharp curse brought her attention back to the bay.

Alexander had dropped his paint-scraper. He studied his hand for a moment and shook his head. He looked around as if searching for a bandage, but apparently finding only his T-shirt, bent to pick it up, and wound it around his palm.

She could hardly leave him bleeding—especially when, prepared as always, she'd brought a small first-aid kit with her and it was unlikely there would be a doctor available on a Sunday in such a small village.

The blood had pretty much soaked through his temporary bandage by the time she reached him but, undaunted, he had carried on working, keeping his left hand—the damaged one—elevated in some kind of optimistic hope of stemming the bleeding.

'*Kalíméra!*' Katherine called out, not wanting to surprise him. When he looked up, she pointed to his hand and lifted the first-aid kit she carried. 'Can I help?'

'It's okay, I'll manage,' he replied. When he smiled, her heart gave a queer little flutter. 'But thank you.'

'At least let me look at it. Judging by the amount of blood, you've cut it pretty badly.'

His smile grew wider. 'If you insist,' he said, holding out his injured hand.

She drew closer to him and began unwrapping his makeshift bandage. As she gently tugged the remaining bit of cloth aside and her fingers encountered the warmth of his work-roughened palm, she felt the same frisson of electricity course through her body as she had the day before. Bloody typical; the first time she could remember meeting someone whom she found instantly attractive he had to be married—and a father to boot.

'It's deep,' she said, examining the wound, 'and needs stitches. Is there a surgery open today?'

'Most of them are open for emergencies only on a Sunday. I'm not sure this constitutes one.'

'I think it does.' Katherine said, aware that her tone sounded schoolmistress prim. 'I'm a doctor, so I do know what I'm talking about.'

His eyebrows shot up. 'Are you really? The villagers had you down as a writer. A GP, I take it?'

Katherine shook her head. 'No. Epidemiology. Research. I'm in public health.'

'But not on holiday? You seemed pretty immersed in paperwork yesterday.'

'My thesis. For my PhD.'

'Brains too.' He grinned. 'So can't you stitch my hand?'

'Unfortunately, no. I could if I had a suturing kit with me but I don't. Anyway, you'll likely need a tetanus shot unless you've had one recently. Have you?'

'No.'

For some reason, the way he was looking at her made her think that he was laughing at her. 'Then one of the emergency surgeries it will have to be,' she said firmly. 'I'll clean and bandage the cut in the meantime. Is there someone who can give you a lift?'

'No need—it's within walking distance. Anyway, this little scratch is not going to kill me.'

'Possibly not but it could make you very sick indeed.' She thought for a moment. 'I strongly advise you to find out whether the doctor is willing to see you. I'll phone him if you like. As one doctor to another, he might be persuaded to see you.'

He was no longer disguising his amusement. 'Actually, that would be a bit embarrassing seeing as I'm the doctor and it's my practice—one of them anyway.'

'You're a doctor?' She couldn't keep the surprise out of her voice. She felt more than slightly foolish, standing before him with her little plastic medical kit. If he was a GP he was probably more qualified than she to assess the damage to his hand. Now she knew the reason for his secret amusement. 'You might have mentioned this before,' she continued through gritted teeth.

Alexander shrugged. 'I was going to, I promise. Eventually.' That smile again. 'I suppose I was enjoying the personal attention—it's nice to be on the receiving end for a change.'

'You really should have said straight away,' she reiterated, struggling to control the annoyance that was rapidly replacing her embarrassment. 'However, you can hardly suture your hand yourself.' Although right this minute she was half-minded to let him try.

'I could give it a go,' he replied, 'but you're right, it would be easier and neater if you did it. The practice I have here is really little more than a consulting room I use when the older villagers need to see a doctor and aren't unwell enough to warrant a trip to my practice. But it's reasonably well equipped. You could stitch it there.'

'In that case, lead the way.'

His consulting room had obviously once been a fisherman's cottage, with the front door leading directly onto the village square. There were only two rooms leading off the small hall and he opened the door to the one on the left. It was furnished with an examination couch, a stainless-steel trolley, a sink and most of what she'd expect to find in a small rural surgery. The one surprise was a deep armchair covered with a throw. He followed her gaze and grimaced. 'I know that doesn't really belong, but my older patients like to feel more at home when they come to see me here.'

Not really the most sanitary of arrangements, but she kept her own counsel. It wasn't up to her to tell him how to run his practice.

He opened a cupboard and placed some local anaesthetic and a syringe on the desk, along with a disposable suture tray. He perched on the couch and rested his hand, palm up, on his leg.

He definitely has the physique of a gladiator, she

thought, her gaze lingering on his chest for a moment too long. She shifted her gaze and found him looking at her, one eyebrow raised and a small smile playing on his lips. As heat rushed to her cheeks she turned away, wishing she'd left him to deal with his hand himself.

She washed her hands and slipped on a pair of disposable gloves, acutely conscious of his teasing appraisal as she filled the syringe with the local anaesthetic. Studiously avoiding looking at his naked chest, she gently lifted up his hand and, after swabbing the skin, injected into the wound. He didn't even flinch as she did so. 'I'll wait a few minutes for it to take effect.'

'So what brings you here?' he asked. 'It isn't one of the usual tourists spots.'

'I was kindly offered the use of the Dukases' villa through a colleague who is a friend of their daughter in exchange for taking care of Hercules and the garden. My mother was from Greece and I've always wanted to see the country where she was born.'

'She was from here?'

'From Ītylo. This was the closest I could get to there.'

'It's your first time in the Peloponnese?'

'My first time in Greece,' Katherine admitted.

'And your mother didn't come with you?'

'No. She passed away recently.' To her dismay, her voice hitched. She swallowed the lump in her throat before continuing. 'She always wanted the two of us to visit Greece together, but her health prevented her from travelling. She had multiple sclerosis.'

'I'm sorry.' Two simple words, but the way he said it, she knew he really meant it.

She lightly prodded his palm with her fingertips. 'How does that feel?'

'Numb. Go ahead.'

Opening up the suture pack, she picked up the needle. Why did he have to be nice as well as gorgeous?

'I hope you're planning to see some of the Peloponnese while you're here. Olympia? Delphi? Athens and the Acropolis for sure. The city of Mycenae, perhaps?'

Katherine laughed. 'They're all on my list. But I want to finish my thesis first.'

He raised his head and frowned slightly. 'So no holiday for a while, then? That's not good. Everyone needs to take time out to relax.'

'I do relax. Often.' Not that often—but as often as she wanted to. 'Anyway I find work relaxing.'

'Mmm,' he said, as if he didn't believe her. Or approve. 'Work can be a way to avoid dealing with the unbearable. Not good for the psyche if it goes on too long. You need to take time to grieve,' he suggested gently.

She stiffened. Who was he to tell her what was good for her and what she needed? How he chose to live his life was up to him, just as it was up to her how she lived.

'I must apologise again for yesterday,' he continued, when she didn't reply, 'You were obviously working so I hope we didn't set you back too much. My daughter's been dying to meet you since you arrived. I'm afraid her curiosity about you got the better of her.'

Katherine inserted a stitch and tied it off. 'Your daughter is charming and very pretty.'

'Yes, she is. She takes after her mother.'

'I take it the beautiful woman on the beach yesterday is your wife?' she said, inserting another l stitch.

When she heard his sharp intake of breath she stopped. 'I'm sorry. Did that hurt? Didn't I use enough local?'

His expression was taut, but he shook his head. 'I can't

feel a thing. The woman you saw is Helen, my cousin. My wife died.'

Katherine was appalled. 'I'm so sorry. How awful for you and your daughter. To lose her mother when so young.' She winced inwardly at her choice of words.

'Yes,' he said abruptly. 'It was.'

So he knew loss too. She bent her head again and didn't raise it until she'd added the final stitch and the wound was closed. When had his wife died? Crystal had to be, what? Four? Five? Therefore it had to be within that time frame. Judging by the bleakness in his eyes, the loss was still raw. In which case he might as well be married. And why the hell were her thoughts continuing along this route?

She gave herself a mental shake and placed a small square dressing on top and finished with a bandage, pleased that her work was still as neat as it had been when she'd sutured on a regular basis.

'What about tetanus?' she asked. 'I'm assuming you have some in stock here?'

'Suppose I'd better let you give me that too. It's been over five years since I last had one.' He went to the small drugs fridge and looked inside. 'Hell,' he said after examining the contents. 'I'm out. Never mind, I'll get it when I go back to my other surgery tomorrow.'

'It could be too late by then—as I'm sure you know. No, since it seems that you are my patient, at least for the moment, I'm going to have to insist you get one today.'

He eyed her. 'That would mean a trip to Pýrgos—almost an hour from here. Unfortunately, Helen has taken my car to take Crystal to play with a friend and won't be back until tonight. Tomorrow it will have to be.'

She hesitated, but only for a moment. 'In that case, I'll drive you.'

'Something tells me you're not going to back down on this.'

She smiled. 'And you'd be right.' She arched an eyebrow. 'You might want to fetch a clean shirt. Why don't you do that while I get my car keys?'

But it seemed as if she'd offered him a lift without the means to carry it through. Not wanting to drive down from Athens —she'd heard about the Peloponnese roads, especially the one that ran between here and the Greek capital—she'd taken a circuitous route; first an early morning flight, followed by a ferry and then two buses to the rental company In hindsight it would have been quicker and probably far less stressful to have flown into Athens.

And now she had a puncture. Thankfully the car did have a spare wheel. She jacked it up and found the wrench to loosen the bolts but they wouldn't budge. No doubt they had rusted.

'Problems?'

She whirled around to find Alexander standing behind her. He had showered and changed into light-coloured cotton trousers and a white short-sleeved shirt.

'Puncture. I'm just changing the wheel. As soon as I get a chance, I'm going to exchange this heap for something better.'

The car the company had given her had more dents and bashes in it than a rally car after a crash. She would have insisted on a newer, more pristine model, but the company had said it was the only one they had available.

His lips twitched. He walked around the car, shaking his head. 'They palmed this off on you?'

'Yes, well, I was tired.' She resented the fact that he

thought she'd let herself be taken advantage of—even if she had.

'Which company did you rent this from?'

She told him.

'In that case, they have a branch in Katákolo, which isn't too far from where we're going.'

'Will it be open on a Sunday?'

'The cruise ships all offer day trips to Olympia from there. Like most places that cater for tourists, everything will be open. Once I've been jagged to your satisfaction I'll make sure they exchange it for something better.'

'I'm perfectly able to manage to sort it out myself.' Did all Greek men think women were helpless?

He drew back a little, holding up his hands. 'Hey. You're helping me. And it's not far from where we're going.'

She was instantly ashamed of herself. He'd done nothing to warrant her snapping at him. It was hardly his fault that he made her feel like a schoolgirl with her first crush.

'I'm sorry. It's just that I'm a bit hot.' She sought a better reason to excuse her behaviour, but apart from telling him that he found his company unsettling she couldn't think of one. 'In the meantime, I still have to change the wheel.' She picked up a rock and hit the wrench. Nothing. No movement. Not even a centimetre.

He crouched down next to her, the muscles of his thighs straining against the material of his trousers. 'Let me do it.'

'I can manage. At least I would if the things weren't stuck.'

He took the wrench from her. 'It just needs a little strength.'

'You shouldn't. Not with your hand recently sutured.'

He ignored her and within moments the nuts were off

the wheel. He took the flat tyre off and silently she passed him the spare.

'I probably loosened them.' He looked up at her and grinned. 'I'm sure you did.' He lifted the new wheel into position and replaced the bolts.

'Thank you,' she said. 'I can take it from here.'

He stood back and watched as she lowered the car to the ground.

'I'll just tighten the bolts again,' he said, 'then we'll be good to go. Would you like me to drive?'

'No, thank you.'

Despite the open windows the car was hot; unsurprisingly, the air-conditioning didn't work either. Katherine gripped the steering-wheel, trying not to flinch whenever a car overtook her, the vehicle often swerving back in just in time to avoid being smashed into by another coming in the opposite direction. Perhaps she should have taken Alexander up on his offer to drive? But if he drove the same way as his countrymen did, being a passenger would be ten times worse. She preferred being in control.

Eventually the countryside gave way to denser traffic and by the time Alexander directed her to a parking spot in front of the surgery she was a nervous wreck, her hands were damp and she knew her hair was plastered to her scalp. She was beginning to appreciate why the car the company had given her was badly dented.

He looked relieved as he undid his seat belt. 'This won't take long but why don't you go for a walk while you're waiting?'

'If you're going to be quick I might as well come in with you.' She was curious to see how the medical services in Greece worked.

While Alexander greeted the receptionist, Katherine took a seat in the small waiting room next to an elderly woman with a bandage on her knee and clutching a walking stick. Alexander turned to her and said something in Greek that made her laugh.

'Mrs Kalfas is waiting for her husband to collect her,' he explained to Katherine, 'so I can go straight in. I won't be long.'

A few moments after Alexander disappeared from sight, a man in his early to mid-twenties, staggered in and, after saying a few words to the receptionist, almost fell into one of the empty chairs. He was good-looking with dark curly hair, a full mouth and olive skin, but his jeans and checked shirt were stained and crumpled as if he'd picked them up off the bedroom floor, too ill to care. His cheeks were flushed and his eyes, when he managed to open them briefly, glittered with fever. Perhaps she should have gone for that walk. All doctors knew that hospitals and GP waiting rooms were bad news for the healthy.

Mrs Kalfas tried to strike up a conversation with him, but he appeared to have little interest in whatever she was saying. Warning bells started to clamour in Katherine's head as she studied him covertly from under her eyelids. Now she wondered if his eyes were closed because the light was annoying him—and the way he kept pressing his hand to the back of his neck as if it were sore alarmed her too. He really didn't look well at all. The receptionist should have let the doctors know that he was here.

Katherine was about to suggest it when he gave a loud moan and slid to the floor. Instantly she was on her feet and, crouching by his side, feeling for his pulse. It was there but weak and rapid. She glanced around but annoyingly there was no sign of the receptionist. Mrs Kalfas was staring, horrified.

'I need some help here,' Katherine called out. 'Alexander!'

The door behind which he'd vanished was flung open and Alexander, followed by a short, balding, overweight man with a stethoscope wrapped around his neck, rushed over and knelt by Katherine's side.

'What happened?' Alexander asked.

'He came in a few minutes ago. I was just about to suggest he be taken through when he collapsed. He's been rubbing his neck as if it's painful or stiff. We should consider meningitis.'

Alexander and his colleague exchanged a few words in rapid Greek and the other doctor hurried away.

The man on the floor groaned softly. The receptionist reappeared and came to stand next to Mrs Kalfas, placing a comforting arm around the older woman. Alexander said something to the younger woman and she hurried back to her desk and picked up the phone.

'It could be a number of things but to be on the safe side Carlos—Dr Stavrou—is going to get a line so we can start him on IV antibiotics,' Alexander told Katherine. 'Diane is phoning for an ambulance.'

Carlos returned and ripped open a pack and handed Alexander a venflon. He quickly inserted it into a vein and, taking the bag of saline from his colleague, attached one end of the tube to the needle. When Katherine held out her hand for the bag of saline, Alexander passed it to her and she held it up so that the fluid could flow unimpeded. In the meantime, Alexander had injected antibiotics straight into one of the stricken patient's veins.

As Katherine placed an oxygen mask over his face, she

was vaguely aware that the receptionist had returned and along with Mrs Kalfas was watching intently. Alexander whirled around and spoke rapidly to the receptionist. He translated her reply for Katherine.

'Diane says the ambulance will be here shortly. She's agreed to take Mrs Kalfas home instead of making her wait for her husband. Seeing she's had a bit of a fright, I think it's better.'

Katherine was impressed with the way he'd considered the old woman, even in the midst of an emergency. Their patient was still unconscious but apart from keeping an eye on his airway there was little more they could do until the ambulance arrived. They couldn't risk taking him in a car in case he arrested.

'You have a defib to hand?' she asked.

'Naturally.'

She wondered what had caused the man to collapse. A number of possibilities ran through her head, meningitis being one, but without further tests it was impossible to know. All they could do now was stabilise him until they got him to hospital.

Diane picked up her handbag and helped the old lady out. Soon after, the ambulance arrived and the paramedics took over. They spoke to Alexander before quickly loading the patient into the ambulance.

'Should one of us go with him?' Katherine asked.

'No need. Carlos wants to go. He's his patient.'

The ambulance doors were slammed shut and it drove away, sirens screaming.

'Are you all right?' Alexander asked.

'Perfectly. Could you make sure they test him for meningitis?'

'Bit of a leap, isn't it? Carlos said Stefan—the patient—

is not only accident prone but there's a few bugs doing the rounds. Besides, I didn't see any signs of a rash.'

'Trust me. Communicable diseases are my area of expertise and that young man has all the signs—sensitivity to light, fever, neck pain. The rash could appear at any time.' Alexander studied her for a moment. 'It couldn't hurt to do a lumbar puncture. I'll phone the hospital and make sure they do all the tests. At least he's been started on IV antibiotics. In the meantime, I'm afraid we're going to have to wait here until Carlos returns. Is that okay?'

'Sure.' She smiled at him. 'You can show me around while we wait.'

The practice was as well equipped as any Katherine had seen. In addition to four consulting rooms, one for each of the doctors, one for the nurses and one for their physio, there was an X-ray room and a sleek, spotlessly clean treatment room. All the equipment was modern and up to date.

'You appear to be almost as well set up as a small hospital,' Katherine said, impressed.

'We never know what we're going to get, so we like to be prepared for the worst. We have, as you can imagine, a fair share of road traffic accidents on these roads and sometimes people bring the casualties here as it's closer than the hospital.' Not quite the small family practice she'd imagined.

'We don't do much more than stabilise them and send them on,' Alexander continued, 'but it can make the difference between survival and death.'

'You have advanced life-support training, then?'

'Yes. We all do. It also helps that I used to be a surgeon.' He picked up the phone. 'Would you excuse me while I phone the hospital?' he said. 'I need to tell them to watch out for meningitis, as you suggested, and Carlos was telling me earlier that one of my patients was admitted there last night. I'd like to find out how he's doing.'

'Be my guest,' Katherine replied. As she waited for him to finish the call she studied him covertly from under her lashes. The more she learned about him the more he intrigued her. So he used to be a surgeon. What, then, had brought him to what, despite the expensive and up-to-date equipment, was still essentially a rural family practice? Had he come back here because of his wife? And how had she died? Had she been a road traffic victim?

While he'd been talking on the phone, Alexander's expression had darkened. He ended the phone call and sat lost in thought for a while. It was almost as if he'd forgotten she was there.

'Something wrong?' she asked.

'The patient Carlos was telling me about has been transferred to a hospital in Athens. The hospital doctor who admitted him yesterday sent him there this morning, but he's left to go fishing and can't be reached. None of the staff on duty today can tell me anything.' He leaned back in his chair. 'I'll speak to him tomorrow and find out why he felt a transfer was necessary.' He shook his head as if to clear it. 'But I have spoken to the doctor on call today about Stéfan. She's promised to do a lumbar puncture on him.'

'Good,' Katherine said.

'So what is your thesis on?' Alexander asked.

'As I said, communicable diseases. Mainly African ones.'

'What stage of your training are you?'

She raised an eyebrow. 'Consultant. Have been for four years. I'm thinking of applying for a professor's post. Hence the doctorate.'

He whistled between his teeth. 'You're a consultant! You don't look old enough.'

'I'm thirty-four.'

They chatted for a while about her work and different infectious diseases Alexander had come across in Greece. Caught up in discussing her passion, she was surprised when she heard footsteps and Carlos came in. She'd no idea so much time had passed.

'How is our patient?' Alexander asked in English, after formally introducing her to his partner.

'His blood pressure had come up by the time I left him in the care of the emergency team at the hospital. They'll let me know how he is as soon as they've done all the tests.'

'Will you let me know when they do?'

'Of course.'

Alexander pushed away from the desk and stood. He smiled at Katherine. 'In that case, let's go and swap that car of yours.'

The car rental company did have another car for her, but it wouldn't be available until later that afternoon.

Katherine turned to Alexander. 'I'm sure you want to get home. Isn't there another rental company in the area?'

'I suspect you'll find the same thing there. The cruise ships come in in the morning and a lot of the passengers—those who don't want to take the bus tour to Olympia—hire a car for the day. They tend to bring them back around four.'

'Damn. That's three hours away.'

'We could have lunch,' he suggested. 'Or, if you're not hungry, we can go to Olympia ourselves. It's years since I've been and it's less than thirty minutes from here. By the time we get back, Costa here should have a car for you.'

He smiled. 'You're in Greece now. You'll find life a lot easier if you accept that here time works in a different zone.'

She hid a sigh. She should be getting back to her thesis. By taking the morning off she risked falling behind the schedule she'd mapped out for herself.

Whoa—what was she thinking? Had she completely lost it? He was right. What was the hurry anyway? It was Sunday and an interesting, *single* hunk was wanting to spend time with her.

'I would love to see Olympia,' she said. And she would. It was near the top of her list of places to visit. It would also be less intense, less like a date, than having lunch.

'Good. That's settled, then.' He opened the passenger door for Katherine. She looked at him and arched an eyebrow.

'I think it will be less stressful—and safer for us all— if I drive,' he said. 'I know the roads better.'

She hesitated, then broke into a smile. 'To be honest, if I never have to drive that heap of scrap again it would be too soon. So be my guest. Knock yourself out.'

It wasn't long before she was regretting her decision—and her words. As far as she was concerned, Alexander drove just like every other Greek driver.

'When I said knock yourself out,' she hissed, 'I didn't mean literally.'

He laughed. 'Don't worry. I promise you driving this way is safer.'

Nevertheless, she was hugely relieved when they arrived still in one piece. Alexander found a space in the crowded car park.

'There are two parts to the site—the ruins of the ancient city and the museum. I suggest we start off in the museum, which is air-conditioned.' He glanced at her appraisingly and his lips twitched. She was wearing navy trousers and a white cotton blouse with a Peter Pan collar, which, she had to admit, while neat and professional were almost unbearably hot. 'It'll be cooler by the time we're finished. If I remember correctly, there is very little shade in the ruins.'

She wandered around the exhibits, trying to concentrate but not really able to. She was too acutely aware of the similarity between the physiques of the naked statues and the man close by.

When they'd finished in the museum they walked across to the ruins. Although it was cooler than it had been earlier, it was still hot and almost immediately she felt a trickle of perspiration gather between her breasts. Alexander, on the other hand, looked as fresh and as cool as he'd done since they'd left the village.

As he pointed out the temples of Zeus and Hera, Katherine began to relax. Perhaps it was because, away from the statues, she could concentrate on what Alexander was saying. He knew a great deal about Greek history and was an easy and informative guide and soon she was caught up in his stories about what life must have been like during the Ottoman era.

When they'd finished admiring the bouleuterion, where the statue of Zeus had once stood, he led her across to the track where the athletes had competed. 'Did you know they competed in the nude?'

Instantly an image of Alexander naked leaped into her head and blood rushed to her cheeks. She hoped he would think it was the heat that was making her flush but when she saw the amusement in his eyes she knew he was perfectly aware what she'd been thinking.

It was nuts. After Ben she'd only ever had one other significant long-term relationship—with Steven, one of her colleagues. When that had ended, after he'd been offered a job in the States, she'd been surprisingly relieved. Since then, although she'd been asked out many times and Sally had tried to fix her up with several of the unattached men she or Tom knew, and she'd gone out with two or three of them, no one had appealed enough to make her want to see them again beyond a couple of dates.

Relationships, she'd decided, were overrated. Many women were single and very happy—as was she. She could eat when she liked, go where she pleased without having to consult anyone, holiday where it suited her and work all weekend and every weekend if she wanted to. Until her mother's death, she had rarely been lonely—she hadn't lied to Crystal when she'd told her she preferred being on her own, but that didn't mean she didn't miss physical contact. That didn't mean she didn't miss sex.

She felt her flush deepen. But sex without strings had never been her cup of tea.

God! She'd thought more about sex over these last two days than she had in months. But it was hard *not* to think about it around all these nude statues. Perhaps it hadn't been such a good idea choosing to come here instead of lunch. Lunch might have been the safer option after all.

A replacement car still wasn't available when they returned to the rental company.

'Really!' Katherine muttered. 'It's almost six.' Unlike Alexander, she needed to cool off, preferably with an ice-cold shower. And to do that she needed to get home—and out of Alexander's company.

'He promises he'll have one by seven. If not, he'll give you his own car.' Alexander grinned. 'I did warn you about Greek timing.'

'But aren't you in a hurry to get back?' she asked, dismayed. 'I mean, you've given up the best part of your day to help me out. You must have other stuff you'd rather be doing. And I should get back to my thesis.'

'Nope. I'm in no rush. As I said, I'm not expecting my cousin and Crystal home until later. And surely you can give yourself a few more hours off?' The laughter in his eyes dimmed momentarily. 'Trust me, sometimes work should take a back seat.'

It was all right for him, he clearly found it easy to relax. But to spend more time in his company, blushing and getting tongue-tied, was too embarrassing. Still, she couldn't very well make him take a taxi all the way back home—even if it was an appealing thought. Maybe *she* should get a taxi home? Now she was being ridiculous! She was behaving like someone with sunstroke. She almost sighed with relief. Perhaps that was it? She clearly wasn't herself. She realised he was watching her curiously. What had he been saying? Oh, yes—something about dinner.

'In that case, dinner would be lovely,' she replied, pulling herself together. 'Do you have somewhere in mind?'

'As a matter of fact I do. It's down by the shore. They sell the best seafood this side of Greece.' He tilted his head. 'You do like seafood, don't you?'

'I love it.'

'Good. We can wave goodbye to the cruise ships and more or less have the place to ourselves. We'll leave the car here. It's not far.'

They walked along the deserted main street. Without the hordes of visitors and now that the shopkeepers had brought in their stands that had been filled with tourist souvenirs, maps and guides, the town had a completely different feel to it. It was as if it were a town of two identities—the one belonging to the tourists, and this typically Greek sleepy one.

The restaurant was situated at the end of a quiet cul-de-sac and it didn't look very prepossessing from the rear, where the entrance was situated. Understated was the word Katherine would use to describe the interior with its striped blue and white table runners and unlit candles rammed into empty wine bottles. But when they were guided to a table on the veranda by the *maître d'*, the view took Katherine's breath away. White sands and a blue, blue sea glittered as if some ancient god had scattered diamonds onto its surface. Alexander pulled out a chair for her beneath the shade of a tree and she sank happily into it.

When Alexander chose the lobster, freshly caught that morning, she decided to have it too. And since he was determined to drive they ordered a glass of chilled white wine for her and a fruit juice for himself.

They chatted easily about Greece and the recent blow to its economy and Alexander suggested various other places she might want to visit. Then he asked which medical school she'd studied at and she'd told him Edinburgh. Surprisingly, it turned out that it had been one of his choices but in the end he'd decided on Bart's.

'What made you decide to study in England?' she asked.

'I was brought up there. My mother was from Kent.' That explained his excellent English.

'So you have a Greek father and an English mother. I'm the opposite. How did your parents meet?'

'My mother met my father when she was working in a taverna while she was backpacking around Greece. It was supposed to be her gap year but in the end she never made it to university. Not long after she and my father started dating, they married. They moved to an apartment in Athens and after a couple of years they had me, then my younger brother. But she always pined for England. My father lectured in archaeology so he applied for a post at the British Museum and when he was accepted, we upped and left. I was five at the time.

'My father always missed Greece, though, so we came back as a family whenever we could, particularly to see my grandmother—my father's mother—and all the other family—aunts and uncles and cousins. Greece has always felt like home to me. Dad died when he was in his early forties. My grandfather died shortly after he did and, as my father's eldest son, I inherited the villa I live in now, as well as the land around it. It's been in our family for generations. Naturally my grandmother still lives in the family home.'

Katherine wanted to ask about his wife, but judging by his terse response in the village consulting room earlier that was a no-go area. 'And where's your mother now?' she asked instead, leaning back as their waiter placed their drinks in front of them.

'Still in England,' Alexander continued, when their waiter had left. 'She hasn't been back since my father died. I don't think she can bear to come anymore. She lives close to my brother in Somerset.'

'Doesn't she miss her grandchild?'

'Of course. However, Mother's life is in England—it's where her friends and my brother and his family are. We visit her often and, of course, there's video chat.' He took a sip of his drink. 'That's enough about me. What about you? Is there someone waiting for you in the UK?'

'No. No one.'

He looked surprised. 'Divorced, then? I'm assuming no children otherwise they'd be with you.'

She hesitated. 'Not divorced. Never married.' She swallowed. 'And no children.'

'Brothers and sisters? Your dad?'

'My dad passed away when I was fifteen. And no brothers or sisters.'

'So an only child. Being on your own must have made your mother's death even harder to handle, then,' he said softly.

The sympathy in his voice brought a lump to her throat. But she didn't want him to feel sorry for her.

'As I told Crystal, I like my own company. I have loads of friends in the UK when—if—I feel the need to socialise.'

'No one who could come with you? We Greeks find it difficult to imagine being on our own. As you've probably noticed, we like to surround ourselves with family.'

'Plenty of people offered to come,' she said quickly. 'But this trip was something I needed to do alone.'

He said nothing, just looked at her with his warm, brown eyes.

'I wish I could have come with Mum before she died, though. She always hoped to return to Greece, with Dad and me, to show me her country, but sadly it never happened,' she found herself explaining, to fill the silence.

'Because of her MS?'

'Yes. Mostly.'

But even before her mother's diagnosis the trip had been talked about but never actually planned. Her parents' restaurant had taken all their energy, money and time. At first it had seemed to be going from strength to strength, but then the unimaginable had happened. Dad had died and without him Mum had become a shadow of herself and had talked less and less about returning to Greece.

It had only been later that she'd realised that her father's death and struggling with a failing business hadn't been the only reasons Mum had been listless. She'd hidden her symptoms from her daughter until the evening she'd collapsed. And that had been the beginning of a new nightmare.

'What do you do when you're not working?' he asked, when she didn't expand.

'I kind of work all the time,' she admitted 'It's honestly my favourite thing to do.'

He frowned as if he didn't believe her. But it was true. She loved her work and found it totally absorbing. Given the choice of a night out or settling down to some research with a glass of wine in one hand, the research won hands down.

Their food arrived and was set before them. Katherine reached for the bowl of lemon quarters at the same as Alexander. As their fingers touched she felt a frisson of electricity course through her body. She drew back too quickly and flushed.

He lifted up the dish, his expression enigmatic. 'You first.'

'Thank you.'

'So why public health?' he asked, seeming genuinely interested.

'I thought I wanted to do general medicine but I spent six months in Infectious Diseases as part of my rotation and loved it—particularly when it came to diagnosing the more obscure infections. It was like solving a cryptic crossword puzzle. You had to work out what it could be by deciphering the clues, and that meant finding out as much as you could about your patient—where they, or their families, had been recently, for example. Sometimes it was obvious if they'd just come from Africa—then you'd start by think of malaria—or typhoid or if they'd been on a walking holiday in a place where there were lots of sheep, making Lyme disease a possibility. It was the patients who made the job so fascinating. When you'd found out as much as you could, you had to decide what tests and investigations to do, ruling diseases out one by one until the only one left was almost certainly the right answer.'

She rested her fork on the side of her plate. 'Of course, it wasn't always a good outcome. Sometimes by the time you found out what the patient had it was too late. And what was the point in diagnosing someone with malaria if you couldn't stop them getting it in the first place? I became really interested in prevention and that's when I moved into public health.' She stopped suddenly. 'Sorry. I didn't mean to go on. But when I get talking about work...'

'Hey, I'm a doctor, I like talking shop.'

'Why did you decide to come back to Greece?' she asked.

Something she couldn't read flickered behind his eyes. 'I wanted to spend more time with my daughter,' he said shortly. 'But we were talking about you. How did your parents meet?' It seemed he was equally determined to turn the conversation back to her.

'Mum met Dad when he was in the armed forces. He was stationed in Cyprus and she was visiting friends there. They fell in love and he left the army and they moved back to Scotland. He tried one job after another, trying to find something he enjoyed or at least was good at. Eventually he gave up trying to find the ideal job and started working for a building company. We weren't well off—not poor but not well off. We lived in a small house bordering an estate where there was a lot of crime. When I was eight my father became unwell. He didn't know what was it was—except that it was affecting his lungs. He was pretty bad before Mum persuaded him to see his GP.' She paused. 'That's when I began to think of becoming a doctor.'

He leaned forward. 'Go on.'

'We used to go, as a family, to his doctor's appointments. We did everything as a family.' Sadness washed over her. 'First there were the visits to the GP, but when he couldn't work out what was going on, he referred Dad to the hospital. I was fascinated. Everything about the hospital intrigued me: the way the doctors used to rush about seeming so important; the way the nurses always seemed to know what they were doing; the smells; the sounds—all the stuff that normally puts people off I found exciting.

'Of course, I was too young to understand that the reason we were there was because there was something seriously wrong with my father. His physician was a kind woman. I remember her well. She had these horn-rimmed glasses and she used to look at me over the top of them. When she saw how interested I was, she let me listen to my father's chest with her stethoscope. I remember hearing the dub-dub of his heartbeat and marvelling that this thing, this muscle, no larger than his fist, was what was keeping him—what was keeping me and everyone else—alive.

'I was always smart at school. It came easy to me to get top marks and when I saw how proud it made my parents, I worked even harder. My school teachers told my parents that they had high hopes for me. When I told Mum and Dad—I was twelve—that I wanted to be a doctor they were thrilled. But they knew that it would be difficult if I went to the high school in our area. It had a reputation for being rough and disruptive. They saved every penny they could so they could send me to private school.

'My father had received a payment from the building company when he left—by this time he'd been diagnosed with emphysema from years of breathing in building dust—but I knew he'd been planning to use the money for a down payment on a mortgage to buy a little restaurant—Dad would be the manager, Mum the head cook—and I didn't want them to use their life savings on me, not if they didn't have to.

'I persuaded them to let me apply to one of the top private schools. My teacher had told them that the school awarded scholarships to children with potential but not the funds to go to the school. She also warned them that it was very competitive. But I knew I could do it—and I did.'

'I am beginning to suspect that you're not in the habit of letting obstacles get in your way.'

Suddenly she was horrified. She wasn't usually so garrulous and certainly not when it came to talking about herself. Over the years she'd become adept at steering the conversation away from herself and onto the other person. Now she was acutely conscious of having monopolised the conversation, and when she thought about it she realised she'd made herself out to be a paragon of virtue when nothing could be further from the truth. Perhaps it was the wine. Or the way he listened to her as if she were the most fascinating person he'd ever met. Her heart thumped. Perhaps this was the way he was with everyone. She suspected it was. In which case he'd be an excellent family doctor.

'So how long have you been back in Greece?' she asked when their waiter left them, after replenishing their water glasses. She really wanted to know more about *him*.

'Just over two years.' His gaze dropped to his glass. He twirled his water, the ice cubes tinkling against the side. 'Not long after I lost my wife. I worked at St George's in

London—As I mentioned earlier, I trained as surgeon before going into general practice—but my wife, Sophia, wasn't really a city girl, so we bought a house in a nearby suburb and I commuted from there. And when I was on call, I slept at the hospital.' A shadow crossed his face. 'In retrospect, that was a mistake,' he murmured, so softly she couldn't be sure she'd heard him correctly. 'Why did you change to general practice?'

His expression darkened. 'I gave surgery up when I decided to return to Greece.'

It wasn't really an answer and she had the distinct feeling he was keeping as much back from her as he was telling her. Had he really been content to give up the challenges and adrenaline rush of surgery to return to Greece to be a GP? But bereavement often caused people to change their lives.

'Was your wife Greek?'

'Yes.'

'Did she work while you were in the UK?' she asked. How had she felt about leaving her country and going to a much colder, much greyer London? But, then, she had been with the man she'd loved and who had loved her. No doubt she hadn't cared.

'She was a musician,' he replied. 'She always wanted to play in an orchestra. She gave that up when we moved to England and taught piano instead.'

'Crystal must miss her terribly.'

'We both do. I see her mother in Crystal every day.' He swallowed and averted his gaze from hers for a few moments. 'What about you?' he asked, eventually. 'Don't you want children?'

He was looking at her again with that same intense expression in his eyes.

'Don't most women? But…' She dropped her head and fiddled with her butter knife, searching for the right words. 'It wasn't meant to be,' she finished lamely. Her heart thumped uncomfortably against her ribs. *Keep the conversation on neutral territory,* she told herself. 'I enjoyed the trip to Olympia. You know a lot about Greek archaeology and history,' she said.

He slid her a thoughtful look as if he knew she was deliberately changing the subject.

'My father was an archaeologist and my wife shared his passion,' he said. 'What chance do you think I wouldn't be? I doubt there is an archaeological site in Greece I haven't been to. Every holiday, when we returned here, that's what we did. I think my wife thought it was her mission in life to educate me.' His face clouded and Katherine knew he was thinking of his wife again. He had loved her very much, that much was clear.

What would it be like—the thought almost came out of nowhere—to be loved like that? To know that there was one person in the world who treasured you above all else? That there was someone you could turn to in your darkest moments, share your deepest secrets and fears with?

It was unlikely she'd ever know.

Katherine sank back into the leather seat of her replacement car, grateful she didn't have to drive back to the villa on dark, twisting roads. Alexander switched on the radio, and the soothing notes of a Brahms concerto softly filled the silence that had sprung up between them since they'd left the restaurant. The lights of the dashboard and the occasional passing vehicle revealed a man absorbed with his own thoughts, his forehead knotted, his eyes bleak. He turned the volume up a little more.

'You like this?' she asked. 'It's one of my favourites.'

He glanced at her. 'It is? My wife used to play it all the time. I haven't listened to it for a while…' He looked away, his mouth set in a grim line.

His wife was like a ghostly presence in the car.

Katherine closed her eyes. Deliberately shifting her focus from Alexander, she wondered how Stéfan was faring. If it was meningitis, he could very well be struggling for his life at this moment. She hoped she was wrong and he just had an infection that would be quickly cleared up with antibiotics.

Becoming aware they had entered the village, she sat straighter in her seat.

Tension seeped between them as he brought the car to a standstill outside her villa. They unclipped their seat belts and climbed out of the car.

As he handed her the keys, their fingers touched. She looked up at him from beneath her lashes, wondering if he had felt the electricity too. Would he ask to come in? Or if he could see her again?

Instead, his voice was as neutral as his words. 'I enjoyed today. Thank you, Katherine.'

Disappointment washed over her. But what had she expected? It was clear he was still grieving for his wife.

'I did too. Good night…'

'Good night, Katherine.'

She winced inwardly as she heard the finality in his tone. Hercules, purring loudly, curved his body around her legs as she opened the front door.

He was some comfort at least.

As the door closed behind her, Alexander thrust his hands deeper into his pockets and, before turning for the short walk home across the square, cursed himself for the fool he was.

Throughout the day he had been aware of the rising of desire he felt for this strait-laced, reserved, intelligent and beautiful woman. But hearing the melody Sophia had played so often had reminded him that Katherine would be leaving too. Even if she hadn't he had only ashes to give her.

No, his first instincts had been correct. It wouldn't be right to become entangled with this hurting woman.

CHAPTER THREE

'YIA-YIA SAYS you must come to our house.'

Katherine started. She hadn't been aware of Crystal coming in. Now here she was again, as bold as brass in her sitting room, as if she had every right to be there. But, then, Katherine conceded silently, she had extended what had amounted to an open invitation.

'Excuse me?'

'Yia-Yia says you helped Baba with his hand so she wants you to come to dinner. She says it's not good for someone to be alone all the time.'

'Yia-Yia? Your grandmother?' When Crystal nodded, she added, 'Does your father know you're here?'

The little girl hitched her shoulders and flopped her arms to her side, her hands bumping against her legs. 'I did tell him.' Her sigh was dramatic. 'He's working on his boat again. He also wants you to come.'

Katherine wasn't sure she believed Crystal. She didn't want to impose herself on Alexander's family—particularly if he'd be there. He'd come to the villa the evening after they'd been to Olympia to tell her that her diagnosis had been correct. Stéfan did indeed have meningitis and was in Intensive Care. But Alexander hoped that, because of her alerting them to look out for meningitis, Stéfan would recover.

She hadn't seen Alexander since then but, to her dismay, she'd found herself thinking about him—a lot—during the week and knew she was in real danger of developing a crush on him. An unreciprocated crush, clearly, and someone like him was bound to pick up sooner or later the effect he was having on her. The ending of their evening together had indicated, more than words could, that he wasn't interested in pursuing a relationship with her. No, if the invitation had been extended by him, it had been out of politeness—from one colleague to another.

In which case it would be better not to encourage Crystal to visit too much.

Katherine managed a smile. 'I'm very busy, Crystal, so...' she picked up her pen pointedly '...would you thank your grandmother very much for her kind invitation but tell her I won't be able to make it?'

But instead of taking the hint, Crystal came to stand next to her. 'What are you doing?' she asked.

'It's a paper I'd like to finish before I go back to work.'

'Like homework?'

'Exactly.' Trying to ignore the child next to her, Katherine made a few more notes on the page. But it was clear Crystal had no intention of leaving any time soon.

She suppressed a sigh and put her pen down. 'Would you like some orange juice?'

'Yes, please.'

When she got up to fetch it, both Hercules and Crystal followed her into the small kitchen.

'I told Baba that Yia-Yia and me thought you must be lonely all by yourself and he agreed. So it's good I can keep you company sometimes.'

As Katherine crouched down to give Hercules some food she felt her cheeks grow hot. It was bad enough, mortifying enough, that Alexander had said that, but for him, his six-year-old and his grandmother to be discussing her was too much. Was that what this dinner invitation was about? A let's-keep-the-solitary-woman-company-for-at-least-one-night-so-that-we-don't-have-to-worry-about-her-being-on-her-own? She swore silently.

It made it more important than ever that she stay away from him; she absolutely refused to be the object of sympathy.

'You can tell your father, as I've already told him, I'm perfectly happy being on my own. I'm not in the least bit lonely.' Why was she justifying herself to a child? If she *did* feel a little bereft at times, it was only to be expected after losing Mum so recently. She handed Crystal the glass of juice.

'I could paint your toenails if you like,' Crystal said. She held up a plastic bag. 'Look. I got three different colours for my birthday from Cousin Helen. Baba says I'm too young to be wearing nail polish.' Her mouth drooped. 'Helen shouldn't have given it to me if I couldn't wear it. What was she thinking?'

The last phrase sounded so much like something her friend Sally would have said, it made Katherine smile.

'If you let me do your nails, it'll make you even more beautiful,' Crystal continued plaintively, and apparently without the tiniest hint of guile.

Katherine knew when she was beaten. 'Okay,' she said.

A smile of delight spread across Crystal's face. 'Can I? Really?'

'Yes, but *only* my toes. I don't wear varnish on my fingernails. A doctor has to keep their fingernails short.' She held up her hands and wiggled them.

'Okay. You sit on the couch and put your feet on this

chair,' Crystal instructed, lugging one of the kitchen chairs over.

Wondering whether she'd made a mistake by agreeing to the child's demands, Katherine slid her feet out of her sandals and placed them on the vinyl-covered seat. 'Like this?'

Crystal nodded. She opened the popper of her little plastic bag and very carefully placed three pots of nail varnish on the table. 'What colour would you like?'

Katherine studied the pots of varnish for a moment. One was deep purple and completely out of the question, even if she intended to remove the polish at the first opportunity, the second was deep red and the third a pale, coral pink.

She pointed to the pink one. 'That one.'

'But I like the red.' Crystal pouted.

Katherine bit down on a smile. 'Okay. Red it is.'

She leaned against the back of the couch and closed her eyes. Crystal's little hands were like feathers on her feet and, to her surprise, Katherine found it very soothing.

'There. Done. Look!' Crystal said eventually. She stood back to admire her work. 'I told you it would be pretty.'

Katherine peered down at her toes. It was as if someone had taken a machete to them, lopping them off somewhere below the metatarsals. There had to more nail polish on her skin and the seat of the chair than on her nails. But Crystal looked so pleased with herself that Katherine quickly hid her dismay. 'Mmm. Quite a difference.'

Crystal tugged her hand. 'Come on, let's show Baba.'

'I don't think your father—'

But Crystal was pulling her to her feet. 'Helen wouldn't let me do hers, but when she sees yours, she will.'

'Crystal! I said ten minutes!' Alexander's voice came from below the balcony.

'Coming, Baba. In a minute.'

'Now, Crystal!'

Keeping her toes spread as far apart as possible, Katherine hobbled over to the balcony and looked down. Alexander was wiping grease-stained hands on a rag. His T-shirt clung damply to his chest and his hair was tousled. Yet he still managed to look like a Greek god.

'Hi, Katherine.' His teeth flashed. 'Sorry I'm calling up, but my feet are sandy, my hands grubby and I need a dip in the sea before I'm fit for company. You are coming to dinner, aren't you?'

Crystal bumped against her as she climbed excitedly onto the rung of the balcony. 'She says not to dinner, Baba, but can she come for a visit? She is much more beautiful now! You have to see her.'

Katherine was about to protest when his eyes locked on hers. 'The part I can see of her already looks pretty good.' For a long moment the world seemed to disappear until there were just the two of them. 'Why not dinner?' he asked, breaking the spell.

'Because I've work to do and, anyway, I don't like to intrude on your family.'

'I assume you take time off to eat?'

'Yes, you have to eat!' his daughter echoed.

'My grandmother will be disappointed if you don't. She's already started preparing her best dishes.'

Alexander's family appeared determined to adopt her. She winced at her choice of words and sought desperately for an acceptable excuse. Apart from the effect Alexander had on her, every time she looked at Crystal she was painfully reminded of what she'd lost.

'Yes, *lahanodolmádes* and *patátes yemistés*,' Crystal added. 'Oh, and *baklavás* for afters! What else, Baba?'

'Crystal, could you please stop interrupting everyone?'

He looked at Katherine again. 'Stay for dinner at least and then you can leave.'

It seemed that she had no choice but to allow herself to be dragged out of the house—it would be churlish to continue refusing not only Alexander's pleas but those of his daughter too. And to be honest, her mouth had started to water when Crystal had been listing the menu. It was a long time since she'd tasted home-cooked Greek food like her mother used to make.

'Yes, then. I'd love to.'

Crystal, victorious, clenched her fist and stabbed her folded elbow backwards. 'Yes-s-s! I'll see you at home, Baba. I'll bring her.'

'Not *her*, Crystal. Dr Burns.'

'Katherine is fine,' Katherine said.

He grinned at her. 'You did bring this on yourself, you know, by being so mysterious and elusive.'

Mysterious? Was that how he saw it? That she was the elusive one? She couldn't help smiling back.

'And you did tell Crystal she could visit. My daughter appears to find you irresistible.'

Her heart plummeted. She preferred *him* to find her irresistible.

The pint-sized tyrant wouldn't even let her stop to put on her sandals, saying severely that she would spoil it all if she tried to put them on too soon.

Alexander's home was set back from the village square and up a steep, narrow path. It was several times larger than hers, with shuttered windows, a cobbled driveway and paths and lush, established grounds. He must have a wonderful view from the wide balconies of his clifftop home.

It took a while for Katherine's eyes to adjust to the dim interior after the bright light and blinding white beach outside. The house was cool, probably because it was shuttered against the heat of the day, although now the shutters were spread wide, allowing a breeze to penetrate the rooms. Despite Crystal hurrying her along, Katherine managed to catch glimpses of her surroundings: engraved, dark wood furniture; colourful striped rugs on polished terracotta tiles; and montages of family photographs, old and new, on white, rough-plastered walls. Crystal swept her into the kitchen where Katherine's senses were assailed with the aromas of garlic, herbs and browning meat.

A plump white-haired woman, bent over the pots steaming on an enormous traditional stove, lifted her head. She smiled warmly at Katherine and addressed her rapidly in Greek.

'Yia-Yia welcomes you and says she's happy you are here, visiting our home,' Crystal translated. 'Please sit at the table.' Without allowing Katherine time to reply, she turned to her grandmother and spoke in Greek, pointing excitedly to Katherine's toes. The older woman leant over and exclaimed. Katherine didn't need to understand any Greek to gather she was praising her great-granddaughter's efforts. Crystal's face said it all.

She had barely sat down before a plate of spanakopita was set down in front of her. Crystal's great-grandmother turned back to her stove, muttering happily.

'Aren't you glad you came?' Crystal said triumphantly. 'Look how pleased she is!'

If the child hadn't been so young, Katherine would have suspected her of engineering the whole situation.

'What's your great-grandmother's name?' Katherine asked.

'Yia-Yia, silly.'

Katherine took a bite of the miniature spinach and

feta pie. She flapped a hand in front of her mouth. 'Hot. *Thermo.* Hot. But wonderful,' she added hastily. Two pairs of dark brown eyes studied her 'No, I mean what should *I* call her?'

'The same as everyone. Yia-Yia. She knows your name. Baba told her. I'm just going to get him!' Crystal said, flying out of the door.

Yia-Yia beckoned Katherine over to where she was working and pointed at the leaves of pastry she had laid out on a baking tray. She brought her fingers to her lips and made a smacking sound. It was clear she was showing Katherine what she was making for supper and that it would be delicious. Katherine could only smile and nod in response.

She was almost relieved when Crystal returned, dragging Alexander in her wake. His hair glistened almost black from his shower and he had changed into a bitter-chocolate T-shirt and cotton jeans. 'Show Baba your toes,' Crystal ordered.

Grimacing to herself, Katherine did as she was asked. She saw the leap of laughter in Alexander's eyes as he dutifully studied her feet. 'Very beautiful,' he said to Katherine, before murmuring so his daughter couldn't hear. 'Do you actually have toes at the ends of those feet? Or should I get the suture kit out again?'

Katherine spluttered with laughter, just managing to turn it into a cough at the last moment. But suddenly Alexander was whooping with laughter and she was too. She couldn't remember the last time she'd laughed like that. Yia-Yia and Crystal looked puzzled for a moment then they were whooping too, Yia-Yia's deep brown eyes almost disappearing in her chubby face.

'What's so funny?' Crystal asked, when everyone stopped laughing.

Alexander tweaked her nose. 'If you don't know, why did you join in?'

'I couldn't help it.' She was hopping from foot to foot. 'I just liked hearing you laugh, Baba.'

The atmosphere in the room changed subtly and the light in Alexander's eyes disappeared, replaced by something Katherine couldn't read.

'If you'll excuse me,' he apologised, 'a neighbour is complaining of a tight chest. It's nothing that staying off cigarettes wouldn't help, but his wife is always happier if I look in on him. I'll be back in a little while.' He turned to his grandmother and spoke to her. She nodded, unsmiling.

'Can I come, Baba?' his daughter asked.

'Of course. You know I always like to have my little helper with me. As long as you stay out of the way and as quiet as a mouse.' He caught Katherine's eye and raised an eyebrow. 'My daughter as quiet as a mouse? Who am I kidding?' he murmured, his lips curving into a smile.

Crystal was out of the door almost before he'd finished speaking.

Once again, Katherine was left alone with Yia-Yia. There was an awkward silence for a moment before the older woman beckoned Katherine to come forward. With a series of hand gestures and nods of the head, she indicated to Katherine that she wanted her help to finish preparing the meal.

'I'm sorry, I can't cook,' Katherine protested. There had never been a need to learn. When her mother had been alive and Katherine had been living at home they'd always eaten at the restaurant. And when she'd moved out and into her first flat she'd taken her main meal at the hospital or had eaten simple salads or pasta for supper. Then, when Mum had become too unwell to be on her own and Katherine had moved back home to look after her, she had fetched Greek delicacies from a nearby restaurant—their own having been sold a couple of years earlier—in an attempt to tempt Mum's failing appetite.

But almost before she'd finished speaking she was being passed a bowl of minced lamb and handed bunches of pungent-smelling herbs. Either Yia-Yia didn't understand what she was saying, or it had never crossed her mind that not all women liked cooking.

In the end it was one of the most peaceful and relaxing hours Katherine could remember spending for a long time. With Crystal's grandmother coaxing her along, while keeping a watchful eye on what she was doing, Katherine stuffed vine leaves and baked rich syrupy cakes. Every now and again the old woman would cluck her tongue and shake her head. At other times she'd nod, murmur something in Greek, and smile approvingly.

When dinner had been prepared to her satisfaction, and Alexander and Crystal still hadn't returned, Yia-Yia took her hand and led her outside to a bench in the garden. For the next ten minutes they sat in peaceful silence as the sun sank in the sky.

After a little while Yia-Yia gestured that they should go back inside. By the time Alexander and Crystal returned, a spread that could have fed eight had been laid out on the dining-room table.

Alexander's dark eyes swept over Katherine and he grinned, making her heart skip a beat. 'Somehow I never quite saw you as being domesticated,' he said.

Catching sight of her reflection in the large mirror on the wall, Katherine realised she was still wearing the flowery apron Grandmother had insisted she put on. Added to her bare feet and splotchy nail polish, she must look ridiculous. Her hair was a mess and clinging to her flushed cheeks. And was that a smudge of flour? Liking to appear neat and tidy at all times, tailored dresses with tights and decent shoes or smart trousers and blouses were what she usually wore. Two weeks in Greece and her colleagues would hardly recognise her. *She* barely recognised herself.

But, oddly, she rather liked the look of the woman in the mirror.

She seemed different from the last time he'd seen her, Alexander thought, studying Katherine from the corner of his eye. But if possible she was even more beautiful. Her blonde hair, bleached white-gold from the sun, had come loose from her plait and damp tendrils curled around her cheeks. A tiny wisp of hair clung to the corner of her mouth and he curled his hands inside the pockets of his jeans to stop himself from reaching out to tug it away. His grandmother's apron and the smudge of flour on her nose only added, somehow, to her allure. But those feet! As he'd said, it looked as if someone had bludgeoned her toes with a hammer.

It had been Yia-Yia and Crystal's idea to invite her for dinner. He'd tried to dissuade them, but his grandmother had insisted that not to, after Katherine had helped him, was not the Greek way. He'd had no choice but to agree. And, whatever he'd told himself, he was glad that she was here.

There was something about Katherine that drew him and despite everything he'd told himself he hadn't been able to stop thinking about her. He wasn't sure what to make of her. Her blue eyes were the colour of the sea at its deepest—more so when sadness overtook her. Was it only the loss of her mother that was causing that look in her eyes? She intrigued him. One minute she'd be the cool professional, like when they'd helped the young man who'd collapsed, the next she'd be blushing at something he'd said or refusing to hold his gaze, ill at ease in his company. And then over dinner she'd seemed to relax. At least until he'd asked her about her private life.

When Helen had found out they'd met and she'd sutured Alexander's hand and they'd spent the day together, her curiosity had known no bounds. That Katherine was also doctor tickled her.

'Perhaps she's like you,' she'd said. 'Maybe she has lost her lover and is here to mend her broken heart.' Helen liked to spin stories, usually romantic ones, about people. 'Yes, it has to be a broken love affair, I'm sure of it.' She'd slid him a mischievous look. 'Perhaps together you can mend your broken hearts.'

Despite himself, he'd laughed. 'You know I'm not interested in getting married again.'

'It's been two years, Alexander. A man like you isn't meant to be on his own. Grandmother won't be around for ever. I have my own life in Athens and as much as I love you both, I can't keep making trips down here every weekend, especially when it means leaving Nico on his own. And once we get married…' She shrugged. 'I won't be able to come so often. Crystal needs a mother. Someone who can be there for her all the time.'

'Crystal has me,' he'd replied tersely. 'No one can ever take Sophia's place.'

Helen was instantly contrite. 'Of course not.' Then she'd smiled again. It was hard for his cousin to stay serious for long. 'Anyway, who's saying anything about marriage?'

Typical Greek women. Always trying to matchmake.

'She is good at cooking,' his grandmother said to him in Greek, drawing him back to the present. 'For an Englishwoman. But she is too skinny. She should eat more.'

He grinned at the older woman. If she had her way they'd all eventually have to join a slimming club. 'I think she looks fine.'

'At least she dresses like a good Greek woman. No shorts up to her bottom like your cousin.'

Under the apron, Katherine was wearing a pair of light cotton trousers and a white blouse, neatly buttoned almost to the neck. No wonder his grandmother approved.

Katherine was looking at him enquiringly and he realised they had been speaking in Greek and excluding her.

'My grandmother says you are a good cook.'

'It's been fun—and informative,' Katherine admitted with a wry smile.

'But why does she seem so sad?' his grandmother continued. 'What does she have to be sad about? She is here in Greece, working in my kitchen, making food, and about to eat a fine meal.'

'Her mother died not so long ago,' he replied.

His grandmother's face softened in distress. She pulled Katherine into her arms and patted her on the back. 'Poor girl,' she said. A bewildered Katherine stared at him over her shoulder and he had to fight not to laugh.

He sobered. 'I told my grandmother that your mother died recently. She is saying she is sorry.'

Katherine gently extricated herself from his grandmother's arms. 'Tell her thank you, but I'm all right.'

'And what about a husband?' Yia-Yia continued. 'Where is he? Has she left him in England?' She clicked her tongue. 'A woman shouldn't leave her husband. Where is her ring?'

'She's not married, Grandmother.'

'And why not? She is old not to be married! Is she one of those modern women who think they don't need husbands? Or is she divorced?' Her mouth turned down at the corners. Grandmother didn't approve of divorce.

'I don't think she's ever been married, Yia-Yia.'

She looked relieved. 'Good. Perhaps she will fall in love with you. Would you like that? I think you like her, no?'

Katherine was watching him, waiting for him to translate, but he was damned if he was going to tell her how interested his grandmother was in her marital status—and her suitability as a partner for him.

'Grandmother is saying she is happy to have you here in her kitchen. She hopes you will come often.'

'Tell her it's lovely to be here.'

To his relief, the business of serving them all dinner prevented further comments from his grandmother. Crystal insisted on sitting next to Katherine, her body pressed so tightly against her Katherine had to find it difficult to eat. Yet she said nothing. She laid down her knife so that she could eat with one hand. Crystal was a friendly child but he'd never known her to form an attachment quite as quickly. It wasn't as if she wasn't surrounded by love.

'So you don't work on weekends?' Katherine asked him. They had taken their coffee onto the balcony. She'd offered to help clear away but his grandmother wouldn't hear of it, insisting it was Crystal's job. Or at least that was what Alexander had told Katherine. Grandmother would have been only too delighted to keep their guest in her kitchen while she cooked some more.

'Carlos—my partner, who you met briefly—and I take turns and we have a colleague who fills in the rest of the time. He retired early so he could spend more time on his thirty-footer, but he likes to keep his hand in.'

'What news about Stéfan?'

'He's still in Intensive Care.'

'But he is going to be okay?'

'I don't know.' He rubbed the back of his neck. 'He's on a ventilator. They think it's a rare type of bacterial meningitis that he has. They're still doing tests.' He stood. 'I'm sorry, but you're going to have to excuse me. It's time for Crystal's bedtime and she likes me to read her a story.'

'Of course. I should get back anyway and do some more work before I turn in.' Her cheeks had flushed. 'Please say good night to Crystal and thank your grandmother for me. I had very pleasant evening.'

'You'll come again?' he asked. She was easy company and he found being with her restful. Actually, who was he kidding? He just liked being with her.

'I don't want to keep intruding,' she said, the colour in her cheeks deepening.

'You're not. Trust me.'

She gave him the ghost of a smile and left.

He watched her pick her way down the steps and into the square. He'd found it difficult to concentrate on his paperwork the last few days. His thoughts kept straying back to her, distracting him. Yes, he thought. She was a distraction—a very enjoyable one—but that was all she would ever be.

CHAPTER FOUR

THE FOLLOWING MORNING, just after dawn had lightened the sky and Katherine had taken her coffee out to the balcony, she noticed that Alexander was back working on his boat. In which case she would work inside, at least until she was sure he'd gone. She'd already had more to do with him than was wise. Relationships, particularly brief flings with attractive Greek doctors still grieving for their wives, had no place on her agenda.

But even as she reminded herself of that, she wondered if she could make an exception. It would be so good to feel someone's arms around her again. Good to have company, good to have someone to share walks and trips with, and who better than a man she would never see again once she'd left here?

She shook her head to chase the thoughts away. She suspected he found her attractive, but that wasn't the same thing as wanting even a casual relationship with her. And just how casual did she want it to be? Unbidden, she imagined him naked, tanned body against white sheets, his hands exploring every inch of her.

She retreated back inside and determinedly fired up her computer. Work. That was what kept her sane. Her paper was what she should be concentrating on.

She edited all day, acutely aware that her attention kept wandering back to Alexander. Just before supper she heard the excited voice of Crystal and, unable to resist a peek, peered out at the bay. He was there again, but this time in the water with his daughter.

She watched as he raised Crystal above his head before tossing her in the air and catching her just before she hit the water. The little girl shrieked with pleasure and wrapped her arms around her father's neck. A few minutes later Alexander, Crystal balanced on his shoulders, waded out of the water, his swimming shorts clinging to narrow hips and lean but muscular thighs.

It wasn't just that she found him sexy as hell. She liked the way he was with his child—clearly she was the centre of his universe and that was the way it should be: a child's happiness should always be paramount. Her chest tightened. What would he think if he knew her secret? Not that she was ever to going to share it with him.

She went into the kitchen and made herself a Greek salad with some of local goat cheese and olives, along with plump, ripe tomatoes she'd bought from the village store. Telling herself it was far too beautiful an evening to eat inside, she took her plate out to the lower veranda. Alexander and Crystal had disappeared, no doubt having gone home to have their evening meal. As the sun sank below the horizon, she sighed. Despite everything she'd told herself, their absence made her feel lonelier than ever.

Alexander excused himself from the game of cards he had been playing and, taking his beer, walked over to the small wall surrounding the village square. Crystal was riding her bike around the fountain in the centre in hot pursuit of the neighbour's boy, her little legs pedalling as fast as they could so she could catch up with him.

Alexander smiled as he watched her. He'd made the right decision, coming back. Crystal was thriving, his grandmother was delighted to have her close by and he was...well, content. As long as his daughter was happy he was too—or as much as he had any right to expect. Sometimes he wondered whether Crystal even remembered Sophia. She spoke of her mother periodically, asking if she were still in heaven and telling him that she knew Mama was watching her from the sky. Occasionally he would show Crystal video footage he'd taken of them on the too-rare occasions he'd taken leave and they'd come here. His daughter would lean forward and watch with shining eyes.

What would Sophia think if she knew he was back in Greece? How would she feel about him giving up his job in London? Would she be pleased that he'd finally, even when it was too late, realised what was important? Would she approve of the way he was bringing up their child? God, he still missed her and, God, he still felt so damned guilty.

He sipped his cold beer and gazed out over the sea. It was then he noticed Katherine. She'd just emerged from the water, her long legs emphasised by the black one-piece costume she was wearing. She dried off then wrapped the towel around her and sat with her back to him, knees pulled up to her chest, staring out at the same sea he was.

Under her prim exterior and natural reserve, there was a loneliness, an aura of something so vulnerable about her he found himself, for the first time since Sophia's death, wanting to know another woman better. But what did he have to offer? He wouldn't, couldn't, get married again. No one could ever match up to Sophia.

He took another gulp of his drink and turned away. Why

had the possibility of getting married again even crossed his mind? The moonlight was making him fanciful. His life was complicated—and full—enough.

Crystal whizzed by him on her bike and waved. Right there was everything that mattered. He glanced at his watch. It was time to get his daughter to bed.

CHAPTER FIVE

As had become a habit, Katherine was sitting outside his house on the bench with Grandmother, after spending a couple of hours cooking with her in the kitchen. She'd closed her eyes to savour the sensation of the breeze on her face, but when Grandmother poked her in her ribs with her elbow she opened them to see that Alexander was coming across the square towards them.

Katherine's heart leaped. Frightened of what he would read in her eyes, she lowered her lids until she was sure she could look at him calmly. She could deal with her developing crush on him as long as he never suspected.

'Hello, you two.' He bent and kissed his grandmother on her cheek and said something to her in Greek that made her laugh. Although Katherine's Greek was improving, when the Greeks spoke to each other it was usually too fast for her to follow.

Alexander grinned at Katherine. 'I've just asked her what she's thinking of, sitting down when dinner's due. She says now she has you to help her, sometimes she can take time off to enjoy the Greek sunshine.'

Nevertheless, the old woman got to her feet and retreated back inside, leaving her space on the bench for Alexander. He took a seat next to Katherine and, like she'd been doing earlier, turned his face up to the sun and closed his eyes. 'My grandmother is right. We all need to sit in the sun more often,' he murmured.

His usual vitality seemed to have deserted him and he looked tired.

'Is everything all right?' she asked.

'No, not really. Stéfan—the man with meningitis—died last night.'

'I'm so sorry. I really hoped he would be okay.'

He opened his eyes and turned to face Katherine. 'So did I, but once he developed multi-organ failure...' He paused. 'We've asked for a post-mortem but, according to the pathologist, it might be another week before they can do it. They have a bit of a backlog as his colleague is off on leave.' He rubbed the back of his neck and frowned. 'I was speaking to one of my colleagues in the area today and he tells me he's had a case too—a couple of days ago, a teenager. He's been admitted to a hospital in Athens.'

Katherine's antenna went on red alert. 'Two cases in a week? Doesn't that strike you as odd?'

'He isn't sure his patient has meningitis. He's going to call me as soon as he has the results of the lumbar puncture. But I'd be surprised if they both have it. As far as I'm aware, meningitis normally affects similar age groups.'

'Usually, but not always. It depends on the strain.'

'We'll find out soon enough. They're giving his patient's family antibiotics prophylactically to be on the safe side.'

'Sensible,' Katherine murmured. However, if Alexander's colleague's patient did turn out to have meningitis, it could be the start of something. Something terrifying.

'Any others you're aware of?' she asked.

'I rang around a few of the practices in the area, but no one else has come across any. I've told them to let me know if they do. I'm hoping these two will turn out to be random, unrelated events—supposing David, the teenage boy, does have it and, as I said, that isn't at all certain.'

He could be right, but there was a way she could find out.

She heard Grandmother calling Alexander from inside and got to her feet. 'Sounds like you're wanted.'

'I thought you'd want to know about Stéfan,' he said, rising too 'After I check in with Yia-Yia, I'm going to see the family of one of my other patients who I admitted to hospital after I diagnosed her with a nasty chest infection.' He smiled wryly. 'It's one of the privileges, but also one of the responsibilities, of being in general practice in Greece. Any member of a family becomes unwell and the rest expect you to see them through it as well. And that usually involves late-night tea and cakes and much discussion.'

Although she was disappointed he was going, the care he took of his patients was one of the things she liked about him. Besides, she wanted to do some checking up of her own.

She hurried back to her house. It was after six in the UK but Tim was divorced and rarely left work until much later.

She dialled the number of the office and was pleased when he picked up straight away. After exchanging small talk for a few moments—yes, she was enjoying her break and, yes, she would be coming back to work as planned at the end of September—she repeated what Alexander had told her.

'I've got a feeling about this,' she said. 'Is there any chance you could speak to your opposite number in Athens and ask him if there have been any more cases reported? I realise I'm probably being over-cautious but it wouldn't hurt to find out.'

'I doubt there will be anyone still there at this time. Will the morning do?'

'It will have to. As I said, it's probably nothing but it's best to be on the safe side. Thanks, Tim.'

He called her back on her mobile just before nine the next morning and came straight to the point.

'You were right,' he said. 'I've spoken to my opposite number in Athens and he tells me there have been reports of ten cases in and around the southern Peloponnese, including the two you mentioned. One or two would mean nothing but ten! It certainly suggests there is something to be concerned about.'

Excitement surged through Katherine. Her instinct had been right! 'What ages?'

'It varies. From teenagers to young adults. As you'd expect, it is the youngest who are most seriously affected. One child—a lad of seventeen—is in Intensive Care in Athens and it's not looking good.'

'The boy in Intensive Care—what's his name?'

'David Panagaris.'

Was he the same lad Alexander had told her about? It seemed likely. Her heart was racing. This is what she was trained to do. 'I could look into it. Could you let the department in Athens know I'm here and would like to help?'

'Absolutely not,' Tim protested. 'You're on holiday. They must have someone local they can call on. It's not as if Greece doesn't have public health doctors of their own.'

'Of course they do, but I happen to be here and I'm an expert in the spread of infectious diseases. I'm probably the most up-to-date person in Europe at the moment and you and I both know it's all much more co-operative now than it used to be. Come on, Tim, you know it makes sense.'

There was a long pause at the end of the phone. 'I guess

it does makes sense,' Tim said reluctantly. 'But is your Greek good enough to ensure you ask the right questions and, more importantly, get the right answers?'

It wasn't. But Alexander's was. 'What about the Greek doctor I mentioned? The one who alerted me to the possibility of an outbreak? If he's prepared to take time out to help me, that would solve the problem of my not being fluent in Greek.' She wasn't really sure she wanted to work with Alexander. It was bad enough catching tantalising glimpses of him most days, without being thrust into his company all the time. But she wanted to do this and she couldn't without Alexander's help. 'I'll need to ask him, of course, but I've no doubt he'll say yes.'

'Okay,' Tim conceded. 'I'll suggest it to my colleague.' Katherine released a breath. 'What more info do you have?'

'In addition to the boy admitted to Intensive Care in Athens, there have been two deaths over the last ten days— your man and a woman tourist from France in her teens. Her family have already repatriated her body. No obvious links between the deceased as yet.'

Her excitement drained away. Three families had lost a loved one or were in danger of doing so. And if there was an epidemic, and there seemed little doubt that was what they could be dealing with, if they didn't locate all those who had come into contact with the sufferers and treat them, more people could die. In addition, they needed to find out where it was coming from so they could reach people before they became unwell.

'Could you give me the names and addresses of the patients? Plus the names of their family doctors, or the doctors who treated them?'

'I'll email them to you straight away.'

As soon as she disconnected, she phoned Alexan-

der's surgery only to discover he wasn't expected in until
later. She flung on some clothes and, without stopping for
breakfast, set off across the square to Alexander's home,
praying he'd be there and not out on a visit.

The sun was already blazing down and she was perspir-
ing by the time she reached his door. She found Grandmother in the kitchen, making bread.

'Morning,' Katherine said in Greek. 'I need to speak to
Alexander. Is he here?' She didn't have time for the usual
pleasantries today.

Alexander's grandmother frowned, wiped her hands on
a tea towel and shook her head. '*Nè*. At work.'

'Hello.' It was Crystal, looking sleepy in pyjamas and
holding a teddy bear. She said something to her grandmother in Greek and went to stand next to Katherine, slipping her hand into hers. 'Yia-Yia says you're looking for
Baba. She says he's gone to his consulting room in the village.' Grandmother had lifted a pot of tea and was holding it up. 'She wants to know if you'd like some tea. And
some breakfast? She's just made some.'

'Please thank her for me and say I'd love to stay but I
really need to see your father. It's urgent.'

The child relayed it back to to her grandmother, who
looked disappointed she'd have no one to feed.

'Is something the matter?' Crystal asked.

'No.' Katherine crouched down and ruffled Crystal's
hair. 'At least, nothing for you to worry about. I promise.'

Leaving the house, she headed back down the flight of
steps and along the street to the rooms Alexander used as
a surgery for the locals.

She tapped on the door of Alex's room and, without
waiting for a reply, let herself in. He was sitting at the

desk, his chair turned to face the window so that he had his back to her. He swivelled around to face her.

'I'm sorry,' he said. 'This isn't a good time.'

'I heard,' she said softly.

He frowned. 'Heard what?'

'About David Panagaris, that is the name of your colleague's patient, isn't it?' When Alexander nodded, she continued. 'I thought it must be him. I gather he's in Intensive Care. I'm sorry.' Without waiting to be asked, she took the seat opposite him.

'Poor bloody parents. Perhaps if they'd brought him in sooner—' He broke off. 'How did you know he'd deteriorated? He was only admitted to Intensive Care last night.'

'My boss phoned me—I phoned him first. Let me explain.'

Alexander said nothing but leaned forward, placing his folded hands on the desk. He looked even more bushed than he had yesterday. There were dark circles under his eyes and underneath the tan he was drawn and pale. She wondered if he'd been up all night.

'As you know, my thesis for my doctorate is on meningitis and other bacterial infections—its spread and containment. That sort of thing. Our unit is one of the biggest in Europe but we have strong ties with others units across the world. We share information on all matters of public health, especially on infectious diseases. Over the last few years increasing numbers of countries across the world have bought into this collaborative approach. It makes sense to pool our resources rather than compete with one another. Africa, for example, has much better information on the spread of malaria, and so on...'

He nodded impatiently.

'When you told me about your cases it rang alarm bells

so I phoned my boss and asked him to contact the public health department in Athens. Apparently, apart from Stéfan and David, there have been eight other cases all in, or around, this area, including another death—a young French girl' She held out her phone. 'My boss has emailed me a list with all their names.'

'Eight other cases?' Alexander looked instantly alert, all traces of his earlier tiredness having disappeared. 'So there is an epidemic?'

'It appears so. The thing is, I've offered to take the lead in looking into the situation. But I'm going to need help. My Greek isn't good enough for me to do it on my own.'

He narrowed his eyes. 'You want me to help?'

'Yes,' she said simply.

'Of course,' he said with no hesitation. 'I'll need to arrange for Dr Kanavakis—my retired colleague—to cover for me, but I don't think that will be a problem. When do we start?'

'Now.'

He raised his eyebrows. 'Let me make that phone call, then.'

When he'd finished he turned back to Katherine. 'Cover's sorted. Now, what else do you know about the cases?'

'Very little. I have the names and addresses of all the patients. Most live in the southern part of Greece. Two come from Nafplio or very nearby. The French girl was on holiday there.'

He leaned back in his chair. 'Hell, that isn't good. A lot of cruise ships come into Nafplio. That will make tracing contacts more difficult.'

She checked the names on her phone. While Alexander had been on the phone she'd downloaded them into a document. 'What else can you tell me about David?'

'His parents live in a village close to Messini. He'd been snuffly and lethargic for most of the morning. They thought it was a cold, but when he deteriorated they brought him in to see my colleague. Unfortunately, he was already showing signs of septicaemia. He was given intravenous antibiotics and they arranged for an immediate transfer to hospital, but he was already in a bad way.' He raked a hand through his hair. 'He's only young.'

He jumped up and started pacing. 'If we do have an epidemic on our hands, none of the children will be safe.' He stopped in front of her. 'Come on. Let's go to the hospital. I'll let his doctor know what's happening. We need to find where the victims have been and who they've been in contact with.' He paused. 'Unless we should split up? You go to see the relatives of the other cases while I go to the hospital?'

'No,' she said, putting her hand on his arm. 'As I said, I might be the expert and know the questions to ask, but you can speak Greek and you're a local doctor. They'll find it more comfortable to talk to you and they might tell you things they wouldn't tell me. You'll also be able to pick up better than I if they are leaving out information that might be important. But what we should do is make sure the health services in Athens have put all the local family practices on alert, as well as warning the general public. Doctors and parents are more likely to be vigilant if they know what to look out for.'

'I'll speak to them, of course. What is the name of your contact there?'

Even before he put the phone down she could see the conversation hadn't gone the way he wanted. His voice had risen towards the end and he appeared to be arguing with whoever was on the other end. A muscle twitched in his cheek.

'They say they've warned the hospitals and practices to watch out for cases of meningitis but they won't put out a full alert on the radio or in the press. They say that if they do, people will panic and rush to the hospitals. They say the medical services will collapse under the strain and it's too early to take the risk.'

'I could phone my boss and get him to put pressure on them,' Katherine suggested. 'Although I suspect they'd do the same in the UK.'

'Be my guest.' He gestured to the phone. 'I doubt it would do any good. They're unlikely to do anything more until there are more cases. They insist the ones we know about might just be random at the moment—a blip, not connected at all.'

'It is possible,' Katherine said thoughtfully. 'We've noted and recorded many cases of infectious diseases in the past that seemed to be part of an epidemic but that turned out not to be. I think we should talk to the Stéfan's parents before we do anything else. As soon as I get the French girl's parents' contact details I'll call them.'

'Fine with me,' he said, picking up his medical bag. 'And I hope to God you're right about these cases not being connected. Stéfan's family is from a village near Sparta. We could go to the hospital in Athens from there.' He took his mobile from his pocket. 'I'll phone Carlos and let him know what's happening.'

The road leading to Sparta was the worst Katherine had ever been on. Travelling through and over the mountains, it was narrow, with barely enough room for two cars to pass safely. In addition, every few miles the road almost spun back on itself through a number of hairpin bends. She could barely bring herself to look. On her side of the car, the road fell away sharply and there were no road barriers to prevent the car, should it have to swerve to avoid oncoming vehicles, toppling over the side. Incredibly, the road conditions didn't stop drivers from overtaking, whether they could see or not.

'What's Crystal up to today?' she asked, trying to unclench her fists.

'She's having a sleepover with a friend a little way up the coast. Her friend's mother is coming to fetch her.'

'Could you slow down?' Katherine yelped, after they took a particularly sharp bend that she'd thought they'd never make.

Alexander turned to face her and grinned.

'If I slow down, it will only encourage other drivers to try and overtake us. They don't care whether the road is empty or not.'

'Please keep your eyes on the road at least.'

Despite her terror and worry about what they would be facing soon, she couldn't help admire the scenery as they whizzed along. Little villages clung to the side of the mountain, the houses often appearing to spill almost onto the road. Small cafés with old men outside, puffing on pipes or playing board games flew by in a blur. To her consternation, Alexander would often take his hand off the steering-wheel to give them a friendly wave as they passed.

At other times, almost out of nowhere, they'd come upon small farm stalls selling flowers or tomatoes or other freshly grown produce from the roadside. At any other time she might have enjoyed the trip and promised herself that once this emergency was over she'd come back—with her own car, of course—and savour the journey.

As she relaxed a little, her thoughts returned to the task in hand. She unfolded the map she'd brought with her and circled each victim's location with her pen. All of them lived in the Peloponnese, apart from the French girl, who had been on holiday there. Nevertheless, it was still a huge area.

'Is there any facility or event you know of that links the victims?' she asked Alexander.

He waited until he'd slowed down to let an overtaking car coming in the opposite direction pass before he spoke. 'None that I can think of. I'd have to study the map. I don't really keep on top of social events these days.'

A short time later, to Katherine's relief, they turned off the mountain road and towards Sparta and the road became wider and straighter.

'The village is about thirty kilometres northwest of Sparta,' Alexander said. 'We should be there in about twenty minutes.'

Katherine's stomach churned. In a short while she'd be facing two very recently bereaved parents and she wasn't looking forward to it.

'What's Sparta like?' she asked, more to distract herself than out of any burning interest.

'Little of the original city remains. Most of the what you'll see as we pass through has been built on top of ancient Sparta.' He glanced at her. 'You know the stories of the Spartans?'

'Only that they were tough and didn't believe in creature comforts.'

'It's grimmer than that. Under a system known as the *agoge* Spartan boys were trained to be as physically tough as possible. They were taken from their families at the age of seven and made to live in barracks. They were deliberately underfed so they'd become adept at living off the land. The boy babies who weren't expected to make the grade were taken to the top of the mountain and left there to die.'

Katherine shuddered. 'Their poor mothers.'

'It was cruel. I can't imagine how they felt, having their sons ripped from their arms. I suspect some ran away with them, even though they risked death to save them.' He blinked. 'It's what Sophia would have done. She'd never let anything part her from her child.'

Katherine's heart lurched. What would he think if he knew what she'd done? She was glad he would never know.

'You should try to visit Mycenae, though,' he continued, apparently unaware of her reaction. 'It's almost intact. It's very close to Sparta—only a few kilometres at the most. It has a less bloody past.'

'Have you been there?' Her throat was so tight she could barely speak.

He glanced at her and smiled. 'Naturally.'

They turned off onto a minor road and continued. It was much flatter here, the land planted with olive trees and vines. But then they turned a corner, drove up a street so narrow it would be impossible for another car to pass, and into a small village square.

Now they were here, her anxiety about facing the bereaved parents returned.

'Are you all right about doing this?' Alexander asked.

'Yes.' She would be. She had to think of the children whose lives they would save rather than the one who was lost.

They parked the car and asked directions from an older man sweeping the square. He laid aside his brush and gestured for them to follow him. It was just as well because although the village was small, it was unlikely they would have found their way to the house, tucked away as it was behind a crumbling wall and almost hidden down one of the maze-like streets.

The house itself, like many of the others in the village, seemed to be built into the rock face.

A woman in a navy-blue long-sleeved dress answered their knock and after Alexander explained who they were, stepped aside to let them in.

Stéfan's parents were sitting in a darkened room sur-rounded by family and friends. They clung to each other and Katherine winced at the grief she saw etched on their faces.

This, she thought, was why she was an academic. Fac-ing other people's pain, when she found it impossible to deal with her own, was something she'd spent most of her adult life trying to avoid. But she couldn't afford to be squeamish—or the luxury of dwelling on her own discom-fort. However much she hated to intrude on their grief, she knew it was necessary.

Alexander introduced them again and very gently ex-plained why they were there. 'I know this is a very diffi-cult time for you, but we need to ask you some questions.'

Mr Popalopadous nodded. His wife seemed incapable of speaking. 'Please,' he said, 'ask your questions. If we can stop this happening to someone else's child...'

Katherine sat down and took Mrs Popalopadous's hands in hers. 'We need to know Stéfan's last movements—where he'd been before he became unwell and who he'd been in contact with.'

She looked bewildered. 'He was a teacher in the local school, but during the holidays he takes—took his boat out or went to the taverna with his friends. None of them are sick.'

Katherine exchanged a look with Alexander. None of them were sick *yet*.

'Should we quarantine the village?' Alexander murmured to her.

She shook her head slightly. 'Not yet.' She knew there was no point in getting ahead of themselves. What they had to do was retrace Stéfan's movements going back at least a week to establish who had come into contact with him. After that they needed to get in touch with those people where possible and make sure they—and anyone who had spent more than a few hours in their company—were given antibiotics.

When Mrs Popalopadous started sobbing again, Katherine leaned forward. 'I know it's difficult, but can you think of anyone apart from his friends or his pupils he might have been in contact with?' She ignored the warning look Alexander gave her. She wasn't unsympathetic to Mrs Popalopadous's grief but what mattered most now was that no one else would die.

Mr Popalopadous answered for his wife. 'No. No one different.' He wrapped his arm around his wife's shoulders. 'Now, I'm afraid you must leave us. We have arrangements to make.'

His dignity in the face of his grief was humbling. But Katherine wanted to press him further. However, Alexander got to his feet and taking her by the elbow forced her to rise to hers too. He scribbled something on a piece of paper and handed it to the bereaved father. saying something in Greek Katherine couldn't follow.

His hand still on her elbow, Alexander ushered Katherine out of the house and to his car.

'I still had questions for them,' she protested.

'For God's sake, Katherine, they've just lost their child. They've told us all they can.'

'You can't be sure of that. It's the things they don't think that are important that might matter most.'

'I gave him my mobile number and asked him to call me, day or night, if anything else does come to mind. I also told them to go to their family doctor and make sure they, and anyone else who might have been in contact with Stéfan, gets antibiotics. I'll call the family doctor to make sure they do—although I'm sure he'll have it in hand,'

'It won't hurt to make sure.' Katherine replied.

After he'd made the call, Alexander turned to her. 'As I thought, he plans to see them later this afternoon. As you can imagine, he's pretty keen that we get on top of this.' He frowned. 'The most likely source of the infection is the high school.'

'But not the only possibility!'

'No, but isn't it better to go with the most likely and work our way out from there?'

He did have a point. 'Perhaps once we've interviewed the other families something will jump out. In the meantime, I'd better get onto my boss and tell him to make double sure that all the medical facilities in the area are on red alert.'

'Shouldn't we do that?' Alexander asked.

'It's more important that we try and locate the source of the outbreak. My boss will liaise with your public heath team in Athens, although we should probably introduce ourselves at some point.'

They got into the car and Alexander turned the key in the ignition. 'Okay. Next stop Athens.'

'How long will it take us to get there?'

'About two and half hours. Less if you stop interfering in the way I drive.'

Katherine gritted her teeth. 'Just get there as soon as you can.'

Happily, it was a far better road to Athens than the one they'd come on. While they were driving, Katherine phoned the French girl's parents. Luckily her French was considerably better than her Greek. But that didn't make the conversation any less painful. Claire's father held himself together long enough to tell Katherine that Claire had been on a short break with her boyfriend in Greece when she'd become unwell. It had all been very sudden—too sudden for the family to make it to her bedside in time. There had been a long pause in the conversation when Claire's father had lost control, but eventually he had, for long enough at any rate to tell her that their family doctor had treated the family and the boyfriend with antibiotics. Katherine repeated what she'd learned to Alexander and they'd sat in silence, each absorbed with their own thoughts. She wondered if Alexander was thinking, like she was, how devastating it was to lose someone you loved—especially when that person was young—like Claire—or Sophia. When, a while later, Katherine's stomach growled she realised she hadn't eaten since breakfast and Alexander would be in the same position.

'I don't know about you but I'm starving,' she admitted.

'Would you like to stop at one of the tavernas?' he asked.

'I'd prefer not to take too long over lunch. I'm keen to talk to David's family.'

'I know a place near here that does pastries and decent coffee. We could pick something up and get back on our way.'

She was pleased he was in just as much of a hurry to get to the hospital as she was. She didn't think she could have beared to have stopped at a café and had a proper lunch, especially when she'd learned that in Greece there was no such thing as fast food served in a restaurant. While most times she appreciated the care they put into their cooking, today wasn't one of them.

When they stopped, she bought some bread rolls and cheese while Alexander downed a couple of cups of espresso in quick succession. She didn't care for the heavy, thick Greek coffee so she bought some fresh orange juice to go with their picnic lunch instead.

She took a few moments to split open the rolls and fill them. Alexander pulled a penknife from his pocket and offered it to her, and she quickly sliced the tomatoes and added them to the cheese. Once she'd done that she handed one of the rolls to Alexander. When she next looked up it was gone. He had to have wolfed it down in a couple of bites.

'Should I get some more?' she asked, astonished.

'No, that will do me for the time being. Shall we get on?'

She wrapped her half-eaten sandwich in a napkin. 'Suits me. I can finish this in the car.'

After they'd been driving for a while she asked, 'How long before we get there?'

He glanced at his watch. 'Another hour.'

She did some calculations in her head. An hour to get there, a couple more at the hospital and then what? A three or a three-and-a-half-hour journey back. They'd be lucky to reach home before midnight and they still had the other families to see.

However, it seemed he was there before her. 'I phoned a colleague while you were in the ladies. He's agreed to contact the doctors on our list and ask the families some preliminary questions. He said he'd call me back as soon as he had some information for us.'

Although Katherine would have preferred to have made the calls herself, she knew that Alexander had made the right decision. Every minute could make a difference—a life-changing difference—for one patient and his, or her, family.

Finally they arrived in Athens. After the peace of the countryside Katherine found the noise of tooting horns and the fumes of the cars that crept along the roads nose to tail almost overwhelming. She craned her neck to see the Acropolis, which dominated the city. It was on her list of places to visit but, like the rest of her plans, it would have to wait.

She was glad Alexander was with her to negotiate his way around the hospital. Although her spoken Greek wasn't too bad now, reading it was a completely different matter and despite many of the signposts being in English, it was still a busy and confusing hospital.

They made their way to the intensive care unit and she listened as Alexander explained to the doctor why they were there. Then he asked for an update on the patient.

'David is holding his own,' he said. 'But the septicaemia means we might have to amputate his hand. We have a theatre on standby.'

Oh, no! The boy was so young to be facing such drastic surgery. His parents must be beside themselves. And indeed, it seemed that they were too distraught to speak to them. The doctor apologised and suggested they come back in the morning when David's condition might have stabilised and the parents be more willing to see them.

'It can't wait,' Katherine protested. 'We have to find out where he's been and who he came into contact with. His family are the only people who can tell us.'

Once more, Alexander took her by the arm and led her away and out of earshot of the doctor.

'For God's sake, Katherine. Their child may be about to go into Theatre. Could you talk to anyone if you were in their position? I'm not sure I could.'

She knew why he was saying that, but she also knew that in circumstances such as these they couldn't afford the luxury of waiting.

'I know it's a bad time, but we need information as quickly as possible.'

'It can wait.'

'No, it can't.' She held his gaze. 'No it can't,' she repeated more softly. 'If you won't talk to them, I'll have to.'

He rubbed a hand across the back of his neck in what, she was beginning to realise, was a habit of his when he was thinking.

'Look, why don't I try to find another, less distressed family member to talk to? There's bound to be at least one here at the hospital—if I'm not mistaken most of the extended family will have gathered by now.'

'Fair enough,' Katherine conceded. 'But if they can't help I'm going to have to insist on speaking to David's parents.'

He nodded and Katherine was left kicking her heels while Alexander went in search of the extended family. While she waited she opened up her laptop and started creating a database. Then she reviewed what they'd learned so far—which wasn't much. They still didn't know what the cases had in common or how they might have come into contact with the virus. It was almost two hours before Alexander reappeared. He looked tired and in need of a shave.

'They decided they had to take David to Theatre and they've just taken him through to Recovery. They had to amputate the fingers on his left hand. Thank God he's right-handed.'

'I'm sorry,' she said. 'But it could have been so much worse.' She waited a few moments. 'Did you find out anything that might help?'

'Not really. I found his aunt, who lives next door to her sister. According to her, apart from school, a party and a trip to the beach he's not been anywhere out of the usual.' He held out a piece of paper. 'She's given me the names of the other kids at the party. None of them are the other victims, though.'

'They might be yet,' she said. 'We need to make sure everyone on that list and their doctors are contacted.'

'I telephoned Diane while I was waiting to hear how David got on in Theatre. She promised to get onto it straight away.'

She was impressed. She'd been right. Alexander was the perfect person to help with the crises.

'What about the other GP? The one you called—has he got back to you?'

'He phoned a few minutes ago. He's spoken to all the doctors, who have agreed to do as we requested.'

Alexander stepped forward and brushed a lock of her hair away from her forehead. The unexpected and tender gesture made her heart tighten. 'We've done all we can for the moment,' he said gently. 'Let's go home. We can discuss what we're going to do next on the way.'

* * *

On the way back. Alexander pulled off the main road. Katherine looked at him, surprised. 'Where are we going?'

'Neither of us have eaten since the rolls we had for lunch. I don't know about you but my brain doesn't work unless it's kept fuelled.'

Katherine had to agree. Now that he'd mentioned food she realised she was ravenous.

A short while later he stopped at a small taverna with tables set out on a veranda upstairs. Despite the hour, and its location, it was thronged with people enjoying meals and drinks in the cool evening breeze of the mountains. Alexander led her over to a table away from the other diners. The view was spectacular. In the crevasses of the mountain hundreds of lights glittered a snaking path downwards towards the sea. When the waitress came Alexander raised his eyebrow in Katherine's direction.

'You order,' she said, reading his meaning. 'I don't care what I eat as long as it's filling.'

Alexander rattled off something in Greek so rapidly she couldn't follow. While he did so she studied him from under her lashes. His earlier tiredness seemed to have disappeared and his usual energy was back. Although she was exhausted, she felt it too. Perhaps it was the urgency of the situation, the need to find answers that was making them both restless.

'So, what next?' Alexander asked, after the waiter had placed their meals in front of them. He'd ordered moussaka and a Greek salad to share. She speared a chunk of tomato on her fork and popped it into her mouth. Delicious.

'We should check in with Public Health in Athens and see if any more cases have been reported.' She laid her fork down, rummaged in her bag, pulled out her mini-laptop and fired it up. 'While you were in with David's parents I made some notes.' She moved it so he could see the screen.

'I've made a table. In the first column I've put the patient's name, the second has the date when they first came to the attention of the medical services and the third has a list of immediate family and friends and anyone else we know of who might have come into contact with them. It's not complete yet—there's bound to be names missing. Next to each name on the list is a column indicating whether they have been given prophylactic antibiotics. The last column is for places they have been in the last couple of weeks and will include swimming clubs, parties, et cetera. By creating a database I can sort the information any way I want. Sooner or later I'm hoping a common link will leap out. In the meantime, I've emailed a copy to my opposite number in Athens.'

Alexander looked impressed. 'You did all that? In, what? A couple of hours. Less.'

Warmth spread through her. Her reaction to him confused her. She couldn't remember a time when she'd felt more at ease in someone's company, yet at the same time her heart raced all the time she was with him.

'It's what I've been trained to do. If I were back at the hospital I'd have access to much more sophisticated programs to do it. On the other hand, entering the data myself helps me to understand it.'

He frowned. 'Is that what they've become? Data?'

'Of course they're not simply data,' Katherine retorted, stung. 'I'm a doctor but also a scientist. Trust me, this is the best way to approach this. Getting too close to individual patients can hinder a person when it comes to seeing patterns.' Hurt, she lowered her glass and pushed her half-eaten meal away. Her appetite had deserted her. 'Give me a moment, will you?' And without waiting for a reply, she stalked away.

Hearing footsteps behind her, Katherine turned. Somehow she wasn't surprised to find Alexander standing behind her.

'Aren't you cold?' he said softly.

'No. It's a perfect evening,' she murmured.

'May I join you?' he asked. When she nodded, he sat down next to her. She could smell his aftershave, almost feel the heat radiating from his body.

'I'm sorry,' he said. 'That was a stupid thing to say. I know you don't see the patients as data.' He grinned sheepishly. 'I'm perfectly aware that underneath the scientist façade beats a soft heart.' He placed a hand over hers. 'Will you forgive me?'

Her heart started pounding so hard she could barely breathe. What was it about him that made her feel that a whole world of possibility lay out there somewhere? She'd accepted that she would remain alone for the rest of her life, which, apart from the sorrow of her parents' deaths and a deep regret about the life she might have had had she made different choices, was a happy one. Then why did she feel she'd been fooling herself all this time?

'What are those lights out at sea?' she asked, to break the tension.

'It's the fishermen. A lot of them like to fish at night.'

'What about you? Is that what you use your boat for? I don't think I've ever seen you go out in it.'

He smiled. 'I've been waiting until I finished repainting it. But normally I go out in it whenever I can. Not just for fishing. I use it to island-hop sometimes. I like taking care of it. It belonged to my father once.' After a pause he continued, his voice soft and reflective. 'When I was a kid and we came to Greece on holiday I used to go out fishing at night with my uncle. Once he wouldn't take me—I forget the reason why. Perhaps he had other plans—but I wanted to go. There was a full moon and only a slight wind—perfect fishing weather. So I waited until everyone was asleep, then I crept out and launched my boat.'

She smiled, imagining the scene. 'Did you catch anything?'

'Tons. There were so many fish I forgot to think about where the boat was, and didn't notice it was drifting. When I looked up I couldn't see the lights on the shore any more.'

'What did you do?'

'I don't know what I was more scared of,' he said, 'being dragged out to the middle of the sea or my father's wrath when he found out I'd been out on my own. I knew the stars pretty well.' He pointed to the sky. 'I knew if I followed the right star it would guide me back to shore. Maybe not here exactly but to somewhere where I could walk or hitch a lift home.'

'And did you?'

'There was only one problem. When I realised I had lost sight of the shore, I jumped to my feet and lost an oar overboard.'

'That must have been a bit of a pain.'

He laughed. 'It was. I tried using the one oar, paddling from one side then the other, but I soon realised that, given the zig-zagging course I was making, it would take days, not hours, to reach the shore. I nearly gave up then. I could have stayed where I was. They would have sent out boats to find me once they discovered I was missing.'

'It's a big sea.'

'And even bigger when you're out there on your own.'

'Were you scared?'

'The thing was, except for the first scary moment, I wasn't. I knew my father would move heaven and earth to find me. I knew whether it took him the rest of his life, whether he had to spend every drachma he had to employ helicopters and search boats to find me, he would.'

'He must have loved you very much.'

'More than life itself.' He turned his head to look at her. 'A parent's love is the strongest love of all. It's only when you have a child yourself that you realise that.'

His words were like a knife straight to her heart. She clasped her hands together and squeezed. He couldn't know how much they hurt her.

'Is that what happened? Did he call the emergency services out?' She was relieved to find her voice sounded normal—cool even.

'No. Thank God he didn't have to. Despite my years in England, I was a Greek boy brought up on legends and myths about Greek heroes. There was no chance I was going to wait for him to come searching for me. I would have died rather than sit there waiting meekly for rescue.' Although he sounded indignant, she could hear the laughter in his voice.

'So, what *did* you do?'

'I decided to try and swim back.'

She laughed. 'You're kidding!'

'It was madness. I know that now, but back then it was all I could think of doing. However I couldn't leave the boat to float out to sea. It was my father's pride and joy. So I threw the fish back. It almost killed me. A whole night's work and the best catch I'd ever had! I jumped out of the boat and, keeping hold of the rope, I swam back to shore.'

'You could have drowned.'

'I knew as long as I kept hold of the boat, I'd be all right. And it worked. It took me a bloody long time but I made it into a small bay just as the sun was coming up. But I still had to get the damned boat back to its proper mooring. So I nicked one of the oars from a boat that was in the bay and rowed home. I've never rowed as fast in all my life. I was determined to get home before my father noticed I was gone.'

'And did you?'

He smiled ruefully. 'Now, that was the thing. I did. At least I thought I did. I crept into bed and a few moments later I heard my father get up. I was pretty pleased with myself, I can tell you. But later, when I went down to the boat again just to check there wasn't any evidence of my night-time excursion, the oar I had pinched was missing and there, in its place, was a brand-new one.' He sighed.

'He must have known what I was up to all along. I bet he was sitting on the wall all night, waiting for me to come home. When he knew I was safe he must have hurried back to bed, and then, when he was sure I was asleep, gone down to check on the boat. Of course, he would have seen instantly that one of the oars had come from another boat and so he made a new one. And you know…' he paused and looked out to sea '…he never once mentioned it. Not ever.'

They sat in silence for a while. 'It sounds as if you have always been surrounded by your family's love. No wonder Crystal is such a happy little girl.'

He looked into the distance. 'I've been lucky, I guess, in so many ways. But the gods like to even the score.' He could only be talking about his wife.

'What about you?' he continued. 'Did you have a happy childhood too?'

Perhaps it was his Greek upbringing that made him talk

like this? Most British men she knew would rather die a hundred deaths then talk about their feelings. Or perhaps it was the night—perhaps everyone found it easier to talk under the cover of darkness.

'Of course my parents loved me. It's just that I think I disappointed them.' The words were out before she knew it.

'Disappointed them? The dedicated, bursary-winning scholar? Did you go off the rails or something when you were a teenager?' He shook his head. 'No, I can't see it. I bet you were head girl.'

Going off the rails was one way of putting it. Off track for a while was perhaps closer to the truth.

She shook her head. 'I was never that popular. Far too studious and serious. I was a prefect, though.'

'There. I was right. And then you went to medical school and here you are about to submit your thesis for your doctorate and one of Europe's top specialists in the spread of infectious diseases. What is there not to be proud of?'

Judging by the teasing note in his voice, he couldn't have known how close to the bone he had come with his questions. She scrambled to her feet. 'I am getting a little cold. I think it's time we went on our way.'

Later that night, she lay in bed listening to the gentle rush of the waves on the shore and thinking about what Alexander had said. She'd tried so hard to make her parents proud, and to an extent she had. Her mother had told anyone who'd listen, sometimes complete strangers, that her daughter was a doctor. In fact, to hear her mother speak you'd think that her daughter was single-handedly responsible for the health of the nation. But what she had wanted most of all, a grandchild she could fuss over, Katherine hadn't given her.

Throwing the covers aside, she went out to the balcony. Alexander was making her think about stuff she didn't want to think about, like loss, and families—and love.

Love. What would it like to be loved by Alexander? It hit her then—she wasn't just attracted to him, she was falling in love with him.

Of all men, why did it have to be him? He was still in love with his wife, that much was obvious. And even if he wasn't, his life was here in Greece and she'd be returning to the UK to pick up hers. But worst of all, if he knew her secret he would despise her. He would never understand why she'd done what she had.

She returned to the sitting room and flicked through the playlist on her iPod. She inserted it into the speakers she had brought with her and as the sound of Brahms filled the room she sat on the sofa and closed her eyes.

What was it with him and this woman? Alexander thought as he stared at the stars from his bedroom window. Why couldn't he stop thinking about her? It wasn't as if he had any intention of having a relationship with her. No one would ever take Sophia's place. Katherine would be returning to the UK soon and he couldn't follow her, she was as much married to her work as he was—there were a hundred different reasons.

Yet he couldn't fool himself any longer that he wasn't strongly attracted to her. Perhaps because he saw his own sadness reflected in her eyes? Or was it because, despite her protestations, he suspected she was lonely and he knew only too well how that felt? It was only when she talked about her work that her reserve disappeared. Her eyes shone and she became more animated. He liked it that she felt passionately about what she did—in many ways she reminded him of the way he used to be. And look how that had turned out.

His mind shied away from the past and back to Katherine.

He liked everything about her—the way she looked, her sensitivity and reserve, the sudden smile that lit up her face, banishing the shadows in her eyes, the way she was with Crystal, slightly awkward but not talking down to her the way many adults did, how she was with Yia-Yia and the villagers: respectful, but not patronising.

When the realisation hit him it was like jumping into a pool of water from a height. Shock then exhilaration. He didn't just like her—he was falling in love with her.

As the plaintive notes of Brahms's Lullaby filtered through the still night air from the other side of the square he went outside and listened. It had been one of Sophia's favourites—something she'd played often. He closed his eyes as an image of Sophia rushed back, her head bent over the keys of the piano, her hair falling forward as her fingers flew over the keys, a smile of pure happiness on her lips. His chest tightened. Sophia. His love. How could he think, even for a moment, that there could ever be anyone else?

CHAPTER SIX

COMFORTED BY THE soothing strains of the music and know-ing sleep would elude her, Katherine studied her database, entering the list of names Alexander had given her.

She stopped when she came to Stéfan's name. He had been the first patient to fall ill. Concentrating on him was key.

There was something about him that was tugging at her memory. What was it? Yes! She had it. The day he'd col-lapsed at the surgery, he'd been sporting a bandage on his right hand. And it hadn't been clean either. It had looked professional, though. Someone had bandaged his hand but not recently. Hercules leaped onto her lap and started purring. She stroked him absent-mindedly as she dialled Alexander's phone. Despite the late hour, he picked up immediately.

'The boy who died. Stéfan Popalopadous? Do you know how he hurt his hand? Did he have it dressed at your prac-tice?' she asked, coming straight to the point.

Alexander mumbled a curse under his breath. 'Hello to you too. No, I don't know how Stéfan hurt his hand. Not without looking at his notes, which, of course, are at the practice. But something tells me that's where I'm going.'

'Would you like me to come with you?' she asked.

'No. That's okay. Keep your phone near you and I'll call you as soon as I have an answer.'

It was over an hour before he called back. She snatched up the phone. 'Yes? What have you found out?'

'He damaged his hand in a winch on his boat. Apparently he often takes people out for trips in the evenings after work. He was treated in Nafplio. He runs trips between there and all the major ports along the coast.'

'Then Nafplio is where we're going. Pick me up on the way.'

Nafplio was pretty, with elegant town houses with balconies that reminded her of Venice. Alexander told her a little of the town's history on the way. During the Ottoman era it had once been the capital of Greece and the Palamayde fortress, which dominated the town, had been a prison during the Greek War of Independence. Now the town was a stopover for some of the smaller cruise ships on their way around the Mediterranean as well as for yachts either in flotillas or in singles. That wasn't good: If one of the transient visitors had come into contact with their patient, who knew where they would be now? Was that how Claire had contracted the disease?

They phoned the doctor of the surgery where Stéfan's hand had been dressed, rousing him from his bed, and discovered that they'd been right. Stéfan had been treated there a couple of days before he'd turned up at Alexander's practice. He'd had a temperature, but it hadn't been raised enough to cause concern.

Now they had their first contact, they could be reasonably confident of tracing the others before they became sick.

Katherine and Alexander exchanged high-fives as soon

as they left the practice. 'You're some public health doctor,' he said.

She grinned back at him. 'I am, aren't I?'

Over the next week, Katherine and Alexander visited all the villages and towns where cases of meningitis had been reported, as well as those of all the contacts they'd traced. Now they knew about Stéfan, it was easier to trace the people he'd come into contact with and their contacts. David, the boy in Intensive Care, had been taken around the coast with a number of his friends as a birthday treat, and the other eight victims, most of whom were recovering, had also taken trips in Stéfan's boat in the days before Stéfan had become unwell. Finally Claire's parents confirmed that their daughter had posted a photo on her Facebook page of Stéfan and his boat shortly before she'd become ill.

Katherine and Alexander set up temporary clinics and spoke to the local nurses and medical staff, advising them what to look out for and what information to give their patients. There had been one new case, but as everyone was more vigilant, she had been admitted to hospital as soon as she'd started showing symptoms and was doing well.

The longer she worked with Alexander the more she admired him. He was good with the patients, kind and understanding with panicked villagers, and authoritative with those who needed to be persuaded to take the antibiotics. It was tiring work and they spent hours in the car, driving from village to village, but she treasured those times most of all. They spoke of their day, what they had to do next, but they also talked about the music they liked and places they wanted to visit.

However, she was aware he was holding back from her, as she was from him. Often it was on the tip of her tongue to tell him about Poppy but the time never seemed right, or, if she was honest, she was too frightened of his reaction. What would he think if, or when, she did tell him? Would he be shocked? Or would he understand? And why tell him anyway? As long as there were no new cases of meningitis she would be leaving at the end of September and so far he'd said nothing, done nothing to make her think he saw her as more than a friend and colleague—albeit one he was attracted to.

She'd caught him looking at her when she'd been sneaking looks in his direction. Unsure of what it meant, she'd dropped her eyes, her pulse racing, finding an excuse to turn away, to speak to someone else.

But apart from the looks, he'd never as much as taken her hand or kissed her good-night. She suspected he was still in love with his dead wife and that no woman would ever live up to her.

The thought of returning to the UK made her heart ache. To leave all this when she'd only just found it. To go back to a life that more than ever seemed colourless and grey. To leave Alexander, his grandmother and Crystal—most of all Alexander—was breaking her heart.

Perhaps it was being here in Greece? Perhaps it was just the magic spell the country had woven around her? Maybe when she returned to the UK she'd be able to see it for what it was: infatuation, brought on by too much sun and the joy of working with someone who cared about what he did as much as she.

But she knew she was fooling herself. She wasn't just falling in love with him—she loved him—totally, deeply and would love him for as long as she breathed. But, he didn't love her. Nothing and no one could replace his wife.

His life was here with his daughter and his family while hers was back in London.

And what if he suspected how she felt about him? That would be too humiliating. Maybe he'd already guessed?.

She threw down her book and started pacing. Perhaps he thought she visited his house as a means to get close to him. And going to the square every evening to share a meal or a beer with him. Wasn't that practically admitting she couldn't stay away from him? God, she'd done everything but drool whenever he was near. She'd virtually thrown herself at him. How could she have been so stupid?

Well, there was only one way to rectify that. She would keep her distance. She wouldn't visit Yia-Yia, she wouldn't go to the square. If anyone asked she would say she was behind with her thesis. That, as it happened, was perfectly true. Besides, what did she care if anyone—least of all him—thought she was making excuses? As long as they didn't think she was some desperate woman trying to snag the local widowed doctor while she was here.

But not to see him? Except in passing? To even think it tore her in two.

She should have known this kind of happiness couldn't last.

Alexander stood on the balcony, a glass of cold water in his hand, his thoughts straying, as they always did these days, to Katherine. He hadn't seen much of her since they'd stopped visiting the affected villages and he missed her. She used to come most evenings to the square but she hadn't been for a while. Was she avoiding him?

Working with her these last weeks he'd come to admire her more and more. She was good at what she did. Very good. If she hadn't been around he doubted that they would have got on top of the outbreak as quickly as they had. Her patience with the affected families, her manner towards the villagers, her determination to speak her faltering Greek to them and the kindness and respect with which she treated young and old alike was very much the Greek ethos. He loved how her forehead furrowed when she was thinking, how her face lit up when she laughed, and most of all the way she was with Crystal. His daughter adored her.

Katherine was almost as perfect in her way as Sophia had been in hers. But she'd be going soon. And the thought of not seeing her again filled him with dismay.

It hit him then. He didn't just like and admire Katherine, he was crazy about her.

So what was he doing here, on his own, kicking his heels when he could be with her?

CHAPTER SEVEN

KATHERINE WAS SITTING on her balcony, watching the sun cast shadows on the sea, when she heard a soft tap on the door. Having come to recognise the sound of Alexander's footsteps, she didn't need to turn around to know it was him. Neither was she really surprised. Deep down she'd known it was only a matter of time before he sought her out.

'Crystal's been looking for you at the taverna these last couple of evenings,' he said softly. 'So was I. And Yia-Yia says she hasn't seen you for a day or two. Are you all right? Not ill or anything?'

The way he was searching her face made her pulse skip a beat.

'I thought I should give company a miss for a while.' Her heart was thumping so hard she was finding it difficult to breathe. 'With everything that has happened, I've fallen behind with my thesis. I'm planning to submit it in the next couple of days.'

He came to sit in the chair next to hers. 'When do you leave?'

'At the end of the month. There's nothing to keep me here longer now the epidemic seems to be under control. I had a phone call from Athens earlier—there's been no more cases reported in the last forty-eight hours. They're pretty confident the outbreak is over.'

'Thank God. If you hadn't got onto it as soon as you did, there could have been more deaths.'

'I was only doing my job. A job I love.'

His expression was unreadable in the light of the moon.

'I never did take you out on the boat, did I?' he said softly.

'No, you didn't,' she agreed. 'But you've been busy. It can't be easy for you, working and being a single father.' God, couldn't she think of anything less inane to say?

'I have Yia-Yia. And Helen when I need her.' He hooked his hands behind his head. 'Although as Helen's getting married in a few weeks it's unlikely that Crystal and I will see as much of her.' He leaned forward. 'I could still take you out on the boat. In fact, we could go later tonight. It's a perfect night for it.'

She didn't think it was possible for her heart to beat any faster but apparently it could.

'You don't have to take me, you know,' she said stiffly.

He looked taken aback. 'Of course I don't have to take you. Why would you think that?' His eyes locked on hers. 'It's not just Crystal who's missed you, I've missed spending time with you too,' he said softly. 'I like being with you. Haven't you realised that by now?' He stood and reached out a hand for hers.

Her heart beating a tattoo against her ribs, she allowed him to pull her to her feet. For a moment she swayed towards him, driven by a need to feel his arms around her. At the last moment she stopped herself and took a step back. Hadn't she told herself she wouldn't make a fool of herself?

He looked bemused, as well he might. How could he

know what was inside her head when she barely did? However, he didn't let go of her hand.

'We should wait until Crystal's asleep, though,' he continued, 'otherwise she'll insist on coming too. If I say no, I wouldn't put it past her to launch a boat of her own and come after us.'

Katherine had to laugh, even if it sounded shaky. 'No one can say she's not your daughter.'

'No.' His expression grew more serious. 'I could do with having you on my own for a bit. My daughter has taken such a liking to you, it's difficult to prise her from your side.'

Her heart catapulted inside her chest.

Why was she worrying about the future? It felt right that he was here, and why not sleep with him if he asked? And she was certain he would ask. She would be leaving soon and although there was no chance of a future for them, why resist snatching a few days of happiness? He need never know her secret. What mattered was here and now and if she could be with him, even for a short while, why not? She'd have plenty time to lick her wounds—to regret what could have been—when she left here. She surprised herself. Greece had changed so much about her.

'We should make the most of what time you have left,' he said, as if reading her mind. 'I could take some leave. We could spend it together.'

'And Crystal? Isn't she expecting to spend time with you?'

'Of course. And she will. I thought the three of us could do some stuff.' He searched her face. 'I know having my daughter around, adorable though she is, puts a spanner in the works, but happily she does go to sleep in the evenings. You do like her, don't you? She's definitely taken a shine to you.'

She wanted to ask him whether he liked to be with her because of Crystal because, much as she was coming to love the little girl, she needed him to want to be with her. But she wouldn't ask him. And what if he said yes? What if he asked her to stay permanently? What would she do then? At the very least she would have to admit that there was a very large part of her life she was keeping secret from him. Perhaps the time to tell him was now, before they got in any deeper. But if she did, what would he say? How would he react?

And what was she thinking anyway? Even if he did ask her to stay, she wouldn't. She couldn't. How could she take on the care of a child after what she'd done? However, didn't he deserve the truth from her, whether she stayed or not?

She was being given a glimpse of a life she might have. A chance to break free from the strait-jacket of the one she'd imposed on herself with its rules, self-denial, hard work and determination. Could she forgive herself—allow herself the joy of loving and being loved? Even for a short while.

He misinterpreted her silence and stood. 'I'll see you about then?'

'What time do you want me to meet you?'

His expression lightened. 'About ten?'

'I'll be there.'

When she arrived at the bay he was leaning against the boat, wearing a black T-shirt and dark jeans with fisherman's boots. He looks a bit like a pirate, she thought, especially with the five o'clock shadow darkening his jaw. He whistled appreciatively when he saw her. She'd been like a cat on a hot tin roof all evening. After discarding several outfits, she'd finally settled on a pair of faded denim shorts and a cheesecloth embroidered blouse she'd purchased in the village. Underneath she wore a lacy bra with matching panties. She'd shaved her legs and moisturised all over.

She couldn't remember the last time she'd felt so nervous and was ready long before she was due to meet him. Unable to change the habits of a lifetime, she'd packed a small bag with a cardigan in the unlikely event it was chilly on the water, and at the last minute had added some fresh fruit and olives, a bottle of wine, a corkscrew and two glasses. It was always better to be prepared.

'Hello,' she whispered. Feeling inexplicably like a naughty child, she suppressed the desire to giggle.

'You don't have to whisper, you know,' he said with a grin. 'It's not as if we're ten years old and stealing a boat.'

'Sorry,' she said in a normal voice. 'Whispering just seemed to go with the moment.'

The boat was in the water, where it drifted gently in the waves, and he was holding on to the rope to stop it being pushed out to sea. 'Why don't you climb in?' he suggested.

She slipped off her sandals and stepped into the sea, shivering as the waves lapped around her ankles, then her calves and above her knees. As her skin adjusted to the temperature, the cool water felt delicious against her overheated skin.

But once she'd reached the boat she stood dumbfounded. How was she supposed to get in? As if reading her mind, Alexander, still holding the rope but gathering it in towards him, waded over until he was standing next to her. Suddenly she felt a pair of strong hands circle her waist and then she was off her feet and he was holding her in his arms. Even in the warmth of the evening air she was conscious of the heat radiating from his body and the clean, fresh scent of him.

He laughed down at her. 'Good thing you weigh nothing.' A slight exaggeration, she thought—she wasn't the smallest of women—but then she was being dropped gently into the boat. A few seconds later Alexander sprang in alongside her. Tentatively she took a seat at the back. He picked up an oar and pushed them away from the shore, before coiling the rope into a neat round and placing it on the bottom of the boat. 'Sit in the front if you like,' he said. 'No, not now!' he added as she stood, making the boat wobble. 'Wait until we're a bit further out. Unless you want us to both end up in the water?'

Feeling a little foolish, she sat back down as Alexander started rowing. The moon was so bright she could see the muscles of his arms bunching with every pull of the oar.

'Are we going to fish?' she asked.

'If you like. But later. I want to show you something first.'

A comfortable silence fell, punctuated only by the creak of the boat against the oars and the lapping of the sea. Katherine trailed her hand in the water.

'Watch out for sharks,' he cautioned.

She pulled her hand out of the water as if she'd had an electric shock. But when she looked at him she saw, from his grin, that he'd been teasing her.

Her skin tingled and she grinned back at him. How she loved this man!

'So, what is it you want to show me?'

'I'm afraid you're going to have to wait and see.' He refused to say any more so she let herself relax, gasping with delight as a shooting star sped across the sky before falling towards the black depths of the ocean. It was if she had been transported into a different world. Happiness surged through her. Everything about being here—being with Alexander—made her feel more alive than she'd ever felt before. As if the person she was when she was with him was a different, more together version of herself on one hand and a wilder, more interesting, version on the other.

It must have been so hard for her mother to leave here when she married. Britain was a colder, greyer place than the one she'd left. Although the way the villagers lived, almost on top of each other and constantly visiting each other's homes, had taken Katherine time to get used to, and she could see how someone used to living in such close proximity with their neighbours, always having someone to call on for support, would struggle to adapt in a strange country with an entirely different culture. Her mother had loved her father very much and, as she'd told Katherine often, she would rather have been with Dad in hell than without him.

A wave of sadness threatened to swamp her mood. At least she was here. In the country her mother had once called home, she felt nearer to her than she'd felt since she'd died.

'You okay?'

Alexander's voice jerked her back to the present. 'Yes. Why?'

'It's just that you looked sad there for a moment.'

She forced a smile. 'Just thinking about my mother and wishing she'd been able come back even once before she died.'

In the distance the tiny lights from other boats bobbed on the sea. Beyond them dark shapes of small islands broke up the horizon.

'Perhaps *you'll* come back—or stay?' he said softly.

Her pulse upped another notch. Was he asking her to?

'I have my work. But, yes, I think will. What about you? Do you think you might ever return to the UK?' She held her breath as she waited for his answer.

'To visit my mother certainly. But I couldn't leave Greece permanently. I couldn't take Crystal away from her grandmother. At least, not until she's older.'

Her earlier happiness dimmed. She could understand him not wanting to separate Crystal from her great-grandmother, not until she was older anyway, but if he felt about Katherine the way she felt about him, wouldn't he want to be with her? Wouldn't he ask her outright to stay?

'Why,' he continued, 'do we always regret what might have been instead of being grateful for the life we have?'

Her heart thudded a tattoo against her chest. She wanted to ask him what he meant. Was he referring to her? What might have been? Or was he talking about his wife?

'Do you regret coming back here?' she asked instead.

'Not at all. It was the right decision for Crystal. Anyway, the UK was too—' He stopped suddenly. 'Too cold,' he finished. She was sure that wasn't what he had been about to say. In unguarded moments his sadness mirrored her own. Even after two years he was still grieving for his wife. But he should find some comfort in the knowledge he had found love—a great love, she suspected—and she envied him for it. More, she envied the woman who had been the recipient.

They lapsed into silence again. Just when she was beginning to wonder where exactly he was taking her, an island with a small bay came into view.

'Is this the place you wanted to show me?' she asked.

'Greece has many beautiful islands, but this is one I like to come to whenever I take out the boat. Not least because no one ever comes here. The only other place I like more is Cape Sounion.'

'Where's that?'

'You mean you don't know? You must have heard of the temple of Poseidon. It's where Byron used to go to write his poetry. I'll take you one day.'

His assumption that they would be spending more time together sent a ripple of happiness through her. She'd waited how many years to find someone like him and she'd had to come to a remote part of Greece to do so. If only she had an inkling of how he felt about her. If only he could love her the way he had loved, and probably still loved, his wife; if only she could make him understand why she'd done what she had, they might have a chance of a future together.

But he would never understand. She was certain of that.

He jumped out of the boat, holding its rope, and held out his arms. She let him swing her into them. As his arms tightened around her she closed her eyes, wanting to savour every last moment. He carried her ashore before standing her gently on her feet.

'So, what's so special about this island?' she asked, when he returned from pulling the boat out of the water. 'You've just told me Greece has hundreds of beautiful islands.'

'Legend has it that a Spartan soldier brought a Trojan princess here when he captured her. I have no evidence that this is the exact place,' he said, holding his hands up as if to ward off her protests, 'but he described it as an island not far from my village whose beauty was only dimmed by the beauty of his wife.' His voice dropped to a murmur. 'He believed if he kept her here, safe, nothing bad would ever happen to her and they could live out the rest of their lives together and in peace.'

'And did they? In your story?' It might only be a legend but she really wanted to know.

His gaze returned to hers, the tone of his voice almost dismissive. 'No. In time he got bored. He missed the excitement and prestige that came with being in the Greek army.'

'What happened?'

'When he was away, fighting in some war or another, his enemies found her here. They captured her and intended to make her a consort. She guessed what they planned so when they weren't watching her, she escaped and ran to the cliff. She threw herself into the sea.'

'Oh, no! And what happened to her lover?'

'As soon as he came back and discovered what had happened, he went mad with grief and guilt. He drowned himself so he could be with her in death.'

Katherine shivered. 'That's so sad.'

He reached for her hand. 'What do you think he should have done? Was he not wrong to bring her here where she was alone and unprotected?' His eyes bored into hers as if her answer really mattered. 'Don't you think he deserved what happened?'

'Well, first of all,' she began cautiously, her reaction was her choice. I don't think she would have agreed to come and live here with him if she hadn't wanted to. She must have known he was trying to protect her the best way he knew how. In the end he was wrong, but that doesn't mean he didn't do what he did for the right reasons. Didn't you say earlier that there is no point regretting what might have been?'

She knew she was talking as much about her own situation as this mythical couple's. 'It's easy to look back on our lives and see what we did wrong, what we should have done—but at the time we can only make the best decision we can in the circumstances.'

'Is that what you really believe? I can't imagine you have much to regret.'

This conversation was getting too close to the bone for comfort. Perhaps it was time to tell him about Poppy. But fear held her back. She couldn't bear it if he judged her or, worse, rejected her. She forced a smile. 'Why do you like the island so much if it has such a sad story attached to it?'

He poured her some wine and passed the glass to her. The touch of his fingertips brushing against hers sent hot sparks up her arm. 'In a way, I guess it is sad. But legend has it that the gods took pity on them and turned them into dolphins. I like to think of them out in the ocean together—always.'

Her heart twisted. So she'd been right. He was still in love with his wife.

He stepped forward and took her face between his hands. 'I don't know why no man has captured you yet. What is wrong with English men?'

'Perhaps it is me,' she said, then could have kicked herself. It was difficult to think straight with him being so close. 'I mean, being too picky.'

He laughed down at her, his teeth white in the dark. 'You should be picky,' he said. He tangled his hands in her hair and, with his thumbs under her cheek bones, raised her face to his. 'You are so beautiful. So perfect.'

No, she thought wildly. *Don't think that!* He mustn't think she was perfect. He'd only be disappointed.

He lowered his head and brought his mouth down on hers and then she couldn't think any more. This was what she'd been imagining almost from the moment she'd first set eyes on him and it was everything she'd dreamed it would be. As his kisses deepened she clung to him, almost dizzy with desire.

When he moved away she gave a little gasp of disappointment. But he lifted her in his arms and carried her over to a soft patch of grass where he laid her down.

'Are you sure?' he asked as she gazed up at him.

'Sure?' She almost laughed. She pulled him down to her. 'What took you so long?' she murmured against his lips.

Later, they lay wrapped in each other's arms, gazing up at the stars. She'd never felt so peaceful, so thoroughly made love to. He'd been demanding, gentle and teasing and had touched her in ways she couldn't remember being touched before, until she'd cried out with her need to have him inside her. She blushed as she remembered how she'd dug her fingertips into his back, how she'd called out to him as wave upon wave of pleasure had rocked her body.

But she didn't really care. This wanton, this woman he'd unleashed, was a revelation to her and she never wanted to go back to the one she'd been before. She smiled to herself. This was what sex should be like.

The moonlight shone on his naked body. It was every bit as she'd imagined—better than any of the Greek statues she'd seen. No wonder she hadn't been able to stop thinking about how he would feel under her hands. A smile curved her lips and she laughed with sheer joy.

He propped himself on his elbow and gazed down at her. Instinctively she reached for her blouse to cover her nakedness, but as she moved her hand he caught it in his fingers. 'Don't,' he murmured. 'I don't think I could ever get enough of just looking at you.'

The new wanton Katherine revelled in the desire she saw in his eyes.

She reached up to him and wrapped her arms around his neck.

As the horizon turned pink and apricot they lay in each other's arms, looking up at the star-sprinkled sky, their hands entwined. 'There's something I need to tell you,' he said softly.

Oh, God, here it was. *This was wonderful but...*

'Remember I told you that I was training to be a surgeon when Sophia died,' he continued.

'Yes.'

'And I said I was working all the time?'

She wasn't sure where this was going. 'I know how competitive the speciality can be.'

'When Sophia fell pregnant with Crystal I was so happy. And so was she. If at times I caught her looking wistful I just put it down to her being homesick for Greece. It suited me to believe that's all it was. Looking back, I think she knew it was the end of her dream to become a concert pianist.

'I was determined to make it in surgery, but you know how it is—the competition is fierce, especially for the top positions, and only the best job in the most prestigious hospital would do me. I had it all planned out. I would qualify for a consultant post then I would apply to the Mayo Clinic in America and do some further training there. I'd already sat my board exams when I was a resident in my final year at med school so getting a post wouldn't be an issue as long as I stayed focussed.

'Sophia backed me all the way. She said she could play

her music anywhere. I knew that wasn't necessarily true—
not if she wanted to play professionally—but I chose not to
listen to that particular voice. I was a selfish bastard back
then—completely focussed on what I wanted to achieve.
I told myself I was doing it for all of us, for me, for Sophia—and for the baby on the way.

'What I chose to forget was that she'd already put her
career on hold for me. A musician's career is, if anything, more competitive than medicine—they have such
a short time to "make it" and she'd already jeopardised
her chances by coming with me to the UK. But, as I said,
I planned to make it up to her. One day when I'd got to
where I needed to go, I would slow down, let my career
take a back seat and let her enjoy the limelight for a while.

'We both wanted a family and I told myself that by the
time I had reached the top, the children would be of an age
to allow her time for herself. There was always going to be
more than one child. We both wanted at least three. Call
me clever, huh? If I'd done the math I would have realised
that if everything went to plan she would have been thirty
three by the time the youngest was born. I thought it was
simple. We'd have children. Sophia would stay at home
until the youngest was six weeks or so and then we'd employ a nanny. And Sophia went along with it. Until Crystal was born. Then she could no more see herself putting
any child of hers into a nursery than she could have left
them home alone. She loved being a mother. If she found
it boring she never said so and I never asked.

'She always made friends easily and the house was always filled—at least so I heard as I was rarely home long
enough to see for myself. It was as if she'd gathered around
her friends to be the family she'd left behind in Greece. I

told myself she was happy. But when I thought about it later, I couldn't remember the last time she'd played the piano. At the time I told myself that that was good—that she wasn't really driven enough to make it as a concert pianist. Why is everything so much more obvious in hindsight?'

Katherine rolled over so she could see his face. 'We all see things differently later, don't we?' she murmured, although every word he'd said about Sophia cut her like a blade.

'I never stopped loving her. She was my best friend, my lover, the mother of my child, but I stopped seeing her— really seeing her.'

The sadness in his eyes twisted her heart.

'She deserved more than I gave her. Perhaps I didn't love her enough. If I had I wouldn't have put my needs so far above hers.'

'She was lucky to be loved the way you loved her. She would have known she was deeply loved,' Katherine whispered.

'I'm glad you told me about her.' And she was. She wanted to know everything about him. Even if hearing about how much he'd loved Sophia hurt.

'I had to. You have to know why I'm not sure I can ever promise more than what we have here tonight. I care too much about you not to tell you the truth about myself. And there's more…'

She stopped his words with her fingertips. The here and now was all they had. After what he'd told her, how could she ever tell him about Poppy? And not telling him meant they could never have more than what they had now. 'Let's not think about the past,' she said. 'Let's only think about now.' She moved her hand from his lips and taking his head between her palms lowered herself on top of him.

* * *

When they returned to the village she led him by the hand up the path and into her home. Her heart was beating so fast she couldn't speak.

He kicked the door closed behind him. '*Agapi- mou*,' he breathed into her neck. 'I want you. I need you.'

She stepped into his arms feeling as if, at last, she'd come home—even if only for a while.

They spent every day of the next week with each other, until Alexander's leave was over. Crystal came to the house often. If Katherine was working, the child would take the colouring book she'd brought with her and lay it on the table next to Katherine's papers, and quietly, her tongue caught in the corner of her mouth, use her crayons to colour in, stopping periodically to admire her work or to study Katherine from the corner of her eye, waiting patiently until Katherine stopped what she was doing to admire her efforts. Increasingly, Katherine would find herself, at Yia-Yia's invitation, at the family home, pitching in to make olive tapenade or some other Greek dish. Then, instead of sitting and looking out at the beach, they'd retire to the bench at the front of the house and sit in silence, enjoying the heat of the sun and letting the ebb and flow of village life happen around them. Katherine's rusty Greek was improving by leaps and bounds and she and Alexander's grandmother were able to communicate reasonably well.

She'd also become confident enough with her Greek to stop to chat with the other villagers when she was passing through the square. Soon small gifts of ripe tomatoes and zucchini, enormous squashes and bunches of fat grapes still on the vine appeared on her doorstep, and before long she had more plump olives than she could hope ever to eat and more bottles of home-made olive oil than she knew what to do with.

She often thought of her mother. It was as if she'd planned this, knowing that Greece would weave its magic around her and that Katherine would discover what she had missed out on in life. It was, Katherine realised, her mother's final gift to her and one she wanted to savour. As it had done during the epidemic, her thesis lay largely ignored—dotting the 'i's and crossing the 't's didn't seem as important as they once had—although Katherine knew she would never submit it until it was as perfect as she could make it. Greece hadn't turned her into a complete sloth.

But she *was* less than perfect here. She no longer blow-dried her hair every morning before twirling it into a tight bun. Instead she wore it lose around her shoulders or twisted carelessly into a ponytail, no longer caring if it frizzed a little around the edges. She felt freer without the tights, the buttoned-to-the-neck shirts, tailored trousers and sensible shoes she'd worn when she'd first arrived. Now it was bare-shouldered sundresses, skimpy shorts and strappy T-shirts. She'd even repainted her nails in the same blood red as Crystal had—leaving Crystal's handiwork would have been a step too far! With Alexander back at work, she saw little of him during the day, but most evenings they drank cold beer and nibbled olives and fresh figs, spoke about work and history while Crystal played in the square. He made her laugh with his amusing stories of the villagers and his patients and although her skin still fizzed every time he looked at her, she was able to relax in his company in a way that she hadn't done with anyone, apart from Sally, in years.

It was, Katherine thought, the happiest time of her life. For once, nothing was asked of her, nothing demanded, no one expected anything of her. Sometimes Crystal came with them and sometimes they went on their own. He took her to Cape Souinon and she could see straight away why he loved it. The ruins of the temple of Poseidon looked out towards the sea and she could easily imagine Lord Byron sitting with his back against one of the pillars, writing poetry.

Often they spent the day on the beach with Crystal, swimming, picnicking and sharing intimate smiles. In the evenings he would call at her house and together they would climb the path to the village square, releasing their hands by unspoken consent moments before they reached it. But it was the nights she longed for most. When his daughter was asleep he'd come to her house and they'd make love, either in her bed or down in the little bay. He'd wake up early and leave her to return to his home so that he'd always be there when Crystal woke up. And every day she fell just a little more in love with him.

She didn't know how she was ever going to say goodbye.

Alexander was whistling as he showered. In a short while he'd be seeing Katherine. It had been a long time, he reflected, since he'd felt this good. Not since Sophia had died.

And it was all down to Katherine. He grinned remembering the night before. How could he ever have thought she was reserved—when it came to making love she was anything but.

Unfortunately his lunchtime date with Katherine was going to be curtailed. He had a patient who needed a home visit. Perhaps Katherine would come with him? He didn't want to waste any of the little time they had left.

But why should she leave?

He stepped out of the shower.

She could come to live with him in Greece. He was certain she would find another job here easily. Or he could find one in England. He quickly dismissed the thought. He couldn't uproot Crystal again. At least not until she was older. Katherine would understand. She knew how important it was for Crystal to be brought up around family.

But would she stay? They would get married of course. The thought brought him up short. Marriage! He almost laughed out loud. He'd been so certain he'd never marry again, but that was before he'd met Katherine. Now he couldn't imagine the rest of his life without her.

Although she hadn't said, he was certain Katherine was in love with him. But enough to marry him? Give up her life in the UK?

There was only one way to find out. 'What do you think, Sophia?' he murmured. 'Do I deserve another chance at happiness?'

CHAPTER EIGHT

KATHERINE WAS PORING over her computer, trying and failing to concentrate on finishing her paper, when there was a knock on the door. No one in the village ever knocked and certainly not Crystal, and although she was expecting Alexander any minute, he always marched in, announcing himself by calling out her name. She quickly saved the file she was working on and went to answer.

When she saw who it was her heart almost stopped beating.

'Poppy?'

Her daughter pushed by her and dropped her rucksack on the floor. 'I'm surprised you know who I am.'

Admittedly, for a brief moment Katherine hadn't. Her daughter had changed so much since the last photo she had seen of her. Gone was her long, golden hair. Gone was the awkward yet beautiful, fresh-faced teenager. In her place was an angry-looking young woman with black spiky hair, kohl-ringed panda eyes and a lip-piercing.

'Of course I know who you are,' Katherine whispered. She'd dreamed of this moment for so long but in her imagination it had taken the form of getting-to-know-you phone calls followed by lunches and shopping trips. In her head, Poppy had been like her as a teenager; demure, well spoken and beautifully mannered. Nothing in her dreams had prepared her for this. But despite her dismay, a warm, happy glow was spreading from her stomach towards her heart.

Poppy flung herself down on the sofa. 'I thought you might be staying in a villa or something. But this place is pokey. I don't see a pool.'

'That's because there isn't one.' She was still stunned. 'But there's an ocean to swim in.'

'Oh, well. I suppose it will have to do. Anything's better than being at home with *them*.'

'Them?'

'Liz and Mike. The people who call themselves my parents.'

Katherine's head was whirling. 'How did you know I was here? Do Liz and Mike know you're with me?'

'I had your email address, remember? I emailed your work address and got an out-of-office reply, so I phoned them and told them I needed to know where you were. I told them it was urgent—a family emergency—and luckily I got through to a receptionist who didn't know you had no family.' The last was said with heavy and pointed emphasis on the 'no'. 'And as for Mum and Dad, no. They don't know I'm here. They don't care where I am!'

'Poppy! They must be out of their minds with worry! You must—'

'All they care about is their new baby. It's Charlie this and Charlie that. God, why did they adopt me if they were going to go and have a baby of their own?'

Mike and Liz had had a baby? Well, it wasn't unheard of for couples who believed themselves infertile to conceive spontaneously when they'd given up all hope of having a child, but Katherine wished Liz had written to tell her.

It had been a long time since she'd heard from Poppy's

adoptive mother. Not since a year ago when Poppy had turned sixteen and Liz had emailed Katherine, telling her that any further contact would be up to Poppy. In the meantime, if Katherine chose to continue writing, not emailing if she didn't mind as Liz couldn't monitor those, she would keep the letters but only pass them on to Poppy when and if she asked.

It hadn't been written to hurt her, although it had. In her heart, Katherine had wanted to argue but in her head she'd agreed. At sixteen Poppy was old enough to decide for herself whether she wanted to stay in touch. Katherine had always hoped that she would decide to—but not like this.

'I didn't know they had another child,' Katherine said. 'That must have been a surprise.'

'They didn't have *another* child. They had a child. I'm not their child. Not any longer. What is it with you lot that you can cast off your children when it suits you?'

'They put you out?' Katherine said, astonished and outraged. 'But that's—'

Poppy stared down at the floor. 'They didn't *exactly* put me out,' she mumbled. 'I mean, they never said in so many words that they wanted me to go—but it was obvious.'

'And they don't know where you are?' Katherine asked, beginning to recover. 'They'll be frantic You need to let your parents—'

'They're not my parents!'

'According to the law, they are. They've probably alerted the police. How did you leave without them knowing? *When* did you leave?'

'Yesterday morning. I said I was going to a sleepover at my friend Susan's'

Katherine was aghast. 'You *lied* to them?'

'Well, I could hardly tell them where I was going, could I?'

'If you're so convinced they don't care, why didn't you try it?' Katherine winced at the tone of her own voice. Now she sounded as snarky as her daughter.

Poppy glowered. 'They have to pretend, don't they, that they care? Even if it's all a big, fat act.'

'Of course they care and they need to know where you are. They need to know you're safe.'

'I don't want to talk to them.'

Katherine retrieved her mobile from her bag and held it out. 'Phone them. Now.'

'No.'

Katherine was tempted for a miniscule moment not to phone Liz and Mike. They might phone the police to return Poppy or at the very least insist Katherine put her on the next plane and she couldn't bear not to steal a day or two with her child. Her child! She gave herself a mental shake. Of course she couldn't possibly do that to Mike and Liz.

'You can't stay here unless you do. I'll have to notify the police.'

Poppy got up from the sofa and picked up her rucksack. 'In that case, I'm off. I should have known you wouldn't want me either. Jeez, I'm so stupid. You got rid of me once. Why on earth would you want anything to do with me now? I just thought you might have a little leftover maternal feeling—if not a sense that you owe me something at least.'

Katherine knew she was being manipulated, but even so, she couldn't let Poppy leave. Not now, not like this. If Poppy walked out her life, would she ever get another chance with her again? And under the sullen exterior Katherine glimpsed the lonely, confused child within. It took all her resolve not to march across the room and envelop her daughter in her arms. Somehow, instinctively, she knew that wasn't the way to handle the situation either. Best to remain calm and reasonable. After all, there must be *some* reason for Poppy to have sought her out—even if part of her motive was to hurt her adoptive parents as much as possible. She had to tread carefully.

'Poppy, please. I don't want you to go, that's not what I meant. I can't tell you how…' her heart swelled '…thrilled and delighted I am to see you.' She gestured towards the sofa. 'Please, sit back down. Let me phone your parents, talk to them. I'll ask if you can stay here for a couple of days. It'll give us a chance to talk…'

Katherine held her breath, her heart beating in her throat, while Poppy considered what she'd said. Now that Poppy was here—here! In front of her! she couldn't bear not to grab this chance to talk to her, maybe hold her… even once.

Just when she thought her daughter was going to bolt for the door, she dropped her bag again.

'Okay.'

Relief made her legs weak. 'Great.'

'But I'm not going back. Ever.'

'We'll talk about it later.' Katherine sat down then stood up again. 'Look, why don't you have a shower—freshen up while I phone Liz and Mike? Then I'll make us something to eat, okay?'

Poppy's contemplated her from under her fringe for a few moments before nodding sullenly.

'I could do with a shower,' she admitted. 'I feel as if I've been in a sauna with my clothes on.' Now that she mentioned it, they did have a faint whiff of body odour. 'Then after that I could do with crashing. Is there a spare bedroom?'

'Yes. Let me get you some towels for your shower and check that the bed's made up.'

'Towels would be good, thanks. I don't think I brought one.'

Katherine hid a smile. It seemed that Poppy had forgotten to forget her manners. And as if she'd realised the same thing, the scowl returned with a vengeance. 'No need to make the bed if its not already. I'm so bushed I could sleep in a pig's pen.'

As soon as she heard the shower running, Katherine dug her diary out of her handbag. She could still hardly believe that Poppy was here. And wanting to stay. It was what she'd always wished for, but in her imagination it had been organised in advance and arranged to perfection. Fear, excitement, nerves—a whole tumult of emotions coursed through her. But first things first: she had to let Poppy's parents know she was safe and well. Flicking through the pages until she found Mike and Liz's number, she sat down on the sofa and rested the phone on her lap. Twice she had to stop pressing the numbers her fingers were shaking so much.

'Poppy?' Liz sounded harassed and hopeful when she answered the phone. Katherine could hear an infant crying in the background. That had to be Charlie.

'No, it's Katherine.' It had been years since they'd spoken, all subsequent communication after the adoption having taken place by letter or email. 'But Poppy is here. Don't worry, she's fine.'

'Katherine? You say Poppy's with you? Thank God!' Liz started to cry. Katherine waited until she was able to speak. 'We've been beside ourselves. We didn't even know if she was alive. She just upped and disappeared.

We thought… Oh, God. She's with you? And definitely all right?'

'She's a little travel weary. Nothing a sleep won't put right.' It was clear that whatever Poppy believed, Liz did care about her.

'Where are you?' Liz continued. 'We'll come and get her.'

'I'm in Greece. Working.'

'Greece? Poppy's in Greece?'

'She found me through my work email.' Katherine lowered her voice and glanced behind her to make sure Poppy hadn't suddenly come into the room. However she could still hear the sound of the shower running.

'She did? Mind you, she's a bright girl—almost too bright for her own good. That's why I wanted her to go to university, but she's not been working… I don't know if she's going to pass her A-levels. She's been going out till all hours despite being grounded and refusing to study. She's changed!'

Katherine smiled wryly.

'I gather you've had a baby. She seems upset about that.'

'Charlie? Oh, I know I've been caught up in caring for him. He's such a demanding baby. Not like Poppy at the same age. That doesn't mean we don't care about her, Katherine. We love her. She's our daughter!'

Katherine winced inwardly. As if she needed to be reminded. Liz broke down again.

'Should we come? No, I can't. Not with the baby—I haven't got around to getting a passport for him…Mike's working… I…' Liz said between sobs.

'She can stay with me for as long as she likes.'

'Oh, that would be a relief. She'd be all right with you.'

They finished the phone call with Katherine promising

to keep Liz and Mike informed and also promising to try and convince Poppy to go home if she could. The problem was, Katherine didn't want her to go.

As she waited for Poppy to re-emerge, Katherine quickly laid the patio table and stood back to survey the results. She cocked a critical eye at the little vase of flowers she'd placed in the centre and hesitated. Too much? Definitely. Hastily she snapped it away but now the plain white tablecloth appeared too plain and unwelcoming so she placed the vase back. For God's sake, she was more nervous than on a first date—but this was way more important than that. Even with this little gesture she wanted Poppy to know how much she cared.

Hurrying back to the kitchen, she tossed the big bowl of salad and added a touch more seasoning. Was it too salty now? Did Poppy even like salt? Or figs, for that matter? Fish? Was she vegetarian, a vegan? She knew absolutely nothing about her, nothing. Not one single iota about her likes and dislikes. Well, perhaps a simple lunch was the place to find out.

The sound of the shower finally stopped. Nervously Katherine paced the small living room, preparing herself for Poppy's reappearance. *Keep conversation light and simple. Ask questions without probing. Get her trust.*

When the front door opened and Alexander walked in, Katherine could only stand and stare at him. With Poppy's sudden arrival, she'd completely forgotten they'd arranged to go out for lunch.

He strode into the room and gathered her into his arms, kissing her softly on the lips. 'I've missed you.' His eye caught the laid-out table. 'Oh, are we eating in, then?' He grinned. 'Smart thinking. I have to go and visit a patient later, but I have an hour or two before I need to leave—'

Katherine wriggled out his arms. 'Alexander, something's come up… Could we step outside a minute? There's something I have to tell you.'

He raised an eyebrow. 'Sounds ominous.' He studied her more closely. 'What is it? Something's really upsetting you. Have there been more meningitis cases reported?'

'No. It's not that.' She took him by the arm. 'We can't talk here.

'Hi. Are you her boyfriend?' Katherine whirled around to find Poppy, wearing only a skimpy towel, draped against the stairpost. When Katherine looked back at Alexander his eyebrows had shot even higher.

'I'm Alexander Dimitriou,' he replied, 'and you are?'

'Hasn't she told you? Well, that doesn't surprise me.' Poppy flounced into the room and sprawled on the sofa, her long thin, legs stretched in front of her. 'I'm Poppy.' She pointed at Katherine. 'And she's my mother. Or should I say the woman who gave birth to me. Not the same thing at all, is it?'

It was one of those moments when the room seemed to take a breath. Behind her scowl, Poppy seemed pretty pleased with herself. Unsurprisingly, Alexander appeared bewildered, and as for her, it felt as if her legs were going to give way.

'Would you excuse us for a moment?' she said to Poppy. 'Alexander, could we speak outside for a moment?'

Still looking stunned, he followed her downstairs and out to the patio. She closed the door behind them.

'You have a daughter?' he said.

'Yes.'

'You have a daughter,' he repeated, with a shake of his

head. 'You have a child and you didn't even mention her. Why the hell not?'

'I was going to tell you about her.'

'When?'

Good question. She had no answers right now. At least, none that would make sense to him.

'I didn't know she was coming.'

'Evidently,' he said dryly, folding his arms.

'I probably should have told you before now.'

He continued to hold her gaze. 'Probably. So where has she been all this time? Most women would mention they had a child and if I remember correctly you told me you were childless.'

'Oh, for heaven's sake,' she burst out, immediately on the defensive. 'It's not as if we— I mean…' What the hell *did* she mean? She couldn't think straight. 'It's not as if we made promises…' Damn, that wasn't right either.

His mouth settled into a hard line. 'Fool that I am, I thought we did have something. I thought it was the beginning.'

Had he? He'd never said. But she couldn't think about that now. Not when Poppy was upstairs, waiting for her. She glanced behind her, caught between the need to return to her child and the need to talk to Alexander. Right now her child had to take precedence. Explanations would have to wait.

'Can we talk about this later?' she pleaded. 'I could come down to the bay.'

He shook his head. 'I think you've just made it clear that you don't owe me an explanation and I doubt there is anything…'

Poppy chose that moment to appear from the house, wearing a bikini and a towel slung casually over her shoulder.

'I'm going for a swim,' she said. 'Where's the coolest place to go?'

'Coolest?' Katherine echoed.

'Where the boys hang out. You don't think I'm going to hang out with you all the time, do you?'

'The little bay just below the house is quite safe to swim in as long as you don't go too far out. Actually, perhaps it's better if you wait until I come with you before you go into the water. And if you're sunbathing, put factor thirty on. The sun here is stronger than you think.'

'I'm seventeen, not seven, you know. Besides, don't you think it's a bit late to do the maternal thing?'

Katherine winced. 'I've spoken to your mother. She knows you're with me. She's been worried about you.'

A faint gleam appeared in Poppy's eyes, to be replaced almost immediately by her habitual scowl. 'Serves them right.'

Katherine sneaked a look at Alexander. He looked confused. No wonder. 'Her mother?' She saw the dawning realisation in his eyes.

'Liz wants you to go home. They miss you,' she told Poppy.

'Well, I'm not going.' Poppy pouted. 'I always fancied a holiday in Greece.'

'We need to talk about that.'

'Whatever.' Poppy yawned, exposing her tongue and, to Katherine's horror, another piercing. She hid a shudder.

'I should go,' Alexander said stiffly.

Poppy sauntered past them and towards the bay.

Katherine turned back to Alexander. 'I'll see you later. Or tomorrow. I'll explain everything then—'

'As I said, you don't owe me an explanation. Hadn't you better go after your daughter?'

'I had to give her up,' she said quickly.

'Did you?' he said coldly. And with that, he turned on his heel.

Alexander left Katherine standing on her patio and strode towards his car. He was stunned. How come she'd never mentioned that she had a child? How old was Poppy anyway? At least seventeen. So Katherine must have been around the same age when she'd had her. Had she been too dead set on a career in medicine to contemplate keeping a baby? If so, he'd had a narrow escape. Thank God he'd found out before he'd proposed. He'd never understand how a woman could give up her child.

But what he found harder to forgive was why she hadn't told him about her. He'd been open and honest with Katherine—sharing stuff that he'd never shared with anyone before—and she'd flung his honesty in his face. He'd let himself believe that finally he'd met a woman who matched up to Sophia, but he'd been mistaken. He'd thought she was pretty damn near perfect. What a fool he'd been. What a bloody fool. He'd come damn close to asking this woman—or at least the woman he'd thought she was—to spend the rest of her life with him. How could have believed he'd find someone as true as Sophia?

He wrenched his car door open with such force it banged against its hinges. Damn.

If Katherine thought that the evening would be spent chatting with her daughter she soon found she was mistaken. Every time she went near Poppy she'd pick up her book and walk away, and, after only picking at her supper she'd excused herself and gone to bed, slamming the door behind her. Left alone, and feeling raw, Katherine had pulled out her photograph album and picked out the photo of Poppy that had been taken on the beach.

What would her life have been like if she hadn't relinquished the care of her daughter to someone else? She would have been the one holding her. She would have been the recipient of those ice-cream kisses. It was something she would never know, although she had questioned it then, when her tiny infant had been gently but firmly tugged from her arms, and she wondered more than ever now.

Early the next morning while Poppy was still asleep Katherine sent a text to Alexander asking him to meet her down on the beach around the corner from her house. She didn't want to go to his home and she didn't want him to come to hers. Not when they could be overheard at either. Whatever he said she owed him an explanation.

He replied almost immediately, saying that he'd be there in five minutes. She tied her hair into a ponytail and applied a touch of lipstick and let herself out of the house.

She was sitting on a rock when he appeared. Her heart jerked when she saw the grim expression on his face. What else had she expected? She *had* lied to him.

'I don't have long,' he said, stopping in front of her, his hands thrust into the pockets of his light cotton trousers.

She leaped to her feet, hating the way he towered over her, making her feel a little like a schoolgirl waiting to be told off by the schoolmaster. 'Thank you for coming,' she said stiffly.

'Look,' he said, 'I can see you have a lot going on at the moment. What we had was fun but as you pointed out, it was never going to be anything but short term, was it? You have your life…' he glanced towards her house '…back in Britain and I have mine here.'

He'd clearly made up his mind about them, then. She'd
thought that after a night to think things over, he'd at the
very least be prepared to listen to what she had to say.

'No,' she said softly. 'I can see that now. I came here to
explain but if that's the way you feel…' She didn't wait for
a response but, blinking back tears, turned back towards
home—and Poppy.

Katherine paused outside her door and waited until she
had her emotions under control before going inside. She
gasped. It looked as if a tornado had hit it. There were
empty cups and plates and a cereal carton scattered over
the work surface. A damp towel was in a heap on the floor,
along with several magazines. Her daughter's bedroom was
in a worse state. Poppy's rucksack lay on her bed, clothes
spilling from it, some on the floor. Instinctively Katherine began to pick up, folding the clothes as she went along.

She called out Poppy's name but there was no answer.
She quickly searched the small villa and the garden, but
there was no sign of her anywhere. Had she decided to go?
But where? Back to Liz and Mike? Or somewhere else?
It hadn't even crossed her mind that Poppy might up and
leave. But if she had, wouldn't she have taken her rucksack? So where was she? Panic ripped through her. What
if Poppy had ignored Katherine's warnings and had gone
swimming and been dragged out to sea? She should never
have left her alone. Underneath that sullen exterior was
bound to be a desperately unhappy girl. Katherine had only
just got her back and she'd failed her again.

She ran outside but there was no sign of her daughter.
However, Alexander was still standing where she'd left
him, apparently lost in thought.

She hurried over to him. 'I can't find her,' she said.

'Who? Poppy?'

'She's taken her swimming things but I looked—she's not in the bay.' She spread her arms wide. 'I can't see her anywhere.'

'I'll check the bay on the other side,' Alexander said. He squeezed her shoulder. 'Don't look so worried, she'll be fine.'

He couldn't know that for sure. She ran around to the bigger bay. On the small stretch of beach was another towel and a pair of sunglasses but no sign of Poppy.

She scanned the bay, searching for her, but apart from a couple of boats the sea was empty. A late-morning breeze had whipped it into frothy peaked waves. Had she gone for a swim and gone out too far?

'Where is she?' She grabbed Alexander's arm. 'We've got to find her.' She began tugging off her sandals.

'What the hell are you doing?'

'I'm going to swim out. I need to find her.'

Alexander gripped her by the shoulders. 'Calm down. Think about it. You'd see her if she's out there.' He cupped his hands and called out to one of the boats nearby. The man called back to him.

'He says he hasn't noticed a stranger, and he's been out here since dawn. He'll ask the other boats just to make sure. Come on, let's check the village. She's probably gone in search of a Coke. Someone will have seen her.

Filled with dread, Katherine followed him back up the steps. He stopped a woman and spoke to her in Greek. She shook her head. They asked several more people and they all denied seeing a young stranger. Katherine's panic was threatening to overwhelm her when the village store owner told them, his expression aghast, that, yes, he'd served a girl with short black hair and an earring in her lip. She was, he said, with Alexander's pretty daughter. The last was said with significantly more approval.

Inside Alexander's house, Grandmother was in her habitual place in the kitchen. In the small sitting room Crystal was lying on the sofa with her feet in Poppy's lap as Poppy painted her toenails. The little girl was giggling while Poppy seemed totally oblivious to the stir she'd caused. Katherine sagged with relief.

Then fury overtook her.

'Why the hell didn't you leave a note to say where you were?'

Poppy looked up in surprise. Immediately her face resumed its belligerent look. 'Why should I leave a note? You didn't and it's not as if you've ever known or cared what I do.'

'While you're staying with me, you're my responsibility. For God's sake, I thought you'd drowned. Your towel—all your things—were on the beach.'

Something shifted in Poppy's eyes. If Katherine hadn't known better she would have said it was regret.

'Well, as you can see, I haven't drowned. I went to the beach and came back to your house for a drink and Crystal turned up. She wanted some company.'

'Poppy's painting my toenails! See, Baba, she's made patterns on them.' When the child turned her face towards them, Katherine noticed that Poppy had also given her full make-up.

Alexander placed a restraining hand on Katherine's arm. 'Thanks for spending time with Crystal, Poppy.' He crossed the room and smiled down at his daughter. 'Have you seen my daughter, Crystal? She's a beautiful little girl with a clean, shining face who never needs make-up.'

Crystal glared at him. 'I am your daughter, silly. And I like my face the way Poppy has done it.'

Grandmother muttered something from behind Katherine. When she glanced at her she couldn't be sure whether it was amusement or disapproval on her face.

Alexander scooped Crystal into his arms. 'I think it's time for a wash.'

'But Poppy is going to do my fingernails next. Then we're going to get dressed up and go to the square.'

'Poppy, we need to go,' Katherine said firmly.

'Oh, all right.' She stood up. 'See you tomorrow, Crystal.'

'That woman is not good,' Alexander's grandmother told him when he returned from helping Crystal to dress. 'What kind of woman gives away her child? I am disappointed. I thought I had found the right woman for you.'

So Poppy hadn't wasted any time in telling Crystal and Grandmother her story. 'We shouldn't judge her, Yia-Yia. Not until we know her reasons.' But wasn't what she'd said exactly what he'd been thinking? Katherine clearly wasn't the woman he'd thought she was. No doubt she'd had her reasons for giving her daughter up for adoption—although he couldn't think what they could be. She'd lied about having a child—that's what he couldn't bring himself to forgive. He'd thought he knew her. Now he knew better.

But a few days later his heart kicked against his ribs when he saw her emerge from the village store.

She hurried along the street, a few steps in front of him, and he was appalled to find that the villagers no longer called out to her or smiled in her direction. Since Poppy had arrived the village had been alight with gossip about her and her mother. Word had it that Poppy had been abandoned as a baby—where, no one could say exactly, but it varied between a hospital doorstep and an alleyway, that she had been taken away from Katherine because she had been unfit to look after her, to all sorts of even crazier versions. One of the other rumours he'd heard had involved Poppy running away from adoptive parents who beat her to a mother who hadn't wanted her in the first place. It seemed now that they knew about Poppy and having made up their minds, they had decided to spurn Katherine. Alexander suspected that most of the gossip had originated from Poppy, who no doubt was making the most of the sympathy she was getting from the women in the village.

He'd seen mother and daughter yesterday, sitting on the downstairs patio. Both had been wearing shorts, revealing long brown legs, both barefoot. When they'd turned to look at him, two identical pairs of blue eyes had stared out from porcelain complexions. It was obvious they were closely related, although, given the gap in their ages, they might have been taken for sisters rather than mother and daughter—even with the radically different hairstyles and Poppy's piercing.

Feeling she was being unfairly accused was one thing, re-igniting their aborted love affair quite another. Nevertheless, it was about time the gossip stopped.

Furious with them, or himself—he couldn't be sure which—he called Katherine's name and ran the few steps to catch up with her. He took the shopping bag from her hand. 'Let me carry this for you.'

She looked up at him, defiance shining in her blue eyes. 'I can manage,' she said. 'You don't have to keep the fallen woman company.'

But behind the defiance he could see the hurt and

his chest tightened. No matter what she said, she'd been wounded badly by the villagers' attitude. She'd told him how much she'd loved feeling part of their small community.

'You'll be a seven-day wonder,' he said. 'Then they'll forget all about it.'

'I'm not so sure,' she said. 'But I won't be judged. Not by them—not by anyone.' She looked at him again. He knew she was including him in her statement and she was right. He had been as guilty as the rest of drawing conclusions without having the facts. 'Neither do I need you to stick up for me.'

'I know. You're perfectly able to do that yourself.' He was rewarded by the briefest of smiles.

'How is the prodigal daughter anyway?' he asked. 'I understand she spends a fair bit of time at my house.'

'She seems to get a kick out of being around your grandmother. She's shown her how to make soap from olive oil, how to dry herbs and how to cook. The things she was showing me before I fell out of favour. Don't get me wrong, I'm sure she's wonderfully patient with her and I'm happy Poppy has someone she feels good around.'

'She tells me Poppy is very good at entertaining Crystal. I suspect my grandmother sees a different side to Poppy than you do.'

She smiled sadly. 'I'm trying to get to know her. I'm trying not to nag, just to make her aware that I'm ready to talk whenever she's ready. I thought that she would have begun to unbend towards me a bit, but she seems as angry with me as she was the day she arrived.' Her shoulders sagged and he had to ball his fists to stop himself taking her in his arms.

'Give her time. She hasn't gone home so being here must mean something to her.'

'I don't think I'm anything more than a bolt-hole to her. And in many ways I'm glad just to be that. I took her to Mycenae the other day. I thought doing things together would help us to bond.' She laughed bitterly. 'I was wrong. It was nothing short of a disaster. She managed half an hour before she sulked off back to the car.'

Despite everything, he had to suppress a smile. 'You know the ruins of ancient cities aren't everyone's cup of tea. Especially when they're teens. From what little I know of Poppy she strikes me as more of a beach girl.'

'But I thought she'd be interested—I would have been at her age. I thought we'd have something to talk about at least. Something that was less emotional than our relationship and what's going on with her back home.'

She looked so disappointed he almost reached out for her. Instead, he dug his hands even deeper into his pockets. But was she really so naïve to think that dragging a seventeen-year-old around ruins was the way build a relationship?

'Have you asked her what *she* wants to do?'

'Of course! I'm not a complete idiot.'

'And her answer?'

'Let me use her exact words. "Duh. To chill."'

Alexander hid another smile. She'd mimicked the little he'd heard of Poppy's truculent voice exactly. 'Then just let her to do whatever she wants. If that means hanging around my grandmother's or sunbathing on the balcony or beach, just let her. She'll come to you when she's ready.'

'I've tried. But every time I go near her she gets up and walks away.' Her blue eyes were bewildered.

'Tell you what,' he found himself saying. 'There's some

caves with amazing stalactites and stalagmites not very far from here. And there's a good beach nearby—shallow, so it's great for swimming—so why don't the four of us go there tomorrow?'

'You must have other things you want to do.' But he could tell by the way her eyes lit up that she liked the idea. She looked like a drowning woman being tossed a float. He hadn't planned to suggest a trip together, but the words were out and he couldn't take them back. Not that he wanted to take them back. A day with Katherine was suddenly irresistible.

'Crystal would like nothing better than to spend the day with her new idol—especially if it involves a boat trip in caves followed by a picnic and a swim. No, I promise you that is my daughter's idea of a dream day and so it's mine too. Do you want me to ask Poppy?'

'I'll do it,' she said, taking her shopping from him. Suddenly she stood on tiptoe and kissed him on the cheek. 'Thank you,' she said.

To Katherine's surprise, when she told Poppy the next morning about Alexander's invitation, she seemed keen to go. She disappeared into the shower and returned an hour later dressed and carrying one of Katherine's bags. In the meantime, Katherine had prepared a picnic with some of the fresh bread she'd bought from the village store as soon as it had opened. She'd also made a fig and mozzarella salad, which she'd put in a plastic container. There were olives, cold meat, soft drinks, and crisps too. She hoped Poppy would find at least some of it to her taste. As she made her preparations her head buzzed. Did Alexander's invite mean he was ready to listen to her? Or was he simply sorry for her? Whatever the reason, she had to at least try and make him understand.

Crystal ran into the room ahead of her father. 'We are going to swim. We're going to see magic caves! And you are coming too.'

'Yeah,' Poppy said, sliding a look at Katherine. 'So she says.' Then her daughter's face broke into a wide smile and picked Crystal up. 'Let's get into the car.'

Alexander looked as gorgeous as ever in a pair of faded jeans and a white T-shirt and Katherine's heart gave an uncomfortable thump. She couldn't read the expression in his eyes when they rested on her. Perhaps at a different time they might have had something—perhaps if she'd been a different person... Timing had never been her strong suit.

'Ready?' he asked.

'As I'll ever be.'

Crystal did all the talking as they drove towards the caves. 'I can swim, you know,' she told Poppy proudly. 'Can you?'

'Of course,' Poppy replied. 'I swim for my school.'

Katherine was surprised. But delighted. They had this in common at least. 'I swam for my school too,' she remarked.

'Whatever.'

Katherine shared a look with Alexander. It would take time, it seemed, for Poppy to unbend towards her—if she ever did.

They parked at the top car park and, leaving their bags and the picnic, walked the rest of the way. The sky was a brilliant blue, feathered with the slightest clouds, and the sea was turquoise against the blindingly white shore.

They bought the tickets for the boat trip into the caves and the children were given life jackets to put on. Poppy looked as if she was about to refuse but clearly thought better of it. Katherine was relieved. No doubt if she had refused, Crystal would have too.

The girls clambered into the front of the boat, with Katherine and Alexander squashed together on one of the seats in the stern. She was painfully aware of the familiar scent of the soap he used and the pressure of his leg against hers. She closed her eyes, remembering the feel of his arms around her, the way her body fitted perfectly against his, the way he made her laugh. She shook the images away. They might never be lovers again, but did him being here now mean that at the very least he was still her friend?

As their guide used an oar to push the boat further into the depths of the caves she gasped. Thousands of spectacular stalactites hung from the roof of the cave, which was lit with small lights that danced off the crystal formations like thousands of sparks.

Crystal turned around, eyes wide, her small hands covering her mouth. 'It is a magic cave, Baba. It's like Christmas! Only better!'

Even Poppy seemed stunned by their beauty. She spent the trip with her arm around Crystal's shoulders, pointing out different formations. Katherine had read about them yesterday after Alexander had extended his invitation and was able to tell the girls how they'd been formed as well as a little history of the caves. Poppy asked some questions, appearing to have forgotten that she wasn't speaking to Katherine. Katherine glanced at Alexander and he grinned back. He'd been right. This was the kind of trip to impress a seventeen-year-old—inasmuch as *anything* could impress this particular seventeen-year-old.

Their trip into the caves finished, Alexander returned to the car for their costumes and their picnic, while Katherine and the girls found a spot on the grass, just above the pebbly beach, where they could lay their picnic blanket. As soon as Alexander came back Poppy and Crystal disappeared off to the changing rooms to put on their swimming costumes.

'Aren't you going to swim?' Alexander asked.

'In a bit. What about you?'

'What are the chances of Crystal letting me just lie here?' When he grinned she could almost make herself believe that they were still together.

The girls came out of the changing rooms and ran down into the sea, squealing as the water splashed over their knees.

'She's a good kid,' Alexander said.

'Yes. I believe she is.'

'What happened to her father?'

Katherine sighed. It was a question she'd been waiting for Poppy to ask. 'Ben? Last time I heard, he was married with three children and doing very well as a lawyer.'

'You must have been very young when you had her.'

'I was seventeen. Sixteen when I fell pregnant.'

'You don't have to tell me anything you don't want to. It's none of my business.'

'No,' she said. 'I'd like to. It's not something I've ever spoken to anyone about, but I think I owe it to you to tell you the truth.'

'I don't want you to tell me because you think you owe me, although I would like to understand. It's not so much that you have a child you gave up for adoption, it's the fact you didn't tell me. Hell, Katherine, I bared my soul to you.'

'I know...' She sighed. 'It's just—it's been a secret I've kept for so long, afraid of what people would think if they knew...'

'I can't imagine the Katherine I know caring about what people think.'

'We all care what people think if we're honest—at least, the opinions of those we love and respect.'

'If they love and respect us, then their feelings shouldn't change…' he said slowly. He was quiet for a long time. 'I promise I'll listen this time.'

'It's a long story.'

He nodded in the direction of the girls, who were splashing each other and laughing. 'Looks like they're not going to be out of the water any time soon.'

Seeing Poppy like this reminded Katherine how painfully young her daughter still was and how painfully young she herself had been when she'd fallen pregnant. A child really.

'Remember I told you that I won a scholarship to high school?'

He nodded.

'I was proud and excited to have won it but I was totally unprepared for the reality. Being there terrified me. Most of the rest of the pupils came from well-to-do families—the children of business people, doctors and lawyers. I was desperately shy as it was, and with my second-hand uniform I knew I stuck out. Unsurprisingly perhaps, they wanted nothing to do with me. I pretended I didn't care. At break times I'd take a book and read it. I knew I still had to get top marks if I wanted to be accepted at medical school.

'I was in my second year when I met Ben. I'd been roped in to swim for the school team in the swimming gala—it was the one sport I seemed naturally good at—and he was there. He was a couple of years older than me, as confident as I was shy, as good-looking as I was geeky—but for some reason he seemed to like me.

'We were friends at first. We spent our break times together, usually in the library or just walking around, talking about history and politics—even then he knew he wanted to be a lawyer—stuff that no one else was interested in discussing but that we both loved to debate.

'Being Ben's friend changed everything. I wasn't lonely any more. I now realised there were people just like me who didn't care about clothes and the latest hairstyle. Then when I was in fourth year and he was in sixth year—he already had a place to read law—everything changed and we became boyfriend and girlfriend. He'd come around to my house. By that time Mum and Dad had bought a small restaurant and were working all hours to get it established, but then Dad died suddenly. Mum, as you can imagine, was devastated and so was I. I clung to Ben and eventually the inevitable happened. We slept together.

'It didn't seem wrong—quite the opposite. It seemed a natural progression. We'd talked often about how, when he was a lawyer—famous and defending the poor and downtrodden, of course—and I was a doctor, the very best, of course...' she risked a smile in Alexander's direction, and was reassured to find he was looking at her with the same intent expression he always had when they talked '...saving lives and discovering new treatments and cures, we'd marry and have a family. But then I fell pregnant. Stupid, I know. We did use contraception but with the optimism and ignorance of youth we weren't as careful as we should have been.

'By that time, he was about to leave to start his law degree and I had just sat my A-levels. I expected, rightly as it turned out, to get all As and I was confident I would get a place in medical school.

'To say we were both shellshocked would be an understatement. We talked about getting married, but we couldn't see how. My parents' restaurant was struggling without Dad and barely making enough for Mum to live on, and she'd been recently diagnosed with multiple sclerosis. Ben's parents weren't much better off. There didn't seem any way to have the baby.'

'What about Ben? Didn't he have a say?'

'Terminating the pregnancy was Ben's preferred option.' She looked over to where Crystal and Poppy were splashing each other and her heart stuttered. Thank God she'd never seriously considered it. 'He said he couldn't see a way of supporting me or our baby—he still desperately wanted to be a lawyer—and one night he told me that if I continued with the pregnancy he couldn't be part of either of our lives.

'We broke up. With the pregnancy something had changed between us. It was as if all that had gone on before had just been us play-acting at being a couple. Maybe if we were older… Whatever, I couldn't blame him. I didn't want to marry him, I knew that then—just as I knew I wasn't ready to be a mother. But neither could I bear to terminate the pregnancy. Oh, I thought about it. I even went as far as making an appointment with the hospital, but when it came down to it I just couldn't go through with it. I knew then I had to tell my mother. It was the most difficult conversation I've ever had in my life. I could see her imagining her and Dad's dreams of a better life for me going down the plughole. She lost it and broke down.

'When she'd pulled herself together she said that she would look after the child. It would mean my delaying going to university for a year but we'd manage. Just as we always had. But she was ill—some days I had to help her get dressed—and even then I knew what a diagnosis of

MS meant. I knew she couldn't help take care of a child—
not when she would need more and more care herself. I
was in a bad way, Alexander. I felt so alone.' She took a
shuddering breath.

'I told her that I had decided to have the baby but that I
was going to give it up for adoption. I'd done my research,
you see. I knew that you could arrange an open adoption.
I would get to pick the parents—ones already pre-selected
by the adoption agency. My child would always know they
were adopted, and although I could never see him or her, I
could write care of the adoptive parents and in return they
would send me updates. If I couldn't keep the baby myself,
it seemed the only—the best—solution.

'My mother tried to argue me out of it—she couldn't
imagine how any child of hers could even consider giving
their child away, and I think she believed I would change
my mind.

'But she was wrong. I refused to imagine it as a baby.
Instead, I pored over the biographies of the would-be adoptive parents. The adoption agency did a thorough job.
There were photographs, bits of information about their
extended families, letters from them. It was heart-break-
ing, reading their stories. I could almost hear their des-
peration. They had to advertise themselves to me—they
had to make me want to pick them.

'When I read about these couples I knew I was doing
the right thing. At least I managed to convince myself
that I was. Far better for the child I was carrying to have
a home with a couple who would be able to give them the
love and attention I couldn't. In the end I picked out one
family. They weren't particularly well off—I wasn't so
naïve that I thought money was all that important—but

they were financially secure. Enough to give my child everything he or she could ever need.

'But more than that, it was them as people who made them shine. They seemed kind, loving and so desperate to have afamily to shower love on. They'd been trying for a baby for several years and were getting close to the age where they'd no longer be able to put themselves forward for adoption. This was, I knew, their final chance of having a child. They also said that they hoped, in time, to adopt an older child, a brother or sister for this one. I liked that. I didn't want my child to grow up, like I did, as an only child. I wanted him or her to have a sibling who would always be there for them. So I picked them. I could have picked any of a dozen couples but I picked them.

'I know you probably can't imagine how anyone could do what I did. But I thought, I really believed I was doing the best thing for her. I insisted on an open adoption—I wouldn't have chosen Mike and Liz if they hadn't agreed to that—because although I couldn't keep Poppy myself I wanted to know that wherever she was in the world she was all right.

'But Mum was right. I hadn't accounted for how I would feel as my pregnancy continued. I began to feel protective of this child growing inside me. I didn't know what to do. I had already committed to giving her up and I knew her prospective parents were longing to welcome her into her family. But even then I thought about changing my mind—even though I knew the grief it would cause them and even though I knew I was too young to bring up a child. I began to persuade myself that with Mum's help we would manage.'

She paused and looked out to sea. 'But then Mum's multiple sclerosis returned with a vengeance. She had to have a wheelchair and she couldn't do even the basics for herself. I wondered if the stress of my pregnancy had made her worse. I felt as if it was all my fault. I didn't know what to do. So in the end I kept to my original decision and gave her up.

'The day I gave birth to her was one of the worst in my life. The labour was easy compared to what came next. They allowed me a few hours alone with her to say my goodbyes. I hadn't realised how difficult it would be. Here was this tiny thing in my arms, looking up at me as if I was the only thing in her world. I felt such an overwhelming love for her it shook me to the core. But how could I go back on my decision then? I was only seventeen. I thought it was unfair to everyone if I did. So I let them take her from me.'

It was only when he leaned across and wiped the tears from her face with the pad of his thumb that she realised she was crying. He waited without saying anything until she'd regained control again.

'I wrote to Liz often and she wrote back, telling me about Poppy's progress and sending photos. I knew when her baby teeth fell out, I knew when she got chickenpox, I saw her in her school uniform on her first day at school. I had more regrets then—seeing the photos of her, watching her grow up, albeit from a distance, made her real in a way she hadn't been before. Of course, by then it was too late to get her back. Mike and Liz were her parents and there was no doubt they loved her and that she loved them.'

He said nothing, just waited until she was ready to continue.

'I sailed through my final year at school and all my exams at medical school. But I worked for it. I hardly went out, hardly joined any clubs or societies, just worked. It all had to be for something, you see? If I'd failed I don't think I could have lived with myself. Mum never spoke of it. It was as if we pretended it hadn't happened. But sometimes I'd see Mum looking at me with such sadness it ripped me in two. I caught her once. About six months after I'd had Poppy. She was in the small bedroom at the front, the one that we kept for visitors. She was kneeling on the floor with a pile of baby clothes in front of her. She was smoothing out each item with her palms, murmuring to herself, before she placed it in a little box. Tears were running down her face. I doubt she even knew she was crying. You see the adoption only became final after six months. I could have changed my mind up until then and, believe me, sometimes I thought I might. But when I thought of the couple who had Poppy, how happy they'd been, I knew I had done the right thing. But I know now that Mum always hoped I would change my mind.

'She didn't see me so I tiptoed away. What was the point in saying anything? Even if I'd wanted to it was too late to change my mind. I had to keep believing I'd done the right thing.

'We never spoke about it. Not once.'

She drew in a shuddering breath. 'By all accounts, she was a happy child. She grew up knowing that she was adopted—that was part of the deal—and I guess it was just something she accepted.

'So many times I wished I could have been there to hold her when she was sick, to hear her laughter, just see her.' She swallowed the lump that had come to her throat. 'But I knew I had given away all my rights. I was just pleased to be allowed into her life—if only in small slices.'

'And have you told her this?'

'I've tried. But every time I raise the topic, she gets up and walks away.'

'Yet she came to find you.'

'I'm not sure she came to find me for the right reasons. When Poppy turned sixteen, Liz said that she would no longer give her my letters unless she asked. She also said that she wouldn't pass on news of Poppy. She thought, at sixteen, Poppy had the right to decide what place, if any, I had in her life. I heard nothing after that. It seemed Poppy had made her decision and I couldn't blame her. I hoped when she was older that she might seek me out.' She laughed shortly. 'I just never imagined it would be now.'

'What made her come to find you?'

'I think it was the new baby. Liz and Mike didn't think they could have children—that's why they decided to adopt. I know they intended to adopt another child, but they never did. About eighteen months ago, Liz fell pregnant—as you know, it can happen long after a couple has given up hope. The child is eight months now. I suspect Poppy's nose has been put out of joint. A baby can be demanding and she's bound to feel a little pushed out. Liz also said she's been bunking off school and her grades have taken a turn for the worse. If she carries on like this then there will be no chance of her getting accepted at university.'

'And that's important to you and to Liz?'

'Yes. Of course. Wouldn't you want the same for Crystal?'

'I want Crystal to be happy. I found out the hard way that success at work isn't the same as having success in life. Nothing is more important than being with your family. Nothing is more important than their happiness. At least to me.'

She felt stung. Somehow she'd hoped that she could make him understand, but it appeared she'd been mistaken. She bent over and undid her sandals. 'I've told you everything. Now I'm going to join the children in the water.'

Alexander watched her tiptoe gingerly into the sea. Her legs had browned in the sun and appeared to go on for ever in the tiny shorts she was wearing. He cursed himself inwardly. She was right. Who was he to judge her? It wasn't as if he had nothing to regret. But he'd wanted her to be perfect—which was rich, given that he was anything but. He still loved her but he needed time to get used to this different version of the Katherine he'd thought he'd known.

'Baba!' Crystal called from the water. 'Come in!' He rolled up the bottoms of his jeans, pulled his T-shirt over his head and went to join them.

It was, Katherine had to admit, despite the tension between her and Poppy and her and Alexander, a happy day—one of the happiest of her life. Despite everything how couldn't it be when she was spending it with the people she loved most? They swam and ate, then swam some more. As the afternoon became cooler, Alexander bought some fish from a boat he swam out to and they built a small fire over which they roasted the fish.

By the time they drove home, Crystal and Poppy were flushed with tiredness and happiness. Poppy had even come to sit next to Katherine when Alexander had taken Crystal away to dry her off and help her change back into her clothes.

'It's cool here,' Poppy said. 'I think I'd like to stay until you go back. If that's all right with you?'

'Of course,' Katherine said, delighted. 'Until I go back

at the end of the month, at any rate. Will you let your mother know?'

'Sure,' Poppy said, and leaned back, hooking her arms behind her head. 'I kind of miss them. Even the crazy baby.'

'They miss you too.' She didn't want to say anything else, frightened of spoiling the fragile truce that had sprung up between them. There would be time to talk in the days to come. At the very least she owed it to Poppy to keep trying to explain why she'd given her up. Maybe Alexander was right. She shouldn't force it. Just tell Poppy she was happy to talk about it and leave it to her to bring it up when she was ready.

Back home, Alexander parked the car in the square and lifted Crystal into his arms. 'Perhaps we could do this again?' he said.

She looked at him. 'Maybe. I'm not sure.' She still felt hurt. They had been friends before they'd become lovers. Didn't that count for anything?

He nodded and, holding his daughter in his arms, turned towards his house. Back home, Poppy also excused herself, saying she had her sleep to catch up on. Katherine suspected that she wanted to phone Liz in privacy and she was glad.

She poured herself a glass of wine and took it out onto the balcony. She'd told Alexander everything. At least now there were no more secrets between them.

She didn't see much of Alexander over the next few days, although Crystal and Poppy continued to visit each other's houses.

Katherine went to call Poppy for supper one day to find

her up to her elbows in flour. 'I just want to finish these baklavas,' she said.

Alexander's grandmother looked at Katherine, shook her head and said something to Crystal in Greek. For one mortifying moment Katherine wondered if she was being told not to visit again, but to her surprise Crystal told her that her grandmother wanted her to come and sit with her outside on the bench by the front door.

Bemused, Katherine did as she asked.

They sat on the bench and Alexander's grandmother reached out and patted her hand. As people passed she kept her hand on Katherine's. Every time one of the villagers passed, her grip would tighten and she'd smile, while calling out a greeting. Many stopped and said a few words to Grandmother and greeted Katherine too, with a 'Hello' and 'How are you?'

So that was what the old lady was up to. Whatever she thought of Katherine's decision to give her child up for adoption, she was, in her own quiet way, telling the other villagers that she supported her. Tears burned behind Katherine's eyes. It was an unexpected, touching gesture from Grandmother and she wondered whether Alexander was behind it.

Speaking of which, he was coming across the square towards them. Katherine's heart leaped. Frightened he would see the desolation in her eyes, she lowered her lids until she was sure she could look at him calmly.

'Oh, hello.' He bent and kissed his grandmother on her cheek. He said something to her in Greek and she laughed. The old lady got to her feet and retreated back inside, leaving her space on the bench for Alexander.

'I think she had an ulterior motive for sitting with me here,' Katherine murmured. 'I suspect she's telling the

village to stop shunning me. Did you have anything to
do with it?'

'No one tells Grandmother what to do, least of all me,'
he said evasively. 'But I need to tell you, I've forgiven you
for giving up Poppy. I'm sure you did what you had to and
for the best possible motives.'

Katherine leaped to her feet. 'Forgiven me? Forgiven
me! How dare you? I wanted your understanding, not your
forgiveness. You're right about one thing. I should have
told you earlier. That was wrong of me. But if you think I
need forgiveness for giving birth to her then you are badly
mistaken. And as for giving her away, you make it sound
like tossing out so much rubbish. That's not the way I felt.
I gave her to two loving, stable parents and it ripped me
apart. You just need to spend time with her to know she's
a young woman any parent would be proud of.'

Tears burned behind her eyes. She didn't even care that
her outburst had garnered a bit of an audience. 'As far as
I'm concerned,' she hissed, 'if I never see you again it will
be too soon.' She whirled around to find Poppy standing
behind her. Her daughter grinned. 'Way to go, Katherine.
Way to go!'

Katherine and Poppy talked late into the night after Poppy
had witnessed her outburst. It hadn't been an easy conversation—there had been no instant falling into each other's
arms, but the tension and angst had begun to ease. There
would, Katherine knew, be many more such conversations
and bumpy roads but they had made a start. It would take
time for them to be totally at ease with one another, but
at least they were moving in that direction. And despite
the rift between her and Alexander, she was more content
than she had been in years.

* * *

'Crystal's great-grandmother isn't well,' Poppy told her a couple of days later. Katherine's heart tumbled inside her chest. She was deeply fond of the old lady but hadn't seen her since she'd made an absolute exhibition of herself by ranting at Alexander in public.

'Do you know what's wrong with her?'

'Crystal says she has a bad cold but she didn't get up this morning.'

If Grandmother had taken to her bed she had to be ill. 'Where is Crystal?'

'I left her at the house. I wanted her to come with me so I could tell you but she wouldn't leave Yia-Yia.'

Katherine snapped the lid of her laptop closed. 'Does Crystal's father know?'

'I don't think so.'

'Come on,' Katherine said, picking up the medical bag she'd brought with her. Luckily she had a whole case of antibiotics left over from the meningitis outbreak. Did Yia-Yia have a chest infection? If she did, it wasn't good. But she shouldn't get ahead of herself. It was possible Grand-mother did have just a cold.

But as soon as she saw her she knew this was no ordi-nary cold. The old woman was flushed and clearly run-ning a temperature.

'Poppy, could you take Crystal to our house, please? Stay there until I come for you. You can go down to the bay if you like but no further. Do you understand?'

Was it possible that the meningitis had come back in an-other form? No, that was unlikely if not impossible. How-ever, until she knew for sure what it was, it was important to keep her away from the others.

For once Poppy didn't argue with her. She took Crystal

by the hand. 'Go fetch your costume. My mum will look after your great-grandmother.'

It was the first time Poppy had called her Mum and a lump came to Katherine's throat. She swallowed hard and made herself focus. She had a job to do.

After listening to Yia-Yia's chest and taking her temperature, which as she'd expected was way too high, Katherine phoned Alexander.

'I'll come straight away,' he said, when she told him.

'I'll give her oral antibiotics,' Katherine said, 'but she could do with them IV to be on the safe side. Do you want me to take her to hospital?'

'Wait until I get there,' he said. 'I'll be thirty minutes.'

While she waited for him to arrive, Katherine wetted a facecloth in cold water and wrung it out, before placing it on Grandmother's forehead. When the old lady tried to push her away she soothed her with a few words in Greek, grateful that it had improved to the point where she could reassure her.

'Alexander is on his way,' she said softly. 'He says you are to lie quietly and let me look after you until he gets here.'

'Crystal? Where is she?'

'Poppy has taken her to my house. Don't worry, she'll make sure she's all right.'

The elderly woman slumped back on her pillows, worryingly too tired to put up a fight.

Alexander must have driven as if the devil himself was behind him as he arrived in twenty minutes instead of the thirty he'd told her. He nodded to Katherine before crouching at his grandmother's side.

'Her pulse is around a hundred and shallow. She's

pyrexial. I've given her antibiotics by mouth. Crystal is with Poppy. I thought it best.'

When Alexander looked up she could see the anguish in his eyes. He took out his stethoscope and Katherine helped Grandmother into a sitting position while Alexander listened to her chest again.

'As I thought. A nasty chest infection. She's probably caught a dose of the flu that's been going around and a secondary infection has set in very fast.'

'Does she need to go to hospital?'

Grandmother plucked at Alexander's sleeve. 'She says she won't go,' he translated. 'She wants to stay in her own home.'

'In that case,' Katherine said, 'that's what's going to happen. We can easily put her on a drip and give her IV antibiotics that way. Poppy and I can help look after her. What do you think?'

'I think it's risky.'

'More risky than admitting her to hospital?'

His shoulders slumped. 'You're right.'

She wished she could put her arms around him and tell him everything would be okay, but nothing in his demeanour suggested he would welcome the overture.

'I'll stay here with your grandmother,' Katherine said, 'while you fetch whatever it is we'll need.'

Later when they had Grandmother on a drip and her breathing was better, Katherine slipped home to ask Poppy to take Crystal back to her father. A short while later she was standing on the balcony when she became aware that Poppy had come to stand beside her. 'Is she going to get better?' she whispered.

'I hope so.' She reached out for her daughter's hand and squeezed it. Poppy didn't pull away. Instead, she leaned into her. Katherine pulled her close. 'We're all going to do everything to make sure she will. But, sweetheart, I think you should go back to Liz and Mike. If flu is going around, I don't want you to get it.'

'But I could have it already and just not be showing the symptoms yet. If I go back I could pass it on to my baby brother.' It was the first time she'd referred to Charlie as her baby brother. 'So I'm staying,' Poppy continued in a tone that sounded much like her own when she wouldn't be argued with. 'I'll help you look after Grandmother and any of the villagers who need help. I can't nurse them but I can cook and run errands.'

Katherine's eyes blurred as she considered her amazing child. 'I'm so proud of you,' she said. 'Did I ever tell you that?'

Poppy grinned back at her. 'And I'm proud of you. Now, shouldn't we get busy?'

'I think it's time I went home,' Poppy said. She'd been a godsend this last two weeks, helping by playing with Crystal while Alexander and Katherine took turns caring for Grandmother. They barely saw each other, the one leaving as the other took over. She'd also helped care for some of the other elderly villagers who'd fallen ill with flu. But Grandmother was much better, as were the others affected. 'I think Mum can do with some help with Charlie.' She looked at Katherine, a small frown between her brows. 'You're okay...' she grinned self-consciously '...but she's still my mum.'

'Of course she is. She's the woman who's cared for you all your life, the woman who nursed you through all your childhood sicknesses. Who was always there for you. Of course she'll always be your mum. But I hope you'll always remember that I love you too. If it helps, think of me as an honorary aunt. Someone who will always be there for you.'

'You know, and I don't mean this to sound horrible, I'm glad you gave me up. I can't imagine anyone except Liz and Mike being my parents. I mean, they get on my nerves sometimes but, you know, they've always been there.'

Katherine winced at the implied rebuke in Poppy's words.

'Would you still have given me away if you had the chance to do it all over again?'

Katherine took her time thinking about her answer. She loved Poppy too much to be anything less than honest.

'I feel so lucky that you are part of my life now—to have been given this second chance to get to know you. And knowing you now, I can't imagine a scenario where I would ever give you up. But back then I didn't know you and I wasn't the person I am now. Remember I was about your age. Half grown up and half still a child. Everything seemed so black and white then.

'I do know that I thought of you almost every day and receiving the updates about you from Liz were the highlight of my year. Wait there. I'd like to show you something.'

She went inside and retrieved the album she always carried with her. She placed it on the patio table. 'Liz sent me a photo of you on every birthday and Christmas. This is you on your first birthday.' She passed a photograph to Poppy. She was standing in front of a birthday cake with a single candle. A hand belonging to someone just out of shot was supporting her and Poppy was grinning into the camera, two small teeth showing. Katherine handed her

several more photos. 'Here you are on your first day at
school, when you joined the Brownies, your first swimming lesson, your first trip to the beach. Liz sent me a letter with every photograph and sometimes a little souvenir
from your life—like this picture you drew when you came
back from a holiday in Spain. I wrote to you too.

'I'm not pretending any of that makes up for not bringing you up myself, but I knew you were happy and so I
could live with my decision.'

'Why didn't you ever get married?

'The right person never came along. One of the things
I promised myself when I gave you up was that I would
concentrate on being the best doctor I could be.'

'And you did.' The admiration in her daughter's eyes
made her want to cry.

'I'm human, Poppy. You of all people know that. Don't
ever think anyone can be perfect.'

'You like Alexander, don't you?' Poppy said out of the
blue. 'And I think he likes you too.'

It felt odd discussing her love life, or rather lack of it,
with her seventeen-year-old daughter.

'He did once, I think.' She leaned across and wrapped
her arms around her child. 'But I've got you now. And
that's more than enough for me.'

Two days later, the tickets home were booked and Poppy
had gone for a nap, exhausted after a day spent cooking
and running errands. Her daughter was truly an amazing
young woman.

Katherine had made supper but Poppy hadn't reappeared. She boiled the kettle and made her some of her

favourite camomile tea. She loved how she now knew these small details about her child.

Taking the tea with her, she tiptoed into Poppy's bedroom. Her daughter was lying spreadeagled on the bed, the sheets tangled in her long limbs. Once more Katherine sent a silent prayer upwards for whatever had brought her daughter back to her.

But something about the way Poppy's face was screwed up—as if she were in pain—made her cross the room and place a hand on her child's forehead. At the feel of cold sweat alarm shot through her. Poppy had been complaining of a sore stomach the night before but this was something more.

Perhaps she had the same flu that had brought Grandmother and some of the other villagers low? Stamping down on the panic that threatened to overwhelm her, she gently shook her daughter by the shoulder. 'Poppy, wake up.'

Poppy opened her eyes, groaned and closed them again.

Her heart beating a tattoo against her ribs, Katherine knelt by the side of the bed and examined Poppy's limbs. To her horror she saw that her legs were covered with a faint but definite purpuric rash. It was one of the signs of meningitis. Worse, it was a sign that the disease had already taken hold.

Forcing herself to keep calm, she ran back to the sitting room and picked up her mobile. Her hands were shaking so badly she was almost not capable of punching in Alexander's number.

To her relief, he picked up straight away.

'Dr Dimitriou.' The sound of his voice almost made her sink to the floor with relief.

'Alexander. Where are you?'

'At home.' He must have picked up the fear in her voice. 'What is it? Are you all right?

'It's Poppy. I need you to come.'

'I'll be there in a few minutes.'

She went back to Poppy's room and tried to rouse her again but once more, her daughter's eyes only flickered. She needed to get antibiotics into her and soon. Perhaps she should have phoned for an ambulance instead of Alexander. But that would take longer. The ambulance would have to come here—at least an hour—and make its way back. And every moment could make a difference.

She sat on the bed and pulled her child into her arms. 'Hold on, darling, please, hold on.'

Alexander was there in less than five minutes, although it felt like hours. He took the scene in at a glance. Katherine looked over at him, anguish etched in every line of her face.

'She feels unwell and has a purpuric rash. I think she has meningitis. Help us, Alexander.'

Although he wanted nothing more than to take her into his arms, he automatically switched into professional mode. He felt Poppy's pulse. Rapid but still strong. She was clammy to the touch but the night was hot. He inspected her limbs and torso. There was a rash but it didn't quite look like the ones he'd seen on patients suffering from meningitis. However, given the recent outbreak, meningitis was still the most likely diagnosis.

'Let's get her to hospital,' he said, picking Katherine's child up. 'You sit in the back with her and phone ahead to let them know we're on our way.'

For once Katherine didn't complain about the way he

drove. She cradled her child in her arms, murmuring words of love and encouragement.

Later that night Katherine sat by the bed, holding her daughter's hand. Poppy had been started on IV antibiotics and it would be some time before they would know whether they'd caught it in time. Alexander had disappeared. He was going to phone Liz and Mike as soon as he'd spoken to the doctors again.

Was she going to lose her daughter again when she'd just found her? Why hadn't she forced her to leave even if she'd felt confident that there was zero chance of her daughter contracting the disease? Had she let her own desire to have Poppy with her get in the way of what was right for her child?

She murmured a prayer. 'God, if you're there, please don't take my child. I'll do anything—give up everything—if only you won't take her.'

A few moments later she heard a soft footfall behind her and looked up to find Alexander smiling down at her. Why was he smiling? Didn't he know she was in danger of losing her child?

'I have good news,' he whispered. 'Poppy doesn't have meningitis.'

'What do you mean? Of course she must have. The aches and pains, the rash…'

'It's the rash that got me thinking,' he said. 'It's very like a meningococcal one but I noticed it was only on her shins. I remember reading something about an illness that can mimic meningitis so I looked it up. Katherine, Poppy has Henoch-Schönlein purpura, not meningitis. When the kidneys get involved it can be nasty but Poppy's kidneys aren't affected.'

'She doesn't have meningitis?' Katherine could hardly believe it.

'No. She'll feel quite ill for a week or two, but I promise you she's going to be fine.'

Katherine's vision blurred as Alexander wrapped his arms around her. 'It's okay,' he murmured into her hair. 'You can let go now. I promise you, everything is going to be okay.'

'How is Poppy today?' Alexander asked Katherine a couple of days later when he visited them in hospital. She was a different woman from the one bent over Poppy's bedside when she'd thought her child was desperately ill. The worry and fear had left her eyes and the steely determination he knew so well was back.

'She's booked on this afternoon's flight to London. I'm going with her.'

'Of course.'

'Thank you for being here.' She held out her hand and he grasped her long, cool fingers. 'Thank you for recognising she didn't have meningitis.'

'Will you come back?'

She smiled wanly. 'I don't think so.'

'I love you, Katherine.' She needed to know that.

There was no response. She just looked at him with her cool blue eyes. 'Do you?'

'I was a fool, an idiot-think of any noun you like and it could apply to me, but I love you, more than I thought possible to love another woman. Just give me a chance and I'll prove it to you.'

She smiled wanly. 'I'm sorry, Alexander, but it's over.' She shook her head. 'I need to go if we're to catch our plane.'

He wanted to reach out to her but the coldness in her eyes held him back. Now was not the time to convince her to give them another chance.

He pressed her fingers. 'If ever you want to come back, if ever you need me, I'll be here.'

CHAPTER NINE

KATHERINE THRUST HER hands deep into her coat pockets and pulled her collar up. Almost overnight, the leaves had fallen from the trees, carpeting the ground.

In a week's time, Poppy would be coming to stay with her for the October school break. Liz and Mike were dropping her off before heading off to stay with Liz's family in the Cotswolds. After Poppy had a week with her, Katherine would drive her daughter up there and stay for the night, before returning to London.

It was amazing how quickly she'd become part of Poppy's family. As she and Poppy had discussed, she never tried to take Liz's place but instead acted the part of the trusted aunt or wise big sister. Poppy had applied to and was starting medical school the autumn after next should she get the grades she and her teachers expected.

Katherine's feet were beginning to freeze as the cold seeped through her boots, but she was reluctant to return home. The solitude that she'd cherished before she'd gone to Greece—before Poppy and Alexander—now felt disturbingly like loneliness.

The crunch of footsteps came from behind her and she whirled around.

At first she'd thought she dreamed him up.

He was every bit as beautiful as she remembered. His hair was slightly longer and he'd lost weight so that his cheeks were more prominent but laughter still lurked in his eyes.

He was wearing a thick trench coat over a thin jersey and jeans and heavy boots.

They looked at each other for a long moment. 'Katherine,' he murmured, and stepped towards her.

She'd been waiting for him to come to her since she'd left Greece. She'd told herself that he would but she hadn't been sure. Then, as the days had turned into weeks, she'd given up hoping.

What had brought him here now? Her heart hammered against her chest.

'How did you find me?' she whispered.

'You do know that Poppy and Crystal still write to each other? Crystal has been giving me regular updates every time your name is mentioned, which is pretty often, or so I gather.'

But it had taken him all this time to come and find her.

'Is Crystal with you?'

'Of course. I left her at the hotel with Poppy. It was Poppy who told me you'd be here and where to find you.'

'Poppy is in London?'

'She met us at the airport earlier.'

'It sounds as if she's decided to meddle. I think she's frightened I'll stay an old maid and she'll spend her adult years looking after me when I'm an old lady. That's why she asked you to come.'

It was a conversation they'd had as a joke—so why was she repeating it? Why was she babbling?

'Poppy didn't ask me to come, Katherine. I wrote to her and told her I was coming to see you and she asked me to keep it as a surprise.' He stepped towards her, his familiar soapy smell turning her bones to water. 'To be honest, I wasn't sure you'd want to see me.'

She stepped back and he halted where he was. 'How is Grandmother?' she asked.

'Looking forward to seeing you again. I think she's decided that you are already part of her family.'

Already part of the family?

He took hold of her collar and pulled her close. 'I've missed you,' he said into her hair. 'More than I thought possible.'

'You don't sound too pleased about it,' she mumbled.

'I am. I'm not. It depends.'

She placed her hands against his chest and although she wanted nothing more than to go on touching him for ever, to be held by him for ever, she pushed him away. 'Depends on what?'

'On whether you feel the same way.'

'I think you know how I feel.' She took a moment to steady her breathing. 'But I won't be with you and have you disapprove of me—or of what I did. I can't go through life thinking and feeling I have to pay over and over for what I did.' She tried to smile but it came out all wobbly. 'I've spent the last seventeen years of my life feeling as if I don't deserve to be happy. Being in Greece, being with Poppy changed all that for ever. I did what I felt I had to do at the time. That was the person I was back then and I can't change her. I'm not even sure I want to.'

'God, Katherine. Don't you understand what I'm saying? I love you. I love everything about you and that includes the person you were as well as the woman you are now. When I met you I didn't want to fall in love with you. I tried not to but I couldn't help it. So I told myself that

Sophia would want me to be happy, would want me to re-marry, especially someone who obviously cared for Crystal.' He looked at her with anguished eyes. 'I didn't tell you everything about Sophia. I have to tell you the rest so you can try to understand why I did what I did.'

He took her hand and led her across to a bench. 'I was six months away from being able to apply for the job in America. In the meantime I had been offered a consultant post at St George's, even though they knew I was going to America. In fact, they said it was one of the reasons they'd chosen me. While I was away they would employ a locum and my job would be kept open for me. It was a flatter-ing reminder of the esteem in which I was held, but at the time I saw it as nothing less than what I was due—what I had worked for over the years.

'But I didn't want to take my foot off the pedal, although I could have. I had the job I wanted—one that was mine for life. I had the post in America. I had done everything I'd set out to do. Now, if there ever was, it had to be Sophia's time. And I was prepared to shoulder more of the child care—or at least that's what I promised Sophia.

'She had an interview for one of the smaller orchestras. It wasn't the career as a concert pianist she'd hoped for but it would have been a start. I wasn't sure. I didn't know if she'd be expected to travel. And it would only have been for eighteen months. But she was so happy to be given the chance. Nervous too. She started playing the piano, prac-tising as if her life depended on it.

'Every hour that she wasn't looking after Crystal she was practising. Often I'd wake up in the night to hear the sounds of Mozart or Beethoven; I can barely listen to their music now. She was in a frenzy—so sure that this was her last chance. It was only then that I realised how much she'd sacrificed for me. And then she fell pregnant again. It wasn't planned, just one of those things, and that was that. Her chance was over.'

He paused for a long moment.

Katherine held her breath as she waited for him to continue.

'It was December and the winter had already been harsh. I left the house early—sometimes before six—but she always got up to see me off. That morning she'd been complaining of a headache. When I think back she'd been complaining of a headache the night before too. But I didn't take too much notice. I was already thinking of a complicated surgery I had that morning. She said she would take some painkillers and go back to bed for an hour or so. Crystal was staying with my mother for a few days. Sophia was thirty-two weeks by this time so I told her that I thought it was a good idea, kissed her and left.' He passed a hand across his face.

'If I'd stopped to look at her, really look at her, I would have seen the warning signs. I was a doctor, for God's sake. A couple of minutes—that's all it would have taken.'

A chill ran up Katherine's spine as she sensed what was coming.

'The roads were bad. The gritting lorries rarely came down the lane leading to our house so I'd taken the four-by-four. She sometimes drove me to the train station so she would have the use of the car, but because she had a headache she suggested I take it. I would leave it at the train station and catch the train from there. It would mean Sophia being without a car, but she said she wasn't intending to go anywhere anyway. She didn't need anything from the village and if she did, she would call me and I could pick it up on the way home.

'I was just relieved to get the use of the car. I needed to catch the six-thirty train if I was to make it to the hospital in time to see my patient before surgery was scheduled to start.'

Katherine's heart was beating a tattoo against her ribs. She sensed what was coming. 'You don't have to tell me any more,' she said softly.

'I do. I have gone over the day so many times in my head, trying to make it come out a different way, but of course that's impossible. We make these decisions in our lives, sometimes ones made in a split second, like the car driver who reverses without looking or overtakes when he shouldn't.'

'And sometimes we agonise over decisions for months but it doesn't mean that they turn out to be right,' she whispered. 'I, of all people, know that.'

'But you've come to terms with your demons. It's taken me this long to come to terms with mine. You need to know what happened so you can try and understand why I reacted to finding out about Poppy the way I did.'

'Tell me, then,' she said softly.

'Surgery that day went like a dream. I had two on my list—both major cases so I wasn't finished in Theatre until late. My secretary had left a note that Sophia had phoned and I tried to call her back, but there was no answer. I assumed she was in the bath—if I assumed anything. I went to see my post-operative patients and planned to try to get her again after that.

'Typically I got caught up and it wasn't until seven that I remembered I hadn't phoned her. I tried again and it went to voice mail. I still wasn't worried. She could be in the bath or in the garden and not heard the phone. She didn't keep her mobile on her unless she was away from home.

'But I was keen to get home—just to reassure myself. I had this uneasy sense of something not being quite right.

'The train seemed to take for ever. I kept trying to get her on the phone and when she still didn't answer I became more and more worried. I wondered if she'd fallen. There was no one nearby—no neighbours for me to call. Sophia would have known their names but I wouldn't even have recognised any of them.

'It did cross my mind to call the police, but I couldn't think of a good reason. My wife not answering her phone for an hour or two was hardly an emergency.

'I collected the car from the station, cursing the snow and praying that the road wouldn't be completely blocked, but nothing was going my way that night. I could only get as close as the lane leading down to the house before drifting snow made it impossible for me to go any further. There was nothing for it but to walk the rest of the way. All this time I was getting increasingly frantic. What if Sophia had gone outside and something had happened? What if she was caught in a snow drift?

'But I told myself that she was too sensible for that. Why would she need to go outside? By that time I was at the house. It was dark—it would normally be lit up like a Christmas tree. It could be a power cut—they weren't infrequent where we lived—but I couldn't fool myself any longer about something being seriously wrong.

'I let myself inside and called out for her. No answer. The lights were working so it wasn't a power cut.

'I found her in our bedroom. She had her mobile in her hand. She was unconscious. But she was alive. I could see that she'd been fitting and now I noticed that her ankles, hands and face were puffy.

'Eclampsia. And I'd been too damn into myself and

my career to even notice. But there was no time to berate myself then. If Sophia was to have a chance of surviving I had to get her to hospital and quickly.

'I called 999. They said they would send an ambulance straight away. I told them they wouldn't get any further than my car and that I would meet them there. They said it would take around twenty minutes to get to me, supposing the roads stayed clear. The baby had to be delivered. If I'd had a scalpel with me, so help me God, that's what I would have done.

'She came round briefly, enough to recognise that I was there, but she started fitting again. I waited until she stopped and then I wrapped her in a blanket and carried her to the car. Thankfully the ambulance arrived at almost the same time.

'They delivered our son. But it was too late. For either of them.'

Katherine wrapped her arms around him and held him. What could she say? All she could do for him was let him talk. No wonder he'd been so shocked when he'd found out about Poppy. Sophia had died bringing a child into the world, whereas, it must have seemed to him, she had casually given hers away.

'If it wasn't for Crystal I don't know how I would have got through the next months. In the end it was Helen stepping in that saved us both. As soon as she heard the news she jumped on the first plane. She was with us before night fell. I was like a madman. That I'd lost the woman who was my very heartbeat was bad enough, but the guilt that she might not have died had I been a different man was worse.

'I stopped going to work. I turned down the consultant job at St George's and the one in America—to be fair to them they told me to think it over, to take my time, but I knew I wouldn't take them up. You see, I no longer felt as if I deserved it. I guess, to be honest, I was sunk in self-pity. So far sunk in it I was wallowing.'

'How old was Crystal?'

'She was three. Old enough to miss her mother but not old enough to understand that she would never see her again and definitely not old enough to understand that this man—who she barely knew, remember—hadn't a clue how to look after her. Even if I had, I was so deep in my trough of self-pity I think I was in danger of enjoying it.

'And when Helen came to stay that gave me more opportunity to wallow. Now she was there to take care of Crystal, there was nothing to hold me back. I drank myself almost unconscious most nights. I rarely got out of bed until mid-morning and when I did I couldn't be bothered getting dressed or shaved. Sometimes I didn't even shower until mid-afternoon.

'God knows how long that would have gone on if Helen hadn't called in reinforcements. It was as if the whole of my extended Greek family had taken up residence. Helen, her mother, my mother and my grandmother too—if my grandfather and father had been alive they would have been there also. I'm pretty sure their disapproving ghosts were in the background, cheering them on and wagging their heads at me.

'Those formidable women kissed and hugged me and then marched me off to the shower. My mother threw every last drop of alcohol down the sink and then Helen and Yia-Yia cooked up a storm. They looked after Crystal, but most importantly they made me see it was my job to care for my child. They fed her and dressed her, but after that it was up to me to look after her.

'Do you know, she clung to them the first time I tried

to take my daughter to the park on my own? She gripped
the sides of the door when I tried to lift her, so in the end
my first trip outside with my daughter since the funeral
was with my whole family in tow. It got better after that.
I still mourned Sophia but my family made me see that
she would have been furious if she'd seen the way I'd gone
to pieces. And I knew they were right. I had stolen her
dreams from her, and what kind of major creep would I
be if I couldn't make a life—a good, loving, caring life—
for our daughter?

'The rest, as they say, is history. I sold everything we
owned in England and ploughed it into a small practice
here in Greece. Then…' he smiled wanly '…I met you.
I fought my attraction to you, but I couldn't help it. You
were the only woman who had come close to measuring
up to Sophia, the only woman I could imagine spending
the rest of my life with. But I felt guilty. It seemed a betrayal of Sophia's memory.

'Then I found out about Poppy and it was as if I didn't
know you at all. As if the perfect woman I had built up in
my mind had disappeared in a breath of wind. I'd put you
on a pedestal' you see. I guess we're not so dissimilar, huh?
Both of us seemed to feel the need to atone.'

Katherine grimaced. 'I no longer feel I have to atone. As
I said, I did what I did and I just have to look at the wonderful young and happy woman Poppy is today to know
I made the right decision. I'm sorry I couldn't be perfect
for you. But, you know, Alexander, I don't think I want
to be perfect.'

'No,' he said softly. 'Of course you don't. You're human.
Like us all.'

'So what changed your mind?'

'Nothing changed my mind. When you told me why

you gave Poppy up I realised why you'd felt you'd had no choice. And when I saw you with Poppy I could see how you felt about her. I was coming to beg your forgiveness when Grandmother became unwell. As soon as I was sure she was all right I was coming to ask you to stay—to marry me. That's when you phoned me about Poppy. I knew it wasn't the time to tell you how I felt. Every ounce of your attention was—quite rightly—focussed on your daughter. I knew there would be time later—when she was better.'

He rubbed the back of his neck. 'What I wasn't so sure about was whether you could forgive me. Then when you were about to leave and you looked right through me, I thought I had ruined any chance I had with you.' His Greek accent became more pronounced, as it always did when he was emotional.

She looked him in the eye. 'You said you forgave me! I wasn't looking for forgiveness. Not from you! How could I be with a man who thought I needed his forgiveness?'

'It was a stupid, thoughtless thing to say.'

'It was,' she agreed. 'I needed the man I loved to love me warts and all.'

His eyes burned. 'So you do love me?'

'I think I fell in love with you almost from the moment I set eyes on you. But I was frightened too. I wanted to tell you about Poppy but I just couldn't. At least, not then. I was planning to tell you, but then Poppy turned up. I never wanted you to find out that way.

'Then she became ill and I couldn't think of anything else. I thought I was going to lose her again. I made a pact with myself, with the gods, to anyone I thought might be listening. If they'd let Poppy live I would give you up. I know it's crazy but I was crazy back then.'

'But when she was better, why didn't you write to me?'

'It took a long time for her to recover completely. I couldn't leave her.' She smiled wryly. 'And I was keeping my pact. Then when she was completely better I wanted you to come to me. I needed to know that you wanted me. The woman I am, not the one in your imagination.'

'I would have come sooner, but I was arranging a job here. I've taken a year's sabbatical. I love you. I adore you. I don't want a life without you. I lost Sophia because I put my ambition before her needs. I won't do that to you. God, woman, put me out of my misery. I have to know if you love me—if you will marry me and live with me. If you say yes, I'll spend the rest of my life trying to make you happy.' A gust of wind blew the leaves around his feet. But she needed to be sure. She had to know she wouldn't be second best.

'What about Sophia?' she asked. 'I don't want to spend my life competing with the memory of a woman who was so perfect. Because we both know I'm not. None of us are.'

'You're perfect to me,' he said. When she made to protest he stopped her words with his fingertips. 'I don't want perfection, my love. It's too hard to live up to.' He grinned. 'But you'll do me. What about you? Can you put up with a man who doesn't always appreciate a good thing when he comes across it?'

She smiled back at him, her heart threatening to burst from her chest. 'You know what? I rather think I can.'

EPILOGUE

THE TINY WHITEWASHED church was perched on a small promontory overlooking the sea. Poppy had helped Katherine find the place where she would marry Alexander. And it was perfect.

It was a glorious spring day and even the small breeze that whipped Katherine's dress around her ankles was welcome.

Crystal could barely control her excitement. She'd been hopping from foot to foot all morning, keeping up a constant flow of chatter. Poppy wasn't much better. Although she'd tried to hide it, she was almost as excited and thrilled to have been asked to be Katherine's bridesmaid—to the extent that she'd removed her piercings in honour of the occasion, although Katherine had no doubt they'd be back in place tomorrow. Not that she cared. Poppy could have turned up in a paper bag for all she cared. All that mattered was that she was here today, celebrating what was the happiest day of her mother's life.

She glanced at the girls. Crystal with a basket of rose petals hooked over her elbow and Poppy holding the little girl's hand. Who would have thought a year ago that she would be standing here with her two children, because that's how she saw them. Crystal and Katherine had other mothers—women who would always be an important part of their lives—or, in Crystal's case, an important memory, but they had her too. And she would always be there for them—to hold them when their hearts got broken, to help them achieve their dreams, whatever those might be, to support them when life wasn't so kind and eventually to help them plan their weddings, if that's what they wished. Whatever lives they chose for themselves, she'd be there cheering them on, as she was certain her mother was cheering her on. Mum would be so proud.

Her gaze turned to the man beside her, more Greek god than gladiator in his cream suit and neatly pressed shirt. She'd earned her doctorate and had accepted a job in Athens for a couple of years. She was almost fluent in Greek now. After that? They didn't know, but they'd be deciding together.

She had the future—a wonderful future—to look forward to, and she'd be doing it with Alexander by her side.

* * * * *

MILLS & BOON

THE HEART OF ROMANCE

A ROMANCE FOR EVERY KIND OF READER

MODERN

Prepare to be swept off your feet by sophisticated, sexy and seductive heroes, in some of the world's most glamourous and romantic locations, where power and passion collide.
8 stories per month.

HISTORICAL

Escape with historical heroes from time gone by. Whether your passion is for wicked Regency Rakes, muscled Vikings or rugged Highlanders, awaken the romance of the past.
6 stories per month.

MEDICAL

Set your pulse racing with dedicated, delectable doctors in the high-pressure world of medicine, where emotions run high and passion, comfort and love are the best medicine.
6 stories per month.

True Love

Celebrate true love with tender stories of heartfelt romance, from the rush of falling in love to the joy a new baby can bring, and a focus on the emotional heart of a relationship.
8 stories per month.

Desire

Indulge in secrets and scandal, intense drama and plenty of sizzling hot action with powerful and passionate heroes who have it all: wealth, status, good looks…everything but the right woman.
6 stories per month.

HEROES

Experience all the excitement of a gripping thriller, with an intense romance at its heart. Resourceful, true-to-life women and strong, fearless men face danger and desire - a killer combination!
8 stories per month.

DARE

Sensual love stories featuring smart, sassy heroines you'd want as a best friend, and compelling intense heroes who are worthy of them.
4 stories per month.

To see which titles are coming soon, please visit

millsandboon.co.uk/nextmonth

MILLS & BOON

MODERN

Power and Passion

Prepare to be swept off your feet by sophisticated, sexy and seductive heroes, in some of the world's most glamourous and romantic locations, where power and passion collide.